Prey for Us

By Geoffrey Neil

Copyright Information

Priorities Intact Publishing

8306 Wilshire Blvd., #7076, Beverly Hills, CA 90211

Cover art by Geoffrey Neil

Edited by Christina Dominguez

Printed in the United States of America

10 9 8 7 6 5 4 3 2 1

ISBN-978-0-9850223-5-8

Contents

For my beloved friend Michelle Martin-Stroup.
All your preyers will be answered.

"Deep vengeance is the daughter of deep silence."

—Vittorio Alfieri

Author's Note

Prey for Us is a thriller whose concepts are underpinned by the stunning, verifiable feats of Ed Leedskalnin.

He claimed to know the secret of the pyramid builders and supported this claim by single-handedly raising and positioning enormous rock blocks weighing up to 30 tons. It's difficult to believe that this small man, weighing approximately 100 lbs., worked alone to quarry, move, and sculpt over 1,100 tons of coral rock using only simple tools. He worked at night, allowing no one to watch, yet he offered tours of his spectacular results to amazed visitors during the day.

Ed Leedskalnin died on December 7, 1951, taking his secrets to the grave. To this day, the phenomenal results of his physics-defying feats stand precisely where he placed them in Homestead, Florida. Many people refer to his creation as the eighth wonder of the world. Search "Coral Castle" to learn more.

What if this special knowledge of the pyramid builders was rediscovered, expanded, and used for a shocking purpose? I daydreamed about this concept for months. My fascination with Mr. Leedskalnin's mysterious methods grew into an obsession, and eventually motivated me to write *Prey for Us*.

Note: I am not funded by or associated with Coral Castle Museum.

Chapter 1

IF THE MAN exiting the liquor store knew how many people Morana Mahker had killed, he wouldn't have whistled at her as she passed by. He would have quietly back-stepped through the door to watch her from inside, waiting until she was long gone before he ventured out. Instead, he followed her and whistled again, louder, raising a six-pack high. "Hey, baby... I got us beer!"

Morana ignored him—a merciful gift he couldn't appreciate. Her long strides carried her deeper into the growing crowd, quickly obscuring the beer man's view of her.

Despite the mid-afternoon heat, people poured from shops and eateries, filling the sidewalk. She weaved her way between them. Most gazed upward, cupping their brows to shield their eyes from the Southern California sun. A few pointed to a place high in the sky where the wind had warped a mushroom cloud into what resembled an enormous, dark fist with crooked fingers melting from it.

To blend in, Morana stopped several times to gape upward with them, listening to the excited onlookers speculate about the cause. They were oblivious to her connection to the massive explosion, and she knew she could count on that for only a few more hours. By the end of the day, her dated headshot and an extended list of chilling crimes would stream to millions of phones, computers, and televisions nationwide. Then, she fully expected the announcement of an enormous reward for her capture.

She kept her brisk pace, comfortably cloaked in her favorite hiding place—the anonymity of a crowd. At six feet tall and featuring cover model looks, moving unnoticed in public was a constant challenge for her, but it had also become a necessary skill. Her knack for makeup disguises and well-practiced adjustments to posture and gait helped her virtually vanish into any group.

Today, loose-fit jeans and a gray cardigan concealed her shapeliness. Sunglasses and a baseball cap pulled low hid most of her face. Her outfit and the timely distraction in the sky limited the attention she drew from those around her—even if it hadn't been enough to fool the beer guy.

The wail of distant sirens jarred her comfortable obscurity. She abandoned the sidewalk at the next block, hurrying to the back alley. She sped to a jog, dodging potholes and vehicle-flattened trash.

She came to the rear of a shoe store after having stopped far enough from it to confirm that no surveillance cameras covered its back wall. She raised her cap brim in the awning's shadow and removed her sunglasses to wipe her eyes. She felt in her pocket and pulled out a wad of cash, counting out $87.

The irony of finding herself homeless sank in. Her failed mission to end homelessness by terrorizing the citizens of Santa Monica into brotherly love had ended in the massive explosion at the bunker that served as headquarters for her vigilante mission.

She put on her sunglasses and continued along the alley until she saw the rear entrance of an electronics store. She kept her head down and passed under a bubble camera mounted above the door. Inside, she selected a prepaid burner phone for $35. At the counter, the clerk paid little attention to her. He split his attention between giving her change and a television mounted from the ceiling showing news coverage of the explosion. On her way to the door, she heard sirens approaching. She waited until the police cars passed before exiting.

She returned to her journey along the alley. After traveling a few more blocks, she found an unlocked back door to a small office building. She entered and saw a restroom sign halfway along a corridor that led to the front lobby. She ducked into the women's restroom. It was empty. She closed herself into a stall, reinserted her phone's battery, and turned it on. She opened her contact app and realized that finding someone in her address book who would be receptive to a call from her would be challenging. She scrolled the list, recognizing people who wouldn't remember her and others who would delight in turning her in for the impending reward for her capture. Then, a name caught her eye: *Clay Thorner*. She smiled.

Clay, a computer hacker and weapons enthusiast, introduced himself to her at a gun show where he had a booth two years ago. After a brief conversation about legal firearm options, Clay escorted her to his car, where he sold her a pristine two-inch, 5-shot .38 Special with a pink finish. Over the next two years, he called on Morana often, presenting new, obscure guns that might interest her each time. He also tried to convince her to join him in several questionable business schemes, which she always rejected. None of Clay's calls concluded without Morana having to dodge an offer to take her to dinner. Maybe it was time for them to spend some time together. Clay had plenty to hide. He was the perfect person to trust.

She popped out her phone's battery again and then dialed Clay on her new burner phone.

"Hello?"

"Hi, Clay, it's Mo," she said, hushed.

"I don't believe it," Clay said. "Is it really you?"

"Yes," she lowered her voice to a whisper.

"What's it been? Years? I thought we broke up."

"Listen, I need your help."

"I knew the day would come!"

"I'm not joking. I'm in a situation… I need to hang out at your place for a bit."

"Dammit."

"What?"

"I'm not in LA. That's always been my luck with you. You finally show an interest while I'm out of town."

"Listen, it's urgent. I could let myself in—"

"Why so anxious? You get evicted?"

"I can't explain now. Can I crash or not?"

"I'm in Miami on business for a tour company I work for."

"When will you be back?"

"Not for a couple of weeks. Did your bleeding-heart mission to end homelessness fail?"

"There's been a setback."

"Tell me what's up, and my place is yours."

"I've got some… trouble. You'll see it on the news later."

"Whoa. What's going on?"

"I'll explain later. You're the only person I can trust. Can you help, or not?"

"Uhhhh, where are you?"

"Before I tell you that, I think we both understand that the law has an equal interest in each of us."

"Wait a minute—you need me, and you're blackmailing me?"

"All I'm saying is that you've helped me before. It won't take long for them to make the connection if I'm caught."

"Hey, I had nothing to do with your previous dirt. You were supposed to only scare that couple I brought to you, not kill them."

"They were horrible human beings. They crushed an innocent homeless woman's skull. They deserved to die. I'm glad you remember that incident because, in the eyes of the law, we're equally guilty."

"There's no proof I was involved."

"Listen, Clay, I just need some temporary cover. Please."

Clay sighed and said, "One night—I'm not letting you tangle me up in aiding and abetting or harboring a fugitive or whatever."

"Thank you. I respect that."

"Do you remember where I live?"

"Yes, and by the way, I also need some cash? Do you have any at your place?"

"You want money, too?"

"I'll pay you back with interest, I promise."

"If you want my help, I need to know where you are—exactly."

Morana hesitated. "I'm on Ventura Boulevard. Near the 405 Freeway."

"Got it. I'm gonna give you directions to McGee's Market," Clay said.

"I don't have ID, and I can't be seen. Why am I going to a market?"

"Trust me." Clay gave her the address. "Get there. The guy at the counter is Benny. He'll be expecting you."

"Wait—don't!" Morana said. "Did you miss the entire part about me being in trouble? I don't need any new friends. I need good cover and some cash."

"If you knew Benny, you wouldn't be worried. He's solid and the best help I can offer."

"Give him an alias."

"Fine. Get a piece of paper and a pen."

"For what?"

"Would you trust me, dammit? You need to write a special number."

"I'll memorize it."

"It's too long."

"Hold on…" Morana came out of the stall and went to the bathroom door. She leaned out and checked both directions. A few people stood in the lobby, talking near an elevator. Some others emerged from a hallway and exited to the street through the glass front doors.

She pressed the phone to her ear as she walked to the lobby. A security guard at a desk faced the front doors. She spotted a camera high on the wall and instinctively tilted her head, flipping her hair to conceal her face from the camera's view. She went to the security desk and motioned to the guard for a pen. A slight smile raised the corner of his mouth as he handed it to her. Morana dismissed it. Even if the guard recognized her, she'd be long gone before he could make a call, and if he tried to detain her, she was prepared.

"Are you still there?" Morana said.

"Yes," Clay said.

"I'm ready."

Clay read her a 34-character string of numbers and letters while Morana wrote it on her palm. "Do you want to read it back to me?"

"No," she placed the pen on the security guard's desk and headed back along the hallway to the back door. "But what the hell is this number?"

"Just give it to Benny. He'll know what to do. Call me when you're done, and I'll get you into my place."

They hung up, and Morana began a four-mile walk to McGee's, abandoning the sidewalk for most of the trek, opting for the safer cover of the back alleys.

When she reached the market, she lurked a safe distance from it, tucked beside a concrete fence topped with razor wire that protected an auto body shop. She watched the McGee's market entrance for a few minutes. Several customers entered and exited, returning their empty carts to the bent cart-return with a crooked sign in the center of the lot.

She adjusted her sunglasses, took off her cap, and finger-combed her hair on her way to the entrance. She spotted a couple of security cameras mounted near the entrance, keeping her face hidden under her cap's brim while passing them. When she pushed the door open, a bell jingled, dangling from some dirty twine on the inside handle.

McGee's had the feel of an old-fashioned mom-and-pop market. Refrigerated beverages and snacks spanned a wall beside several well-stocked aisles of food and fresh produce. The aroma of fresh coffee and the visuals of antiques mounted high on the wall gave the space a homey charm.

Morana spotted another exit on the opposite side of the store. The entrance where she stood provided a clear view of the cashier at the far end of the center aisle. A short, dark-skinned man with straight, jet-black hair sat on a stool while reading a newspaper. Behind him, cigarettes and magazines were stacked to the ceiling on the back wall. The man looked over his glasses at her. "Afternoon."

Morana waved and nodded as she approached him, still scouring the store for risks.

The man slid the newspaper aside, stood, and folded his hands on the counter.

"I'm looking for Benny," Morana said.

"You found him." He examined her more closely.

"Clay sent me."

"Of course he did," Benny said, grinning as he looked her up and down. He came around the counter and motioned for her to follow him.

"What you need is back here."

Morana kept her distance from him as they entered a dim hallway.

Benny stopped at a doorway with a curtain. A sign above it read *Restroom*. He pushed back a curtain and held it for Morana.

She hesitated, leaning to see into the small room. In addition to another door on the back wall, it contained a Bitcoin ATM.

"Clay said you'd be suspicious," Benny said.

They stepped inside.

Benny pointed to the ATM. "That's what you want." He went to it and tapped the screen a few times. "Enter your number, and win a prize." He chuckled as he left her, disappearing through the curtain.

The screen was set to *Withdrawal*. Morana typed Clay's cryptic code into the on-screen box. The machine hummed before spitting out $300 cash. Morana peeled off $40 and pocketed the rest.

She returned to the main store and saw that Benny had reopened his newspaper at the cashier's counter but was now on the phone. The bell on the front door jingled, and Morana backed into the hallway until she saw it was an elderly woman pulling a small metal cart with some empty shopping bags on the bottom.

Morana moved to a rack of baseball caps. She picked one with the smallest logo, and as she approached Benny, he ended his call.

Morana placed the cap on the counter.

"Get what you needed?" Benny asked.

"Yes." She pointed to the hat. "Just this."

She felt a pang of something. Benny was no longer looking at her.

"I have one more thing for you," he said.

"No, this is all I need…" Morana said, looking at him suspiciously.

"Clay said you don't want to be seen. I have something that will help. Follow me."

A tinny voice that sounded like a small speaker came from the other side of the counter. Benny reached under the counter and muted it. When he turned his back, she leaned over the counter and saw a small TV tucked underneath.

"First time to my store?" he asked, pushing through swinging doors to the back of the store.

Morana stopped outside the doors, letting them swing shut.

Benny poked his head back out. "C'mon, the quicker we are, the less likely you'll be seen."

"Thanks, but I have all I need."

Benny pushed the door open, raised a pistol to her chest, and said,

"No, I think you need to stay. You will come in here and do it slowly and quietly."

Morana raised her hands.

Benny braced the door open with his foot. He motioned with the gun for her to enter.

Morana eased by him, stepping into a storeroom filled with store inventory stacked high on the walls. In the corner, an overhead sprayer hung over an industrial size sink. Rinsed produce sat off to one side. Another wall of shelves was lined with rolls of shopping bags and packaged product inventory. A beer can, and an over-filled ashtray sat on the adjacent wall above a cluttered desk. The far wall had an exit door to the rear of the store.

Benny used his free hand to shove her shoulder, moving her deeper into the room. He pulled his phone from his pocket and said, "Yes, I'm still here... You need to hurry."

Morana turned to face him, keeping her hands raised.

Benny leered at her.

The gun was just out of her reach. She took a small step closer.

Benny stepped back and raised the gun from her chest to her head. He pulled the phone from his ear and said, "I wouldn't test me. You'll lose." His attention went back to the phone conversation. "... Yes, I'm sure... Do you want me to tie her?"

Morana coughed.

"What? Say it again..." Benny pressed the phone to his ear harder.

Morana coughed again.

"Shut up!" He snapped at her. "Say it once more... do you want her tied?"

When Benny turned his head slightly to hear, Morana lunged, swinging her fist downward, connecting with his wrist. The gun fired into the floor. She hooked her arm around his neck, slammed him onto his back, and then rolled, pinning his gun arm to the floor.

Benny twisted, trying to mount her, and when he swung his leg over her, she landed a solid blow to his groin. His hand released the gun, and he howled.

He twisted onto his stomach and clawed for the gun, but Morana mounted him, grabbed his wrists, and pulled them high up his back.

"Ow!" Benny screamed. "You're breaking my arms."

"That breaks my heart," Morana said. She squeezed a fistful of his hair and pressed the side of his face to the floor. "Shut up. Don't test me. You'll lose."

Benny nodded, his nostrils flaring.

Morana held his wrists with one hand and stretched to grab a phone charger cord that dangled from the desk near the floor. She yanked it free and tightly bound Benny's wrists. She picked up his phone from the floor. The screen showed an open call for *1 minute 16 seconds*... The call ID displayed only a number, no name. She ended the call.

She got the gun and put it to the back of Benny's head. "Was it Clay?"

"What?"

"Was Clay on the phone?"

"Uh... yes. He wanted me to get you."

"You hesitated. You're lying."

She threw the phone. It shattered against the wall. She grabbed a canvas shopping bag from a nearby stack and slipped it over his head.

"Please!" Benny begged. "I wasn't going to harm you." He tried to buck her. She slammed his head to the floor again and rode him until he stopped struggling.

"You're already too late," Benny said. The bag muffled his voice. "Even if you run now, you won't get away."

Morana pressed the gun to his head. "We could have been friends, Benny." She pulled the trigger twice. His shirt and the bag contained most of the splatter. On the third trigger pull, the gun only clicked. She released the magazine. It was empty. *Only two bullets?*

She pulled out his wallet. $133 cash. She stared at it momentarily before tucking the wallet and cash back into his pocket.

She considered cleaning her fingerprints from the scene until she heard the store's front door handle bell.

"Benny?" The man's voice seeped through the double doors. Morana quietly slipped out the market's back door.

Sirens grew louder as she sped up to a full sprint toward the end of the alley. She turned onto a residential street, her long strides taking her past several homes before cutting across a lawn at the end of a cul-de-sac.

She slipped between houses and scaled a chain-link fence before crossing through several more backyards. The wail of sirens from the market's direction grew louder.

She turned onto another street and slowed to a jog as some kids on bicycles passed her in the opposite direction. Her heart pounded, and her lungs burned. A siren blared closer than the others, and she ducked behind a row of hedges until it passed at a nearby intersection.

She casually walked to the street, and when she was out of view from the house, she resumed her sprint, zigzagging away from the sirens through several more blocks until she came to the neighborhood's edge.

A quarter mile ahead, she saw signs for shops and eateries. One was a pharmacy, and she slowed as she neared the parking lot. After catching her breath, she went inside. A female cashier was preoccupied with scanning boxed items with a barcode gun as she arranged inventory in a glass cabinet behind the counter.

Morana was relieved to see no television on in the store. She was sure that a reward photo of her would go viral any time now. She walked to a clothing aisle, noting three security cameras mounted high to cover the cashier, the entrance, and the pharmacy counter. She picked out a sweatshirt, sweatpants, a knit cap, sunglasses, another burner phone, and several makeup items and went to check out. As she approached the cashier, she observed the woman.

"All ready?" the cashier said, fumbling with the sweatshirt to find the tag.

Morana nodded, adding a large water bottle from a fridge beside the checkout counter.

"Sounds like something big is going on out there," the woman said, glancing up at the ceiling. Another helicopter flew overhead. More sirens sped past the pharmacy.

Morana nodded, paid with cash, and exited the store. She put on her cap and sunglasses. Another helicopter passed overhead, racing toward others already hovering over McGee's Market in the distance.

She moved to walk along the opposite side of the road, holding her breath to guzzle the water. Looking back, she noticed that the pharmacy cashier had followed her outside and now stood a few steps from the entrance, shielding her eyes while gazing up at the helicopters.

Morana sped up to a jog, twice squatting to tie her shoe with her back to the road as police cars screamed by.

She came to the overpass of a wash and climbed over the guardrail and down an embankment that took her below it. The wash floor had only a trickle of a stream that snaked through mud and plant debris.

A short distance away, a shopping cart sat, partially filled with aluminum cans. Morana looked up to see underneath the overpass. Several bundles of blankets bound with knotted grocery bags were tucked into a crevice where the overpass met the slanted concrete. She climbed the ramp of concrete for a closer look. Alongside the bags, a homeless woman lay amidst the clutter of having camped there for several days. She was curled up with her eyes closed and wore a thick, tattered coat, and fingerless gloves. Her toes jutted through an open flap at the front of her shoe soles.

When Morana nudged the woman's shoulder, she stirred without opening her eyes. "Hey there," Morana said, gently caressing the woman's cheek with her fingers. The woman opened her eyes and looked up into Morana's sunglasses.

"Sit up, angel," Morana said. Morana took hold of her jacket and pulled her into a sitting position.

The woman's confusion quickly became fear. "Whatchu doin'?" She pulled her coat from Morana's grasp and tried to scoot away.

"I won't hurt you. I promise," Morana said. She stepped closer and smoothed the front of her jacket, then fingered the hair from the woman's eyes. "What's your name?"

The woman's face drained some of its terror while keeping its suspicion. "Janelle... Whatchu want?"

Morana sat beside her and said, "Sweetheart, have I got a deal for you."

Having swapped as much of her attire as was practical with Janelle, Morana said goodbye and slipped a twenty-dollar bill into Janelle's pocket. She returned to the thin stream of water at the bottom of the wash, rubbed dirt in her hair, and then shook it out, leaving clumps of it matted. She smeared mud on her face and neck, then wiped most of it off.

"Thank you, angel," Morana said as she climbed past the woman up to the road. Janelle waved, flashing a toothless grin.

Having transformed her appearance enough to distinguish herself from whatever photos would soon be plastered across all media channels, she continued her trek along the street toward Clay's house.

As she strolled along in her new, grubby wardrobe, she was relieved that several pedestrians she passed averted their eyes the moment they were within talking distance.

She continued to a bus stop and waited. A slight wind shift reminded her of the pungent stench that exuded from Janelle's clothes. While not pleasant, the aroma would be helpful for privacy.

She called Clay on her burner phone, hoping he would answer the unfamiliar number.

"Clay, here."

"It's Mo. Surprised to hear from me?"

"Not at all. Did Benny help you?"

"He was more than happy to help me go to prison."

"No!"

"He said you tipped him, so I will be waiting for you when you return home."

"No, no, no—son of a bitch. Mo, that's bullshit. I swear I had nothing to do with whatever he did."

"I know. Fortunately for you, he's a crappy liar, but I fixed his honesty problem."

"Don't tell me you killed him…"

"He pointed a gun at me, Clay."

"God, I can't believe this."

"I had no choice."

"He was a friend."

"He was my enemy, but we can debate that later. I'm on my way to your place. Do I need an alarm code?"

"Why don't you hold off for a while? If you get tracked, we'll be connected, and I'll be useless to you."

"Calm down. They won't be able to track me to your place, and if they could, I'd be long gone before they get there. All I need to know is if your house has an alarm."

"No alarm, but it's well secured. You should wait until dark."

"Wait a while? You're kidding, right?"

"Mo, I swear I'm not setting you up. I have nosy neighbors. If you want to deal with that, go to my place in broad daylight. If I were you, I'd tuck myself inside a dumpster until dark. I saw the news. That explosion was you?"

"Get me safely into your house, and I might share more details."

"Fine. Call me when you're there, and I'll tell you how to get in."

Chapter 2

AS MORANA BOARDED a bus, the driver gave her a withering glare. Any type of look from strangers was better than recognition.

She rode to a stop four blocks from Clay's house, walking the rest of the way to his street. She remembered from her previous gun purchases from Clay that his house was the fourth from the intersection. As she approached the front yard, she recognized the fountain, now filled with stagnant green water, and its rim splattered to a solid white from bird droppings. The lawn had grown out and died. The end of his street had a yellow *Dead End* sign that effectively limited vehicle cross traffic.

She noticed that the window shades were drawn at the house across the street from Clay's, but there was a narrow crack at the bottom. A suspicious sedan with tinted windows resembling a vehicle a detective would drive was parked in front. Although she didn't like the risk, remaining exposed on the streets would be a more significant risk.

Dusk was settling in, and waiting for nightfall seemed more ridiculous than ever. She walked past the house twice for surveillance, then after a final look up and down the street for any potential spectators, she hurried across Clay's lawn. Dried leaves and grass crunched under her feet on the way to a side gate she quietly opened and latched behind her.

Clay's backyard was as neglected as the front. Insect hulls dangled on a tangled cobweb that connected a couple of dusty patio chairs and a table. Overgrown ivy concealed the house's back wall. Trees blocked the view of one neighbor. She peered through a knothole in the wooden fence on the opposite side and saw no sign of any backyard activity.

She went to Clay's back door and tried the knob. Locked. She found a garden trowel in a rotting wooden workbench that Clay had buttressed against the back wall of the house.

She used the trowel to pry open a thin crack at the base of a window. The smell of stale air infused with pine freshener seeped through the opening. The breeze caused the drapes to shift. She cupped her eyes against the window to see inside. From the narrow visible angle, Clay's house looked like it had been ransacked. Empty water bottles, papers, and pillows littered the floor.

If his car was in the garage and she could find the key in the house, borrowing it would help her more than he knew.

In the suburb of Oakchester, Florida, Clay tugged his tie loose to air out his sweaty neck. After spending the last hours at the office briefing a client about an upcoming tour he had arranged, he entered his apartment. Before the door closed behind him, he'd already kicked off his loafers, sending them tumbling to a place under a corner table. He pulled a cold beer from the fridge, sat on the sofa, cracked open the beer can, and drained half of it. He leaned back and sighed.

He set the beer aside and turned on the TV, flipping through the channels. He found one that showed the breaking news from Los Angeles he had heard on the radio. There it was in color—an aerial view of an explosion in the west San Fernando Valley. Helicopters circled an enormous cloud with fire and a crater at least a block wide below it.

Clay sat forward and turned up the volume. The wide shot from a helicopter zoomed in on familiar streets—only a few miles from his home. He got up, went closer to the TV, and saw the reason for Morana's paranoia.

A $1,000,000 reward with her photo appeared on the screen. "Oh, my God!" he said, interlocking his fingers on his head. He remembered seeing Morana with longer hair—sometimes. But the color would change from day to day. In this photo, she looked much younger than Clay knew she was. Even when she wasn't on the run, he remembered how Morana transformed her appearance daily. Whenever she arrived at his place to pick up a gun she had ordered from him, he felt silly asking if it was really her before opening the door. Anyone trying to identify her from the photo on the TV was a long shot. He grinned, knowing he was the only person who knew where she was.

He took out his phone and returned a call to the number Morana had used to reach him earlier. It rang with no answer. He flopped back onto the sofa and watched the news media working themselves into a frenzy over this story. He changed channels, watching stations competing for the newest details of the story. By the time he had finished his beer, every major news broadcast had featured the same photo.

He found a number for Morana in his phone's address book and called it, even though it was over a year old. No answer. He tossed his phone aside. Morana was in trouble, and she needed him. From the time he met her, Clay had wanted her, but she had no interest in dating him. But perhaps her new predicament would bring hope if he could be heroic in her time of need. Who knew what could happen? If she weren't adequately grateful for his help, her bounty would burgeon by the day, and he could eventually cash her in for quite a nice bonanza. Clay laid back and dozed off, relishing his unexpected leverage and letting his fantasy go wild.

About an hour later, his phone vibrated, waking him. He patted his hand beside him until he felt his phone. He opened one eye and squinted at a security app on the screen that blinked red.

"Now what?" he said, sitting up. The app was linked to a camera system at his house in Los Angeles. He went to the corner table and opened his laptop. A video feed split the screen into eight parts, showing each room and his house's exterior front and rear. Motion on one feed caught his attention. The guest bedroom's window was open, and the drapes flapped in the breeze. Then he saw movement in another feed. "Dammit, you don't listen!" he said.

He saw Morana standing beside the refrigerator in his kitchen. She looked directly at the camera. Clay called his home phone. He heard the ring through his laptop. Morana ignored the phone and kept her eyes on the camera.

"Pick up!" Clay yelled.

Morana left the kitchen and went to the den. He enlarged the den feed to full screen. He called the burner number again.

Morana pulled her phone from her pocket. "What?"

"I warned you to wait until dark. If Mrs. Ramden across the street saw you, expect a police ambush anytime now."

"That's why I need to borrow your car. Where's the key?"

Clay laughed. "I saved your ass, gave you money, and now you want my car, too?"

"Look, I appreciate your help, but I need to use it to get some distance from here after dark. You can report the car stolen. When you come back, I'll tell you where you can find it for a miraculous recovery."

"I saw the news. A car is the wrong move. You are safer there than anywhere."

"Clay, I can decide what is safe. Can I borrow your car or not?"

"The answer is yes, but first, I want to show you something that might make you reconsider."

Morana turned to the camera. "I'm listening…"

"There's a bookcase in the living room."

Morana left the den and stepped over the clutter in the hallway to enter the living room. "You need a maid," she said.

"The mess will all make sense in a minute. The bookcase to your left," Clay said, clicking to a different feed on his laptop.

The window shades were drawn, but enough light came through the edges for Morana to see a small barrister bookcase against the wall. "Where's the light switch?" she asked, sliding her hand beside the doorframe.

"There's a flashlight behind the books on the top shelf of the bookcase. Get it, and then pull the bookcase away from the wall."

Morana found the flashlight and held it between her teeth while she slid the bookcase from the wall. Etched on the hardwood floor beneath it was a rectangular seam outlining the base of the bookcase. A metal pull-ring was connected to a chain at the edge.

"Pull the ring up," Clay instructed. "You have to pull hard."

As Morana pulled, the rectangular section of the floor raised on a concealed hinge. Cool air drifted up from the darkness below.

"There's a string under the edge. Pull it."

Morana kneeled and swept her hand inside the opening. "Before anything explodes when I pull this, you should know I'm worth more alive than dead," she said.

Clay laughed and said, "The only thing that is about to explode is your mind, baby!"

Morana grasped the string and pulled it. Lights came on, illuminating a sea of green in the opening below her. She kneeled and leaned into the opening, and looked around Clay's hidden basement, converted into a massive grow room. Thick bushes of cannabis, fed by a grid of plastic tubes, were lined wall to wall in perfect rows. A rope ladder hung from one edge of the opening, swaying in a breeze.

"Go on down and meet my babies," Clay said.

Morana smiled. "Why am I not surprised?" She climbed down the ladder and stepped off. She looked around the edges of the ceiling, homing in on a camera in the corner. She waved.

"Why is your face muddy?" Clay asked.

"Long story," she said, leaning closer to a plant. "Why can't I smell this?"

"I'm glad you said that. It means the neighbors can't smell it, either." Clay said. "Negative airflow. Look down."

At Morana's feet, vent slats lined the floor. The soft hum of fan blades visible through their slats pulled the air downward.

Evenly spaced ceiling fans above her head created a gentle downdraft, quivering leaves under pods of LED lights that sprouted in clusters from the ceiling like upside-down bouquets.

"I'm impressed. Feels nice in here," Morana said as she moved to the edge of the room.

"It *is* nice in there." Clay laughed. "The air conditioning pushes through a carbon filtration system layered with state-of-the-art ionizers and Ozonators. By the time any air in that room leaves the house, it's cleaner than the air in a surgery room. All the environmental control equipment is in a room behind the door to your right."

Morana sidestepped through the plants toward the hum of machinery behind a door. "Nice setup," she said. "Clever."

"If you had dated me, you could have had a piece of this."

"My loss," Morana shrugged.

Clay laughed, "I live down there when I'm home, which is rarely lately."

"Interesting hobby, Clay," she said. "I can't say I'm shocked."

"I'm going to choose to take that as a compliment. It hasn't taken off yet, but it will. I'm doing what I can to fund a decent retirement."

"Who tends to it while you are gone?"

"I do. It's all automated. If I have a serious power or water problem, I have a contact who can stop by to take care of things. That hasn't happened yet."

"Was it Benny?"

"No."

"Good."

"Look inside the cabinet on the far wall."

Morana went to it and opened a gun vault with what looked like thirty long guns in rows, cable-locked through their trigger housings. Below them was a large assortment of pistols, also locked. "Nice. Why are you letting me see all this?"

"So you'll trust me. Is it working?"

Morana looked around the room and then up to the opening in the ceiling as the rope ladder swayed in the breeze. "I'm encouraged."

"That answer is good enough. You want work? From what I see on the news, you're definitely between jobs."

"I appreciate yet another job offer from you, but this isn't my type of gig, Clay."

"The weed is nothing compared to the gigs you've been playing."

"What I did wasn't dirt. It was for a good cause."

"You killed. That's not dirt?"

"Don't lecture me."

"Fine. Believe it or not, I have something to show you that's much bigger than you can imagine, and the timing is perfect."

"No more money schemes, Clay."

"It's not a scheme, I swear. I'm gonna blow your mind. If you come to Florida and give me a chance, you can use my car."

"I don't want to fuck you, Clay."

"I'm not talking about that. Seriously, there's something spectacular I want to show you. I swear it will be worth your while."

"Clay, you know I hate surprises."

"I'll make a deal. If you see this and aren't as excited about it as I am, I'll give you my car. I'll sign over the damned title to you. As America's most wanted, you'd be smart to leave the state, anyway."

"Where's the key?"

"Number 159. Under the stalk."

Morana walked along the narrow aisle until she came to the #159 sticker on the side of a plant. She wormed her finger into the dirt, pulled out a plastic case, and removed the car key from it.

"Thanks," she said, holding it up for Clay to see.

"Good. Hold on a minute," Clay said.

A printer connected to a computer in the room's corner startled Morana when it hummed to life and spit out a piece of paper. She picked it up.

"That's my address," Clay said. "There's some more cash for gasoline in the bottom drawer of the computer desk."

"Thanks," Morana said.

"Mo, listen to me. I can't over-hype this. You need to get here."

"Don't beg."

"I'm never going to see you or my car again, am I?"

Morana blew the camera a kiss.

Chapter 3

FIVE DAYS LATER, when Clay arrived at his apartment, he pulled his briefcase from the back seat of his car. A voice behind him said, "Hi, stranger."

He turned and saw a tall blonde woman with a duffel bag over her shoulder. She wore a black leather jacket, jeans, sunglasses, and an unmarked black baseball cap pulled low.

He frowned and said, "Can I help—" but then smiled. "Mo?"

"I thought you'd be happier to see me," she said.

Clay grinned. "You scared the shit out of me!"

"You should have expected me."

"Not so soon."

"I made good time. It wasn't exactly a leisurely drive." She pulled the brim of her hat down lower. "Can we finish chatting inside?" She pointed to Clay's apartment building.

As they climbed the steps to the second level, Clay said, "Why won't you answer my calls? You're using a goddamn burner phone I sure as hell can't trace."

"I wouldn't bet that you couldn't. I wasn't ignoring your calls if it makes you feel any better. I dumped that burner phone in Phoenix."

"How long have you been here?"

"Long enough to profile a few neighbors while waiting for you to get home."

Clay laughed as he opened the door for her and looked her up and down as she passed by with her fingers tucked into her pockets. She dropped her duffel bag to the floor beside the door.

Clay opened his arms to hug her. She passed by him and went to his kitchen. "I've been dreaming about your shower," she said, walking to the hallway.

"That's flattering. The bathroom's that first door."

Morana came back for her bag. Clay followed her into the hallway. "I put fresh linen on our bed."

Morana stopped in the bathroom doorway and rolled her eyes at him.

"I only have one bed—I'll be good."

"Your sofa will be a luxury for me." She stepped past him to look into a small second bedroom Clay had set up as an office. A desk held two computers, a laptop, a printer, and several other devices with flashing lights. She returned to the bathroom and looked disgusted in the mirror before swiping her finger across each eyelid. She twiddled her fingers in a wave as she closed the door. After a shower, she emerged wearing a mocha-colored v-top under a jean jacket and black leggings. She entered the front room while leaning to the side, finger-combing her wet hair.

Clay got up from the sofa where he had been watching TV.

"Feel better?"

"A hundred percent," she slurred, with a hair band pinched between her lips. "Have I told you how much I hate sleeping in cars?"

"Well, this extended-stay corporate housing isn't exactly palatial, but I'm glad I could solve that problem for you."

"Thank you—I mean it," she said, flipping her hair back and pulling it into a ponytail.

"My pleasure." He looked her up and down. "Nice outfit. I see you made time to shop on your trip."

Morana shook her head. "I grabbed these at a yard sale outside Pensacola. You know I hate shopping—except for guns." She looked down at herself.

Clay nodded with approval. "Is that what my Bitcoin got you?"

"Look, I'll pay you back."

"I'm not worried about that."

"Then why are you looking at me that way?"

"Because—look at you... You're hot."

Morana sucked her teeth. "Tell me more about this new pyramid scheme you want to rope me into?"

"Keep on joking, Mo. I made a couple of calls while you were in the shower. Now that you've brought me my car, I can return my crappy rental. Afterward, I got the okay to show you something special at 6 o'clock."

"What is it?"

Clay leaned against the door frame. "I'm not going to tell you beforehand, but my offer to give you my car if you aren't impressed stands."

Morana put on some lipstick and rubbed her lips together. "I accept the offer."

†

While driving to Clay's mystery destination, he drummed his fingers on the steering wheel and occasionally grinned at Morana.

"What?" she asked. "Am I overdressed?"

"Not at all. I will introduce you to maybe the most reclusive guy you have ever met."

"I like him already," Morana said.

"His name is Thane Sykes. He's young, probably early twenties. He's one of those mad genius types. If I'm right about this, you'll blow his mind, and what he can do will blow yours."

"What does he do?"

"If we're lucky, he'll give you a demonstration. He's got a house but spends most of his time in the garage tucked in the back that he's converted into a workshop. He invited me over last week and showed me one of his projects. Mo, I'm still in shock from what he showed me."

"Does it involve guns?"

"No."

"Computers?"

"No."

"Then why do you know him?"

"He's my boss's nephew. Occasionally, my boss makes Thane come to the office to run errands and do other odd jobs. He forces him to walk around the office and ask every employee if they want their car washed. He might be one of those savants because, I swear to God, the poor guy looks tortured having to talk to people. By the end of each visit, you can see in his face how badly he wants to get away."

"And you think he'll be okay with me because…"

"Just listen, so anyway, about the third time he came to the office, I felt sort of bad for him, so I tried to be cool with him—you know— friendly. He seems sensitive to everything, so I make sure not to shake his hand. I don't force him into conversation like the others do. I always tip him really well when he washes my car. Last month, I gave him car wash money and whispered, 'Skip my car, but tell your uncle you did it.' I actually got a faint smile from him for that. Now, when he visits the office, he comes to my desk first."

Morana kicked off her shoes and crossed her feet on the dash. "Would you just tell me what he showed you already?" she said.

"Hold on—we're almost at his place. A couple of weeks ago, his uncle sent him to the printer to pick up an order of brochures for a corporate Egypt tour we booked for a client. So, I'm in the parking garage helping him transfer these boxes to my car. When we loaded the last box, I thanked him. Then he points to one brochure taped to the side of the box in my trunk and says, 'I know how they did that.' I couldn't believe he started a conversation, so I said, 'You know about 4-color offset printing?' He says, 'No, those.' He taps his finger on the two pyramids on the brochure. I laughed. He gets all serious and says, 'I'm not kidding,' like I had offended him. I said, 'I'm sorry, buddy. You know how they built the pyramids?' He looks around to make sure no one is watching and pulls a crumpled photograph from his pocket. Mo, I swear on my mama's life I damn near fainted."

"What was it?" Morana yelled, smacking Clay with the back of her hand.

"You'll see in a minute—I hope." Clay wrung the steering wheel as he turned onto another street. "So, Thane invites me to his place to see this special thing he's got. I wonder why he's so open with me, and when I get there, he tells me he's in some sort of trouble, and he's afraid to tell his uncle. Apparently, he had an accident with his truck a few months ago. He had no insurance. The guy he hit drives a Maserati and hired a pit bull of a lawyer. They've been harassing him for money to cover property damage and medical treatment for injuries that Thane says would have been impossible. So now these bastards are threatening to sue him. I can guarantee you that speaking publicly in a court of law would probably make his list of top three worst nightmares. This legal problem makes him sick, and he's freaked out that his uncle will find out."

"Why?"

"The boss can be tough with all the staff, but who knows how he is with family? I told Thane I would see what I could do to help him."

Morana smiled. "So, you're bringing me here for charity work?"

"Not at all. Mo, I'm telling you that when you see what he does, you'll know an accident settlement will be the last thing he needs to worry about. Trust me."

Clay turned onto a residential street lined with bungalows. "His place is right up there," Clay said, pointing. "I need to tell you some ground rules for this meeting."

Morana smiled. "You're going to tell me how to behave?"

"I'm serious—Thane is sensitive. Offend him, and he'll clam up, and we won't see anything—probably ever."

"Fine. What are your rules?"

"Don't force him to talk to you. He doesn't like to talk. Don't touch anything. He hates that. We'll leave our phones by the door. He hates electronics and is worried someone will record what he does. Keep your hands in plain sight."

"Is he armed?"

"Quit joking. Just smile, nod, and be polite, alright?"

Morana gave Clay a long look and said, "Could he recognize me?"

"I doubt it."

Morana winced.

"He hates the news, and he doesn't care about money. Does that help?"

"Okay," Morana said. "As long as you understand that if he recognizes me, I'll know it and have to kill him."

"Quit fucking around, Mo." Clay turned the car into a driveway.

"I'm not kidding," Morana said. "I can't believe I agreed to let you drive me to a mysterious location. If you've arranged an ambush, I'll make you sorry before they take me."

Clay drove slowly along the narrow driveway that flanked the house. The headlights lit up a pergola wrapped with a blanket of honeysuckle thick with white and yellow blossoms. As they passed through it, dense foliage scraped the car before opening like a stage curtain to the rear of the property. A fenced-in backyard contained several solar panels angled upward on stands in the center amidst untended grass and weeds. The driveway led to a detached garage opening to a space wide enough for only two parallel cars. A small red pickup truck was parked outside the garage's roll-up door.

Although there was room to park beside the red truck, Clay parked in the driveway beside the rear corner of the house. "C'mon," he said, getting out.

Morana stayed in the car, craning to look around with her hand tucked into her bag.

Clay came around to her side and thumped the window. "Would you relax? C'mon. I hope he hasn't changed his mind."

She got out, and they walked to the garage entry door. Clay knocked. The words *Go Away* were almost completely worn from a grass doormat.

While they waited, Morana kept her back to the garage, scanning the property behind the house. Trees and hedges on all sides of the backyard obscured it from the neighbors. Weather-worn paint that used to be white curled from the house and garage's exterior walls. All the windows were covered from the inside, and one was cracked. A few weeds had pushed through the cracked asphalt in front of the garage door.

The space in front of the garage was too narrow for the red truck to turn around, and dark tire marks ran the length of the driveway, showing where the old pickup truck had regularly backed to its position at the garage door.

"It actually looks like a place where a genius would live," Morana said.

"Wait until you see the inside—if he lets us in… Thane, buddy, it's me…" Clay knocked again, then used his fingernail to scrape some rust from the door hinge.

Morana moved closer to the truck to examine it. A small Chevy at least fifteen years old and decorated with plenty of dents, dings, and mismatched tires. She dropped to one knee and looked underneath, noticing a small pool of liquid below it. In the truck's bed, some metal poles were tied in a bundle and tucked neatly beside a chain wrapped around a wooden dowel. Water beaded on a black bed liner, likely explaining the puddle beneath the truck.

When Morana returned to where Clay stood, the small garage door opened a few inches, revealing darkness inside.

Clay put his mouth to the opening. "Thane? It's me." His voice echoed. There was no answer. Clay eased the door open and leaned in. "Thane?" He motioned for Morana to follow, and they stepped inside and stopped.

A single bright light bulb hanging from the opposite side of the garage lit the wide-open space of a pristine workshop. On the far side, clean countertops were below screwdrivers, hammers, crescent wrenches, and other simple tools that were wall-mounted with perfect spatial precision and sorted by size. The bulb hung from a long wire extending into the exposed wooden ceiling beams.

Clay and Morana stood on a large black area rug embroidered with images of golden padlocks. Cabinets lined the entire length of the back wall. More cabinets hung over a long, clean work surface on the wall opposite the entrance.

Various decorative doors hung on the shop's walls in a tapestry, each with a chain and key hanging from its knob. Contemporary doors, painted in bright colors, contrasted with numerous polished antique styles.

Below the light bulb, a small black man stood beside a waist-high cube positioned like a desk. He wore khaki pants, a dark green polo shirt, and an afro picked and shaped into a perfect sphere. He leaned with both hands onto the block, examining some papers spread on it.

Morana moved toward the man.

Clay grabbed her arm. "Thane, hey buddy," he called out. "You had me worried for a minute when you didn't answer! I thought you had forgotten we were coming."

Thane briefly raised his head and looked over silver-rimmed rectangular glasses.

Clay cleared his throat. "I brought my friend. Is it okay if we come over there?"

Thane gave a slight nod before returning his attention to the papers.

Clay pointed to a small table beside the front door that held a small plastic bowl. He fished his phone from his pocket and dropped it into the bowl. "Put your phone in there."

Morana hesitated.

Clay's widened his eyes at her. "Just do it. Don't make him ask."

Morana pulled her phone from her bag and placed it in the bowl.

As they crossed the garage toward Thane, Morana realized that the window coverings were nothing more than brown construction paper roughly taped in place, apparently for privacy.

"We left our phones by the door. No photos, we swear." Clay held up his hand, and his nervous laugh echoed.

Thane nodded again, remaining engrossed in the papers on what now appeared to be a cube of rock. Thane shuffled the papers and closed them into a folder.

"Buddy, this is the woman I told you about," Clay said, thumbing toward Morana. "She's completely trustworthy. You can call her Mo."

"Hi," Morana said. She stepped forward and reached out to shake, but Clay grabbed her arm again.

Thane looked up and down Morana with no change of expression.

Off to one side, a cat emerged from beside a cabinet. It was a Chausie cat, brown with a black tail and black pointed tufts on its ears.

"That's Gus," Clay said to Morana.

The cat stopped and inspected Morana and Clay, then strolled to Thane and rubbed against his leg before sauntering off to another part of the garage.

A faint car horn sounded outside. Thane's shoulders jerked, and he stood up straight.

The horn sounded again, longer.

Thane ran around the cube, running past Clay and Morana. "Don't move," he said as he raced out the entry door.

"What the hell?" Clay said, looking at Morana.

"I'd say he's a little tense," she replied. "Maybe he ordered delivery, and he's starving." She moved to the workbench to examine the tools.

Clay went to the door and looked out. Dusk was deepening to night, making it difficult to see detail, but he could make out Thane talking to a man midway up the driveway behind Clay's car. From Thane's gestures, the conversation seemed heated.

Clay rejoined Morana beside Thane's makeshift desk. A few moments later, Thane returned and closed the entry door behind him. "You shouldn't have parked in the driveway," he said.

"I'm sorry, buddy. I'll move it right now." Clay headed for the door.

"No!" Thane sidestepped to block Clay. "Don't go out there. It's fine this time. Leave it."

Morana had moved toward the wall, her hand concealed in her bag.

"Do you have company?" Clay asked.

"You saw them?" Thane looked concerned.

Clay exchanged a glance with Morana and then said, "I couldn't see clearly."

"Did they see you?" Thane asked.

"I don't think so. Would it be a problem if he did?"

"Maybe—I don't know." Thane wrung his fingers, opened the door a few inches, and looked out before closing it again. He locked the knob and deadbolt.

"Buddy, I didn't mean to cause a problem," Clay said.

Morana came to stand beside him.

Thane said, "It's okay, forget about it." He passed by them and returned to his cube desk.

"I don't like this," Morana whispered.

Clay flashed a frown and put his finger to his lips. "Relax, he does not know who you are." Clay cleared his throat and said, "Buddy, if you remember, we talked about someone who might help us with your situation. I asked you to trust me. Do you remember that?"

"Yes," Thane said.

"Well, this is her." Clay put his hand on Morana's shoulder. She shrugged it off.

"I changed my mind," Thane said.

"What?" Clay said. "Listen, buddy, she keeps a secret better than anyone I know. You said that was important, right?"

Thane looked at Morana and said, "Are you a lawyer?"

Clay looked at Morana, coaxing her to answer.

"I'm not," she said.

"Then you can't help me," Thane said.

"No, you're wrong about that," Clay said, clasping his hands in a prayer sign. He looked like he might cry. "You asked for my help. She's fantastic and trustworthy."

"I need a lawyer."

Morana watched the interaction between Clay and Thane, then tugged Clay's arm. "I'm intruding. I don't want to make him uncomfortable. We should go."

"Wait!" Clay said. "She's better than a lawyer. If you won't accept her help, then can you at least show her, you know, the thing you showed me?"

"She knows?" Thane asked suspiciously.

"No—I swear!" Clay held up his hands. "I promised I wouldn't reveal it, and I haven't."

"Show me what?" Morana asked.

"It's nothing," Thane said.

"I don't know what Clay wants you to show me," Morana said. "But I certainly don't want to make you feel uncomfortable." She turned to Clay and said, "We're done here. Let's go."

Thane moved to the opposite side of the cube desk so that it was between himself and them. He was about to speak when Clay said, "Buddy, I hate to pressure you, but I really think Mo could not only help you with your problem, but she's a privacy and camouflage expert." He looked around the space. "She could help you make your shop virtually disappear if you wanted her to."

Thane crossed his arms with his hands squeezed into fists. His lips tightened.

Morana hit Clay with her hand and said, "It's obvious that he's uncomfortable." She looked at Thane and said, "I respect secrets. I wish you the best of luck."

"Thane, buddy, for God's sake, listen…" Clay moved closer.

"Drop it, Clay," Morana said. "Don't nag him." She turned to Thane. "I can see that you and I are a lot alike. I apologize for Clay's pushiness." She turned to Clay, "Let's go."

"How?" Thane said.

"I beg your pardon?" Morana said.

"How are we alike?"

Clay crossed his fingers behind his back.

Morana looked around the shop. "Well, I don't like my photograph taken. I often don't trust technology. I despise a messy workspace—by the way—your shop is cleaner than any museum I've visited." She pointed at Clay. "And we have a common friend who is easily excitable and doesn't always know when to back off."

Clay rolled his eyes.

Thane stared down, fidgeting with a pencil on the desk.

Morana detected a hint of a smile. "And you are quiet," she added. "My favorite people are quiet. I don't know how long you've lived here, but the way you have prioritized your privacy, I love it."

"What do you do?" Thane asked.

Clay cleared his throat.

"I, uh, I'm between jobs," Morana replied.

"What did you do before?" He pushed the pencil aside and folded his hands.

Morana glanced at Clay. He motioned for her to hurry and answer.

"I was a manager—for an advocacy group that assisted the underprivileged."

Thane nodded, staring down at his interlocked fingers.

Morana said, "If you don't mind me sharing one suggestion..."

Thane nodded.

"Your solar panels in the backyard appear to be relatively new. The contrast between the clean solar array tucked out back in a yard that isn't— forgive me—well maintained could lead to suspicion that you are powering something covert."

"People don't see them," Thane said.

"Maybe not the neighbors, but satellites do. Images are high definition and available to virtually anyone." Morana said. "You might replace them with some more discrete solar shingles." She pointed up. "Roof shingles are available in what they call flexible, non-translucent luminescent concentrator material. They'll generate as much or more power than your current array. From the sky and the street, your house will blend in perfectly with nobody knowing you use solar power."

Clay grinned, pointing at Morana while looking at Thane, and said, "See?"

Thane slowly nodded and then said, "Thanks."

"You're welcome," Morana said. "I'm sorry for the unsolicited advice. It was nice to meet you." She turned and walked toward the door.

Clay mumbled, "Dammit," and followed her. "I'll call you, buddy," he said over his shoulder.

As they reached the door, Morana reached to retrieve her phone from the bowl.

Thane whistled from across the shop, startling both of them. Morana and Clay turned. "Oh, my God!" Morana gasped. Clay said, "That's it!"

Chapter 4

MORANA AND CLAY stood frozen, gawking at what they saw Thane doing.

"What the hell?" Morana said.

"What did I tell you?" Clay whispered.

The solid cube of rock that Thane used for a desk hung suspended in midair, its base level with Thane's shoulders. He spread his fingers, and with a slight push, the massive block slowly rotated. After allowing it to turn completely, he placed his hand on it, slowing the rotation to a stop.

Morana covered her mouth while Clay grinned, looking back and forth between her and the block. "Buddy, is it okay for us to approach?"

Thane nodded.

Morana followed Clay, and they moved closer. A faint hum came from somewhere above them. Thane pointed to an area on the floor a few steps away, directing them to stand there.

Morana bent down to look underneath to confirm that the block had no other connections.

Thane pressed two fingers against the corner of the block. Again, it rotated with the smoothness of gliding on ice. Only a thin, limp wire attached to the bottom corner wound to the wall behind Thane. Nothing else appeared to be connected to the block.

Behind Thane, high atop a cabinet, Gus looked down at them, the black tufts of his ears resembling sharp little horns. He didn't share their amazement.

Thane moved to the opposite side of the block, and it descended slowly to within ankle-height of the floor, and then walked around it, coming back to them as he slid his open hand on its surface.

"Is this magic?" Morana asked.

Thane looked at her and shouted, "No!"

The block dropped. Upon impact, its weight shook the garage's foundation and rattled the windows. Dust shot out from the rock's base.

Morana and Clay jumped back.

"Geez!" Clay gasped.

Thane scowled at Morana and raised his finger to her. "It's not an illusion."

"Don't even suggest that again," Clay said to her.

"I'm sorry," Morana said quietly. "I didn't mean to offend you. It's just that I've seen so many things that seem—"

"This is real," Thane said. "According to Newton's third law of motion, there is always an equal and opposite reaction to every action. Magicians want you to believe they've dodged this law, but they can't. No one can. And neither have I in this case."

"I understand," Morana said. "Please accept my apology."

Thane went to a closet at the side of the room and pulled out a broom. He returned and swept the dust from the base of the cube.

Clay said, "Thane, are you open to some questions?" he asked.

Thane's expression softened. Morana's apology and the sweeping seemed to have settled him. He gave a slight nod, then returned the broom to the closet.

"Good. Go ahead," he said to Morana. "Ask anything about the *science* of it." He pointed to the block.

"What does that block weigh?" she asked.

On his way back to them, he said, "This one is 4,059.19 kilograms or 8,948.98 pounds," Thane said. He leaned onto the block with both hands. "It's composed of coral limestone, which has a density roughly equal to 3,474.48 pounds per cubic meter. This block is precisely 1.81 cubic meters."

Morana leaned to see the wire running from the block's bottom corner to the wall. "What lifted it?" she asked.

"Me and the earth."

Morana and Clay exchanged a confused glance.

Thane spread his fingers on the rock again. The faint hum resumed. Thane guided the rock with his hands as it lifted again. He raised it higher this time, elevating it above his head.

Morana and Clay were already clear of the rock but stepped back further.

"Please don't drop it again," Morana said.

"I won't," Thane said. He lowered the block gently, bringing it to rest on the floor.

"How did you learn this?" Morana said.

"Master Edward Leedskalnin."

"Who is that?" Morana said.

Thane puffed a laugh, as though Morana should have known. "He was a true geomancer."

Morana looked at Clay for help.

Clay said, "From what Thane has taught me, a geomancer has a special understanding of the earth and its gravitational fluctuations based on patterns they can see on the ground. Edward Leedskalnin had this gift and moved tons of rock using simple tools. When he passed away, he left his writings, and Thane, here, has studied them, right, buddy?"

Thane nodded.

"Amazing," Morana said. "Can you help me understand the physics involved?"

"Probably not," Thane said.

Morana laughed and said, "I'm not insulted!"

"You shouldn't be," Thane said. "It requires a certain… aptitude."

Morana crossed her arms and said, "Try me."

"Alright," Thane said, "The physics at play in what you've observed involves vortex energy. Exploiting our unique position on one of the earth's diamagnetic vortex points provides an anomaly of telluric grid dynamics." Thane rested his hand on the block. "I have harnessed a function of linear, geometric magnetic flows at the atomic level by manipulating their convergence with diamagnetic gravity vortexes. This interaction allows adjustment to the resultant magnetic flux, effectively subjugating this object's centripetal acceleration, which attenuates its gravitational constant."

Morana raised her hands. "I give." She laughed.

Thane didn't.

"Let's keep the questions simple for now," Clay said. "Tell her how large a rock you can lift." He nudged Morana with his elbow.

"Theoretically, from this location, I could lift between 7.3 and 7.4 kilometers square of coral limestone," Thane said.

"Unbelievable," Clay said, grinning.

Thane went to a cabinet on the back wall, retrieved a green file folder, and brought it to Clay. "This is the information you asked for about the accident."

Clay took it and thumbed through a few of the documents inside. "Okay, buddy, but I really think you should reconsider letting—"

Thane cut him off. "You can show her." He pointed to Morana.

"Thank you. I promise she's trustworthy," Clay assured him.

"I hope so," Thane said. He looked at Morana and said, "Please keep all this secret."

Morana raised her right hand. "I swear. Thank you for trusting me."

"You're welcome."

"May I touch the block?" Morana asked.

Thane stepped back and motioned for her to help herself. She slid her hand along the porous surface that felt like a sandpaper texture. Its edges and corners were cut perfectly square with amazing precision and showed no visible chip of any size. She tried and failed to move it with both hands but couldn't nudge it. The rock felt every bit as heavy as Thane claimed.

When she finished walking a complete circle around the block, Thane went to the entry door. Gus followed him. Thane unlocked the door, opened it, and looked out. When he stepped aside, Gus raced outside.

"I have some work. Maybe you should go now." Thane said, opening the door wider.

"Oh, of course," Clay said. "Let's go, Mo. Buddy, I'll contact you after we review this information." He and Morana went to the entryway and retrieved their phones from the bowl. Thane held the door open for them as they exited.

Morana poked Clay's arm. "You never told me how cute he was."

Thane blushed as he closed the door and locked it.

Chapter 5

MORANA SAT QUIETLY, staring out the passenger window on their ride back to Clay's apartment. Several times, she blurted, "Oh, my God," as her head gently swayed with the car's movement.

Each time she said it, Clay replied, "Right?" unable to stop grinning as they considered what they had witnessed in Thane's garage.

While stopped at a traffic signal, Morana said, "It's incredible. And you swear it's not magic?"

"You heard the man. Thane hates magic! He's a scientist. I knew you'd be blown away," Clay said.

"All that physics stuff he said is an actual description?"

Clay held up his right hand and said, "It's one hundred percent authentic and accurate. Nerd-speak, I swear to God."

Morana slapped her leg and said, "I wish I could've recorded what he said. So tell me what you're thinking. What do you think this is good for?"

"Are you kidding me? Thane has figured out some anti-gravity mechanism, hasn't told a soul, and you're asking me what it's good for?"

"Yes, I am."

"The better question is: what *couldn't* you use it for? Movers, construction, civil engineering, hell, we could reroute rivers by building enormous dams in hours. And we'll finally be partners."

"So, why am I involved?"

"Because I'm generous, and I wanted to include you."

"Don't bullshit me, Clay."

"What?" Clay feigned being insulted. "Why wouldn't I?"

"Because you'd make twice as much on whatever scheme you plan if I wasn't involved. So why did you bring me into this?"

Clay cleared his throat. "Thane won't tell me anything about it—at all. The way I see it, he never will."

"You saw him refuse to tell me, too."

"Yes, but you're good at getting people to help you. You're persuasive, and he likes you—I can tell. Did you see his face when you said he was cute? I want you to get him to tell us how he moves those damned blocks."

"A legit business? Have you forgotten that I'm a fugitive?"

"Doesn't matter. Nobody on earth can chameleon better than you. We'll get you a new identity—we can change your name. In less than 24 hours, I can hook you up better than the federal witness protection program. I have connections that owe me. Trust me."

"I don't trust you. I only trust myself. And you still haven't told me exactly what you want from me."

"You convince him to tell you in a way we can understand. Then we patent the shit out of it and monetize it in a legit business."

Morana looked out the window briefly and said, "Clay, I don't know if he can make it simple. You heard him—he talks like he's collaborating with Einstein."

"You've got to try. I've visited him three times since he showed me, and he won't let me *watch* him work."

"Interesting," Morana said, twirling her hair around a finger. "What split are you thinking?"

"Fifty-fifty, baby," Clay said, pointing between them.

"What about Thane?"

"What about him?"

"What is his cut?"

"I don't know," Clay said, shifting in his seat. "We'll keep him happy."

"Clay, he gets a fair cut."

"Money isn't important to him," Clay said. "Thane wants his privacy more than anything else. If we can help him maintain that and ensure he has enough to work on his experiments in private for the rest of his life, we've made his dreams come true."

"I'm not ripping him off, Clay. You should know how I feel about that sort of exploitation."

"Okay, we give him a cut."

Morana glared at him.

Clay cleared his throat and added, "A fair cut… a third."

"Good," Morana said. "If you want me involved, that's how it will be, especially since you want me to do the initial heavy lifting—so to speak."

"If you get him to spill his secret, I'll agree to anything because money will be the least of our worries. Can you even imagine the potential revenue from this?"

"Yes, it's enormous."

They rode in silence for a few minutes, and then Clay chuckled.

"What?" Morana asked.

"You have no problem killing people like you did on your mission in LA, but a complete stranger not getting paid what you think he deserves pisses you off."

"Fair is fair. And for your information, I've never lifted a finger to anyone who didn't deserve it—unless doing so contributed to a greater cause."

"I understand. Are we... good?" Clay exaggerated a nervous glance at her.

"So far," Morana said. "If I'm going to work on Thane, I need to see his accident documents."

"I like how you're thinking," Clay said. He pulled the green folder from under the driver's seat and gave it to her. "Frankly, I think it's a scammer. Thane feels like the accident was staged. I think he was set up."

Morana flipped through the papers. "Interesting... Can you get me the full background on the driver? I need a full profile, including all addresses he visits regularly."

"What are you thinking?"

"Can you do it or not?"

"If I'm helping you, I'd just like to know in advance if you plan to do something illegal."

"What do I have to lose? Can you do it or not?"

"Mo, if you get too extreme and Thane gets any more paranoid, we'll get no info from him. And then, if it makes his potential legal problem worse, our entire plan is shot."

"Do I tell you how to operate your computers?"

Clay didn't answer.

"Then shut up and let me do what I do. I plan to give Thane one less thing to worry about. A hunch like the one I feel now has never been wrong."

Chapter 6

THE NEXT MORNING, Morana woke up to the sound of slurping interlaced with the clinking of Clay's spoon in a cereal bowl.

"Morning," Clay said.

Morana gave a halfhearted wave before she got up and went to the restroom. She returned minutes later, having changed, and pulled her hair back.

She came and sat beside Clay at the table.

"Have you figured out how to get Thane to talk to us?" he asked, crunching on his cereal. He offered her an overripe banana.

"Yes, we need money." She took the banana.

"How much?"

"We'll have to work with what's available. Of the two of us, you're the only partner in a position to fund our startup costs."

"It's funny how you use the word partner, then tell me I need to come up with the money."

"You know I'm broke." She peeled the banana and took a bite. "You knew that when you asked me to help you."

"I get that. As long as you understand, I get proportionate equity if I carry the financial risk."

Morana stopped chewing and gave him a skeptical look. "Do you know the absurd revenue potential this thing has?"

"I'm just saying…" Clay raised his shoulders

"I can see that your greed probably ruined all your other schemes. This is what I missed by not working with you before?"

"Okay, okay, okay," Clay said. "How much cash are you thinking?"

"Not much. I need simple supplies, clothes, makeup, and a few tools—to start. And, frankly, you could use some groceries. Five thousand should cover it. I can get us started."

Clay went to his bedroom. When he returned, he counted out $2,500 into her open hand. She folded the cash and tucked it into her pocket.

"That's half," she said.

"It's all I have on hand. I'll cash out some Bitcoin for the rest." He opened a phone app, jotted an extended code onto a napkin, and gave that to her. "This will get you the other half. Don't spend it all in one place."

He pulled a phone from his pocket and gave it to her.

"I'm supposed to trust this?" she asked.

"God, Mo, it's a dead phone that was registered to me!" He popped the back cover off and inserted a battery. After the phone rebooted, he turned the screen toward her and pointed to an icon. "Use this app to message me. It'll encrypt our text conversations. I'll activate the calling service for this phone tomorrow."

"I don't need the phone, Clay."

"Just take it."

"I prefer burners."

"They're not encrypted."

"Anonymous communication needs no encryption."

"Suit yourself." Clay got up and picked up a tablet from the countertop. "So this morning, I got the profile information you wanted on the guy harassing Thane."

"Let me see." She took the tablet from him and scanned the details. "He's going after Thane for—how much?"

Clay looked over her shoulder and pointed to a place on the screen. "He's trying to get $10,000 from Thane, but that makes no sense. According to the records I found, Everett Paige is a successful stockbroker worth about $60 million. And the dirt under his mansion in Arborcliffe Estates is worth at least $3 million, yet he's going after Thane for 10,000? Something doesn't add up."

"Thane can't pull together ten grand?" Morana asked.

"You saw his truck as clearly as Everett and his lawyer must have. They've got to know he doesn't have any money."

Morana thought momentarily and then said, "Can you get me a full panel on Everett?"

"What do you mean?"

"His email addresses, phone numbers, mortgages, calendar, and anything else I can use for a profile. The deeper you can drill down, the better."

Clay took the tablet back from her. "Although I'm incredibly uneasy about what you'll do with this information, it's all on the following pages." Clay swiped through several screens. "Social media passwords, banking passwords, and a hundred other logins."

Morana said, "Beautiful." She took the tablet to the sofa and began reviewing the details of Thane's harasser.

Clay said, "The guy is boring, but he's made a few enemies in online forums arguing about politics. He doesn't cover his tracks very well for being such a jerk. I guess when you're that rich, lawyers fix any problem."

"How did you get all of this information?" Morana said.

"Getting scoop is my thing."

"No, seriously—this is great. I need to know your capabilities. How did you do this?"

"This one was easy. I emailed an attachment to his secretary earlier this morning and then phoned her to verify its authenticity."

"An attachment?"

"Yes, I asked that she open it to make sure it was viewable. It was a tax form I told her Everett had ordered. She opened it, and a little piece of malware I authored granted me access to Everett's world. I pulled all her browser-saved passwords and hacked their router with little effort. Everett wasn't in yet, so I took a quick tour of his computer after blanking the monitor. I think I have everything except a blood sample from the guy."

"Nice work, master hacker. I'll take it from here." She got up and went to the fridge.

"The sooner, the better on whatever you plan to do," Clay said. "Thane is freaked out and thinks he's going to prison and will lose his precious garage. He'd rather die than lose it. So, until this issue is out of his life, you can bet he won't say a word about how he does anything in there."

"Where are the papers Thane gave us?"

"I'll get them," Clay said, heading for the bedroom. "I have to get ready for work." He disappeared into the hallway.

With Clay out of sight, Morana crept to the table and picked up his phone. She quickly opened his contact list and found Thane's number. She memorized it, locked the phone, and then jotted the number on the other side of the napkin with the Bitcoin code. She tucked it into her pocket just as Clay returned.

He handed her the papers. His mobile phone rang. He checked the number and said, "Dammit. I have to take this…" He left the room again.

Morana heard a tense conversation from behind his office door. Clay's voice was muffled, not clear enough to understand. She poured herself some stale cereal and sat at a table, leafing through the printouts on Everett.

When Clay exited his office, he said, "We need to put everything on hold."

"Why?"

"I have to go to LA." He pocketed his phone and sighed.

"You're kidding…"

"I wish I was."

"When?"

"Now. I tried to get out of it. One of our clients is booking a Fiji tour, and the boss wants me to meet their organizer in person at their LA office first thing tomorrow morning. It's a big contract. Also, I've got a busted water pump in the house, according to my monitoring app for the nursery, so I need to tend to that while I'm there."

"Can I stay here?" Morana asked.

"Sure, But I don't want you working on Thane until I return."

"Why not?"

"I want to be here, and I want to be involved. I introduced you. I'm funding this thing."

"Clay, timing is key. I can have all the info we need from him before you get back."

"Why don't you listen?"

"You asked for my help. Let me help."

Clay went into the bedroom and slammed the door. A few minutes later, he came out with a couple of packed bags and said, "You aren't going to wait for me, are you?" Clay said.

"You'll thank me later."

Morana drove Clay to the airport in his car. As they neared the terminal, she said, "There's one more thing. "

Clay didn't answer. He shook his head and looked out the passenger window.

"I need access to your guns," Morana said. "There is no way you wouldn't have some."

"I knew this was coming."

"Then just save me some time and tell me where you've stashed them."

"Listen, Mo, as creative as I've been with laws, I can't afford to get tangled up in whatever you're planning that needs a gun."

"We're already tangled, Clay. You've harbored me, so we're both wanted by the law. They want me more than you at the moment."

Clay raised his hands and said, "I really hate it when you threaten me, Mo. I'm doing you a favor!"

"You shouldn't feel threatened. Our ability to harm each other is equal. Mutually assured destruction. That power keeps us both safe."

"That's so soothing," Clay said.

"You know I'm not reckless. Quit trying to manage me. You do what you're good at. I'll do what I'm good at, and things will be perfect for us."

They arrived at the airport, and she pulled the car to the curb. Clay opened the door and paused before getting out. "Check my bedroom bookcase. Look inside the thickest books."

"Thanks."

Clay grabbed his bags from the trunk and stooped to the passenger window. Morana rolled it down. "I'll be calling the apartment from my house. Caller ID will have my name, so answer. Be careful."

"I'm never careless."

Clay waved over his shoulder as he walked toward the terminal entrance.

"Clay!" Morana called out. He stopped and looked back.

"Thanks. I appreciate—you know—everything."

✝

On the drive back to Clay's apartment, Morana stopped and purchased an additional burner phone after intentionally leaving the phone Clay gave her stuffed between his sofa cushions. At the apartment, she went to his bedroom and scanned the bookcase for the thickest books. She pulled them out: a Glock, a Smith & Wesson, and a Beretta. At the top of his closet, under some linen, she found a few boxes of ammunition.

Later that afternoon, Morana used her new burner phone to call Thane. The phone rang ten times with no voicemail pick up despite Clay's claim that Thane rarely left his shop. She tried again a couple of hours later and let the phone ring fifteen times before she hung up. She double-checked the number she'd written on the napkin to see if she might have dialed the wrong digit.

After spending some time in Clay's home office researching on a computer Clay left out for her, she tried calling Thane again.

"Hello."

"Hi, Thane?"

"Who is this?"

"It's… Mo, Clay's friend. We met last night. You showed us—"

"I remember."

"Good. How are you?"

Thane didn't respond.

"…Are you there?"

"Why did you call?"

"Okay… I want to talk to you about your situation—with your truck. I think I can help."

"Where's Clay?"

"He had to leave town for a few days unexpectedly. I just took him to the airport."

"I know."

"Pardon?"

"He told me already."

"Then why did you ask?"

"You were honest."

"Yes, of course… was that a test?"

"Are you dating Clay?"

Morana pulled the phone from her ear and frowned at it. "Did he tell you that?"

"Yes."

"That's not true."

"So, you're saying that Clay lies?"

"What I'm saying is that Clay sometimes exaggerates. Listen, Thane—"

"If you're not dating him, he lied to me. Maybe I can't trust him."

"I wouldn't go that far. His intentions are usually good."

"Can you help me without Clay?"

"Absolutely—your trust would mean a great deal to me."

"What do you have to tell me about the accident?"

"Listen, Thane, could I stop by later this evening to show you?"

"Why can't you tell me now?"

"Based on what I've learned, I'd rather not share it on the phone."

"Do you think my phone is bugged?"

"No, I'm not saying that. But I don't want to take risks because privacy is so important to us. Talking in person is safer."

"I thought so."

"You thought what?"

"I thought you would refuse to tell me on the phone. That's good."

"Was that another test?"

"You passed."

Morana laughed. "Then, can we meet?"

"When?"

"How about now? I could be there in about a half hour."

"Today isn't good. Maybe tomorrow."

"Fine… But can you answer one question for me?"

"Maybe."

Morana pressed the phone to her shoulder as she walked to Clay's office. She pawed through some notes she had jotted beside the laptop. "Is it true that Ed Leedskalnin built a perpetual motion holder?"

"How do you know that?" Thane asked.

"I was so impressed by what you showed us. I researched and tried to grasp some of Master Leedskalnin's concepts, but I couldn't understand all the technical information in the YouTube video. I hesitated to ask you because I assumed your explanation would be above my head."

"Interesting," Thane said.

"So, have you ever tried that experiment?" Morana asked.

"Of course. Many times."

"After our call, I plan to buy some copper wire and bolts to see if I can replicate one of Ed Leedskalnin's magnetic current experiments."

"Really?"

"Absolutely. I'll let you know how it goes. Wish me luck."

"Where will you get supplies?"

"Hold on, I wrote it down…" Morana turned the laptop toward her and typed quietly, Googling hardware stores. "I'm going to… Perry's Hardware on 17th Street," she said.

"Be sure the copper wire is at least 20-gauge—do you really plan to attempt this?"

"Absolutely. It fascinates me. By the way, can you recommend a battery size for magnetizing six half-inch bolts?"

There was no reply.

"Thane?" Morana said.

"Maybe I have extra supplies. Why don't I help?"

"Oh, I couldn't impose…"

"We're meeting anyway, so why not?"

"But that isn't until tomorrow. I'm so excited about this. I had planned to try it right away."

"If you can wait, I'll give you a demonstration using better hardware than you can purchase."

"Sounds wonderful. It's a date!" Morana said. "What time should I arrive?"

"Seven o'clock."

"Can I bring any supplies?"

"No, don't. And knock first," Thane said.

"I promise. See you then."

Morana drove to a local coffee shop with Clay's laptop and connected to the wireless network before opening her Tor browser. She spent the next hour researching Edward Leedskalnin's experiments and writings. She studied his life and interests and reviewed more of his experiments that fans had recreated on YouTube.

When she drove back to Clay's street, she heard a news report about the nation's search for her and an increase of her reward to $1.25 million. She pulled to the side of the road, a safe distance from Clay's apartment building, and waited a few minutes, watching for anything suspicious.

She took out her phone and reviewed her photograph of the street in front of the apartment building before she had left earlier. Most of the cars were still in position, except a red Camry with tinted windows parked almost directly across the walkway to the building. She would have paid little attention to it, except that the tinted driver's window was open a couple of inches, and someone inside flicked out a cigarette. Anyone waiting in a parked car within a hundred feet of anywhere she went was a suspect. She made a U-turn and drove away, confirming in her rearview mirror that the car didn't follow her. To wait out the threat, she worked with a pocket mirror to fine-tune her disguise and then went shopping to purchase several items for her meeting with Thane.

It was almost dark when she returned to Clay's place. Although the Camry was gone, she still parked a block away from the apartment building. She exited the car and climbed from the driver's seat to the passenger seat.

Instead of taking the front sidewalk to Clay's apartment, she walked along the edge of the building to the back, where a laundry room opened directly into the apartment's courtyard. This allowed her to get to Clay's staircase from a rear walkway not visible from the street.

She pulled a pistol, keeping it hidden, then unlocked the front door. After checking to see if any neighbors were watching, she stepped inside and raised the gun, clearing each room of the apartment.

There's no way Clay would send the authorities to Thane's house. He would know that a raid on Thane's property would ruin any opportunity to learn the secret of Thane's mysteries. Morana was confident that Clay knew that.

Turning her in from the privacy of his own apartment was a different story. She went to the front window and peered through a crack in the blinds. The red Camry had returned, parked in perfect camera position. If somebody was in the car, their position to view Clay's apartment was perfect. Her paranoia grew.

She knew the guns hidden in the hollowed-out books couldn't be the only guns Clay had, so she ran to the bedroom and scoured it, lifting all the floor rugs and moving pictures, searching for hidden compartments. She flung his bed linens back and kneeled, drawing her hand along the edge of the mattress. She felt a roughly sewn flap on the side of the box spring mattress. She pulled it open and pulled out a metal box. She opened it, revealing a foam-lined case that contained four more handguns—one with a suppressor. On the opposite side of the mattress, she reached into another slit and pulled out box after box of ammunition. She emptied a large duffel bag full of tour brochures in the room's corner and loaded the weapons and ammunition into it.

She went to Clay's office and rifled through his desk drawers, finding some credit cards and cash that she pocketed. If her hunch was wrong, and Clay had been forthright with her, she'd see that this loan was repaid in full—with interest. If he had betrayed her, the money would be the smallest portion of his repayment.

As she slung the duffle bag over her shoulder and stepped into the hallway, a shadow passed by the front window on the walkway out front. The figure slowed near Clay's door and then continued. She tiptoed back into the bedroom. She set the duffle bag on the floor, pulled the pistol, and took a position in the hallway with a clear view of the front door. If an ambush was imminent, she'd make them sorry. While she waited, something caught her eye. An electrical socket on the wall beside her had unusually large screws. She squatted for a closer look and noticed that the top screw wasn't a screw but a lens.

After waiting a few more minutes, she eased through the apartment's front room. A cabinet knob on the television console was off-color. She pulled it open. The glass knob was connected to a tiny camera on the inside. "Bastard," she said.

She held her gun in the ready position and crept back to the hallway, keeping her gun aimed at the front door. She sidestepped into the bathroom and found small cameras behind the medicine cabinet mirror, inside the tissue box aimed toward the toilet, and in the shower head.

She backed into the bedroom and pulled the sheets from the bed. Clay's landline rang. The caller ID showed his LA phone number.

She slung the duffle over her shoulder and answered. "I'm only answering your call to tell you I'm about to entertain your guests, and I'm not feeling hospitable."

"What are you talking about?" Clay said. "I just landed in LA, and I'm calling to check on you."

Morana turned off the bedroom light and opened the sliding balcony door. "Aren't you watching? I found the cameras, Clay."

"Mo, tell me what's going on?"

"I gotta go." She hung up, placed the heavy duffel bag on the balcony, and then tied the bedsheets together. She connected one end to the balcony railing.

Someone pounded on Clay's front door. She tucked the gun into her jeans, slung the duffel over her shoulder and rappelled from the balcony.

As she neared ground-level, a voice said, "Hey, what are you doing?" Clay's downstairs neighbor had come out onto her patio.

"Fire drill," Morana said as her feet touched down. She ran to the back of the property and disappeared into the darkness.

Chapter 7

MORANA TOTED HER heavy bag for a mile and a half to the outskirts of the suburb until she found a highway overpass. Plastic cups, dirty towels, and syringes were scattered on the ground below. The area was vacant today, so she decided to stay here for the night, making herself as comfortable as possible. She laid down after pulling a pistol from her new cache of weapons. Although the ground wasn't comfortable, she was tired, and the temperature was comfortable. Soon, she fell asleep.

The following day, she was up before dawn, using her burner phone to search for a used car. She found some local listings. One of them was a private party selling a used 1999 Ford Expedition with nearly 200,000 miles on it. The ad offered it at $1500. Morana took a bus to within a few blocks of the seller's address, walking the rest of the way. After a brief negotiation, the seller agreed to her offer of $985 cash.

Her first stop in her new ride was at a restaurant. She staked out at a distance for an hour before driving into the parking lot. This was ideal because the restroom doors were only three steps from the side entrance.

She entered, washed up, and changed clothes before making other brief stops to prepare for her meeting with Thane. The first was at *Better Safe Spy Shop*, in the back of an industrial center. She browsed through their wide selection of security, surveillance, and counter-surveillance equipment. She eventually paid cash for bug detectors, an ambient sound amplifier, and a battery-powered micro-video recorder easily adjustable to fit into almost any small device.

She found some high-resolution photos of Ed Leedskalnin with her phone, setting up an online order for a large poster of one of them from a local copy shop.

While waiting for the shop to process the poster, she used Clay's password information to log into Everett Paige's email. Scrolling his Inbox, she saw email messages from his broker to confirm stock trades, a few real estate marketing, and messages from his assistant. One message from his wife caught her eye.

Honey,

Ashwell Interiors will stop by to measure our lounge next week.
They want to take measurements for the new floor while we settle on
a hardwood. Tell me which of the attached samples you like.

XO

Morana saved a screenshot of the message on her phone and then made a couple more shopping stops to update her wardrobe with clothing and makeup for disguises. After purchasing a burger at a drive-thru, she headed to Thane's place.

Her phone rang. The caller ID read *Sykes.*

"Thane?"

"Yes."

"What's going on?"

"We need to reschedule."

Morana clapped her hand to her forehead. "Oh, no, what happened?"

"I don't have much time to talk. There's something I have to do. Maybe you could come at 8 o'clock instead of 7 o'clock."

Morana sighed with relief. "Yes, I can do that. Are you okay? You sound stressed."

"No, it's fine. I think I can finish by 8 o'clock."

"It's okay, don't worry. I'll call you when I get there. If you don't answer, I will wait in my car until you return, okay?"

"Yes, that's good. And don't park in the driveway."

"I promise I won't. Is anything wrong?"

"I have to go."

"Thane? Thane?"

The line was dead.

When Morana turned onto Thane's street a half hour early, she parked a couple of blocks away and waited until 8:01 PM before dialing Thane's number.

Thane answered, saying, "I'm ready. Where are you?"

"Great, I'm turning onto your street. I'll be there in a couple of minutes."

"Don't let yourself in. Be sure to knock so I can open the door for you."

"Of course."

Morana exited her Explorer wearing a crimson blouse, black leggings, and a black leather shoulder bag. She pulled a gift bag and a long cardboard cutout from the back seat and headed to Thane's driveway. She passed through the honeysuckle foliage hanging from the pergola and emerged to the rear of the property. She listened for sounds coming from the garage as she passed by Thane's truck to the entry door but heard only crickets.

She leaned the cutout against the side of the garage, then came to the entry door and knocked, concealing the gift bag behind her. Unlike her first visit with Clay, Thane answered the door immediately. He wore the same khaki pants and dark green shirt she remembered from her first visit. His afro was combed out and perfectly shaped. He panted, wearing a taut expression.

"Hi there, Mr. Sykes," Morana said. She tilted her head and smiled.

Something moved near her feet, startling her. Gus darted out the open door. He ran to the corner of the yard and leaped to the top of the wooden fence.

"Hi," Thane said. While catching his breath, he looked up and down at her, taking in her outfit, avoiding eye contact.

"Is everything okay?" Morana asked.

"Why?" Thane said, looking past her to the house.

"You seem a little frazzled, that's all." Morana looked over her shoulder, too. The house lights were off.

"No, I'm fine." Thane wiped his forehead on his sleeve. He leaned slightly, trying to see what Morana held behind her back.

She brought the bag to her front and held it out to him. "I brought gifts for you."

Thane pushed his glasses higher onto his nose and slowly took the bags. "Why would you get me gifts?"

"Uh…" Morana tapped her cheek and looked up, smirking. "Because I wanted to."

Thane pushed the door wider for her and stepped back inside the garage.

When she entered, stepping onto the black area rug with golden embroidered locks, Thane closed the door behind her and locked it. He looked down into the bag. "Can I open it now?" he asked.

"I would love for you to!" Morana clasped her hands.

"Over here." Thane walked to the work block on the opposite side of his shop. Before following him, Morana said, "I'm leaving my phone here." She dropped her phone into the bowl by the door.

"Thank you," Thane said, examining the gifts as he set them on his work block.

Morana saw a wooden armchair a few feet away with a windbreaker draped over its back. A neat stack of magazines and a spool of packing tape was on the seat. She remembered seeing these items on their first visit, and they had remained untouched.

She pulled a small black clutch from her bag, and while Thane removed a gift from the bag a short distance away, she subtly tucked the clutch on the stack of magazines, aiming its torn seam toward Thane's work area. She had inserted the micro-video camera's lens inside the seam, concealed in the bottom of a lipstick dial.

She crossed the shop to join Thane and reverently approached the work block to stand on the opposite side, facing him.

Thane examined a plain brown box from the gift bag. He held it up high for a better view.

"Go ahead!" Morana said. "Open it!"

Thane opened the box flap and pulled out a large brown plastic key the size of a lunchbox tucked among packing shreds. He looked at it, puzzled, examining each side for a clue about its function. He knocked on it. The plastic sounded hollow. "What is this supposed to be?"

"May I come around and show you?"

"Sure," Thane said, frowning at the key.

Morana came to him, and when he looked up at her face, she stepped back to lessen the conspicuousness of her six-inch height advantage.

"There's one more piece to this gift," she said, reaching into her bag. She pulled out a tiny door the size of a cigarette lighter and handed it to him. "Instead of a key opening a door, this is a door opening a key."

Thane slipped the small door into the slot of the key container and opened it, revealing hundreds of paper cutouts of doors of every style. Thane grinned as he shook them out onto the work block. He pawed through them, removing a few to rotate and move them to a row.

"What is its purpose?" Thane asked, tapping the key container.

"Fun. It's just a novelty. I noticed your amazing decorative doors and keys." Morana pointed to the workshop's walls. "So, when I saw this key container, I knew you should own it."

"That was kind. Thank you," he said, gathering the cutouts together. He took them to a drawer, then returned to the block. He took the large plastic key to a nearby wall and placed it on a shelf inside a cabinet. "Ready to begin the experiment?" he asked, returning to her.

"Not yet—there's one more thing…"

Thane looked at her suspiciously.

"Wait there," Morana said. She exited the garage and returned moments later, carrying the cardboard piece she had leaned against the side wall. She brought it to Thane, keeping the face of the display hidden.

"What is it?" he asked.

Morana put her hand on her chest. "I don't know what you'll think of this, so my heart is beating so fast right now." She rotated it for him to see, revealing a full-scale cutout of Ed Leedskalnin.

Thane's eyes widened, and he beamed. "Where did you get this?"

"I made it for you." She unfolded a piece of cardboard at the bottom to stand up on its own.

While Thane marveled at the cutout, Morana pulled a deflated plastic ball from her bag. She blew it up to the size of a small melon, revealing a model wrapped in a high-definition photograph of the earth, complete with its bright blue oceans, cloud cover, and land. She connected it to the Leedskalnin cutout's upraised hand and steadied it. "Do you like it?" She clasped her hands under her chin and held her breath.

He stepped closer. The cutout was within an inch of Thane's height. He smiled, reached out, and touched Master Leedskalnin's shoulder. "This is remarkable."

Morana exhaled. "Whew! I hoped you would like it," she said. "Where should we put it?"

Thane reverently picked it up and carried it to the corner of the shop where he stood it upright, facing his work block. He stepped back and rested his chin on his hand, smiling. "Thank you for this," he whispered.

Morana came to him. "You're welcome. I didn't have Master Leedskalnin's name put on it because I wanted to keep this private. The printer asked me who the man was. I didn't tell him."

"People don't realize what a great man he was," Thane replied, stepping away to examine the model from a different angle. "If anyone asks you again, please share his name."

"I thought you wouldn't want that."

"Master Leedskalnin kept his methods private. He freely shared his results. He shouldn't be a secret."

"I understand," Morana said. "But, for now, consider this a private gift from me to you."

"Thank you," Thane opened a cabinet and raised to his toes to reach a key that hung with several others from a nail inside. He pulled it off and tore a piece of clear tape from the dispenser below. He pressed the key to the hand of Ed Leedskalnin, adjusting the angle so it looked natural, and then taped it there.

"May I ask why you collect doors and keys?"

"Leverage intrigues me."

Morana frowned. "I don't understand."

"A tiny key can open an enormous door with little effort."

"Does that apply to how you lifted the block?"

Thane crossed his arms. His expression tightened.

"I'm sorry. Forgive me for prying," Morana said. "I hope you take it as a compliment that I'm completely fascinated by your work."

Thane didn't answer. He returned to the work block. "Clay said I could trust you."

"Of course, you can. I can tell you Clay *isn't* lying about that," Morana said with a small laugh. She raised her right hand. "I swear I won't say a word, but if you don't mind my asking, what do you think would happen if word got out about what you can do?"

Thane shrugged and folded his hands on the block. "That should be impossible, right?"

"Of course, but I just wondered—"

"Why consider it if it's not something that should happen?" Thane cut her off.

"I'm sorry." Morana raised her hands. "I won't ask again."

The tension drained from Thane's face. He spread his hands on the block and leaned on it. "Let's get on with the experiment you wanted to re-create," he said, walking to a cabinet. He removed a tray loaded with copper wire, bolts, magnets, a large battery, and several tools and returned it to the block. He removed a U-shaped piece of metal and began coiling a copper wire around its base. "Please sit here," he said, dragging a chair to a place beside the block.

Morana sat.

Thane rested his hand on the edge of the tray and said, "Today, we will recreate a perpetual motion holder."

Morana bit her lip to avoid smiling at the awkward formality of Thane's introduction.

For the next twenty minutes, he recreated the Leedskalnin experiment, explaining every piece of hardware and every step.

Morana committed little of what Thane said to memory, occasionally nodding and conveying as much interest as possible. Thane became utterly absorbed in the topic, smiling when he described Master Leedskalnin's successes with related experiments. He eventually announced that the demonstration was complete and held up the result of metal and wires that remained fused even after removing a connected battery. "We have created a permanent magnet," he announced. "You can examine it."

Morana clapped and leaned in for a closer look. "If you can't answer this next question, just tell me to back off. But without giving away your secret, is this experiment related to the method you used to lift this table?"

"You found my description of the physics involved challenging to understand, remember?"

"Yes, but now I've studied a little, and you've given me this wonderful tutorial."

"This wasn't a tutorial. It was a demonstration," Thane said, his voice tense. "I wasn't teaching, I was demonstrating."

"I'm sorry—please forgive me," Morana said.

Thane carried the tray back to the cabinet, his lips pursed. As he tried to slide the tray onto the cabinet shelf, he bumped the corner, and the tray fell, spilling all its contents on the floor.

"Oh, no!" Morana said, running to him. She kneeled to help.

Thane said, "No, I can fix it."

When Morana reached for a magnet, Thane snapped, "No, don't touch it. I don't need you..."

Morana pulled her hand away and stood. She backed away while watching Thane carefully pick up and position each item, creating neat rows on the tray. When he finished, he carefully slid it into the cabinet.

When he returned to her, he said, "We're finished." He sat in the chair and rocked, staring at the entry door.

"So... are you asking me to leave?" Morana asked.

Thane stopped rocking. "The demonstration is finished." He ran his thumbnail along a groove in the block, keeping his eyes on the door.

Morana said, "Thane, there's something important we need to discuss."

"Maybe this isn't a good time," he said.

"I'm sorry I asked about the block again. I didn't mean to upset you. But I need to review some information with you about your accident situation." She opened her bag and pulled a piece of paper from it. She placed it on the block in front of him.

Thane briefly glanced at it and went back to digging the groove.

Morana pushed it closer to him. "I think you should see this. I don't want to panic you, but this Everett Paige has used judgment liens in several cases before yours."

Thane stopped and said, "What does that mean?"

"A judgment lien can be created if someone wins a lawsuit against you. If you cannot pay, the judgment is recorded against your property."

"That can't happen!" Thane said, standing.

"I'm afraid that it will happen if we can't settle this issue with Everett."

Thane grabbed his hair. "How can I settle?"

"$10,000 solves your problem."

"I don't have that kind of money."

"Then he'll seek a judgment to squeeze it out of your property."

"That can't happen," Thane said. "Please don't let that happen."

"I might prevent that if I can convince Everett to change his mind."

"You mean—contact him directly? Are you a lawyer?"

"No, but I can be persuasive."

Thane cringed. "Maybe we should wait for Clay. He knows how to negotiate. He's in sales and told me to wait for him before I talk to you."

"He did?" Morana's jaw clenched.

"Yes, and he said you might not keep my work a secret."

"Really..." She took a deep breath. "Thane, although both Clay and I could help you, I'm better equipped to help in this situation than he is. I would *never* violate your privacy. Don't forget how adamant Clay was when he told you I was an ideal person to help you with the situation."

"Still, maybe we should wait. Clay said he'd be back in town soon."

Morana cleared her throat. "So, when did he tell you that I might not keep your secret?"

"He called me right before you got here. He said he has a new plan to make this problem disappear."

"Listen, Thane, Clay, and I worked together. He and I may seem at odds, but we aren't."

"Then why did he tell me to call him when you leave? It feels like you two are competing."

"Thane, let's take the stress off you. Why don't we forget that Clay and I are working together for now? Suppose you could only choose one of us. You can wait for him to return to town, but we don't know how long he'll be gone. I'm already here, ready to help, and timing is critical to getting this problem resolved for you."

Thane resumed rocking in the chair, studying his thumbnail. "Why are you so willing to help me?"

"Because I like you... and you have impressed me with your amazing demonstrations. I wouldn't want anything to prevent you from continuing your work, and from what I can see, it wouldn't take much time to fix this for you." She tapped her finger on the paperwork. "I think this Everett person is trying to scam you, and I hate that sort of injustice more than anything."

"And what do you expect in return?"

"What else would I want?"

"I'm not disclosing how I raise the blocks," he said.

"I haven't asked you to disclose it."

"I saw your reactions when you saw what I did. You don't even know me. Why else would you want to help me?"

Morana smiled. "I'll make you a deal. Let me see what I can do to help you with this problem. If I haven't completely resolved it before Clay returns, I'll bow out, and he can take over."

"I suppose that would be fine," Thane said.

"I have just one more question about your case—hold on, it's in here, somewhere…" Morana dug into her bag again, rummaging through it with one hand while tilting the opening in the light to see inside. "I can't believe I might have forgotten…" She began pulling out all the bag's contents. A hairbrush, wallet, spare T-shirt, lipstick, and an eight-inch hanger wire bent into a helix.

"What's that?" Thane asked, pointing to the wire.

Morana picked it up. "Oh, this is for a different experiment of Master Leedskalnin's I was going to ask you about. I forgot the name."

"Was it called the unipole helix experiment?"

"Yes, that's it," she said, still digging. "I must have forgotten that paperwork." She began stuffing the items back into her purse.

Thane said, "May I hold that?"

She handed the wire helix to him.

He held it up to the light. "You need two of these. This one is too small and feels like an alloy."

"Oh," Morana said.

"You know, I have supplies for this experiment, too," he said, handing it back to her. "I've done it a thousand times…"

"I'm sure you have."

"Maybe I could show you that one, too."

Morana checked her watch. She knew that doing the experiment now would eliminate an ideal reason to return another day. "I'd love for you to show me, but I have other obligations tonight and tomorrow night. Is there any chance I could visit the following evening?"

Thane twisted his mouth and drummed his fingers on the block several times. "What time?"

"Will seven o'clock work again?"

"Sure."

"Wonderful. I'll bring us dinner... What do you like to eat?"

"You don't have to do that."

"I want to. What is your favorite restaurant?"

"Sometimes I get Chinese food from Dragon's Nest."

"Do you have it delivered?"

"No!"

"Of course not," Morana said. "Shall we eat there?"

"No, I only order takeout. They know my order."

"Great."

As Thane escorted her to the door, Morana said, "I bet few people know how much you and Master Leedskalnin have in common."

Thane blushed.

When they passed the chair near the entryway, she glanced down at the clutch she had tucked. Its aim seemed perfect. Accidentally forgetting her clutch might prove productive and provide a reason for an extra visit to stop by if Thane discovered it. If not, she would be the first to view how Thane performed a marvel of physics.

Thane opened the door and said, "Goodbye."

Gus strolled in, rubbing against Thane's leg before slinking into the shadows along the wall.

Morana stepped outside.

"I knew you were in there!" A woman's voice echoed from the side of the garage.

Morana moved to look around the corner of the garage.

Thane followed her.

They saw a woman with her chin raised over the back fence that separated their backyards.

"I knew you'd come out soon because you have company," she said.

Thane mumbled, "Meet Mrs. Perkins."

"I'm sick and tired of telling you to stop the strange noises you create at night. If you don't stop, I'll report it."

"What noises?" Thane said.

The woman raised her finger. "You know what noises. The hissing from your garage constantly wakes me. Our community's official time for quiet enjoyment is from 10 o'clock PM to 6 o'clock AM. You are violating it."

"I apologize."

"And a couple of nights ago, there was another explosion, too."

"There are no explosions," Thane said.

"Oh? I have proof. The last one was so strong that my Bradford Exchange Commemorative Hummingbird Plate fell and shattered into hundreds of pieces. You're lucky I didn't call the police."

"Hold on a minute," Morana said, moving closer to the woman. "The man apologized and told you there was no explosion."

"Who are you?" Mrs. Perkins snapped.

Morana glanced at Thane. "I'm a friend. Don't you think involving the police is extreme? After all, here we are, resolving the situation in a neighborly way."

"His ruckus keeps me awake. You know all the neighbors are talking about you," Mrs. Perkins said, glaring at Thane.

"Aren't you a piece of work?" Morana said.

"Say whatever you want, but he'd better heed my warning."

"You've made your point."

"You've been warned," Mrs. Perkins said, dropping from view.

Morana and Thane went back to the front of the garage. "Friendly neighbor," she said.

"She doesn't like me," Thane replied.

"Does she complain often?"

"More so recently. She always has a new complaint. She used to harass me about an overgrown tree that she claimed was infringing on her property. When I trimmed it, she began complaining about the occasional sounds from my garage."

"What do you think she's hearing?"

"The explosion she said she heard was during your visit when I intentionally dropped my work block during the demonstration. I've only done that a few times. She mistakes the vibration for an explosion."

"I see." Morana checked her watch. "I better get going." She walked down the driveway toward the street, then stopped. "Oh, can I use your restroom before I go?"

"Uh," Thane looked at the house. "I suppose."

"Unless you have a restroom in your garage…"

"No, it's fine." Thane led her to the house's back door. He pulled a key from his pocket and unlocked a deadbolt and the knob lock. "Wait a minute."

"Sure," Morana said, showing her urgency by dancing in place.

Thane opened the door and squeezed through, closing it promptly behind him. Morana tried to see inside, but a curtain blocked the view. A light flicked on.

After about a minute, the door opened. "C'mon in," Thane said.

Morana entered a bare kitchen with no table, chairs, microwave, stove, or refrigerator. An opened bottle of Wild Turkey bourbon and a crumpled paper bag sat on a center island.

Thane led her to the hallway, where Morana smelled fried food.

Thane said, "Second door on the right." He pointed, but then, when Morana walked down the hallway, he followed her, stopping outside the bathroom door.

Morana said, "Are you going to supervise?"

"No," Thane said, blushing. He went back to the kitchen.

When Morana finished, she stepped into the hallway and clasped the bathroom knob to keep the latch quiet. She tiptoed to the bedroom doorway. A queen-size bed with disheveled linen lay crookedly on the floor. Beside it were two empty shot glasses beside an open bag of tortilla chips. A used condom lay beside the pillow. A spool of paper towels had unrolled across the floor from the base of the bed.

She continued along the hallway to the other bedroom with a pile of clothes pushed into the corner and a stack of framed pictures leaning against the wall on the floor. She turned on the light and leaned into the room.

"Why are you looking in there?" Thane startled her from the end of the hallway.

"I just wanted to see your adorable home."

"You should go." He stepped back and motioned toward the kitchen. Morana went to him and, at the hallway intersection, made a right turn toward the front door.

"No, this way," Thane said, pointing toward the back.

"I'm parked on the street in front," Morana said.

"I know. This way will be better." He escorted her to the back door and followed her outside.

Morana stopped and said, "Thank you for everything you showed me tonight, Thane. I look forward to our next visit in a couple of days."

"You're welcome," Thane said, looking around the backyard.

"Thane, is everything alright? You seem nervous."

"I have a lot to do. I need to get to work."

"Okay." Morana walked to the driveway.

Thane followed and watched her pass through the pergola and onto the street.

Morana waved over her shoulder at him. She had walked far enough to move out of Thane's view and stopped. After waiting a few moments, she crept back toward Thane's driveway, using a tree near the edge for cover. He was gone. She hurried across his front yard to the corner of the house. She leaned close to the large front window's edge and listened. The draperies had a sliver of an opening on either side, allowing her to see a limited portion of the living room. The light was on, and fast food containers littered the coffee table.

After waiting a few minutes, she saw Thane enter the living room with a dishrag draped over his shoulder. He carried a black trash bag and a broom. He hurried around the coffee table, grabbing and stuffing the fast food containers into the trash bag as quickly as possible. He stumbled over the edge of the couch as he hurried to get to the other side. He brushed crumbs from the sofa and coffee table onto the floor before he swept them up. He then pulled the towel from his shoulder and polished the coffee table. When he finished, he stood back and examined it from several angles before he brushed crumbs from the sofa onto the floor. After completing this task, he walked to the hallway, and the living room light went off. The master bedroom light came on, but the window coverings were flush, preventing Morana from seeing inside. Morana watched, realizing that Thane had more than one secret.

Chapter 8

MORANA DROVE BACK to Clay's apartment and pulled to the side of the road three blocks away. She dialed Clay.

He answered on the first ring. "Dammit, Mo, would you tell me what's going on?"

"I'm calling to remind you that the reward for turning me in is nothing, and I mean *nothing*, compared to the profit we will make from what Thane can do."

"What do I have to do to convince you I'm not turning you in?"

"You're not winning any Oscars, Clay. I ditched your leeches, but I'm sure you already knew that."

"Wait a minute—if someone followed you to my place, I didn't set that up. Oh, God, we're screwed."

"They were amateur, Clay."

"Mo, tell me what you saw."

"They were driving a Camry. I didn't wait around to ask for ID. Your balcony made a more comfortable exit."

"That was my brother," Clay said. "Don't scare me like that."

"Why didn't you tell me he was coming to your place? You knew that if he cornered me, he'd be dead."

"I didn't know he was going to show up. He's been trying to fix our strained relationship. He lives over in Coral Gables and found out I was in town on business. I made the mistake of telling them where I was staying. He said he might stop by. It's just like him not to call first. If you had answered the phone I gave you, I could have cleared this up sooner."

"I'm not carrying that phone anymore. It was too fancy."

"Fancy?"

"By fancy, I mean bugged."

"Tracking is not bugging. All phones have built-in tracking with the 'lost phone' function."

"So, you *were* tracking me?"

"Mo, I didn't look until you wouldn't take my calls. I needed to see if you were okay."

"Why don't you check the video feed from your living room?"

"What?"

"I found your cameras, and I must admit, some of your placements were clever."

"So what? You saw some cameras! Those are strictly for security."

"In the bathroom?"

"I hide valuables everywhere."

Morana laughed. "The fact that you are an atrocious liar is probably my best reason for trusting you."

Clay was quiet and then said, "Listen, I'm sorry. I haven't reviewed any of the footage. Let's put this behind us. I promise you that I won't record or track you."

"I don't need your word. I'm finished with your place."

"Is this why my car is parked far from the apartment?"

"I figured you watched that, too."

"That GPS tracking is built-in, not my doing. Mo, whether you believe me or not, I'm not trying to turn you in."

"Drop it, Clay."

"Fine. Did you visit Thane?"

"Of course."

"Why won't you wait until I get back?"

"What are you so worried about?"

"I'm the one who brought you in and introduced you to Thane. This is supposed to be a joint venture. Going on without me ruins the 'jointness' of it."

"Listen, if I wanted to cut you out of this deal, you'd be dead. I'm honoring the fact that you introduced me to Thane. Your technical proficiency is useful, and I'm gambling that you're smart enough to keep our business quiet. So, if you're so worried about me learning the secret and hoarding it from you, you can rest easy. Why don't you just come back?"

"If getting Thane's secret was certain, I'd quit my job this minute. But if getting the scoop about how he moves these blocks doesn't pan out, and I screw up this tour account, my boss will fire me for sure."

"Then it looks like you need to trust me on this," Morana said. "I'm reaching out to Everett Paige tomorrow."

"Could you do me a favor and not kill him?"

"I'll let you know how it goes."

✝

As a safety precaution, Morana spent the night in the back of her Explorer. The following day, she parked behind a bookstore and connected to its Wi-Fi. She used her Tor browser to log into Everett's webmail. She scanned his historic email messages and found several names that he corresponded with frequently. With little effort, she discovered several plans made by Everett that would take him to public places. One email message was from his assistant, confirming his lunch the following day at the *Sa Bon Restaurant* in Bayfield. She scrolled through a few more pages of information Clay had gathered until she found his vehicle registration. He drove a black Maserati Ghibli. She noted the license plate.

After gathering the information she needed, she put on heavy makeup and a shoulder-length blonde wig and drove to *Sa Bon Restaurant*. She parked a safe distance away and walked back after driving past the entrance twice to scope it out. She noticed the restaurant had valet parking next door in a parking garage shared by a business center. She went into the parking garage and scouted it out, noting the vehicle and pedestrian entrances and exits.

She returned to the street, sat on a bus bench opposite the entrance to the restaurant, and spent a few minutes watching the uniformed parking attendants valeting cars for the lunch crowd at *Sa Bon*.

After observing for almost a half hour, she entered the restaurant. A gentleman in a suit stood just inside the entrance, resting his hand on a podium. When he saw her, he smiled and said, "Welcome! And how many will be dining for lunch today?" He reached for a stack of menus.

"I'm not here for lunch," Morana replied. "I'm shopping for venues to host an important event. Do you mind if I look around?"

"By all means, ma'am," the man said, coming out from behind the podium. He made a sweeping motion with his arm toward the main dining room. "Shall I call someone to give you a tour?"

"That won't be necessary. I know what I need," Morana said as she passed by him.

"Very well, then," the host said, smiling as he returned to his podium.

Morana wound her way between the tables in the main dining room until she reached the rear of the restaurant, where she noted the restrooms, kitchen entrance, and a hallway to a rear exit through which she left. From the back alley, she saw a door to a stairwell for the parking garage next door.

She returned to her car and drove to a nearby shopping mall where she used cash at several stores to purchase a dinner outfit, elastic bandaging, gauze, a pair of black gloves, a new wig, and more makeup. She stopped at a Post Office, taking some blank peel-and-stick mailing labels from a wall tray. She now had everything she needed except a good night's rest. Tomorrow morning, she'd have a little chitchat with a special person before joining Everett for lunch.

Chapter 9

THE PAIGE HOME sat in the exclusive Arborcliffe Estates, only steps from the beach. The 8,000-square-foot mansion was part of a sprawling estate with a tennis court and an infinity pool glistening in the morning sun.

Morana parked on the street and walked up the curved driveway, briefly taking in the spectacular view of the ocean. She carried a leather binder, a tape measure, and a pen. She rang the bell at the front door.

A thin woman in her mid-40s, wearing business attire and with a mobile phone pressed to her ear, opened the door. "Yes?"

"Are you Mrs. Everett Paige?" Morana said.

"Who's asking?" She looked at Morana suspiciously.

"I'm sorry. I'm from Ashwell Interiors, and we wanted to take some measurements."

The woman frowned and turned away. "Let me call you back," she said, ending her phone call. When she turned back to Morana, she said, "But you said you weren't available until next week."

"Your husband…" Morana opened her binder and scrolled a tablet with her finger, "Everett?"

"Yes."

"Well, he called us this morning and asked if we could start sooner. Under-promising and over-delivering is the philosophy that's given us a waiting list. Usually, our clients are thrilled, but if this is a bad time, we'll be happy to reschedule."

"No, no, it's fine. I'm just surprised, that's all. That's unlike Everett."

Morana covered her mouth and said, "I hope I haven't ruined a surprise."

"No, we've discussed this project. You haven't ruined anything."

"Still, I apologize for arriving unannounced. I will arrange a nominal credit on the order for the inconvenience."

"Amazing," Mrs. Paige said, staring at the binder Morana held.

"May I?" Morana said, pointing inside.

"Oh, of course—I'm sorry," Mrs. Paige said. She stepped back and held the door wider for Morana to enter.

They entered, and Morana stopped, looking around a grand foyer bathed with sunshine that poured through a skylight. Morana clutched her chest as she pivoted and said, "I love your choices, Mrs. Paige."

"Please—call me Rachel. And thank you, but I must give credit to our designers." As Rachel led Morana down the hallway toward the back of the house. They entered the lounge. "Here we are. So, how long have you been with Ashwell Interiors?" Rachel asked.

Morana reached back and pulled the door closed. "Today's my first day!" she replied, grinning.

✝

Three hours later, lunch service was busy at *Sa Bon Restaurant* when Morana returned. She had completely transformed her appearance, wrapping her arms, thighs, and torso with a layer of gauze wrapped in an elastic bandage. The padding straightened the curve of her waist, adding what looked like 25 to 30 pounds of weight. She wore an oversized, light green blouse, long skirt, and wedge sandals that complemented an auburn wig.

She took a large black purse and went to the parking garage elevator next door. While she waited for it to open, she pulled one of the large mailing labels from the purse. She smiled at the photograph of Everett's children she had printed on it. When the elevator door opened, she stepped out and held the door, scanning for any spectators. She was alone—for the moment. She peeled the adhesive from the back of the photo, then reached into the elevator to avoid being seen or recorded by its security camera. She swept her hand around the button panel. She felt the smooth glass, about the size of a book, above it and stuck the photo onto the glass, rubbing it firmly in place. She leaned in and verified that the sticker covered the interior security camera. The placement was perfect.

She returned to the street and waited on a bus bench to watch the valets at work. She didn't have to wait long before Everett's black Maserati pulled to the curb. He got out wearing a navy suit, opened the trunk, and laid his jacket inside before handing the key over to the valet. Morana noted his dark, slicked-back hair, white cuff-linked shirt, and yellow tie. She waited ten minutes before crossing the street to enter the restaurant.

"Welcome," the host said, greeting her with a smile. "How many for lunch?"

"I'm meeting a guest who had a reservation. Can you tell me if Everett Paige has arrived?"

The host scanned the names. His finger stopped midway down the list. "Yes, ma'am, he has. Please follow me. I'll take you to him."

"No, that's okay. I'm an old friend, and I'm here to surprise him."

The host grinned and said, "Absolutely, ma'am, enjoy." He bowed slightly and held his arm toward the dining room.

Morana entered, scanning the tables as she walked. She quickly spotted Everett. He sat conversing with another man at a table in the center of the dining room. A waiter was leaving their table after having delivered appetizers to them.

Morana pulled a tablet from her purse and approached them. "Hello, gentlemen. Is everything to your satisfaction this evening?"

The men paused their conversation to look at her.

"Yes, fine," Everett's guest said dismissively.

Morana approached Everett's side of the table and said, "Are you Mr. Paige?"

"Who's asking?"

She leaned closer, "Forgive my intrusion… If I could have a moment with you—there may be an issue with your vehicle, sir."

"Do you mean an accident?"

"An accident is a stronger word than I'd use for what has happened," Morana said. She turned to Everett's guest. "My apologies."

"Why don't you just tell me what the hell happened?"

"Sir, it would be best to show you. I assure you we can resolve this situation to your satisfaction. Please follow me."

Everett stood up, wadded his napkin, and threw it on the table. He followed Morana to the rear of the restaurant, where she opened the back door and held it for him.

When Everett turned toward the wrong parking lot, Morana said, "This way, sir. It's a busy day. We lease spaces for overflow from the secure garage next door. It's only a few steps."

Everett followed her. "How much damage is there?"

"Frankly, the damage is difficult to see, but the policy of our restaurant is to inform our guests of valet incidents promptly." She led him into the small elevator foyer of the parking garage.

When the elevator door opened, Morana held the door for him. When he stepped in, she pressed an index card that read *Out of Order* over the call buttons before joining him inside.

The elevator closed them in. Morana pulled black gloves from her bag and wiggled her fingers into them behind her back. She slipped her hand back into the bag and squeezed a pistol grip. "And, of course, your dinner will be on the house tonight," she said.

Everett rolled his eyes. "If I find any damage on my car, more than my dinner will be 'on the house,' I can promise you that."

Morana pulled the emergency stop button. The elevator car jerked to a stop between *P1* and *P2*.

Everett said, "What the hell are you—"

Morana grabbed Everett's throat and slammed him back against the wall while raising the gun and pressing the suppressor to his temple.

"Fight me, and your end will be quick and quiet."

Everett slowly raised his arms.

Morana slipped the purse strap from her shoulder. It dropped to the floor, and she kicked it into the corner.

Everett's eyes were wide, and his mouth locked open. "My wallet is in my back pocket," he said. "Please, take whatever you want—"

"Shh, shh, shh, the first thing I want is a little chit-chat with you."

Everett nodded.

Morana pulled the pistol from his forehead. A white ring on his skin left by the suppressor faded. She held the gun steady while grabbing a handful of his collar. "How much money did you make last year?"

Everett said, "I don't know... I did well."

Morana squeezed his collar tighter and slammed him against the wall again. "Vague non-answers agitate me, so I'll ask again. How much money did you make last year?"

Everett raised his chin, his face turning red. "Somewhere around 2 and a half."

"Is that $2.5 million?"

Everett strained to nod.

Morana whistled. "And what is your sweet car worth?"

"Around 75K."

"I saw you arrive. I like that car. It's beautiful."

"It's yours," Everett said. A twinge of hope appeared on his face at the possibility of a deal.

"That was easy, wasn't it?"

Everett nodded.

"Has your Maserati been in an accident before tonight?"

Everett hesitated. "Of course not."

"The damage to your vehicle didn't happen tonight. It happened a few weeks ago."

"I—I don't understand."

"Thane Sykes. Do you know him?"

"No."

"You're demanding $10,000 from him for an accident you told me never happened."

Everett looked confused.

"Let me help you remember," Morana said. "He drives a truck. Short, adorable, young, black man. He allegedly caused $10,000 worth of damage to your Maserati, and you can't remember his name or the accident?"

Recognition spread across Everett's face. "I can explain that…" He started to raise his hand, but Morana pressed the gun to his forehead again.

He squeezed his eyes closed and, through clenched teeth, said, "I swear that was my lawyer, not me."

"The demand came from you."

"I'll return the money!"

Morana hesitated. "Wait, he paid you?"

"Yes, but I can make it right. Let me go, and I'll—"

"Shut up! When did you receive this money?" she said, squeezing his neck harder.

Everett's face reddened. He grunted, "Wire transfer. Can't breathe."

Morana loosened her grip.

Everett gasped and coughed. "I got a notification a couple of hours ago. It's on my phone."

Morana lowered the gun to his chest as she reached into his pocket. She removed his phone and backed to the opposite side of the elevator, keeping the gun aimed at him. Everett told her the unlock code and said, "Open the email. See the confirmation message."

Morana scrolled Everett's inbox and found the wire transfer message. The sender's name was listed as C. Thorner. When she recognized Clay's name, she masked her surprise. Clay would only put up ten grand to gain a trust advantage over her with Thane.

"There's another email," Everett said. It came a minute after the wire.

Morana opened the message.

> *As per our conversation, I need a letter stating that you are releasing Thane Sykes from all liability in the accident referenced in your demand letter. You are to send the signed letter to my PO Box listed above.*

Morana clenched her teeth and pocketed the phone. She moved closer to Everett, raising the gun to his head. When she had come within reach, Everett swung his arm upward, landing a blow to her arm. The pistol fired into the ceiling. He head-butted Morana. When she fell back, he dove onto her, but she raised her feet and caught him in the gut, deflecting so that he slammed into the wall before crashing to the floor. They both struggled to their feet. Morana dropped the gun and grabbed his wrists, kneeing him in the groin. When he bent forward, she sidestepped, took hold of his forearm, and used her leg to sweep his feet from under him. He fell to his back, and she mounted him.

Everett wriggled under her, trying to buck her off until she delivered an elbow to the side of his head, dazing him long enough to fish a stun gun from her purse. She pressed the stun gun's prongs into his gut and delivered the voltage.

Everett released a vibrating scream as his whole body stiffened.

Morana clapped her gloved hand over his mouth. He rolled to his side when she released the trigger, gasping for breath. He held his hands out in surrender. She rolled him face down. "This could've been so clean and easy, but you've made it messy." She pressed his face to the floor.

"Please—I'll cooperate!" Everett said.

"Oh, of course you will," she replied. She pulled his arms behind him, pulled zip ties from her purse, and secured his wrists.

"I said I'll give the money back," Everett said. "What else do you want? I can pay it back with interest. Please!" he shouted.

"You're noisy," she replied.

She pulled a bandana from her bag and gagged him before pulling him into a sitting position.

"You're lucky that I won our first and last tussle. If you had won, you would have only hurt her." Morana pointed to the photo of his wife printed on the label she had stuck to the elevator camera window.

Everett struggled to raise his chin from the floor to see it. His face contorted with a new confused terror when he saw his wife's image. He grunted something through the gag.

"Yes, I stopped by your place this morning. Rachel was incredibly hospitable, and we had a nice little visit that I feel was productive."

Everett screamed through the gag and kicked his feet against the floor.

"Oh, you want to know if I've harmed her? Not yet. She's safe in her car—for the time being. Don't worry. Her seatbelt is securely fastened." Morana turned her phone so that Everett could see it. A live feed from a micro camera mounted to the dash of Rachel's Lexus played on Morana's phone. The camera was mounted under the rearview mirror and displayed the car's interior. Between the driver and passenger seats, Rachel was fastened in the center of the three rear seats. Her wrists and arms were bound tightly with a rope attached to her waist. She wore a blindfold and a gag. When Morana noticed that Rachel's body was limp, and her head hung to one side, she frowned and said, "That's odd…"

Everett watched the horrifying footage of his wife's stillness.

Rachel's head rose, and she tried to shift herself, writhing under her restraints.

"Ahh, much better," Morana sighed. "I tried not to restrict her breathing but thought we might have lost her." Morana laughed, turning the phone to Everett so he could see a few moments of his wife's struggle. "I realize that Florida rarely gets cold enough for a remote car starter to be practical, but it was the only gift for Rachel I had. Her car is parked far from foot traffic but with an excellent public Wi-Fi signal. You'll notice that up here in the screen's corner," Morana pointed for Everett to see, "the rear window is pinching a hose attached to the car's tailpipe. The car will automatically start in 13 more minutes unless I'm holding this phone to type in the code that will snooze the fumes." She put her lips close to Everett's ear, "It's how a girl stays prepared in case your cooperation flags, and you make things messier—can you blame me?"

She pulled Everett to his feet. "When I remove the gag, you won't make a sound. I'm taking your arm, and you'll go where I lead you."

Everett's nostrils flared, and he nodded furiously.

After she removed his gag and freed his wrists, Morana pulled the emergency stop button on the elevator panel. The elevator car finished its descent, and the door opened.

Morana led Everett by the arm, guiding him around the corner to her Explorer. "You should be happy there was no actual damage to your car tonight—just like there wasn't with Thane."

She opened the door and forced Everett inside, cuffing his wrist to the passenger door handle. "We're going for a little drive."

Chapter 10

MORANA AND EVERETT sat in the parking lot of his bank.

"Any withdrawal over $10,000 requires paperwork," he said.

"You'll withdraw $9,980 and pull 20 bucks from the ATM. When I get the 10 grand, you'll get the location of your wife's car."

Morana waited while Everett walked into his bank. She had his mobile phone in one hand and her burner phone in the other, ready to start his wife's car at any sign that Everett might have gone off script.

Fifteen minutes later, he returned, got into the car, and tossed a zipped cash bag onto her lap. "There. We're done."

Morana opened the bag and counted the money while Everett wrung his hands. She reached around the seat and tucked the cash into a duffel bag.

"Now, where's my wife?" Everett said.

Morana folded her hands in her lap and sighed. "There's something you need to understand. Thane is unaware that you received this dirty money. He's unaware that you have returned it. By returning the money, your net financial loss is zero. Thane has suffered a net emotional loss worth far more than $10,000. The weeks of stress and anxiety your dishonest demand put him through come at a price, so the score between you and him has not been settled."

"Tell me what you want. $10,000 more?"

"I'm willing to ignore that imbalance on the condition that Thane never sees or hears from you again. Do you understand?"

"Yes," Everett said, swallowing hard. He raised his hand. "I swear!"

"I hope you are sincere because if Thane experiences the slightest twinge of discomfort because you contact him again, then I'll dispense with your son, Devon, while his cute-as-a-button sister, Kimmy, watches. Then I'll obtain and dispense with Rachel. Finally, we will have a follow-up visit to watch the results of your poor judgment on video together."

"No, please," Everett begged. The color had drained from his face.

Morana stared at him. "I want to believe you, but I must feel certain of your sincerity."

Everett's lip quivered. "I swear to God I won't say a word."

"Good for you. If that changes, please be certain I will slaughter you last and slower than the others."

Everett raised his hands. "I *swear* Thane will never hear from me again."

"It's time for you to get out."

"But my wife—you promised."

Morana raised her burner phone. "You'll get a text with her location."

"But—"

Morana started the car. "If I were you, I'd get out of this car now. You won't like where I take you."

Everett jumped out and slammed the door. He backed away from the SUV as Morana drove away.

In her rearview mirror, she saw him straining to see the license plate she had removed on her Explorer.

She drove to a quiet suburb, pulled to the roadside, and called Clay.

He answered and said, "Don't hang up on me again. We need to talk. Listen—"

"No, you listen. Everett Paige isn't a problem anymore," Morana said.

"That's great news. What happened?"

"Again, your acting sucks, Clay. He told me about the wire transfer and showed it to me on his phone. You paid the ten grand without telling me," Morana yelled.

"I couldn't tell you. Thane swore me to secrecy."

"You must tell me everything or our deal is off."

"Wait, did you kill Everett?"

"Not yet."

"I called Thane from the airport before my flight. He was freaking out, about to go insane over this accident thing. He told me he would do anything to resolve it, so it was the perfect opportunity to make a deal. He told me that if I could make the problem disappear, he'd show me how he moves the blocks."

"He said that?"

"Swear to God."

"After selling me on helping you with this project, you pull this stupid stunt by trying to pay off Everett for an advantage?"

"Mo, I knew I could tell you after I had the secret. Look, we won't make a dime unless we know how he moves those blocks. Resolving this accident for Thane was the perfect leverage for getting him to talk."

"Gratitude won't make Thane reveal anything," Morana said.

"Thane is motivated by fear. Something's going on with him that has him on edge. By the way, does anyone live with him there?"

"Not that I'm aware of. Why?"

"I saw some strange things in his house last night."

"He let you in? He never lets me go inside."

"I had to use pressure. I needed the bathroom."

"What did you see?"

"I'll tell you when you get back. Speaking of that, when *are* you coming back?"

"It'll be a few more days. I've sold my house out here in LA."

"You're kidding. You're moving to Florida—permanently?"

"According to you, it will be worth it. I can stay in the corporate apartment for as long as I need to while I find a new place to buy. I thought about it on the flight. California has become too weed-friendly, eroding my profits." Clay cleared his throat, "market share. Plus, I don't want the hassle of getting licensed, so the house's equity offers more cash."

"How long will that take?"

"I already have three offers."

"Congratulations."

"If we are as successful as you predict, I'll be able to buy a much bigger house, right?"

"Only if you quit interfering with my plan for Thane—a plan that will work."

Chapter 11

AFTER PICKING UP food from The Dragon's Nest the following evening, Morana parked on the street a half block from Thane's house. She wore denim shorts and a white tank top. She carried the food sacks containing Thane's "usual" order and her selections.

When she came to the garage door, she noticed it was already ajar. A note taped on the doorknob read, *Come in, Mo.*

She sidestepped in to avoid bumping the sacks and stopped on the golden lock entry rug.

Before she could close the door, Gus ran outside.

"Thane?"

He stood from behind his block desk on the other side of the garage.

"I'm sorry. Gus ran out when I opened the door," she said.

"That's okay. He needed to go out."

Morana said. "I have dinner." She held up the food. "Shall we go eat in the house?" She tilted her head toward it.

"No," Thane said, coming to her. He took one sack of food.

"I'm leaving my phone right here in the bowl." Morana dropped it in with an exaggerated gesture.

"Thanks." Thane headed back to his work block.

Before Morana followed, she glanced down at the chair where she had left her clutch with the micro-camera. The magazines were still stacked on the seat, and the jacket draped over the back, but the clutch was gone. If Thane had moved it immediately after her last visit, there was no way the lipstick camera could have captured any footage of Thane working.

"I've set the table for us," he said, placing the sacks of food on the floor beside the block.

"Where?" Morana said, looking around.

Thane pointed up.

Above them, a large rock slab the width of a dining room table was hoisted to within inches of the ceiling.

"Please move to that carpet," Thane said, pointing to a green throw rug a few steps away. She sidestepped to it, trying to keep her eyes on the suspended block. "What is that?"

A faint hum began, and the slab smoothly descended with no sway. It came to rest on the work block, using it as the foundation. Once in place, the slab became a table and already held two place settings with silverware, pressed and folded cloth napkins, and wine glasses.

Thane stood by with his hands tucked into his pockets, and he wore a satisfied expression, watching Morana grin as she took in the scene. He walked around the table, gently unclipping a thin, barely visible wire from the corner of the slab.

"What is that?" Morana asked.

Thane only smiled as he let go of the wire, which retracted into a small black box between the open ceiling beams. He dragged a nearby chair to the table opposite his chair. "Please sit," he said, motioning for her to step closer.

Morana didn't press him for an answer. She came to the table and spread her hands on it. "This is beautiful."

"Thank you. Let's eat," he said, pulling the sacks from the floor and placing them on the table's edge.

Morana took a seat, unable to remove the grin from her face.

They began opening the food containers, and after looking inside a couple of them, Thane froze, staring at them and then at the remaining sacks they had yet to open.

"Is the order okay?" Morana asked.

Thane looked inside each of the other containers. He said, "It's the wrong order."

"Oh, no," Morana stood up. "I just told them to give me your usual order. I'm so sorry—I'll go back."

"No, it's not your fault. I have two usuals."

Morana tilted her head. "Pardon?"

"They gave you the order I placed for my uncle."

Morana said, "I have to admit, I was surprised by the amount of food. I was looking forward to watching you finish it. Why would they give me your uncle's order if I told them it was for you?"

"I take him food from Dragon's Nest every week—sometimes twice."

"You deliver it to him?"

"Every Thursday."

"That's why the owner told me I was late for it," Morana said.

"They know I need my uncle's order by 6:00 PM."

"Why?"

"Never mind, it's okay. This order has more food than we can eat." Thane opened another food container.

Morana stared at him until he finally noticed.

"What?" he said.

"Why do you get food for your uncle?"

"I don't mind."

"I only ask because ordering delivery would be easy for him."

"I told you, I don't mind," Thane snapped.

Morana held up her hands. "I'm sorry."

Thane handed her a plate and utensils.

They served themselves food from the cartons. Thane slurped noodles loudly enough to make Morana stop chewing. She chalked up the etiquette lapse to the rarity of dining with guests. She said, "You know you are adorable when you get flustered."

Thane blushed and stopped chewing, fighting a smile. He held up a finger and, after swallowing, said, "You're pretty all the time."

"Thank you, Thane!"

"You're welcome." He stared at his plate briefly, then said, "There's something else I need to tell you."

Morana served herself more noodles. "I'm all ears."

"I received some good news today. Maybe it was because of you."

"Well, if it's good news, I hope so!"

"But I don't know how you could have done it so quickly." He pulled a folded envelope from his pocket and handed it across the table to her. "This was taped to the house's front door this morning."

While Morana opened and unfolded the letter, Thane rubbed his hands together, then clasped them as he watched her lips moving while she silently read the letter, line by line.

She read the last sentence aloud. "… After further examination of the vehicle incident on the sixteenth of May… we are releasing you from any liability for damages in the vehicle collision—Thane, this is wonderful!"

"Are you responsible for this?" Thane asked.

"The honest answer is… probably."

"How?"

"I did contact Everett Paige. I convinced him to meet me in person. And we discussed his claim and the situation it has put you in. I emphasized the futility of pursuing you for money and explained several ways his aggression could end up being a losing proposition for everyone involved."

"You make it sound simple."

Morana said, "Much like how you lift these blocks, it's easy if you know what to do."

Thane laughed. "Fair enough."

"Sometimes reaching out to someone in person can make all the difference. Nonverbal, face-to-face communication is so much more powerful than letters."

"Thank you for helping me," Thane said, taking the letter back from her. He carefully folded it, tucked it back into the envelope, and held it to the light to ensure it was still inside. He took it to a drawer and slid it under some other papers. On his way back to the table, he said, "Your reaction to the letter is better than Clay's," Thane said.

Morana stopped. "Clay knows?"

"He's been calling a lot. Today, he called right after I found the letter."

"Really?" Morana forced a smile.

"Yes. When I told him about it, he only said, 'Good for you.' That's it. I guess the two of you haven't been talking because he wanted to know if you knew."

"What did you tell him?"

"I told him you were still trying to help me, but I didn't know if you knew about the letter."

"Clay can be unpredictable," Morana said. "I wouldn't worry about his lack of enthusiasm."

Throughout their meal, Morana felt relief and concern that Thane hadn't mentioned her purse or the lipstick-concealed camera. His relief about resolving the situation with Everett seemed to have been an ideal distraction—unless he planned to drop that on her later. If Thane knew she had breached his precious privacy, there was no way he would have allowed her to stay for dinner, no matter how grateful he was about her success with Everett.

When they finished eating, Thane announced it was time for the experiment and reconnected the thin wire tether to the bottom corner of the table slab.

Morana cleared off the table, filling a plastic trash bag. She slowly carried the bag toward the entry door to dump it in the bin she had seen outside the garage. On her way to the entry door, she tried to scan for her missing clutch. With her back to Thane, she held her head steady, scanning either side of the path, checking beside some stacked tires, sawhorses, giant spools of wire, and chains that Thane had positioned in neat rows on the floor. She saw no sign of the clutch.

When she reached for the doorknob, Thane said, "Wait. Keep the trash bag in here. We'll need it after the experiment."

Morana used the opportunity for another brief search for her clutch on her way back to him.

Thane slid his hands into his pockets as the faint hum from above resumed. The slab that had been their makeshift dining room table smoothly ascended, returning to its original position between the open beams within inches of the ceiling.

"Aren't you afraid that could fall?" Morana asked as she came to stand beside Thane.

"No." Thane shrugged and walked to his workbench.

Morana followed him. "Can you at least tell me—in general—if you've discovered some sort of anti-gravity mechanism?" she asked.

"Nice try," Thane said, wagging his finger at her. "I will tell you it involves gravity, but anti-gravity is too blunt to describe the process." He opened a drawer, removed several items for the experiment, and placed them on a tray. He brought the tray to his work block and set it down. "Let's begin."

On the floor beside Thane's chair, Morana noticed some travel magazines and brochures for tours of Egypt that she hadn't seen during dinner.

"What's this?" Morana asked, picking up a colorful, tri-folded piece with the Great Pyramid on the front.

"Clay gave me those before he left. He said he wants to send me to visit Egypt."

Morana poked her tongue into her cheek and said, "Unbelievable. Do you plan to accept his offer?"

"I've always dreamed of visiting the Great Pyramid. I want to touch it."

"Why do you think Clay is offering you such an elaborate gift?"

Thane shrugged. "Maybe because he'd like to go, too. He's been generous with me. He tips me well. When I told him I knew the secrets of the pyramids, he said he'd like to visit them in person with me."

Something out of the corner of Morana's eye pulled her attention from Thane. Behind him, about ten feet away on a shelf, sat her clutch. She moved to one side, positioning Thane between her and the clutch so she could examine it while still facing him. It was tucked between the wall and a small metric scale. She considered pointing it out to him and then decided against it when she realized that its new placement was at a perfect angle and closer to Thane's work area than it had been on the distant chair on which she had placed it. If the clutch remained in its new position for one more day, it could make all the difference in obtaining telling footage of Thane's secret work in the shop. If she was lucky, the camera had already recorded plenty of footage from its first location and now might give her some prized footage from an entirely new angle.

"Hello," Thane said, waving his hand in front of her face. "Are you ready?"

"Oh, I'm sorry. Absolutely," she replied.

Thane took some aluminum foil-wrapped wooden sticks, wires, and tools from the tray and arranged them. When the setup was complete, he said, "Today, I will show you an experiment Master Leedskalnin performed to illustrate the Biefeld-Brown Effect."

"I can't wait," Morana feigned interest.

Thane launched into the experiment, performing each step with the same scientific jargon he had used in the previous experiment.

Morana's thoughts returned to Clay's conniving and how he had been working entirely out of bounds to pander to Thane. Perhaps he hadn't intended to completely cut her from the picture, but his attempts to win a contest for Thane's loyalty couldn't be more flagrant. Her angst diminished when she considered her experience with Thane so far. There was no way a trip to Egypt would get Thane to give up his secret. And asking Thane directly only fanned his paranoia, making him clam up. This task would require more than coaxing.

Thane was still focused on the experiment and eventually levitated a small metal apparatus after applying an electrical current to a plate below it. Morana made a show of amazement that seemed to please him.

When he finished, he said, "I have some work to do. You should go."

Morana released a small laugh, still unaccustomed to Thane's occasional raw bluntness.

He walked her to the door, and when he opened it, Gus ran in. "Thank you for the food," he said.

"My pleasure." Morana took her phone from the bowl. "I hope I can see you again soon."

"Maybe that can happen."

"Great, I'll give you my secret phone number," she said.

"Why is it a secret?" Thane asked, looking at her suspiciously.

"You've already forgotten that I guard my privacy almost as much as yours." She took a piece of paper from beside the phone bowl and jotted her burner number on it. She handed it to him before going outside.

"Thanks," Thane said, smiling.

As Morana walked away, she waved goodbye over her shoulder and noticed that Thane's smile had deepened as he watched her.

She stopped. "Why are you looking at me that way?"

Thane brought her clutch from behind his back, holding it up for her to see. "Did you forget this?"

"Oh, my God!" Morana said, infusing as much surprise as possible into the words. "Of course! I've been looking everywhere for that."

She came back and took it, studying his face for any sign that he might have gone through its contents, but Thane telegraphed nothing in his expression. "Now you probably know more about me than you wanted to," she said.

"Why?"

"What a girl carries in her purse says a lot about her."

Thane flashed a frown. "But if I had examined its contents, how would you ever trust me again?"

Morana tucked it under her arm. "Of course. That is so admirable."

"My mom taught me to never look inside a woman's purse. It's private. For me, a woman's permission is the virtual key to her purse."

"Well, I can tell you there isn't much to see unless you are into pocket mirrors and lipstick! You are a true gentleman."

Thane slid his hands into his pockets and rocked on his heels, still smiling at her.

Morana hesitated, trying to sense any suspicion from him. If Thane had gone through the purse and discovered her micro camera, then he was testing her honesty at this moment. If she failed the test, regaining his trust would be impossible. She needed to erase the possibility of suspicion developing if Thane didn't already have it. She cleared her throat. "Thane, do you want to look inside my purse?"

He cocked his head. "Why would I care what's in your purse?"

"I don't know—you said my permission is the key, and I know you love to use keys!"

"It isn't necessary for you to show me what's inside."

"I know, but I *want* to show you," Morana eased past him to re-enter the garage.

Thane shrugged and followed her, then watched as Morana emptied the contents of her clutch into the phone bowl. She pawed through the items, holding up one at a time. A pack of chewing gum, keys, tissues, hair clips, a granola energy bar, a pocket mirror, a pamphlet about Edward Leedskalnin, and lipstick.

Thane didn't seem interested in any of the items. Instead, he kept his eye on Morana until she had finished.

"You didn't have to do that," he said.

"I wanted to use my virtual key."

"Do you feel better?" Thane said.

"Yes, I do, thank you," Morana said.

"Good, because I have work to do."

When they went outside, they heard Mrs. Perkins. "There you are. I knew you'd come out eventually," she said.

"Not again," Thane mumbled.

They went to the side of the garage and found her peering over the fence at them again, this time shining a flashlight down into Thane's yard.

"Can we help you?" Morana said.

"You can't," she said, swatting her hand at Morana. "Thane, I told you before to keep your damned cat off my property. I just caught it digging itself a new toilet in my African lily garden less than five minutes ago."

"Sorry," Thane said.

"Yes, you're always sorry, but you do nothing to stop it," Mrs. Perkins shouted. "If that cat keeps destroying my garden, I'll make sure *you* are sorry."

"Hold on," Morana said, stepping closer. "Next time you see the cat, why don't you just call him instead of yelling threats at him after the fact?"

"He doesn't answer my calls, even when I know he's home. I can hear the phone ringing over there," she aimed the flashlight at the house, "and over there," she aimed it at the garage. "Anyway, his damned cat is ruining my African lily garden. If you don't believe me, come and look."

Thane waited behind while Morana approached the fence and looked over it. Mrs. Perkins wore a pink bathrobe and fluffy slippers. She pointed at three rows of tall green stalks about knee-high, each clustered at the top with blue and white flowers, some of which toppled. "You think my lilies would be safe on private property, but apparently, they're not."

"I'll try to keep my cat away," Thane hollered as he came to stand beside Morana. "Let's go, Mo. Nothing will make her happy."

Mrs. Perkins aimed the flashlight at the place on the fence behind which she thought Thane stood. "Oh? If your cat doesn't stop destroying my flowers, I'll be more than happy to trap that varmint."

"What a bitch!" Morana said.

Mrs. Perkins gasped, putting her hand to her chest. "I beg your pardon?"

"If you keep harassing my friend, you *will beg* for my pardon."

"You don't intimidate me, lady." Mrs. Perkins yelled. "Thane, I know more about what you're doing in there than you think."

"She doesn't know anything," Thane said to Morana.

"Oh, yes, I do. I've recorded it, and I'm going to share it with the authorities."

"Stop harassing me!" Thane yelled.

"Shh, shh, it's okay," Morana said.

Mrs. Perkins's face dropped below the fence, and they heard her cussing as she stormed toward her house.

Morana took his hand and guided him back to the front of the garage.

Chapter 12

AS MORANA DROVE from Thane's house, she rested her hand on the clutch she had tossed to the passenger seat. She nibbled her lip while reviewing her strange conversation about it with Thane. Something didn't feel right.

She pulled the car to the side of the road and then unzipped the clutch. She removed the lipstick that contained the micro camera. The lens at its base and its SIM card were still in place. She wondered if Thane was technically savvy enough to remove, view, and copy the footage before returning it to the clutch.

She turned the lipstick dial until it clicked and detached. The micro camera fell onto her lap, still attached to its tiny circuit board. If Thane had opened it, he had done a masterful job of perfectly reassembling it. If the camera functioned properly, she'd enjoy a fascinating movie of Thane's secret work with the blocks, even if it ended with him reaching for the camera.

She passed a busy hospital, pulled into its parking lot, and parked. With her laptop in hand, she found a seat near a power outlet in the corner of the crowded waiting room. She booted up and inserted the micro camera's SIM card. Her leg bounced while she waited for the video file to appear. She took a deep breath, willing it to hurry.

When the video box popped up, the footage flickered a few times at the beginning of the recording. Morana held her breath. A moment later, she saw herself walking to Thane, who stood at his work block. Perfect. The camera had not only worked, but she could confirm that her camera placement had been excellent as they were centered in the shot.

She watched Thane perform the experiment. She saw him drop the tray and watched his reprimand when she tried to help him pick up the items. She fast-forwarded to where Thane walked her to the door, passing right by the camera before moving out of the shot.

A minute later, the footage showed Thane returning to his workbench alone. He began jotting something on paper. Occasionally, he paused from his writing to look up, tapping the pencil on his chin or the block while thinking.

For over an hour, he stood there, writing, drawing, and thinking. His only movement from the block was picking up a small ruler from a pen holder on a countertop.

Morana fast-forwarded through another hour of the recording until the footage went black. Her heart jumped. She rewound it. The last visible footage showed Thane putting the pencil down before he ducked out of sight behind his work block. A moment later, again, complete darkness. Morana checked at the video time counter—it was still running. She fast-forwarded 10 minutes, then 20, then an hour. Finally, after one hour and twenty-six minutes, the footage resumed, showing Thane standing on the opposite side of the block. All the footage of his movement to that location had been blacked out. Morana's heart pounded as she wondered if Thane had doctored the video.

She rewound to a place right before the footage went dark and watched it slowly, studying each frame. Thane put the pencil down and slowly ducked until the block obscured him. During the next moments, she realized the lights hadn't turned off. The last three frames before the screen went dark showed motion. An object moved upward, blocking the camera lens. She zoomed in and saw that the footage went dark, but not completely black—and it was textured. Something in the shop had moved to block the camera. It remained motionless for too long to have been Gus.

She sped to a point after the footage resumed, but after Thane reappeared, the camera stopped. *Dammit.* The camera's memory card was full. With no options to lower the resolution, she was limited to capturing only two and a half hours of recorded footage.

Another idea came to her. She slammed the laptop closed and hurried from the hospital. She started her car and crossed her fingers on the slim chance that her lost footage might not be needed.

Chapter 13

MORANA SPENT THE night hunkered down under blankets in the back of her Explorer, parked inconspicuously in a crowded motel parking lot. Her frustration with the failed attempt to capture video footage of Thane working had prevented any sound sleep.

She needed a better solution. After fishing her phone from her bag, she dialed Clay.

"I hope this is you," Clay answered, groggy.

"A trip to Egypt is incredibly generous."

"It's 4:30 AM here. What do you want?"

"I need something, but before I get to that, why didn't you invite me to Egypt, too?"

"Hilarious—so I gave him a trip. He'll love it, and with my company discount, it'll cost next to nothing, so the extra cash made sense. I was planning to tell you."

"You should leave the finessing to me—unless you were trying to hide all this from me."

"It's not like that, Mo. Is this your way of asking me to cancel the trip I promised Thane?"

"No, it's too late for that. The disappointment would distract him too much."

"Mo, what's the harm in doing something good for Thane? I thought I was rather generous."

"You fail to realize that fear will squeeze more out of him than excitement or gratitude, and it will do it faster."

"You want to scare him into talking?"

"I'm not going to hurt him. If things keep going as planned, we can eventually make him thrilled after a brief rough patch. Your gift is a distraction."

"Whatever you say."

"Good. Now, I need your handiwork. I need a camera to record on battery for over 24 hours."

"Now you're a fan of my surveillance?"

"I was never against it. I just don't want to star in it."

"Fair enough. Tell me what you want to do."

Morana told him about the micro camera in her clutch and leaving it in Thane's shop. She updated him on the mysterious footage and the recording limitations of her memory card.

"Nice effort," Clay said, "but you need better hardware."

"You mean more like the camera in your shower head?"

"I mean something with a live feed option to skip the need for any media. The lipstick was a fair idea, but we can go smaller. I know something that will blow your mind."

"See? Now, that's why I agreed to work with you. Tell me where to buy it."

"Hold on, you don't just purchase something like this off the shelf. I need to tweak it."

"This can't wait until you get back."

"It'll have to. There's no way we can—"

Morana's phone beeped with another call. The ID read: *T. Sykes.*

"I have to take this call."

"Who's calling you?"

"Goodbye, Clay… Hello?"

"Mo, this is Thane."

"Hi, Thane! What a delightful surprise."

"Can you meet me?"

"I knew you'd miss me soon." Morana laughed.

"I need you to come back to my shop."

She grinned. "Of course. Do you want to have dinner again tonight?"

"No, I need you right away."

"Is something wrong?"

"Yes."

"What is it?"

"Just come here."

"Of course—I'm on my way."

"Thank you. Please hurry."

"Can you tell me what this is about?"

"No. I can't." Thane hung up.

Morana started the car, made a U-turn, and sped up. Her mind raced, sorting through the possibilities for Thane's urgency. The tension in his voice made her wonder if he was hurt—perhaps an accident with a block. Given his extreme secrecy and the fact that he gave her an exclusive look at his block-lifting demonstration, she might be the only person he'd be willing to call for help.

When she turned onto his street, she slowed to check the cars parked on his block. Only a couple of them had an unobstructed view of Thane's house, and those cars were empty. Despite Clay's greed, Morana knew he wouldn't set up a law enforcement ambush on Thane's shop. If this was a setup, snagging her quickly and quietly before she entered, Thane's property was the only way to get her, and she was ready.

She parked a block and a half away, packed her bag with a few items, and tucked a pistol into a concealed holster under her belt. She hurried along the sidewalk, scanning in all directions. As she closed in on Thane's driveway, she slipped one hand into her bag, gripping a second pistol. She turned and jogged the last steps toward the garage. She passed through the pergola and stopped at the corner of the house. The rear of the property was quiet, and she saw no smoke, no broken windows, and no evidence of a physical emergency. The garage doors were closed. Although she expected Thane to be inside, the sun's reflection on the windows prevented her from seeing any glow behind the brown paper that covered them. She passed by Thane's truck and went to the door. As she reached for the knob, the door opened.

Thane stood there, his face taut. He wiped tears on his arm.

"Thane, what's happened?" she asked.

He motioned for her to enter and quickly closed the door behind her.

She looked around the shop. It was as pristine as ever. Everything appeared to be in order.

"It's not over," Thane said. "I got a phone call."

"About what?" She asked, placing her phone in the entryway bowl.

"The accident."

"Everett Paige called you?" Morana stared at him in disbelief.

"No," Thane said. She followed him to his work block. She sensed motion above one cabinet. Gus's tail curled and flicked as he looked down at them from his perch on a blanket.

"I got a voicemail," Thane said, picking up his landline handset. He dialed and put it on speaker.

> *Listen, Sykes, I don't know how you intimidated my client, but I'll be damned if this is over. I'd say to watch your back, but I don't give useless advice. I'm coming for you.*

The message ended.

"It's Everett's attorney," Thane said.

Morana crossed her arms. "Why is he involved?"

Thane put his finger to his lips. "I don't want to discuss it in here."

"Why not?"

Thane pointed to his ear.

"Is he listening?"

"I hope not," he whispered, tension etched into his face.

"How would he be listening?"

Thane shrugged and whispered, "I worry."

"This makes no sense to me," Morana said. "I met with Everett and put this issue to bed."

"This situation is bigger and more complicated than I thought. You were so effective with Everett. I was hoping you could help me with his lawyer, too. I don't have anyone else to call."

"Listen, Thane," Morana said, coming around the block to stand beside him. "Of course, I will do whatever I can."

"Thank you." Thane wrung his hands. "I wish I had money to pay you."

"Don't worry about that. I agreed to help you resolve this situation. I always finish any job I take, and this one isn't finished. Maybe you can pay me in experiment demonstrations."

Thane relaxed and said, "If you can help me solve this problem, I'll give you all the demonstrations you want!"

"Deal." Morana held out her hand. They shook.

"If I'm going to help you, I must learn more about this attorney. Is his information included in the file you gave Clay?"

"Only his firm," Thane said. He watched Morana as she looked up and tapped her chin in thought. "What is it you do for a living?" he asked.

"Well…" Morana paused. "I'm between jobs right now, temporarily helping Clay with a personal project. Why do you ask?"

Thane strolled around to the opposite side of the work block and fiddled with the phone, spinning it a few times. "You not only found Everett in no time, but you also convinced him to drop his claim so quickly and effectively. I wonder how you did it." When Morana didn't immediately answer, Thane set the phone aside and looked at her.

"That's an interesting question," Morana finally said, scratching her neck. "I tracked him down by using public records. I met him face-to-face. We had a brief conversation where I explained that his attempts to pursue you for the $10,000 would be futile and costlier than the payoff. By the end of our discussion, he agreed with me."

Thane mustered a small smile.

Morana drummed her fingers on the work block. "But I didn't realize he was only half of the problem." She pointed to the phone. "You need to take the voicemail message seriously."

"I do."

"Then let me help you with some security measures to make your garage safer. It may seem trivial, but at a minimum, we should install an additional deadbolt on the door."

"No, that isn't necessary."

"But you were trembling after listening to it."

"That was more anger than fear."

Morana came to him and took his hand. "I'm concerned about your safety." She pointed to the entryway. "What if he kicks your door in? What will you do?"

"I would defend myself."

"How?" Morana asked. "Please don't be offended, but physically, you're not…"

Thane laughed. "I'm less vulnerable than you think."

"Do you carry?"

"Pardon?"

"A gun—do you have a gun?"

"No, nothing like that."

Morana let go of his hand and leaned onto the block. "All I'm trying to do is keep you safe while I help you resolve this dangerous situation with Everett's lawyer."

"Follow me," Thane said, leading her out of the garage. He pointed to a place for her to stand a short distance from the door.

Morana went there and folded her arms.

"Wait there," Thane said. "Don't try to see into the garage."

Thane went back inside and closed the door. A moment later, the large garage door opened to ankle height, a red brick slid out, and the door came down to rest on it. Gus squeezed out under the door, ran to the side fence, scaled it, and disappeared to the other side.

Morana fought the urge to move closer.

Within a few seconds, air rushed out from under the door, scattering the fallen twigs and leaves accumulated there. A small dust cloud grew and faded across the driveway.

She heard Thane's footsteps approach the entry door, and it opened.

"Come in," he said.

She stepped inside, looked toward his work area, and covered her mouth to muffle a gasp.

Thane closed the door behind her and locked it.

A section of the garage's foundation, larger than a vehicle, hung suspended in midair. The smaller work block rested atop the larger block. Together, they formed a two-tier pyramid hoisted to within inches of the ceiling. Below them, a crater mold was deep enough to be dark at the bottom.

Morana stood transfixed by the massive tonnage that levitated perfectly still. She noticed a thin wire draped from the bottom corner of each block to a black box mounted on the ceiling. The faint hum had resumed.

"Follow me," Thane said. "It's safe." He walked toward the edge of the mold.

Morana broke from her trance and approached him, staying back a few steps.

"You've already seen the work block that I use as a desk," Thane said. "This larger one is called the Gateway block." He squatted on the edge of the mold and hopped down into it. The edge came up to his chin. He looked up at Morana and said, "Come in with me, and I'll show you more."

Morana squatted, keeping her eyes on the colossal gateway block as though she expected to fall at any moment. She dangled her feet inside the space and scooted closer to the edge. She recalled how the smaller block had shaken the garage and rattled the windows when it fell only a few inches. Thane had hoisted this block that looked 10x larger, well above her full height.

Thane watched Morana assess the obvious risk against his assurance. "If you want to see more of my work, you'll need to trust me," his voice echoed. He turned and went to the distant corner of the Gateway block's mold. A thin string of lights outlining a square blinked on around his feet. The lights cast speckles on his legs and the nearby crater wall.

"What… is this?" Morana asked.

"I'm safer than you think. There's much more to see. I'm offering you an opportunity, but if seeing more isn't worth the risk of stepping under 80 tons of suspended rock, you can leave—taking my word for it."

Morana took a final look up at the massive block and shuddered. Despite Thane already being in the block's mold, everything about stepping under it felt unreasonable. "Thane, I want to see whatever you are willing to show me, but I don't mind admitting that this scares me."

Thane slipped his hands into his pockets. "I can't prove you are safe unless you accept some danger."

"And if you are wrong?"

"It would be too quick to hurt." He smiled.

"Not funny, Thane." She took a deep breath and hopped down into the space. The edge of the crater came to just below her shoulders. "I feel like a bug under a big shoe," she said, hurrying to Thane's side.

"Stand closer and stay within the boundary," he said, pointing down to the lit outline.

She moved to within a couple of inches of Thane and faced him. He seemed perfectly comfortable with her having invaded his personal space.

He looked at her face and said, "You will feel movement. You must not panic."

Morana hooked her arm through Thane's. A sharp click came from somewhere near their feet. The square they stood on descended. Morana squeezed Thane's arm as they descended, swallowed into the darkness.

"Ouch," Thane said.

"I'm sorry," Morana said, loosening her grip on his arm as they sank deeper into the pitch-blackness of the shaft.

"Be sure to not touch the walls of the shaft. The interference could cause a rapid drop."

Morana pulled him closer, staring upward as the lit opening above them shrank. "What are we on?"

"It's a lift block. It's like an elevator without the safety features."

"That's not encouraging," Morana said, resuming her grip on Thane's arm.

"It doesn't require an elevator's safety features as long as we follow the rules."

"I'm feeling compliant," Morana said. "Where are we going?"

"To a special place."

After they had descended about fifteen feet, the lift block slowed to a stop. Thane clicked on a flashlight, illuminating the shaft wall. A black panel the size of a wallet had come into view. Thane pressed it, and the lift block descended the same distance again until another black panel appeared. He repeated this process nine times. With each press of the panel, they traveled deeper from the surface. The shaft's opening shrank to a distant square of light above them.

"How much further?" Morana asked, loosening her grip on him.

"Approximately four meters," Thane replied. Moments later, an opening slid up beside them. Thane aimed the flashlight into the open space of a chamber the size of a small bedroom, completely encased in the same rock as the shaft walls and the blocks up in the garage. A thin string of pinpoint lights like those around the edge of their lift platform blinked on, lining the ceiling's edge. The lights illuminated the bare chamber with an ambient yellowish glow.

Morana lifted her foot to step off the platform, but Thane stopped her.

"Wait," he said. Another click came from a place near their feet. Morana looked down, trying to determine what had caused it. Thane's hands were out of his pockets, resting comfortably at his sides.

"Look up there," Thane said, pointing up.

Morana did so and saw the square opening of the shaft slowly dim and then go black as the large Gateway block descended in the garage. When its bottom edge reached the top of its mold, air rushed through the shaft, rustling their clothes and Morana's hair. The flow of air stopped when the Gateway block stopped in its mold.

Thane stepped into the chamber first and extended his arm for Morana to join him. "Welcome to my sub-lair," he said.

"Wow," Morana said. She reached out and touched the wall and then the ceiling.

Thane moved to the opposite side of the chamber and flattened his hands on the wall, rubbing in circles along the gritty surface.

Morana pivoted, taking in every detail about the space. The walls were composed of the same solid rock as the blocks in the garage. When she looked closer, she noticed they had been placed so precisely that their hairline seams were barely visible.

"What do you think?" Thane asked.

"I'm so overwhelmed, I almost don't know what to ask," she said.

Thane smiled. "This is a place I've created. There's no evidence of its existence above ground. I appreciated your concern for my security when we talked a few minutes ago," he pointed up. "...but assault and burglary aren't a concern for me when I'm down here."

Morana sensed motion and turned to the shaft they had just exited. The opening to the lift was gone, and a solid column of rock accelerated upward, filling the shaft and sealing them in.

"What's happening?" she asked.

Thane said, "There goes our ride," he laughed. "Whenever I'm in the sub-lair, I raise the lift block to eliminate the shaft's airspace. Filling the shaft prevents any possibility of detection of my route to the sub-lair by anyone on the surface."

"Unbelievable," Morana said. "I knew you valued privacy but underestimated your preparation for it."

After about a minute, the rock within the shaft slowed to a stop, and with a barely detectable bump, it locked. Morana went to it and touched it.

It was difficult to distinguish the column of rock that had filled the shaft from the wall blocks on either side.

Thane said, "Something about the absolute subterranean isolation in solid rock that appeals to me. Does that make you uncomfortable?"

"Not if you are with me." Morana patted the wall. "I used to work in an underground facility not long ago, but this is extreme. It's truly amazing."

"I appreciate your enthusiasm, but I want to ask that you not share anything you see down here."

"Of course, I won't," Morana said. "This is worth protecting at any cost." She drew her finger across the rock that now filled the lift shaft. "How can the rock below the lift rise to fill the shaft if you aren't on the lift to press those panels?"

"The shaft-triggers are only necessary if the lift carries more weight than its own."

"Amazing," Morana said. "So, there's a place below us deep enough to house a column of rock that can fill the entire shaft?"

"We're over a hundred feet below ground. But we've descended only halfway to the floor of my work."

Morana reached up to the string of lights. She gently tapped a bulb with her fingertip. "So, how do you get power to this... sub-lair?"

Thane pointed upward. "Most is provided by the solar panels mounted in the backyard, supplemented by the garage's wired power. Eventually, I'd like to develop an independent power source for the sub-lair."

Morana pivoted and said, "I'm stunned."

"I thought you would be." Thane smiled wide enough to show teeth.

Morana laughed. "So, did you expand an underground cave that already existed?"

"No, I quarried every square inch of space you see down here."

"How?"

"Block by block."

"Where do you take the blocks?"

"I discard them."

"Where?"

"Sorry, I can't tell you that. But I will tell you I use my truck, and the block discards are well hidden. If anyone discovers them, it would only generate more questions than answers."

He pointed to the corner of the chamber where three knee-high rectangular blocks were stacked against the wall. "I can remove three per night, one at a time. Each is approximately a cubic meter, weighing 3,474.48 pounds, which is the payload limitation of my truck. Depending on the day, I can quarry and clear four or five cubic meters."

Morana remembered that, aside from the relatively new bed liner, the worn truck looked like it was running its last miles. That Thane claimed to have moved the immense tonnage of rock by making multiple trips with his small beat-up truck only impressed her more.

"Where are your tools?" she asked, knowing the question was likely on the cusp of what Thane was willing to disclose.

"Stored away." Thane motioned toward a narrow opening that Morana hadn't noticed at the end of the chamber.

"Can you show me the tools?"

"No."

Morana feigned a pout, and Thane laughed.

"What about ventilation?" she asked.

He pointed to a small round hole high in the wall where a fan's spinning blades pulled in cool air from the darkness behind it. "The sub-lair's air is completely exchanged every nine-and-a-half minutes."

"But I thought there was no sign of this place up at ground level."

"You'll have to trust me when I tell you that the intake and exhaust vents are virtually impossible to detect on the surface."

"How do you know the overall structure is safe? Could it collapse?" Morana asked.

"Of course—if I've made the slightest miscalculation. Fortunately, that isn't likely." Thane strolled around the chamber, smiling up at the ceiling seams. "We are standing in the belly of a solid coral limestone sheath over a mile and a half wide, varying from fifty to two hundred meters deep. From the surface, there is no way to reach us using 'known' technology without weeks of drilling and knowing where to drill. We're encased in millions of tons of solid rock in arguably one of the most private places on earth. I think of it as being protected inside earth's clenched fist."

The explanation included more words than Morana had ever heard Thane use at one time. Her amazement was interrupted by his reference to being undiscoverable. Down here, Thane was in a position of absolute power over her. If he couldn't or wouldn't lift the huge Gateway block high above in the shop and then operate the lift to raise them back to the surface, escape from this place was impossible.

"What if we get stuck down here?" she asked.

"That's an understandable concern, but I wouldn't worry. I've got you covered—so to speak!"

Morana looked at him. It was the first time she had heard Thane tell a joke. He laughed, and she noticed his face was completely transformed. His smile had not faded since they had stepped from the platform. It was as though descending into this bizarre catacomb had infused him with a new personality.

"Follow me," Thane said, shocking her by reaching for her hand. He led her to the opposite side of the chamber, humming and caressing the walls with his free hand as they walked. They entered a corridor about the same length as the garage.

Partway along the corridor, Thane pressed on the faint outline of a square in the wall. A large block a few inches taller than he ascended, disappearing into a slot in the ceiling and creating an open doorway to a dark space. Thane leaned inside, feeling with one hand for something.

"What moved that door?" Morana asked.

"The same mechanism you've been observing with the other blocks and the lift—nice try."

The lights blinked on, revealing another chamber. Morana followed him inside. A mattress with unmade bedding, like the one in the house, was on the floor. A box of tissues and a clock sat on a small block positioned as a bedside table. A larger block set against another wall held some papers, pencils, and a coffee mug. The space was lit by more thin lights strung around the edge of the ceiling.

A hollowed-out space on the wall opposite the bed contained a mini-fridge underneath several shelves carved from the rock that held crackers, fruit, cereal, and other packaged foods. Its electrical cord was strung to the corner and up the wall, joining the wire that powered the lights.

"This is where I live," he said.

Morana released his hand and moved to the center of the room, looking around with her hands on her hips.

"Can I offer you a drink or a snack?" Thane asked.

Morana laughed. "I don't want to pillage your stash."

"I have plenty," Thane said, handing her a bottle of water from the fridge. "I spend so much time here that it made sense to stock food. I have provisions to last well over a year."

"Are you a doomsdayer?" she asked.

"I've heard of them. That doesn't describe me—at least not by its typical definition. I'm not worried about a nuclear war ending our world. I'm concerned about an invasion of privacy ending mine."

"I'd say your precautions are… extraordinary," Morana said.

"I want to show you something else," Thane said. He led her through an arched opening into an adjacent chamber, slightly smaller than the bedroom. Inside the room, three steps descended to a square pool the size of a hot tub. Its far edge was flush to the wall, and the water level was only a couple of inches lower than the floor.

"Don't tell me you built a pool!" Morana said.

"Not exactly," Thane replied. "I can only take credit for discovering it. You are looking at a Floridian aquifer." He kneeled beside the water. "I knew it was possible, but I was still surprised when I hit the water while quarrying this space."

Morana kneeled beside him and wiggled her fingers into the water. "Do I feel motion?" she asked.

Thane removed a paper from his pocket and tore off a corner. He dropped it on the edge of the pool closest to the center of the room. The paper drifted at walking speed until it bumped against the wall and bobbed a few times before the current pulled it under and out of sight.

"Where does the water go?"

Thane shrugged. "I don't know."

"Is it drinkable?" Morana asked. She stood and walked around the edge of the pool.

"With proper filtration, it's delicious. Taste it."

She laughed. "No, I'll stick to the commercial water," she said, raising her bottle. "Thane, this place is unlike anything I've ever imagined. It's truly surreal."

Thane beamed. "I can tell you it's always extraordinary every time I see it."

"I'm sure." She watched him briefly before adding, "There's no place you'd rather be, is there?"

"Is it that obvious?" He ran his thumbnail along a groove in the wall. "I never feel freer than when I'm locked down here. Returning to the surface has become a chore."

"Interesting," Morana said. "So, Thane…" She paused.

"Yes?"

"We are free to say anything we want down here without worrying about eavesdropping, right?"

"I can guarantee that."

"Then, can you please tell me anything else about the voicemail message? I want to understand why this person is after you, and I sense I'm missing something."

Thane's cheery expression dissolved, and he folded his arms. "The person who left the voicemail message is a guy who has been after me for a long time."

"As in—a stalker?"

"Not exactly."

"Do you know this person?"

Thane fidgeted with his hands."His name is Waylon Snells. We met when we were both eight years old."

"Wow."

Thane said, "Let's go back in here." He led her back into the bedroom and sat on the mattress.

Morana sat beside him. "I want to know more. How do you know him?"

Thane opened his mouth and hesitated, struggling for words.

Morana put her hand on his back. "If it's too difficult to share, you don't have—"

"No... I want to." He took a deep breath and said, "Waylon began teasing me in third grade, but it got much worse in middle school. He was always the strongest boy in class and flaunted it. He called me 'Thane the Pain.' He stole money, school supplies, whatever I had that he wanted. He beat me up at least once a week."

"That's awful."

"He must have heard the term 'super predator' and liked it, so he referred to himself as a super predator. If he saw me in the hallway between classes, he pointed his finger and repeated, 'Behold my prey,' until I looked his way. He stole my lunch at least once a week. He'd eat whatever dessert my mom put in and ruin the rest by throwing it into the waste bin behind the school. He'd beat me up if he didn't like what my mom had packed."

"And the teachers allowed this?" Morana asked.

"I learned to keep my mouth shut. If I reported him, he punished me. Everywhere I went, he was there. In the hallway, lunchroom, and the schoolyard, he would shout, 'Behold my prey!' I'd hear it in the distance, and he kept saying it repeatedly until he caught up with me. Other kids were afraid of him, too." Thane wiped his eyes on his sleeve. "One time, he found a tuna can on the ground beside the trash area. The open lid was still attached. He threw the can at me. The lid hit me here, and I needed stitches." Thane pointed to a scar above his eyebrow. "For the next few days, while I was bandaged, he'd sit behind me in class and whisper, 'Something's fishy.' He always taunted me like that until he got the reaction he wanted from me."

"What about your parents?"

"I grew up without a father. I didn't want to tell my mom because she'd tell the teachers, and Waylon would punish me. When she saw bruises and the cut from the tuna can, she reported it to the principal. I made something up, but the principal picked my story apart until I confessed the truth. Waylon got reprimanded and, as usual, took it out on me." Thane wiped his eyes again. "Waylon once drew and cut out pretend tickets and tried to sell them for a quarter each to a show he called 'Thane Pain.' When the other kids wouldn't buy them, Waylon went into the classroom when everyone was gone for lunch and put a ticket inside every desk—except mine. I didn't know it, but the back of the ticket had the time and place: after school, behind the gymnasium at the head of a trail that Waylon knew was my route home from school. On that day, rain left the trail muddy and thick with puddles. I first noticed more kids than usual gathered at the trail's edge. I didn't know why they were there. Waylon stepped out from among them when I approached, threw me face-first into the mud, and sat on me. I tried to get him off me while he acted like he was riding me like a rodeo horse. A few of the kids laughed. Most were stunned and backed away. He shoved my face into the mud and said, 'Look, you can't even tell the little nigger's dirty.' He wouldn't let me get up until I ate some of it."

Morana put her arm around him and said, "Thane, I'm so sorry that happened to you. I can't believe no one defended you."

"Most of the kids that ran away continued watching from behind the science building. One girl, Sarah Parsman, stayed behind and tried to defend me. She pushed Waylon off me. He threatened to make her eat mud, too. She ran to get help, but I knew Waylon would be finished with me before any adults could arrive to stop him."

"And no one in authority at your school did anything to help you?"

"The first time he threatened me for reporting him, he kept his word and punished me with a beating. The second time I reported him, he set fire to a custodial closet and put matches and lighter fluid in my backpack. He told the principal that he saw me running from the closet and to check my bag. They found the items. Not only did I get in trouble, but it was also the first and only time I remember my mom being afraid of me, even though I denied it."

Morana stared at the wall, her jaw tight.

"Most of what Waylon did was more embarrassing than physically painful—except..."

"Except, what?"

"Probably the worst thing."

Morana squeezed his hand. "You don't have to tell me more if it makes you uncomfortable."

"No, I'll share it. It doesn't feel uncomfortable to tell you. I once got permission to leave the class to use the restroom. Waylon must have gotten permission to leave class right after I did. He entered and startled me. I was at the urinal. My pants were at my knees. He rushed me. He threw me to the floor before I could pull up my pants."

Morana squeezed her eyes shut, bracing for it.

"He had something on his fingers. He wrestled me and wiped something on my—all over me down there. I couldn't fight him off. I was terrified. He laughed while washing his hands and went back to class. The cream he smeared was menthol, and it tingled and then burned. I tried to wash it off, but the water and soap worsened it. I couldn't go back to class like that. I stayed in the restroom for over an hour trying to clean myself and got in trouble for skipping class." Thane took off his glasses to wipe his tears.

Morana rubbed his back. "You shouldn't have had to go through that. I wish we could reverse what he did to you. Nothing angers me more than seeing the suffering of someone innocent."

Thane gathered himself and said, "Obviously, I survived, but I know the experiences scarred me deeply." He rested his chin on his knees. "My mother promised me he'd be gone someday, but he never goes away."

Morana took a tissue from the bedside stand and wiped his eyes. "I'm betting that your mother was right."

"In my dreams," Thane said. He cleared his throat. "I couldn't wait for the day I'd graduate from high school because I knew we would go our separate ways, and I'd be free. He used to tease me, saying he could always find me no matter where I tried to hide. I never dreamed his abuse would continue after we were grown up. Now it has happened."

"What sort of schoolyard bully continues until they are an adult?"

"Part of this situation might be my fault."

"How can you say that?"

Thane leaned back on the bed. "I looked him up and discovered he still lives in the area. He's a big-time injury attorney. He has a billboard on Kingman Road. On it, he's grinning with the same sneer he used to give me. He's holding his fist up. The caption reads, *Get What You Deserve!*"

"He's *that* guy? I've seen the ad," Morana said.

"It's the perfect job for him and made him rich. He has radio ads, too. Whenever I hear one, it reminds me I can't escape him. One of his radio ads invited people to stop by his firm's booth at a career fair." Thane stopped talking.

"And?" Morana said.

"Now I know it was a mistake, but I went. I wanted him to see that he hadn't ruined me. Something inside me wanted to confront him—to show he hadn't won. I thought that would help me, but it didn't."

"What happened?"

"He was there. I remember approaching his table. He was sitting. I felt anger welling up in me. I can't remember everything I said, but things didn't go as planned. He stood to look down at me like he used to. He folded his arms like he used to. He leered at me with the same smirk I remember. I yelled at him, and then he threatened me."

"How?"

"Something about finding out where I lived. A few days later, the supposed accident happened, and he was back in my life."

"But how is Everett involved?"

"Waylon and Everett are friends. I think Waylon used Everett for payout in many fake accidents, like the one they staged with me."

Morana rested her hand on Thane's shoulder. "Waylon is cruel. You are so smart and handsome. I can't imagine anyone having an urge to hurt you."

"Then you're unusual."

"Why do you say that?"

"I know I'm not exactly good with people. My mom used to call it a social deficit. As a boy, the awkwardness of interacting with classmates made me a frequent target." Thane's eyes welled up again. "As an adult, my self-doubt makes almost every interaction awkward. That's why I love the quiet solitude of the sub-lair." He twirled his glasses.

They sat silently for almost a minute. Morana kneeled to face him. "Please look at me," she said. "You may not believe this, Thane, but I was bullied, too."

"You're right. I *don't* believe you."

"Swear to God." Morana raised her hand. "Mine happened in my teen years. I was tall, my body developed early, and that got attention from the boys the other girls wish they could attract."

"Then you should have been popular."

"You would think so, but the girls were jealous and felt threatened. I rarely started conversations with the popular girls. That only isolated me more from them. When their boyfriends flirted with me, things got worse. The girls ganged up and shouted things at me in the hallway and cafeteria. They reported lies to teachers to get me in trouble." Morana paused.

Thane put his glasses back on and pushed them higher on his nose.

His eyes locked on her as he soaked up her words.

"One day, these mean girls drove by while I walked home from school. One threw a soda out the car window, and it hit me. I have a scar to this day." Morana hiked the back of her shirt up and twisted, exposing the skin on the side of her back. She looked over her shoulder. "Here, look, there's a faint discoloration." She moved closer to him.

"I believe you," Thane said, briefly looking before averting his eyes.

"It's okay," Morana said. She took his hand and gently spread his fingers on her back, moving his fingertip in a circle on her skin. "Can you feel that?"

"It's just… warm skin. I don't feel a scar."

"Well, it's there," she said. She let go, and her shirt dropped. "I sometimes notice it in the mirror when I get dressed. Anyway, I decided to not be a victim anymore, so I got even with them." Morana scooted back to lean against the wall. She crossed her legs and studied her nails.

"You can't stop there. What happened?" Thane asked.

Morana laughed and said, "Sorry, I was reliving it… I seduced several of their boyfriends and secretly took some… useful photos."

Thane's mouth opened, and then he smiled.

"I gifted a photo to each girl on the same day. I knew they'd be furious. As expected, three of them confronted me in the gym locker room, but I was ready. I first went for the tallest, mouthiest one and took her to the ground. The other two ran away, but I had the one I wanted."

"What did you do to her?"

"That's not so important. The bottom line is that—"

"But I want to know what you did to her," Thane said, looking earnestly at her.

"Well, I had a pocket knife."

"My God," Thane said.

"I forced her face down and wrung her long blond hair into a ponytail before slicing it an inch from her scalp. I ran from the gym through a side door. To this day, I believe the teachers overreacted by calling an ambulance. Our tussle drew blood from her nose and mouth. I didn't plan for that, but she wouldn't listen when I told her to be still."

"Wow," Thane said. His eyes had glazed over as he envisioned Morana's story.

"The principal wanted to expel me, but I persuaded him I had been the victim of their bullying for weeks. He agreed to only suspend me. During my time out of school, I went to each of the girls' houses at night to see into their lit bedrooms from outside. I taped a thinly braided lock of

Tammy's hair with a note outside each of their bedroom windows."
"What did the note say?"

"Stay out of my hair, and I'll stay out of yours."

Thane laughed and shook his head.

"You approve?" Morana asked.

He nodded. "You so rarely hear about bullies getting what they deserve. They always seem to get away with it." He looked up at the corner of the ceiling in thought. "Did the note work?"

"Like a charm."

"They never bothered you again—at all?"

"Ever!"

"I don't think Waylon has enough hair for me to do that." They laughed.

"You know," Morana said, "I've never shared this story with anyone. I hope I can trust you to keep it between us. I wouldn't have mentioned it, but based on what you've shared, it seemed right to tell you about my experience since we've both been victims."

"I won't tell anyone," Thane promised.

"Thank you. Bullying is my trigger. It's one of the few things that can make me lose my temper. I'm your best advocate if you're a victim and a friend. I wish I could heal you," she said. She came back to him and sat beside him on the mattress. They hugged.

"I'll probably never get even with Waylon. I'm left to hope that fate takes care of it. Before his constant radio commercials, I would look him up. Rarely, maybe once a year."

"Why?"

"I hate to say it, but I sometimes hope to discover that something's happened to him, and he's gone forever so I can be free."

"Gone as in... dead?"

"That sounds horrible, doesn't it?" Thane grimaced.

"Given what you endured, I can't blame you."

"I hope my dream of freedom will come true someday. I'm superstitious. My dreams and nightmares come true. I dreamed about having my own workshop," he pointed up. "I dreamed about learning the secret to Master Leedskalnin's teachings. That happened, too. But the nightmares always seem to have the best chance of becoming real, and I feel like I can't stop them. Each time I looked Waylon up, I was afraid doing so would bring him back into my life—and it has."

"Thane, what if we could confront Waylon together?"

"Except that I want nothing to do with him. Seeking contact has brought nothing but problems for me. I only want him out of my life."

"After your confrontation at the job fair, you've rekindled his memory of you. It will take a long time for him to forget you. Now, he wants to hurt you—or worse. That was clear in the voicemail message. I won't let that happen. I won't let anyone hurt you."

"That's kind of you, but you can only do so much."

Morana said, "I just—" She paused, searching for the right words.

"What is it?"

"I don't want to alarm you."

Thane looked puzzled.

Morana took a deep breath and said, "I make it a point always to be ready to protect myself." She patted her hip.

"What do you mean?"

"I carry."

"You mean a gun?"

Morana gave a slight nod.

"Oh." Thane stared at her hip.

"Have you ever used a gun?" Morana asked. She stood and stepped back to avoid towering over him.

"No. My mom owned one but never allowed me to shoot or touch it." He stood and came closer to her. "Where is your gun? I still can't see it." He stared at her thumb hooked through her belt loop.

"It's a concealed holster." She raised the front of her shirt, reached under her belt, and slid out a compact pistol she had retrieved from Clay's stash.

Thane stepped back.

"Does my having a gun bother you?" she asked.

"I'm not against guns, but I need to ask you not to bring guns into the sub-lair."

"I promise it's safe." She released the magazine and checked the chamber to verify that it was unloaded. "Would you like to hold it? Here…" She held it out by the slide, offering him the grip.

"No."

"I only carry for personal protection. I told you I wouldn't allow anyone to hurt you, and I keep my word." She re-holstered the gun and adjusted her shirt to conceal it.

"So, you're prepared to kill someone?" Thane said.

"Only if I had no other choice."

Thane said, "The gun is a bigger risk to you down here than it is to me."

"Why?"

"If it were to discharge and kill me accidentally, you'll be trapped here—forever."

"Won't the lift block still work?"

"What an interesting response," Thane said, smiling.

Morana held up her hands. "I'm sorry, that sounded horrible."

"The lift block won't work without me." Thane opened his arms and pivoted. "Another problem is that firing a gun down here would cause structural damage that I'm unwilling to accept."

"But it's solid rock."

"Composed of coral limestone that shatters like glass. The potential for injury from a ricochet is enormous. You must be as careful to avoid shooting me as I have been to avoid crushing you."

Morana looked again at the pristine walls, floor, and ceiling.

Thane said, "Cutting and quarrying this space took thousands of hours. I could have finished sooner, but I was unwilling to compromise on precision."

"If damage occurred, couldn't you repair it?"

"Firing the gun isn't an option," Thane snapped. "Your weapon has no practical function in this environment."

"I'm sorry. No, of course not."

As quickly as Thane's anger flashed, it vanished.

Morana went to him and cupped her hand on his cheek. "Sweetheart, I understand your concern. I don't need the gun to help you."

"We should go back up," Thane said, going to the doorway.

As they exited the bedroom, Morana said, "How many people have seen the sub-lair?"

"This has been an exclusive tour."

"I'm honored. But I have to ask... why me?"

They rounded the corner and entered the lift chamber. Thane looked up and rubbed his throat. "Because you take what I do seriously. Your interest in Master Leedskalnin's experiments is admirable. I believe you when you say you love privacy. You've shown me respect. And probably the most important reason is that I don't want to put the additional locks on the garage you wanted me to. Rather than giving you a series of vague objections, I concluded I should show you. I hope it wasn't a mistake, but I committed to it despite the risk."

"There won't be any risk," Morana said, embracing him with his cheek pressed against her breasts.

When she let go, Thane blushed, looking down.

To cut the awkwardness, she said, "So, are you sure Clay knows nothing about the sub-lair?"

"I'm sure."

"Good."

"Why does that please you? You don't trust Clay?"

"Sometimes Clay," Morana paused, "let's say he has difficulty containing his excitement."

"I've observed that, too."

"How so?"

"I like Clay," Thane said. "He is always kind to me at my uncle's office, and he offered to help me with the accident situation, even if that help amounted to introducing me to you. I told him about my discovery and then showed him. I knew it was impressive, but I didn't realize how it would affect him. He was excited—I expected that. But then, after he left, he started calling frequently. And then, in the following days, he dropped by without calling in advance. He seems to lack self-control."

"Don't worry. I will talk to him," Morana said.

"No, please don't! I only shared that because you know him. I don't want to offend him. He is aggressive. In retrospect, I should have kept quiet about my discovery."

"But then we would never have met."

"True."

"Are you sorry you showed me?" Morana asked, wincing.

"Not yet."

She laughed. "That's okay. I accept your suspicion while I prove my loyalty."

The solid column of rock that had filled the lift shaft began sliding down in the wall beside them, startling Morana. She had not seen Thane press or manipulate any object in the chamber. "How did you start that?" she asked.

"Sensors."

"Can you be more specific?"

"No."

"Even though you won't share your secrets with me, I still want to thank you for trusting me enough to share your private worlds."

"Worlds?"

"Yes, the world in which you were victimized by Waylon and this wonderful new physical world you've created." She gently kissed his cheek.

Thane stood frozen for a moment. "You're welcome."

"I wonder if I could stay here with you—for a little longer," Morana asked.

"How much longer?"

"What if I said… Overnight?"

Thane's head jerked at the suggestion.

"I'm good company—I promise," Morana coaxed, fingering a button on his shirt.

"But I don't know where you would sleep."

"Where do *you* sleep?"

Thane turned away and laughed. "Mostly in there." He pointed toward the bedroom.

"Well, I'm an extremely low-maintenance guest. I can be comfortable almost anywhere."

"I don't know."

She took his hand. "I've enjoyed my time with you so much. We've only been down here a short time, yet I'm feeling sad about leaving. Can we spend more time together—back in your room?"

Thane let go and wrung his hands. "Maybe you can visit another time."

"Alright, I accept your invitation since you are so adamant that I come back."

Thane laughed, visibly relaxing.

The top of the lift slid into view, slowing smoothly to a stop.

"You first." He pointed to the opening.

Morana stepped onto it. Thane joined her and turned so that his back was to her. Morana said, "Do you mind facing me? I'd feel more comfortable."

"I suppose," Thane said, laughing nervously.

Morana pulled him closer. "It'll be easier to avoid touching the wall if you hold me."

Thane took her hand and pressed the black panel button on the shaft wall with his other one. The large gateway block lifted high overhead, and air from the sub-lair chamber rushed past them and up the shaft.

When the Gateway block stopped, the lift ascended smoothly, raising them toward it. Beside them, the opening to the sub-lair chamber vanished, and the shaft went dark as they ascended toward the small square opening of light ten stories above them.

Morana pulled Thane's arms around her waist. She gently rested her chin on the top of his head. She caressed his back.

At the first lift stop, Thane delayed pressing the wall panel.

Morana kissed his forehead. She took his head in her hands, and they kissed.

"I hope that didn't make you uncomfortable," Morana said.

"It didn't." Thane freed one of his hands to press the wall panel, taking them closer to the surface. The shaft's opening above grew larger, and more light poured in. After three more stops, the lift stopped in the garage at the base of the Gateway block's mold.

Thane hesitated. "I guess we should get off." He let go of her, but Morana continued to hold him.

"Can I make a request?" she said.

"Of course."

She lifted his chin to her with a finger and said, "Please don't make me wait too long for my next sub-lair visit."

Thane smiled and nodded. He turned away to hide his arousal.

Morana stepped off the lift. "Whew." She walked to the side of the Gateway block mold and climbed back up to the garage floor, moving around the edge to Thane's workbench, where she saw a small lamp beside a stapler and a penholder on the edge of the countertop. She removed one of three identical black pens from the penholder and tucked it into her pocket.

Thane eventually climbed out of the Gateway block mold and said, "I need you to step outside for a minute."

"Of course," she said, heading for the door.

Thane followed her and closed the door.

In the next minutes, she heard a faint hiss. When it stopped, Thane opened the door for her.

The Gateway block no longer hung in the air when she entered the garage. It was back in the foundation, with a barely visible seam around its edge. Thane had also lowered the smaller work block to the floor, where it resumed its role as a desk. He stared at her.

"What's the matter?" she asked.

Thane didn't answer. He stood motionless.

"Have I made you uncomfortable?"

"No, not at all." He glanced around the shop. "Something is not right," he said.

Morana looked in all the same places Thane looked but saw nothing different.

"Someone has been in here," he said, walking a few steps away.

"How do you know?"

Thane pointed to the large garage door. "And someone touched the window cover." A corner of the brown paper that covered the window was folded back, exposing a sliver of light that streamed in at the pane's edge. He returned to the entrance where Morana stood and examined the ground near her feet. "It happened while we were below."

"Are you sure?" Morana asked.

"Look, right there," Thane said, his voice tense. He pointed to the black area rug with the golden locks on it. Besides the few prints left by Morana and his shoes, a half dozen large shoe prints traversed it, some with the toe pointing in and the others pointing out. "This is bad," Thane said. He threw the door open and went outside.

Morana followed him.

Thane pointed to the windowpane with the altered paper. "Look! It's a hand-heel print." Thane got closer to it and pointed to an oblong dust smudge on the edge of the window.

Morana watched Thane scratch his neck, leaning for a better angle to examine the evidence of trespassing.

"Are you sure that smudge wasn't there before?"

"It was *not* there! This is *new!*" Thane shouted.

"Okay, I'm sorry," Morana said. "Sweetheart, calm down. That isn't going to help you." She looked around the backyard. Most of the property behind the main house was fully exposed, with no place for anyone to hide. The only hidden area was a narrow space behind the garage and a narrow walkway along the house wall opposite the driveway.

Morana slipped her fingers around her pistol as she walked around the corner of the garage. She pulled out the pistol and sidestepped along the wall when she was out of Thane's view. She peered around the rear corner. It was clear. She holstered the gun and went back to Thane.

"And look here," Thane said, still sleuthing for evidence. He had moved along the garage wall to a place behind his truck. "Look! More shoe prints, and they're unique." He used his finger to draw an oval around one of them. It had a tic-tac-toe pattern surrounding a logo that resembled a leaf. "And look, here's a knee print," Thane tapped his finger on the concrete beside the impression. "Somebody kneeled and looked under the door after I vented it!"

"How do you see this?"

"Because of the sprinkling!" Thane brushed past her and walked to the main house's back door. He leaned close to the knob, examining it. When Morana approached him, he said, "Here, too—there's a grab. Someone checked this door."

"Thane, I hope this question doesn't anger you, but can you tell me what the sprinkling is?"

"It's a sprinkling. I sprinkle. There's no tricking it."

"I beg your pardon…"

"It's powder—just lightly. It always tells the truth."

"I think I understand," Morana said, stepping closer. "What type of powder is it?"

"I make it. It's part talcum, part brown rice powder. It's difficult to see unless you know what to look for."

"So, you use this powder—"

"Everywhere. I use it everywhere," he said, jiggling the knob.

"But what good is the powder if it only tells you something happened after the fact? We need to get you a camera system."

"No! I hate cameras. Cameras ruin privacy. I don't want my privacy invaded. My powder may seem primitive, but its reporting is flawless."

"Okay, I'm sorry I suggested it." She tried to take his hand, but he pulled back and said, "What if it was Waylon?"

"It's another reason to be with you—so I can protect you."

"Will you shoot him?" Thane said, pointing to her belt.

"We're not in the sub-lair anymore. And that's another reason I think I should stay with you."

"No."

Morana took his hand. "Let me protect you."

"I don't need protection right now. I need privacy."

"How can you enjoy privacy if you know Waylon could return and hurt you?"

"I want to be alone," Thane said louder, pulling away.

"What an interesting conversation…" a voice startled them both. Ms. Perkins peered over the back fence, eavesdropping. "I knew you were up to no good!"

Morana bristled. She spun toward the woman. "You bitch!"

Thane took her arm and said, "Leave her."

Morana pulled free of his grip and stormed to the fence.

Mrs. Perkins's head dropped from view.

Morana looked over and saw Mrs. Perkins standing safely away amidst her prized African lilies.

Morana held an icy stare on her.

"What?" Mrs. Perkins said. "Why are you looking at me that way? I document everything I see over there, and I will also document what I just heard." She pointed to Thane's garage. "Something's wrong with what's going on in there, and I think it's high time the authorities learned about it."

"Let me tell you something…" Morana said.

Thane came up behind her and said, "Mo, the footprints are a bigger problem—please." He led her toward the front of the garage and whispered, "She constantly threatens but has never actually called anyone to complain."

Morana looked over her shoulder at the fence as they retreated and said, "After the harassment you've suffered from Waylon, the last thing you need to deal with is harassment from this hag."

"Thank you. Maybe now that you've intimidated her, she'll leave me alone."

"It would be her best option," Morana said. "Can I call you later?—I mean sooner?"

"I have to figure some things out. I'll call you instead."

"Please call me soon." Morana hugged him, walked up the driveway through the pergola, and disappeared around the corner.

Chapter 14

THE NEXT MORNING, Morana pounded on the front door. She had waited for over a minute after ringing the doorbell three times.

"Just hold your horses," a voice echoed from inside, followed by footsteps. The door's floral window curtain parted. Mrs. Perkins peered out, scowling. "What is it? Are you soliciting?"

"No, it's Thane's friend."

"No, it isn't."

Morana looked down at herself. "I know I look different."

"Is that your car in my driveway?" she said, tapping the window.

"Yes, I'll only be a minute."

"There's plenty of room on the street. And why did you back in?"

Morana glanced over her shoulder at her Explorer, parked only inches from the garage door. "Let me explain. I have a gift for you." She held up a package the size of a dictionary, wrapped in white paper with a blue ribbon.

The curtain closed, and a deadbolt unlocked. Mrs. Perkins opened the door and beamed at the package. "For me? Oh, my!"

Morana said, "I apologize for not calling first, but I won't take much of your time—May I come in?"

"Of course," Mrs. Perkins said, stepping aside. As Morana passed by, Mrs. Perkins reached for the package, but Morana didn't hand it over.

Morana looked around a home that had the dated, mismatched furniture and clutter of a hoarder. The collection of rare plates that Mrs. Perkins mentioned at the fence was stacked on shelves along the short hallway. A card table sat amidst several easy chairs and two crooked sofas in the living room.

"Why would you get me a gift?" Mrs. Perkins asked, pointing to a sofa for Morana to sit.

"It's my way of making things right after our discussion in the backyard." She sat and placed the gift beside her.

Mrs. Perkins sat across from her at the end of a sofa wrapped in clear plastic. "I suppose we could put that behind us," she said, eyes locked on the gift again.

"Before you open your present," Morana rested her hand on it, "I wanted to chat with you a little."

"About what?" Mrs. Perkins asked, clasping her hands in her lap. "I've already agreed to keep the past in the past. Let's move forward."

Morana said, "I appreciate your willingness to move on, but first, I want to apologize about the noises you've been hearing in Thane's garage, and we'll do our best to control our kitty cat. Unfortunately, I'm afraid I can't help you with the tragic loss of your plate."

Mrs. Perkins raised a finger. "Now, it wasn't just any plate. It was a Bradford Exchange Commemorative Hummingbird Plate—extremely rare."

Morana closed her eyes to emphasize the feeling of loss. "I can't tell you how much your story has disturbed me. I'm here to make it right."

"Don't I wish everyone was as thoughtful as you are?" Mrs. Perkins said, still eyeing the gift, now on Morana's lap. "You know, your consolation is so kind. I'm glad you have the maturity to show some decency. Thane won't say two words to me and refuses to lift a finger to solve the problem. His cat is more destructive than gophers. I toil for hours in the scorching sun to grow and nurture some of the most sophisticated and delicate flowers, and that horrible varmint digs them up, leaving his disgusting poop nuggets everywhere. Would you put up with that?"

"Absolutely not." Morana grimaced.

"And then, after using my garden as a toilet, that cat stalks and kills my beautiful birds perched on my feeder. I know the damn cat has killed at least three times this month. A trail of feathers always leads straight to that garage door."

"Are you sure it's Thane's cat?"

"Of course, I'm sure—there's no denying that it's Thane's cat with its tufted ears and long hind legs. It doesn't even climb the pole. I've seen it jump higher than the height of a man."

The corners of Morana's mouth went down, and she nodded, "Impressive."

"Impressive? These innocent birds are simply trying to get a bite to eat."

"The cat is, too," Morana said.

Mrs. Perkins sucked her teeth and swatted her hand toward Morana. "It's called cat food. Maybe your friend should look into it instead of murdering my birds."

"Just to play devil's advocate, maybe you should consider that the cat enjoys hunting and catching prey more than eating from a bowl."

"I don't care what appeals to it." Mrs. Perkins wagged her finger.

"Now, you can't tell me Thane isn't aware of what his cat is doing. If he doesn't keep that damned cat off my property, I swear to God, I'll trap it. Let's see how that works out." Mrs. Perkins made a gesture of wiping her hands clean.

"I promised to keep this brief, so I want to get to the real reason for my visit," Morana said, twirling the gift on her lap.

Mrs. Perkins sat up straighter.

"When we had that conversation by the fence, you mentioned knowing more about what Thane was doing in his garage than he thought you did. You said you had documented it. What did you mean by that?"

"Well... I just," Mrs. Perkins stammered.

Morana interrupted. "Remember that I'm Thane's best friend, and I can't get him to tell me what he does in that garage, so perhaps we can swap notes and help one another."

Mrs. Perkins looked surprised. "So, you're coming to *me* to find out what Thane is doing in there?" She laughed.

Morana shrugged. "I've asked him, but he refuses to say anything. Tell me what you've seen or heard. Perhaps you've looked over the fence while he was transporting something unusual—or anything?"

"I can tell you one thing for sure... whatever he's up to, I'm sure it isn't legal."

"Be specific. I need to know exactly what you've seen or heard."

"He keeps that garage locked up and the windows covered like a crack house. How could I possibly know what's going on in there?"

"You said you had documented it."

"Suspicions. I've documented my suspicions. And if he thinks I have more than suspicions, well then, all the better. Maybe he'll stop being such a nuisance. By the way, I'm not the only one who's suspicious. All the neighbors are, too."

"So, you have no evidence, recordings, or documentation about what Thane is doing inside his garage."

"Aha! If he sent you here to make sure I didn't know what he's doing, that tactic won't work. If he doesn't control his creature and stop the strange late-night noises, I will be a bigger problem for him. I'll call the city."

"Why the city?"

"His garage is a hazard, and you know the saying: *If you see something, say something.*" Mrs. Perkins retrieved a piece of paper from a narrow foyer table in the hallway. She returned, placed it on the coffee table, and tapped her finger on a phone number. "I told you I would."

"But Thane hasn't done anything illegal."

"I wouldn't be so sure. I doubt he got a permit for those solar panels he's rigged in the backyard. And a tree on his side of our common fence almost touches the power lines. I've told him to trim it because it's a fire hazard."

"You'll report these things because of the cat?"

"Absolutely. Hopefully, that won't be necessary." She glanced at the gift.

Morana cleared her throat. "Mrs. Perkins—"

"Call me Eloisa."

"Mrs. Perkins, I'm going to ask you one more time. Do you know anything about what Thane does in his garage?"

Mrs. Perkins took a moment to think. "Nothing for sure yet, but you better believe I'll find out."

Morana tore the wrapping paper from the gift, exposing a plain brown box.

Mrs. Perkins raised her finger. "But I thought that was for me…"

"Oh, it is. And you shouldn't be surprised to learn that it will fix the cat problem." Morana reached into the box and pulled out a Glock 43 with a 3.3-inch micro-suppressor. She aimed it at Mrs. Perkins's gaping mouth.

Chapter 15

AN HOUR LATER, Clay's phone rang. He put it to his ear. "Where the hell have you been?"

"How did you know it was me?" Morana replied

"The way you rotate burners, any unfamiliar number is you. Has Thane given up the goods yet?"

"No, but he showed me more of what he can do, and I'm having a hard time believing what I saw."

"Bigger than lifting that rock?"

"Imagine being a little kid excited about the turnstile at the entrance of Disneyland because they thought that's all there was."

"Wow. So, what did he show you?"

"There's no way I can explain it on the phone. All those times when you said, 'trust me' to get me to come out and see the rock lift, I'm telling you to trust me about Thane's potential."

"I'll be back tomorrow."

"Already?"

"The housing market is crazy out here. My place triggered a bidding war, and I ended up closing a deal well above my asking price."

"Great. We can use the money."

"We? That money's going back into a new place."

"You'll like my plan for the money better, but we can wait to discuss that when you get back. Meanwhile, I need information on a new person."

"Who's on death row now?"

"Funny. Get me the works on Waylon Snells."

"Who's that?"

"He's Everett's lawyer. Now that Everett has dropped his demand— no thanks to your clumsy $10,000 payoff—this Waylon Snells has continued to pursue Thane."

Clay paused. "Snells—Snells—isn't that the lawyer from the radio? '*I'll Help You Get What You Deserve*'—that guy?"

"That's him."

"I don't remember seeing that name on Thane's paperwork."

"It only had his firm's name."

"Okay, I'll need a day to pull his info."

"No, I need it today."

"Impossible. I'm coming back tomorrow. I'll hand it to you in person then."

"That could be too late. Snells is threatening Thane, and I need to get to him. He's already been scoping and door rattling at Thane's place. I need this info yesterday."

Clay sighed. "If I get you what you need, can we date?"

"Goodbye, Clay."

Chapter 16

THE NEXT MORNING, Morana woke up in the back seat of her Explorer to the sound of her phone. She reached between the front seats and grabbed the phone from the console. "Hello…"

"Mo, it's Thane."

"Do you miss me already?" she said, yawning.

"Can you come back?"

"What's wrong? You sound stressed."

"I was right. Waylon came onto my property, and he came back again."

"How do you know? Did he try to break in?"

"Yes, and… he hasn't left. Can you come back?"

"Wait, you say he's still there?"

"Yes."

"Are you okay?"

"Temporarily."

"I'm on my way. Tell me what is happening."

"Please, hurry back. I have to hang up now."

"No, no! Stay on the phone with me!" Morana said, climbing into the front seat. "Thane… Thane, are you there?"

The line was dead.

Morana started the car and sped to Thane's house, trying to call him back several times.

When she turned onto his street, she was relieved to see no police activity. Still, rather than breaking Thane's rule and pulling into the driveway, she parked near the corner and ran half a block in broad daylight despite the risk. She crossed his front yard and went to the corner of the house. She peered down the driveway. She could only see a small corner of the garage. She moved closer, concealing herself behind the pergola, and slid her hand onto her gun under her beltline. She sidestepped to the rear corner of the house. As the garage came into view, she saw that the large roll-up door was open behind Thane's truck. Inside, Thane fidgeted and paced in the shadows. She pulled out the gun, held it behind her back, and called out, "Where is he?"

Thane looked in her direction but didn't see her.

She stepped into view, and he waved for her to come closer.

Morana held her gun in the ready position as she approached.

"You don't need the gun," Thane said.

"Where is he?" she said, joining him to stand under the open roll-up door.

"Over there." Thane pointed to the entry area where the phone bowl was located.

"I can't believe it," Thane said, grabbing his afro as he paced in a circle in the center of his shop.

"I don't see him," Morana said, creeping toward the entryway. Despite Thane's instruction to put it away, she kept her gun out and ready. Something had changed about the garage's interior—more than the additional light streaming in through the large open door. "Thane, I'm so confused. Where is he?"

Thane walked past her, leading her toward the entry door.

"I didn't want to do it." He pointed. "He's below that."

Morana looked where Thane pointed. The work block had been moved from the center of the shop and was buttressed by another, larger block in the entryway, blocking the door. Morana noticed the familiar thin wire connected to its bottom corner. It draped in a long arc up to the black ceiling box.

Morana stared in disbelief. "My God, you've crushed him?"

"No, I shafted him."

"What does that mean? Thane, I am so confused. Please tell me exactly what happened."

"He's under the block… trapped in a shaft. I never wanted it to come to this. I told him to leave, but he refused. I gave him plenty of warning."

"How did you get him in there? A trap door?"

"Technically, it's a trap floor. This entire entryway is the top of an eighteen-ton block I designed for a rapid drop."

"You moved eighteen tons quickly enough that he couldn't jump off?" she asked.

"Yes, I can drop it twenty feet in less than five seconds. He wasn't quick enough. He tried to jump off. He caught the edge with his fingers but couldn't hang on."

"You never showed me this."

"I'm glad I didn't need to."

Morana laughed. "Me too. He *is* alive, right?"

"Watch." Thane squatted beside her and placed his hands on the smaller work block. The faint hum resumed. With little effort, the block slid, creating a thin opening to the dark shaft beneath it.

Waylon's shouts immediately echoed from below. "Don't be an asshole, Sykes. This shit isn't funny. You better get me out of here." His footsteps echoed as his shoes scuffed the bottom of the shaft.

Thane picked up a small flashlight from the table beside the entry door. He returned, and they kneeled beside the block. Thane aimed the flashlight into the opening.

This shaft was substantially larger than the shaft created by the lift block they rode to the sub-lair. About 20 feet below, Waylon stood, wearing a business suit. He glared at them, shouting and pacing like a trapped wild animal. When the flashlight lit his face, he raised his hand to block the light. "Dammit, you fucking runt. It's not a game. You're facing serious consequences if you don't get me out of here *now*!"

Thane stared back without answering.

Waylon snatched the crumpled black throw rug with the golden locks on it that had been swallowed up with him and hurled it upward at them. It fell back onto him, and he flung it from his shoulder. He screamed, "You do not know how much shit you're in, Sykes!" Waylon lunged at the wall with one foot, launching himself upward and clawing as high as he could on the wall in a futile attempt to grab the top edge.

Thane said, "Fight me if you want to, but you'll still lose. Sound familiar?"

"I swear I'm gonna make you sorry for this, you mud bug."

"Go to hell!" Thane yelled.

Morana watched the exchange and then tapped the block with her hand. "Thane, I need you to close this opening right away."

"Who's that?" Waylon shouted. "Who's the woman? Hey, lady, I'm injured. You need to call the police, or you'll make a fine accessory to kidnapping."

"Thane, close this now!" Morana said.

Thane hurried to the opposite side of the block, squatted, and shoved it. As the narrow opening closed, Waylon shouted, "You're gonna pay for this, you scrawny nigger!" The block sealed the opening, muting him.

"Charming," Morana said. She stood and crossed her arms.

Thane stood and brushed some dust from his knees. "Why did you want me to close the shaft so quickly?"

"Did Waylon have a phone?" she asked.

Thane looked puzzled. "I assume he does."

"Could Waylon have used his phone after you trapped him and

before you sealed the shaft?"

"I—don't think so. I feared Mrs. Perkins would hear him yelling, so I covered the shaft. It took twenty, maybe thirty seconds. He was yelling at me during that time, so he couldn't have been texting."

"So, you lifted and moved your work block across the garage and sealed the shaft in 30 seconds?"

"Yes, probably less."

"We should assume he tried to place a call or send a text after he was trapped. If he succeeded, it's possible he could already have help on the way."

Thane said, "No, there's no way any mobile frequency could penetrate this rock." He patted the top of the block.

"We just opened the shaft a few moments ago."

"An aperture of that size," he held up his fingers, "couldn't possibly allow sufficient signal for transmission." Thane sounded more like he was trying to persuade himself.

Morana winced and said, "If he tried to send a text message, a small opening might have been all it needed to transmit."

"I still disagree."

"Fine, then there's a bigger issue. Now that you've trapped him, what do you plan to do with him?"

"I don't know. I was only trying to defend myself. It happened so quickly. I didn't know what to do, so I called you."

"What do you *want* to happen to him?"

"I want him punished."

"We can do that."

"What do you mean by we? I meant turn him in to the authorities for trespassing and attempting to assault me."

"You would bring the police into your garage?"

"No, not here. I want you to help me take him out and deliver him to the police from the house."

Morana looked up and sighed. "Sweetheart, that won't work. If you turn him in, he'll make good on every charge he just promised to file against you."

"But he's at fault here! He assaulted me. I was defending myself! He isn't hurt."

"That won't be his story. It is illegal to use a trap floor as a defense against trespassers."

"I didn't build it for that purpose. The trap floor is how I extract the larger blocks from the sub-lair. When he chased me, I panicked. It was all

I could do."

"You and I know that's true, and he knows that's true. But he also knows the law and will use it as a weapon against you. He'll claim injury from assault and battery by you. And to support this claim, all he needs is expert testimony from one or more of his sleaze-bag physician his firm uses in their injury cases."

"No, that can't happen!" Thane shouted. "You see? He's bullying me again." Thane kicked the block.

"You know what fixes all of this?"

"Please tell me."

"Confirming that he could not text after you dropped him."

"Why does that fix it?"

"Because it removes any need for us to hurry. It removes the chance that anyone is on their way. It gives us a world of options."

"Then we have to get his phone," Thane said, scratching his neck.

Morana said, "The problem is that even if a text message didn't transmit before he was sealed in, that message would surely transmit the moment we open the shaft. We need him to turn the phone off and to give it to us before we let him out."

"But he'll never agree to that."

"It might be easier than you think," Morana said. "Wait here." Morana went to the garage door, leaned out, and looked around. She went around the side and found a looped garden hose hanging from its fixture. She unwrapped it and pulled the hose around the corner and back into the garage, where Thane waited.

"What are you doing?" he asked as she snapped the hose to uncoil a kink.

"Encouraging him to give up his phone."

"You can't do that!" Thane said.

"You said a small crack won't allow him to get a signal. Move the block to give me a half-inch opening to the shaft."

"We can't do that," Thane said.

"Listen, Waylon's desperation to avoid drowning is greater than our desperation to get his phone. He'll give up the phone before the water reaches his ankles. I promise this won't add to the charges he's threatened."

"It isn't about the charges. There's no drainage at the base of this shaft. You'll flood the sub-lair."

"What about the aquifer? Won't that prevent flooding?"

Thane said, "I haven't quarried ducts to the aquifer, and I don't have a sump pump." He took the hose from her.

Morana put her hands on her hips. "I don't expect to need more than a few gallons to get him to comply—nothing a mop won't clean."

"No, no, no!" Thane said. He dragged the hose back outside. "Flooding the shaft is not an option."

"Okay, okay. No water." Morana raised her hands to calm him.

They came back into the garage. Thane closed and locked the large roll-up door.

Morana sat on the work block and crossed her legs. "Then the best option is to do nothing. We wait for his phone battery to die."

"But that could take a day or more."

"So?"

"You mean we just leave him in there?" Thane pointed.

"What concerns you about that?" She hopped off the block. "Are you afraid you will offend him?"

Thane nibbled his lip and swept his foot back and forth on the floor.

"Think about it," Morana said. "if he somehow got a text off, and someone shows up, we simply turn them away."

"What if it's the police?"

"Okay, suppose he dialed 911, and they traced his call to this location. The police might show up, but what will they find?" Morana opened her arms and pivoted, looking around the shop. "Waylon could be shouting at the top of his lungs right now, and we hear nothing. Your masterful job concealing your work within a normal-looking garage is incredible. Anyone looking will search for Waylon will see that he is not here. They'll have no clue you can move that block so easily. Say nothing, and visitors will know nothing."

Thane said, "I don't want visitors. I don't want to risk making this situation worse."

"And you won't—as long as we wait for the appropriate time to remove him from the shaft." She came closer to Thane and said softly, "You shared with me some horrific stories about how he victimized you. The power dynamic between you and Waylon has been completely reversed for the first time since you were children. It's also the first time he cannot harm you. He's obviously not hurt, and forcing him to wait longer won't do any more damage than he'll already claim he's suffered. How often did he restrict your movement or force you to endure situations you didn't want to be in? Or to do things you didn't want to do? How much of your time has he wasted over the years? When I think of what he's done to you, I have no problem waiting for that battery to die." She cupped his cheek in her hand. "And if he suffers from fear and boredom down there, I hope it begins with a fully charged battery."

Thane strolled to the opposite side of the garage, thinking. When he returned, he rested his hands on the block, drumming his fingers. "There may be another way. I need you to step outside."

"What are you thinking?" Morana asked.

"I have an idea. I'm going to access him from below. That way, it won't matter if his phone is on."

"I need to go with you."

"No. It won't take long—I'll be safe."

"Thane, listen to me. He'll kill you if he somehow gets loose from you below."

"Trying to kill me would be suicidal for him. He'll never get out. I'll make sure he knows it."

"Just take me with you. I'll have him begging you to take his phone."

Thane shook his head. "There's no way I will allow him to harm me. Please wait for me outside."

"I just saw you move this work block. Can't I watch you move the Gateway block?"

"No!" Thane snapped. He pointed to the door. "You can wait in the house if you want to. If anyone shows up, please don't let them come back here. If I can't get the phone from him, I'll take you to help me get it."

Morana went to the door, but before she could reach for the knob, a firm knock echoed throughout the garage.

"Please, God, no," Thane said.

Morana peeked through the crack at the edge of the paper that covered the window. She stepped back from the door and looked at Thane. "It's the police."

Chapter 17

THE UNIFORMED OFFICERS standing outside the garage door knocked again harder.

Thane stared at the door, frozen, with his mouth open.

"Do not panic," Morana said.

"You can't let them in," Thane said.

"We have to."

"I don't want to lose everything!" Thane's face went flush.

"You won't," Morana said. She went to him, grabbed his shoulders, and then pointed to the work block that concealed Waylon in the shaft. "Listen to me… Waylon is screaming at the top of his lungs now, right?"

"Probably," Thane said.

"And we hear nothing. The police won't either."

"But what if they know he's here and want to search my shop?"

A louder knock on the door echoed.

"Why wouldn't we let them? They sure as hell won't find him. And remember, they don't have a right to search without a warrant, and they couldn't have gotten one so quickly. Concentrate on feeling surprised and confused about anything they ask. Do you understand?"

Thane nodded, backing away from the door.

"Come closer," Morana motioned to him. "It will be okay. I'll do as much of the talking as possible."

Although she hid it from Thane, Morana's concern about opening the door matched his for a different reason. She had transformed her facial appearance so that it was unlike any of the photos of her shown in the media. But suddenly, the disguise felt inadequate for a face-to-face conversation with the police. Several options for a quick escape if things went wrong raced through her mind. She opened the door wide enough for part of her face.

The officers stepped closer, one of them casually resting his hand on his holstered gun.

"Can I help you, officers?"

"Yes, ma'am. Are you the resident here?"

"One of them," Morana said. She opened the door a little wider.

The officer exchanged a glance with his partner. "We rang the bell at the house. No one answered." He thumbed over his shoulder. "We're involved in an investigation and want to ask you a few questions."

She heard a creak behind her. She looked back at Thane, who had sat in a chair, and shook his head with his face buried in his hands. "I suppose that would be okay. What are you investigating?"

"Mind if we come in?"

Morana stepped back and opened the door fully. She caught Thane's eye and winked.

As the officers came inside, Morana hoped that the dimness of the garage interior would work in her favor.

"Afternoon, partner," the first officer said to Thane.

"He's... my boyfriend," Morana said.

The second officer glanced at Thane, and then his eyes swept Morana from feet to face as he passed by her. They took positions a few paces apart beside the garage wall, looking around the space.

Thane took a couple of deep breaths as quietly as he could. Morana went to him and gently squeezed his shoulder. "Can you tell us what this is about?" she asked.

"We're investigating a homicide."

"Oh, my God!" Morana said, covering her mouth.

Thane frowned, looking back and forth between the officer and Morana.

"What? Where?" Morana said.

"Your neighbor to the rear of your property."

"Can you tell us what happened?" Morana asked.

The second officer said. "Not yet. CSI is still finishing up its work. We need to know if you saw or heard anything suspicious from that property during the last 48 hours."

"No, not that I can think of," Morana said. She looked at Thane.

He said, "I haven't seen Mrs. Perkins for a few days."

"So, you knew her?" an officer asked.

Morana smiled to conceal her gritted teeth.

"Not well at all," Thane said.

The other officer said, "Can you tell us if you've observed any unusual activity on her property or visitors she may have had—especially anyone unfamiliar?"

Thane opened his mouth to speak, but Morana interjected, "Not recently. I can count the times we've ever spoken face-to-face on one hand. I know she loves her flowers and once gave us a delightful tour of her beautiful African lily garden."

Thane nodded to confirm, looking wide-eyed at the officer.

"Have you both been in town the last couple of days?"

Thane wrung his hands.

Morana answered, "Yes, we've been here. We spend most of our time working here in my boyfriend's shop. I haven't seen or heard anything, have you, honey?"

"No," Thane replied, but the word sounded like a grunt.

One officer motioned to his partner to follow him to the door. "We're canvassing all the neighbors to gather any other leads. If you see or hear anything that could contribute to our investigation, we'd appreciate it if you'd call us."

"Absolutely," Morana said. "This is all so unnerving." She covered her face with her hands. "That poor, poor woman."

"We're sorry to have to give you this news," the officer said.

"Thank you for stopping by," Morana said. "We're so grateful for the job you do, and we hope to see more of a presence from you in our neighborhood."

"Thank you, ma'am."

Morana feigned a shiver, rubbed her arms, and said, "I just can't believe it."

The officers went outside and walked down the driveway to the front of the house.

Morana came to the doorway and watched them walk out of sight. She turned to find Thane standing right beside her.

"I thought they were here for Waylon," he said.

"Me too," Morana said, taking a deep breath.

"That was amazing," Thane said.

"What?"

"The way you directed them. I thought they would ask questions leading to Waylon, but you kept them from doing that."

Morana smiled. "You played an important part by remaining calm, so we work well as a team. If you had panicked, it would've been impossible to have kept their visit as short as it was. It's too bad about Mrs. Perkins, isn't it?"

"Yes, I wonder what happened to her," Thane said, looking up as he contemplated. After a moment, he said, "I should feel worse than I do about her death, but she was so mean. I hate to say this, but people who are that mean are sometimes mean to the wrong person."

"So true. You better hurry with whatever you're going to do." Morana pointed to the work block.

"Shouldn't I wait for a while in case the officers return?"

"If they try to come back, I'll intercept them. Just be as quick as you can." She went into the garage and picked up her bag.

"I will. My plan will take me between ten and fifteen minutes. You wait over there," Thane said, pointing toward the rear of the house. "Watch for my signal to come back."

"Got it," Morana said. She stepped outside, and Thane closed himself inside the garage.

As Morana walked toward the house, she slowed and looked back when the wide garage door slid up to ankle height behind her. A red brick slid out, propping it. Thane then flung talcum powder along the edge of the open garage door and smeared it with his hand.

She had to smile. Thane's trespassing detector was primitive yet very effective.

She waited at the house's back door for a couple of minutes, watching the garage for any other activity, but she saw and heard nothing. She crept back to the propped-open garage door and squatted. "Thane?" she called out.

No answer.

She kneeled and looked under. "Thane?"

Still no answer.

If Thane had descended to the sub-lair, going into the garage for a quick look around would be safe. She put her face near the ground to look inside. A thin haze of talcum powder hung in the air. The entire foundation of the shop was intact, and it seemed impossible that Thane could have raised the Gateway block and descended and resealed it so quickly.

She tried to raise the door, but it was locked where the brick had propped it. She went to the entry door. It was unlocked. She opened it and peered inside.

She walked across the garage toward Thane's workbench, holding her breath. There was no way for her to reach the countertop without passing over the sealed gateway block. She knew that at any moment, it could lift. She ran across the Gateway block, grabbed Thane's pen holder, and quickly swapped a black pen with an identical pen that contained a micro video camera. She looked at the roll-up garage door on the brick and saw a padlock Thane had fastened through the metal railing on its edge to lock it in place.

She moved to the center of the shop where the work block was usually located and used her phone to take photos of the shop, including Thane's workspace and the bottom of the partially opened garage door.

On the floor beside a cabinet, she found the opened sack of talcum powder Thane must have used. She grabbed a fistful and sprinkled and smeared it, covering her tracks as she backed toward the entryway.

After exiting the garage, she sprinkled more powder outside the front door and smeared it, just as Thane had. She thought for a moment and then went to the house's back door. After a final listen for any sound from the garage, she went inside. "Hello?"

The house was quiet. She cleaned herself off at the kitchen sink and then checked her watch. Her escapade in the garage had used only 2 to 3 minutes of the 10 to 15 minutes Thane said he would be in the sub-lair. She left the kitchen, walked down the hall, and entered the main bedroom. Once again, the bedsheets on the mattress were tangled, and two torn condom wrappers lay on the floor a short distance away. Three empty beer cans, one of them crushed, had replaced the shot glasses she remembered seeing beside the head of the mattress. Either Thane was renting out his place as an Airbnb, or she had much more to learn about him.

She helped him by making the bed. When she pulled back the sheets, she found two used condoms underneath. She grabbed a paper towel from a loose roll beside the beer cans and picked up the condoms and their wrappers, discarding them in the bathroom trash across the hall. She returned to the bedroom and made the bed, tucking the sheets tight. She flipped the pillow and fluffed it, centering it on the mattress.

In the hallway, she opened a linen closet. Thane's bedding supplies were sparse, but she found a faded blue sheet with worn edges at the bottom of a small stack of bedding. She took it to the kitchen, where she used a knife to cut the sheet into arm-length strips, tucking each into her bag.

Looking out the window, she saw no sign of Thane yet, so she hurried out the front of the house and jogged to her car parked at the end of the block. She opened the back and retrieved a stun gun and some other small items, concealing them in her bag before hurrying back to the house. She went inside and double-checked the front door lock. The large sliding garage door still rested on the brick when she exited out the back door. Thane hadn't returned yet. She took a seat on the step and waited.

Her phone buzzed with a text message from Clay.

Waylon drives a red Mercedes.

Thanks, I already have him.

How?

Long story.

Don't kill him.

If he doesn't make me.

You owe me. Protect Thane & wait for me. I'm on my way.

Don't come here. All under control. Stay away.

Chapter 18

A HISS CAME from the garage door opening, sending talcum powder swirling into a cloud that slowly drifted across the driveway as it dissipated. Thane's fingers curled under the door and raised it knee-high.

Morana stood, slung her handbag over her shoulder, and approached slowly enough to avoid startling him.

Thane kneeled and looked under the door. "Did anyone come?" he asked.

"No, but the front door was unlocked."

"You went inside?" he said, crawling out from under the door.

"Uh, yes, we agreed that if the police returned, I needed to handle them. How can I do that without being able to hear the doorbell?"

"I never gave you permission to go inside." Thane hurried to the back door of the house.

Morana chased after him. "Thane, what's going on?"

Thane flung the door open and ran inside.

Morana followed him, entering the kitchen just as he disappeared around the corner. "Thane?"

She followed the sound of his footsteps to the hallway.

Thane stood outside the bedroom door, looking in. "Did you go into this bedroom?" he said,

"Yes. I made your bed for you."

Thane grabbed his hair. "You shouldn't have done that," the words squeezed through his teeth.

"I was only trying to be helpful."

"You need to go make the bed like it was. Exactly like it was. Hurry."

"What? That's impossible. It was a mess."

Thane palmed his forehead. "You know how important privacy is to me."

"Thane, I'm confused. If privacy is so important, why would you leave your front door unlocked, especially after being physically threatened?"

Thane forced his hands into his pockets and took a deep breath. "It's complicated."

"Do you have someone special that you haven't mentioned? If so, there's no need to hide it. I'm happy for you."

"No, it's not like that. I'm only saying you had no right to go in there." Thane pointed into the bedroom.

"I apologize." She stepped closer to him. "The stress on your face right now... I'm worried about you. If something is going on that could be dangerous to you, I want to know about it." She took his hand. "Don't forget that based on the personal experiences we've already shared with each other and that we've agreed to keep secret."

"What happens inside this house doesn't concern you. Especially in the bedroom. Please stop asking."

"Understood." Morana stepped back with her hands up.

"We have to get back to the garage and focus on Waylon." He led her to the large roll-up door, kneeled, and crawled into the garage. He motioned for Morana to follow.

She got down and rolled inside. As she stood and brushed talcum powder from her legs and hips, she saw the hoisted Gateway block. Despite having seen it before, the immense cube suspended in midair was as mesmerizing as it had been the first time.

"Did you get Waylon's phone?" she asked.

"No, but he's available for conversation."

Thane went to the entryway and shifted the work block, creating a one-inch opening to the trap floor shaft.

"Why are you opening that?"

"That block creates a virtually airtight seal. We must vent the shaft, or the trap floor block cannot descend to the sub-lair." Thane returned to the large garage door, lowered it to the brick, and padlocked it. He went to the Gateway block mold and hopped down into it. "Hurry, we can't waste time."

Morana came to the edge of the mold and jumped in with less trepidation than before, still looking up suspiciously at the Gateway block. She went to Thane and stood face-to-face with him on the lift. It sank almost before she had put her full weight on it.

Morana put her arms around him and held him close.

Thane kept his eyes upward, gauging their progress. "I never imagined wanting the lift to move faster, but now I do," he said.

"Can't you lower the Gateway block back in place before we reach the bottom?"

"No, the principle I explained about the trap floor block also applies here. Consider this a rather blunt example of Newton's third law of motion—that every action must have an equal and opposite reaction. In this case, the change in air pressure below the Gateway block must be equalized by the air pressure above it. Without venting the virtually perfect seal in the shaft by opening the garage door, the garage windows would blow out, or worse, the lift platform would lock up, and we'd be entombed in this shaft without my tools."

"Please don't let that happen."

Thane smiled.

The shaft grew darker as they descended deeper into the earth's fist. When they slowed to a stop, the sub-lair lift chamber lights blinked on. Thane and Morana stepped off the lift. Air rushed through the shaft and into the sub-lair almost immediately, blowing their clothing as the Gateway block dropped into its mold a hundred feet above them.

Morana could detect nothing Thane might have done to trigger the Gateway block's movement. She decided not to ask—this time.

Thane led her from the chamber to a short corridor she hadn't seen before. He gently drew his fingertips along the wall until they reached a dead end. He pressed both hands against a wall block the size of a door. It smoothly pivoted with no sound, opening to another pitch-dark chamber.

Morana grinned. "Amazing."

Thane said, "Wait here." He stepped into the chamber and pushed the door block with one hand. It pivoted and stopped, sealing him inside.

Morana waited for over a minute before gently pushing the block's side. It wouldn't pivot. A thin seam that outlined the block blended so well she couldn't have seen that the block was a door. She pressed harder and then shoved, putting all her weight into it. The block didn't budge. "Funny, Thane… Are you coming out?" she yelled. She put her ear to the seam and held her breath. If Thane answered, she couldn't hear it.

Moments later, the door block pivoted, opening to a chamber that was now lit. Waylon's shouts echoed inside. "…tired of your little game, Sykes."

Morana's jaw clenched.

Thane ignored Waylon's threat. "Come in," he said to Morana.

Inside the chamber, the ceiling, walls, and floors were carved precisely as all other surfaces in the sub-lair and lit with identical thin strands of LED bulbs.

"You have no idea the charges you are facing, little nigger." Waylon's voice was crystal clear.

Morana didn't see him as she looked around what seemed to be an empty chamber. "Where is he?"

"He's up there," Thane said, pointing to a corner of the ceiling on the opposite wall.

Morana looked up and saw Waylon's face pressed against a narrow opening along the top of the far wall.

"That wall supporting him is the base of the trap floor," Thane said.

Morana dropped her handbag beside the door and rushed toward Waylon. "You son of a bitch…"

"Wait!" Thane said, rushing after her. He grabbed her arm.

Waylon's face pulled back into the darkness of the space.

"It's okay," Thane said. "When he has no control, his words have no impact on me."

"Who's the woman?" Waylon's voice came through the dark opening.

"She's—"

"I'm his girlfriend," Morana answered.

Thane smiled and looked down.

"Right. You expect me to believe that?"

Morana glared up at him. "Give me your phone."

Waylon laughed. "Not gonna happen."

"Do what she says. Give her the phone," Thane shouted.

Waylon scooted to the opening and slid his hand out, waving his phone a few times before pulling it back in. "You get me out of here, and you get my phone. But that's not happening unless I see some daylight."

Morana raised up onto her toes, trying to see him through the darkness. Through clenched teeth, she said, "Thane, can you give Waylon and me some private time?"

"What will you do?" Thane asked.

"I'll be persuasive."

"You're hot, sweetie, but the most persuasive thing you can do is to open this hole. That's the only thing that might persuade me to drop some of the charges you both are racking up."

"Please, sweetheart, give us a few minutes," she said to Thane, keeping her eyes locked on the opening.

Thane went to the chamber entrance. "I'll leave the door open."

"No, we need some private time," Morana said.

Waylon laughed.

Thane hesitated. "Okay. Press the side of the door when you are ready to exit, and it will open."

"Are you sure it will work?"

"Do you want to test it?"

Morana went to the door and pushed on the edge. With barely any force, the enormous block pivoted. "It didn't work for me from the outside," she whispered.

"I know. I locked it briefly," Thane said.

"Okay," Morana said. She picked up her bag from the floor beside the door.

Thane whispered, "What will you do?" as he tried to look into her bag.

Morana squeezed the bag closed. She took his hand. "Please trust me. We'll have the phone in no time."

"Don't damage any of my rock surfaces with whatever is in your bag," Thane said.

"I promise."

Thane left the chamber and closed the door.

Morana pulled a stun gun from her bag and held it up in the light, examining it.

"Whoa!" Waylon said. "Hold on. Listen, I've offered you a diplomatic solution here... You can have my phone if I get out of here. It seems like a fair deal."

Morana pulled a flashlight from her bag before dropping it in the center of the floor. She walked toward the slat, aiming the flashlight to illuminate Waylon. He had removed his suit jacket and was on his hands and knees, the side of his face pressed to the opening to see into the chamber. "You realize police are on the way, don't you?" he said.

Morana reached a place right below the opening and raised her hand. "Give me the phone willingly."

Waylon scooted forward and pressed his face to the opening. "Before you make things worse, you need to understand that we can both get what we want out of this situation."

"How about you give me the phone, and you live a while longer?"

"Was that a death threat?"

"No, it was an offer. But I can see it lacks appeal. Let me sweeten it." Morana raised the stun gun with her other hand, aiming it through the narrow opening at him. A bright laser dot jiggled on Waylon's shirt.

"Wait!" Waylon yelled. "I don't know what you two think my phone will get you, but it has nothing useful to either of you. You can't possibly think you will get away with—"

Morana fired. The probes pierced Waylon's abdomen. His vibrating scream resonated throughout the chamber for seven seconds. When she released the trigger, he writhed, cursing her with a spit-filled string of profanities.

"Here's a new deal for you. I want the phone in exchange for... nothing," Morana said calmly.

Waylon panted. "That deal's... not... fair."

She squeezed the trigger again until Waylon's screams became hoarse. When she let go, she said, "I'm working on my patience. As you can see, my threshold is embarrassingly low."

Waylon threw the phone out. It crashed on the floor, spinning to a stop face down a few steps from her.

"There's the fucking phone," he groaned.

Morana took hold of the stun gun's wires and snatched the probes from him before picking up the phone. She slowly turned it over to check for damage. The corner was dented, and the screen had a diagonal crack. "For your sake, I hope this phone is still usable," she said, pressing the button to turn on the screen. "Lock code?"

"9999 You got what you wanted. Now let me out—please."

Morana scrolled through the phone's apps and contacts and then slipped the phone into her pocket. "That was a good start." She went to her bag, pulled out the bed linen strips, and draped them over her shoulder. "But there's so much more I need from you."

Chapter 19

THANE SAT ON his mattress in his bedroom chamber, wringing his hands. For years, he had fantasized about getting even with Waylon. Being in an unexpected position of power exhilarated him more than he had imagined it would.

He went to the aquifer chamber, sat on the step, and watched the rippling water. Morana had been alone with Waylon in the trap floor chamber for over twenty minutes. If she was making things uncomfortable for Waylon, that was fine with him. Eventually, he heard Morana's voice echo from the corridor. "Okay, Thane, we're ready."

He hurried out of the bedroom and down the corridor. Morana stood in the open doorway of the trap floor chamber. Her shirt was untucked. "Whew," she said. She swept back the hair stuck to her forehead and then wiped her hands on her jeans.

"Did you get his phone?" he asked.

"Of course," she said, tapping her pocket. They went into the chamber.

Waylon's legs hung out of the open slot, dangling at the top of the far wall. His ankles were bound with the strips of bed linen.

Thane moved closer to the wall, looking up to examine the bindings that secured Waylon's ankles. "How did you do that?"

Morana patted the wall below Waylon's feet. "I told you—I was persuasive. Now it's safe to lower this block so we can take him out."

"What about his hands?"

"They are bound behind his back the same way." Morana handed him the flashlight.

Thane stepped back and raised the flashlight above his head, aiming it into the opening.

Waylon grunted through a thick cloth gag tied behind his head. He jerked his shoulders, struggling to free his hands.

"How did you tie his hands through that small opening?" Thane asked.

"It's easy—if you know how!" She winked at him and then pulled the phone from her pocket for Thane to see. "He threw it and cracked the screen, but it still works." She held it for Thane to see.

"Did he send a text message?"

"Yes."

Terror flooded Thane's expression. He covered his mouth and said, "How is that possible?" When he tried to take the phone, Morana clenched it, turning the screen for him to see.

"It looks like he only *tried* to send a text message, but it failed to transmit, just as you suspected."

The screen showed a *Failed: Retry* indicator beside a text addressed to Frank Mercelli.

"That's his partner at his firm," Thane said.

Need help @ Syke's place quick

"Erase it now. That can't transmit—ever!" Thane said, reaching again for the phone.

Morana pulled it away and said, "Don't worry. No one will ever see that message." She let Thane watch her delete it and then turned the screen to him so he could verify that it was gone. She slid the phone back into her pocket. "Come with me. I need to tell you something privately," she said, leading him from the chamber.

After they were outside, Thane closed the door and said, "I was going to ask you to leave so I can raise him to the surface."

"That's a bad idea," Moana said.

"Why? We have his phone, and he's bound, so we can safely turn him over to the police."

"Turning him over to the police will guarantee that things worsen for you."

"But we agreed that was the plan?"

"No, we agreed he deserved to be punished. Thane, when I was alone in the chamber with him, he threatened to have kidnapping charges filed against you, and he told me exactly how he could accomplish that."

"That's ridiculous. I didn't kidnap him."

"He says he can prove it."

"Then what are you suggesting?"

"We've confirmed that no one is looking for him, and he can't be found. I'm suggesting we keep him until we are sure you won't be charged for kidnapping."

"He trespassed and attacked me. I defended myself. I didn't kidnap him. I'm the one who should press charges."

"Listen to me," Morana said, grabbing his shoulders. "I agree with you, but the law defines kidnapping as detaining someone against their will. Technically, the instant you dropped him through the trap floor was kidnapping. And if he claims any injury, he'll construe his ride on the trap floor as assault."

"So, it's illegal for me to protect myself?"

"There are no guarantees with our justice system."

"I don't know what to do!" Thane looked like he might cry.

"First, let's stay calm. If we don't release him, no one can prove he was ever in your garage—even with the search warrant."

"Search warrant? What are you talking about? That can't happen! Waylon forced his way into *my* shop. I told him to leave, and he refused. He chased me and grabbed my shirt. *He* should be charged with assault!"

"Except that you'd have to produce evidence that he assaulted you. And if he claims an injury and shows so much as a scratch after we turn him in, you're looking at assault and battery. And then you can expect to be served a search warrant that will allow investigators to dismantle your shop for evidence."

"This can't be happening..." Thane pressed his back to the wall and slid to the floor.

"He's a lawyer," Morana said. "The law is his toolbox, but he uses it as an arsenal. You've seen from his professional success that he's good at it. If he gets out of here and succeeds, you'll be left to hope that a judge has great latitude in sentencing."

"Sentencing?"

"Depending on the severity of the charges. We can't know that yet, so why risk it?"

"If I go to jail instead of him, then the law is completely wrong."

"I agree, but even if a trial exonerated you, Waylon threatened you. Whatever you said to him at the job fair must have ignited a personal vendetta against you. He said you are a dead man. Has he ever threatened to kill you before?"

"Not outright like this," Thane swallowed.

Morana nodded, watching Thane absorb the full impact of his dilemma.

His voice quivered as he said, "I was only trying to protect myself. The trap floor was the only way I could keep him from getting to me."

Morana sat on the floor beside him. "Listen, you did exactly what I would have done. You took a drastic measure to protect yourself, and because of that, you escaped harm."

"From what you're saying, that's only temporary. Everything about this is unfair."

"And Waylon is counting on it remaining unfair. Was it fair for him to shove your face in the mud years ago?"

"Of course not."

"Was it fair for him to offer tickets for the other kids to watch?"

"No."

"What about all the other times he beat you up? When did Waylon ever play fair?"

"Stop it!" Thane covered his ears. "You helped me with this—you're in on it with me."

Morana gently pulled his hands down. "That's true, I am. And that's how you can be sure I won't give poor advice. I'm worried that a poor decision would end your magnificent work in the sub-lair. If I were you, I'd be willing to do whatever is necessary to prevent that."

"Which is what?" Thane's voice cracked.

"Waylon knows he has intimidated you by threatening to use the law as a weapon. But he hasn't realized that his position is far worse than yours."

"How?"

"We can ensure that Waylon doesn't press charges."

"I'm listening."

"Have you ever heard the saying the only way to deal with a bully is to stand up to him?"

Thane nodded. "My mom used to say that."

"She was right. I told you how I stood up to the girls who teased me. The way I retaliated against them may have been extreme, but it worked, and they never teased me again."

"But if I retaliate against Waylon, it could get me into more trouble."

"Only if anyone discovers it." Morana put her arm around him. "You haven't stood up to him yet."

"What do you mean?"

"Do you know what the term V1 means?"

"No."

"V1 is the maximum speed at which a pilot can abort take off. It's the point at which maintaining full throttle and committing to fly becomes a safer option than attempting to stop. Aborting takeoff after V1 risks disaster."

"Okay." Thane looked at her suspiciously.

Morana said, "When you dropped him into the trap floor shaft, and then I bound him, our plan for Waylon passed V1."

"I still don't understand. What am I supposed to do?"

"I'll answer that with a question. What is a perfect outcome for you here?"

"That Waylon would leave me alone forever, and I would never have to see him or hear his voice again."

Morana shrugged and said, "That's only possible if he never leaves the sub-lair."

Thane laughed.

When Morana didn't join in, he frowned. "What do you mean— never?" He slowly shook his head. "You can't be serious."

Morana strolled a few paces from Thane, then came back, tapping her chin. "Based on your history with Waylon, we're in a zero-sum game. That means the only way for either of you to win is for the other to lose. One of your lives is about to be ruined, and there's no way around it. You are in the power position. You get to decide who deserves protection. Considering everything he's done to you and that he's made it clear it will never end, I suggest you protect your life and freedom. By doing that, your problem goes away forever."

"Whoa! Are you suggesting... You can't be serious."

Morana came closer to him. "I realize the idea may seem jarring initially, but let's think about it. Fate is offering you a rare opportunity to even the score for crimes he committed against you, which he thinks he got away with." She took his hand and softened her voice. "Everything happens for a reason. From what you've shared, he put himself in this position by his actions."

Thane took a deep breath. "I've always dreamed of getting even, but..." He nibbled his lip. "In all my fantasies of getting even with him, I never actually—you know—went all the way. I don't think I could live with myself."

"You can live with the fact that you protected yourself, or you can continue letting him abuse you for the rest of your life," Morana interlocked her fingers on her head, watching him.

Thane sat quietly, then said, "It's true that there is zero chance he will ever leave me alone."

"If it's any consolation, there is also zero chance anyone would ever know about anything you did down here."

"That might be true, but if we release him, I can make sure there is no evidence to support his claims. I'll fill the trap floor shaft. I'll make it impossible for them to discover the trap floor or the sub-lair."

"Let's say that plan succeeds, and investigators find nothing. Do you honestly think Waylon will forget the miraculous things he's seen you do today? What if he hires private investigators, and they get a photo of you moving a block? If that leaks, you'll need the police for crowd control to prevent reporters and curious spectators from camping in front of your property for a glimpse."

As Thane listened, the anxiety on his face deepened. "I hate him more than anything." He wrung his fingers.

Morana put her arm around him. "Imagine your life without him."

"I imagine it every morning when I wake up."

"Sweetheart, do you remember when I promised I wouldn't let anything happen to you?"

Thane nodded.

"Let me keep that promise. Let's end this now. Waylon attacked, and you defended yourself. If we turn him over to the police, you can't trust the justice system to see it that way, so make sure the justice system doesn't see it at all."

Thane stared at the floor, motionless for almost a minute, before he said, "If he were to die, how would it happen? I don't think I could bring myself to... you know... do it."

"If that's your concern, there's more than one way to insulate you from that part if that will help. What if we set things up so that I cause an unfortunate accident?"

"So, you would do it for me?"

"Without hesitation. Nothing triggers me more than the type of abuse you endured at the hand of this monster."

Thane covered his face.

Morana patted her hand on the chamber door. "I've never seen an opportunity so safe and so perfect as the one you have here. The possibility that he could use his knowledge of the law to continue his abuse and to end all of your amazing work infuriates me."

"You still haven't said how you would do it," Thane said.

Morana paused. "Slowly lowering a block onto him comes to mind."

Thane cringed. "I couldn't use the blocks that way."

"Then show me how to lower one."

Thane thumbed at himself. "I control the blocks. Only me."

"Of course. I'm sorry." Morana stepped back. "I should have ended him when I had him alone in the chamber. I considered it, but he's more indebted to you than me."

Thane sighed and said, "I need to think about this."

"What else is there to think about?"

"I don't know—this solution feels disproportionate. It seems like killing someone is a steep price for abuse."

"Then consider something else. Do you believe you're the only person Waylon has bullied?"

"Of course not."

"Then what about his other victims? And what about his future victims? What would they beg you to do if they knew you were in this position? How many of them would give anything to trade places with you now? Add up all the pain he's caused, and ending this monster will perfectly apply Newton's third law of motion."

Thane scuffed his foot on the floor a few times. He took a deep breath and said, "You're right."

Morana smiled. "You deserve the power for once. Remember how he restrained your arms and legs while tormenting you? Now he's restrained, and I think it would be good for you to spend a few minutes letting him realize the role reversal."

Thane nodded. "I suppose that would be fair."

"It's more than fair." She patted the chamber door.

Thane pushed it open, and they went inside.

Waylon's legs shifted when he heard them.

Morana said, "Lower him enough to step out of the shaft." She pulled the stun gun from her bag.

Thane looked at it. "Is that how you got him bound?"

Morana raised the gun to her shoulder and blew the tip. "The right tool makes any job easy."

Waylon kicked his heels against the wall, yelling something unintelligible through his gag.

"Please wait outside," Thane said.

"Sweetheart, please. I want to support you."

"You've given me plenty of support," Thane said, pointing to the door. "I'll let you back in after I pull him from the shaft."

"Okay," Morana said, offering him the stun gun.

"I won't need that."

Morana tucked it back into her bag and said, "Although he's bound securely, you should still keep your distance." She slung her bag over her shoulder and went to the door. Before exiting, she said, "Leave this open in case you need me?"

"No, all I need now is some privacy," Thane said, aiming a flashlight into the space that contained Waylon.

Morana stepped out into the corridor.

Thane came to the door, and as he pushed it closed, Morana said, "Trust nothing he says."

Chapter 20

MORANA RETURNED TO Thane's bedroom. The door was still open. She took Waylon's phone from her bag and dropped the bag on the mattress. She pulled the memory card from her burner phone and inserted it into Waylon's phone. The photos she had taken of the garage interior displayed beautifully. She copied the photos to Waylon's phone, then selected an image that showed most of Thane's work area. She attached it to a new email message and sent it to Waylon's email address. A spinning hourglass appeared for 10 seconds before a message displayed:

Send failed… Retrying…

Morana smiled, turned off the screen, and tucked the phone into her bag. While she waited for Thane to finish extracting Waylon from the trap floor shaft, she wandered between the aquifer room, the bedroom, and the corridor before returning to rest on the mattress. She laid back and listened to the occasional trickle of the water in the aquifer room.

After waiting a while, she checked her watch. After having seen Thane so easily manipulate the blocks, the simple task of removing Waylon from the shaft had gone longer than she expected.

She left the bedroom and went to the door of the trap floor chamber. She tried to push it open, but it wouldn't budge. She pounded on it with the butt of her hand, knowing that the door was thicker than her body and that there was no chance Thane would hear her.

She returned to the bedroom and waited another half hour before returning. This time, she kicked the door. "Thane! Are you okay? … Let me know you're okay… Thane!"

She pressed her ear to the door and held her breath. A possibility came to mind, sending a chill up her spine. What if Waylon somehow broke free of his restraints and lost his temper with Thane? He might not realize Thane was his only way out of the sub-lair. If he killed Thane, she and Waylon would also die, separated but entombed in the sub-lair forever.

She rechecked her watch. Something had to be wrong. She wiped the sweat from her hands and paced in the corridor. The sub-lair's silence and Thane's absence spiked her anxiety. She went to the aquifer, splashed water on her face, and then dried it on a sheet from Thane's bed.

An hour later, Morana had retrieved her bag from Thane's bedroom and sat with it on the floor in the corner of the lift chamber, trying to breathe deeply and slowly to stave off panic. She had pressed and kicked every block on the small cubicle's floor, walls, and ceiling, but nothing triggered the lift.

She wiped her face on her sleeve and then felt the slightest air movement. She held her breath, listening. "Thane?"

She heard a foot scuff from around the corner. She quietly got up and sidestepped toward the corridor.

"Thane?" she repeated.

She looked around the corner.

"I'm here," Thane said. He stood outside the doorway of the trap floor chamber. He held a flashlight at his side. Its beam had dimmed from white to yellow and flickered on the floor by his feet.

"Thank God!" Morana said. She rushed to Thane and threw her arms around him, rocking him. "You had me panicking!"

"Why?"

"You said it would be quick!"

"Things didn't go exactly as planned," Thane replied.

"How so?" Morana pushed the door to enter the chamber, but it didn't budge.

"What didn't go as planned?" she asked, using both hands to push the door harder.

When Thane didn't answer, she turned back to him. "What's going on?"

Thane wore an odd smile. He said, "Waylon is no longer a threat."

Morana grabbed his arms, containing her excitement. "You took care of him?"

Thane nodded. "His days of harassing are over."

Morana hugged him tightly. "I'm so proud of you." She gently pushed him to arms-length. "It was the right thing to do."

Thane said, "Follow me. We need to get to the surface."

"Why? I want to see him—for closure and all that!" Morana said, laughing as she patted the chamber door.

"Not now. The sooner we get to the surface, the better." He turned and walked toward the lift chamber.

"Why? What's going on?"

"I'll tell you on the way," he said, leading her back to the lift chamber.

"Thane, should I be nervous?" Morana nearly tripped over him.

"Not if everything you've told me is true."

"What does that mean? Thane, please clue me in. I want to know exactly how it happened in there. Did he fight you?"

In the lift chamber, the lift column already sped downward in the center of the wall. "How did you trigger the lift?" Morana asked, pointing to it.

Thane turned to her. Ignoring her question, he said, "When I lowered Waylon's block to remove him from the shaft, I noticed he had loosened his gag with his tongue and teeth."

"And?"

"And he told me something—something disturbing."

"Okay…" Morana cocked her head. "And?"

"We had an interesting conversation. He told me you used your time alone to interrogate him."

Morana frowned. "He said that?"

"Yes, he told me you tried to force him to describe exactly how I lowered him."

Morana poked her tongue into her cheek and shook her head. "The bastard. That's not true, Thane."

"He said that you were adamant that he must have seen how I manipulated the blocks while I had him alone. He said you became furious when he couldn't describe the process."

"He's lying," Morana said. She tried to take Thane's hand, but he pulled away and stepped back.

"He said you tortured him with the stun gun for an answer."

"That's a lie." She reached out to him again.

Thane stepped back.

"Don't you see he was trying to trick you?"

"He warned me to be careful with you."

"Thane, we agreed he is a liar and will say anything to get what he wants. Apparently, he's proven that."

"If he was lying, how would he know anything about your desire to learn my secrets?"

"Are you trusting someone who has abused you most of your life? Wouldn't it make more sense to believe someone who's never hurt you?"

"That doesn't answer my question. How did he know you were trying to learn my secret?"

Morana froze, blinking. She cleared her throat and said, "Waylon heard you insist I leave the chamber while you worked. My curiosity must have been obvious. Can't you see he's saying these things to create a conflict between us?"

"And how would conflict between us benefit him?"

"If he can get us to turn on each other, it's the only way he could get one or the other of us to help him out of here."

"I suppose that's possible." Thane chewed his cheek.

"It's more than possible. It's the truth."

Morana stepped closer. "Sweetheart, listen... you know I respect you, and I know how important the privacy of your work is to you. I would never violate that trust by telling him anything—even if I knew."

Thane's expression remained unchanged as he looked at her.

The shaft in the wall beside them opened as the lift's floor slid down into place.

Thane took a deep breath and slowly sighed. "It's time to go," he said, motioning for her to go first.

"You don't believe me, do you?" Morana asked.

"I'll tell you what I don't believe: I don't believe Waylon told you anything about how I lowered him into the chamber."

"Because I didn't ask him!" Morana said, crossing her arms.

"It wouldn't have mattered if you had."

"Why do you say that?"

The lights blinked off, and the chamber went pitch black.

"What happened?" Morana said. She reached out to where Thane had been standing, but he wasn't there. She moved away from the open shaft. "Did we lose power?"

Thane didn't answer.

"Thane? Where are you? What's happening?" She reached behind her and stepped back until she felt the wall. "Thane? Sweetheart?"

The chamber was silent.

"Thane, where are you? It's not funny. Now I *am* afraid... Thane?" She couldn't mask the tension in her voice.

Air rushed through the chamber, and a hiss came from the lift shaft. Morana remembered the sound from the Gateway block.

"Please don't leave me!" she shouted.

Thane's reply cut through the darkness. "Whether or not you interrogated Waylon doesn't matter. What you see now is what Waylon saw."

"Okay," Morana said. "You've made your point... please..."

The lights blinked on. Thane stood with his hands in his pockets in his original position as though he had teleported there. "We need to leave right away. Please step inside."

Morana leaned into the lift shaft and looked up into the darkness. "I know it's safe, but I'd feel more comfortable if you boarded with me."

Thane smiled. "Are you afraid?"

Morana forced a laugh. "Should I be?"

Thane didn't answer. He stepped onto the lift and scooted to the edge to make room for her.

She picked up her bag from the floor and joined him.

Thane pressed the button on the wall of the shaft, and the lift began its ascent from the sub-lair. When the opening to the lift chamber disappeared, Morana and Thane rode in almost complete darkness except for the tiny square of light from the distant shaft opening above.

Morana put her arms around Thane and whispered. "Sweetheart, please listen. I need you to believe that I didn't interrogate Waylon. Everything about this sub-lair is a mystery to me, and I'm comfortable with that as long as I have you with me."

"Good," Thane said.

"I could prove he lied if you hadn't killed him."

"I never said I killed him."

"But..."

"Waylon is gone," Thane said.

"But you said you took care of him."

"No. I said I took care of the problem."

"Then what did you do?"

"I let him go."

"Oh, my God!" Morana let go and clapped her hand over her mouth. "Thane, how could you do that?"

"Please don't raise your voice to me."

"I'm sorry! But I can't believe you set him free."

"It wasn't my plan, but we conversed when he loosened his gag. That's what took longer than expected."

"But what about our plan? What about justice? We talked about how he would never stop abusing you. The last thing I told you before I left the chamber was not to trust him."

"I know. And I didn't. I know what you wanted me to do. I actually liked the idea of getting even with Waylon, but the price I'd have to pay if the solution you suggested went wrong was too high."

Morana laughed in disbelief. "There was no possibility his body would ever be found, and I would have gladly handled everything for you if you didn't want to be the one to do it. Do you really think he'll forget all this? Do you think he still won't come after you?"

"We came to an agreement."

Morana tilted her head back and closed her eyes briefly, focusing on keeping her voice steady and calm. "What were the terms of the agreement?"

"It couldn't have been more basic. In exchange for his freedom, Waylon agreed to not file any charges against me and to leave me alone—forever."

"And you trust his word?"

"He gave it to me in writing and signed it." Thane clicked on a flashlight, pulled a crumpled piece of paper from his pocket, and handed it to her. He held the dim flashlight for her while she smoothed the paper on her leg, then read it out loud.

> *I, Waylon Snells, will not pursue criminal prosecution of Thane Sykes for temporarily and accidentally detaining me against my will. I fully recognize that his action was taken in self-defense and without malice. I apologize for all the harm I have caused him. I will respect his privacy and will not interfere in his life in any way from this day forward.*
>
> *Sincerely,*
>
> *Waylon Snells*

"Thane, he's a liar. He won't keep that agreement." Morana squeezed the note into her fist and then opened it again, hoping its meaning had changed or that, somehow, she had missed something. She pretended to reread it while her mind raced.

Thane said, "He said this written agreement is as good as a restraining order. He swore to me that if he violates it, I'm the one who will have a legitimate legal case against him."

"Sweetheart, you've been suckered."

"No, I haven't because I don't believe a word Waylon says—or writes. I know this paper is worthless."

"Then I'm confused. Why did you accept it from him?"

The lift came to a stop about thirty feet from the surface. Instead of pressing the button on the shaft wall to ascend to the next level, Thane waited and said, "The moment I opened the shaft where he was trapped, I felt sick to my stomach. I felt bullied by the circumstances forcing him into my creation—the sub-lair. Waylon's eyes got big as he looked around my chamber. I felt like he was again experiencing a special part of me he had no right to experience. It brought back the old feelings of him taking something that was mine."

"Then killing him would have resolved that," Morana said.

"I couldn't bear having his body stored permanently in the sub-lair. And if we took his corpse to the surface, it becomes potential evidence, forfeiting the sub-lair's advantage of absolute secrecy. Either way, Waylon continues to haunt me, possibly sending me to prison even after he's dead. At least this way, I know he's gone, and I keep my physical freedom." Thane pressed the final shaft button. As the lift approached the surface, more light filled the shaft.

Morana shook her head, looking up. "I hate him for what he's done to you. I desperately wanted to see him pay for it."

"You're the first person I've seen get as angry at Waylon as I get." Thane aimed the flashlight at her hand that had gone into her bag. "What are you doing?"

"Did you consider he could be waiting in the garage for us?"

"I told you not to bring guns into the sub-lair. Waylon is gone."

"Maybe you're right, and he's gone. But if not, you'll thank me."

They rose into the garage, knowing they'd be in full view of anyone who might wait there. Morana bent her knees and pulled her gun from the bag, holding it ready. The lift slowed to a stop, perfectly level with the base of the Gateway block cavity. Near the entrance, they saw the trap floor had lifted back into place.

Thane pointed to the entry door left ajar. "I told you he'd be gone."

Before they stepped off, Morana said, "You realize he can still, and probably will, tell the world what he saw here, right?. There's nothing in your agreement about that."

"I'm counting on him not having the opportunity."

"What does that mean?"

"Give me Waylon's phone. I saw you put it into your pocket," Thane said, extending his hand.

"Why?"

"Please, just give it to me."

Morana tucked the gun into her concealed holster and pulled the phone from her bag.

Thane took it and slid it into his pocket. Then he took Morana's hand and pressed a car key into it.

"What is this for?" she asked.

Thane patted his pocket. "I have Waylon's phone, and now you have his car key."

"How did you get this?"

"I made it part of the deal to release him."

"So, you're saying—"

"I'm saying he's on foot with no phone and couldn't have gone far. And if I timed the movement of the trap floor well enough, it would have brought him to the surface of the garage." Thane looked at his watch. "approximately 90 seconds ago,"

"You expect me to go get him?"

"When you said you could handle him, I believed you."

"When I said that, I had the advantage of the sub-lair, but you've squandered that."

"I don't have a problem with anything you want to do to him. In fact, I hope you make him suffer. But it can't happen here. I can't accept the risk."

Morana looked at the key, then slowly looked at Thane. "So, you let him go, hoping I would deal with him somewhere else?"

"I can hope."

"But you let him get away. Why didn't you keep him restrained? I would've gladly taken him somewhere else."

"After he convinced me to let him go, and after everything you said you wanted to do to him, I couldn't be sure that you wouldn't kill him on the spot, right there in the sub-lair." Thane pointed toward the trap floor.

"I'm much more controlled than that."

"I'm sorry, it's like this. I want to experience the relief you described, but I can't do it here. If you can do to him what you said you wanted to, it would mean so much. I don't know what I could do to express my gratitude because I'd owe everything to you." He opened his arms and pivoted, looking around the shop.

"Are you serious?" Morana asked again.

Thane nodded while going back to the lift. "He couldn't have gone far, but there won't be much time. He could be knocking on a neighbor's door to make a call or to get a ride at any moment."

Morana ran to the entrance. She stopped in the doorway and turned back to Thane. "If he slips away, your life is in grave danger. I advise you to lock this door and not leave until you hear from me."

"I understand," Thane replied. "I'm putting my trust in you." The lift dropped, and he disappeared into the floor.

Chapter 21

MORANA IMMEDIATELY NOTICED that the back door was open a few inches. With Thane on his way down to the sub-lair and given his desperate request, Morana ignored his order to stay out of the house. She pulled her gun and cleared the backyard before crossing to the back corner of the house. She sidestepped to the open door and waited, listening. Footsteps scuffed inside from the room beyond the kitchen.

She eased the door open with her foot and stepped inside, clearing the kitchen.

As she crept to the hallway entrance, the footsteps stopped. Something crashed to the floor around the corner. Morana lunged into the hallway, aiming at a figure standing in the den.

"Not a move!" she shouted.

"No! Wait! Don't shoot!" Clay dropped his phone and raised his hands.

"What the hell are you doing?" Morana said, lowering the gun.

"God, you scared the shit out of me!" Clay said. He clutched his chest, catching his breath.

"You chose a horrible time to break into Thane's place."

"I didn't break in. The front door was unlocked, so I came in looking for you and Thane. Where were you?"

"We have to go." She took his arm and dragged him toward the front door.

"But where are we going?"

"We had Waylon, but he's on the run again." She showed Clay the key. "Thane got him to give up his key, so he's on foot, and we need to catch up to him." She opened the front door.

Clay followed. He looked at the key, turning it over a few times.

"Hurry," Morana said, holding the door for him.

Clay said, "But this is a BMW key."

"So?"

"He didn't drive here in his BMW. He has the Mercedes."

"How do you know?"

"Because I already told you he drives a red Mercedes, I tagged his car with a GPS tracker on my way in. I'll show you…" They went outside and stopped on the porch. They scanned the street. Clay frowned. "It was parked right there a few minutes ago." He pointed to an empty place at the curb.

"You've got to be kidding me," Morana said.

Clay walked toward the empty place at the curb. "I'm telling you, the red Mercedes was parked right there. I checked the VIN to confirm it." He pulled out his phone.

"Shit!" Morana said, kicking the porch railing.

"Wait a minute," Clay said, looking at his phone. "It might not matter. The tracker app is working," Clay said, tapping his phone. "He's on Cumber Street headed south. Let's go."

Dusk settled in as they sped from Thane's house. "Maybe now you can tell me why the hell we're chasing this guy," Clay said.

Morana told Clay about Thane's years of abuse at Waylon's hand. She told him about Thane's recent attempt to confront Waylon at the job fair and how it only rekindled Waylon's abuse. Finally, she alluded to the hidden labyrinth Thane had created beneath his garage.

"You're saying there's no way to detect this place even when standing in the garage?" Clay asked.

Morana laughed. "Not a chance, and if you knew how deep underground it went—Clay, I'm telling you, it's a perfect world for the ultimate privacy."

"So, why would Thane let Waylon escape?"

Morana sighed. "He's scared and wants to limit culpability to me, so he didn't want anything to happen on his property." Morana studied Clay's phone, mounted on a cradle between their seats. A dot representing Waylon's car moved westward on a map. "Dispensing with Waylon is a much bigger deal than resolving Everett's fake accident, and Thane knows it. He didn't say it directly, but he looked me in the eye and said he wouldn't know how to repay someone who had saved everything for him. We need to be his salvation."

"Listen, Mo, I have no ethical problem making a shit-ton of money with you, but if you're talking about—"

"I'm talking about doing whatever is necessary to gain access to a literally earth-shattering technology. If Thane needs some pest control, then that's what I'll give him. He'll understand exactly how he can pay me back."

"Right." Clay drummed his fingers on the steering wheel. "If Waylon is on the run, why can't we just forget about him? He'll never find or be able to access this underground place you are talking about."

"Waylon has seen too much. If he talks, or worse, goes back on his agreement and pursues charges, investigators and the media will swarm Thane, and I think we both know how tragic that would be. Make a right turn here," she pointed at the phone. "He's still going west."

Clay rounded the corner. "Mo, I told you I don't need to get tangled up in any felony situations."

"It's too late. You've harbored me. I've used your guns. You are tangled up tightly. But for now, you are with me, and we are allies, so you don't need to worry about it."

"Is that supposed to give me confidence?"

Morana shrugged. "Have I been caught?"

"Fair enough, but I don't have your kind of luck."

"I don't believe in luck. Listen to me, Clay," Morana said, turning to face him. "If you do what I tell you, I guarantee you'll get more satisfaction and money by working with me than any other job you could dream of getting. If you don't want to participate, let's shake hands and call it off now."

"And if I say no?"

"Thane and I will do fine working alone, so you need to decide if you're all in because a half-ass effort will surely get us caught."

Clay sped up to make a yellow light. "I'm in," he said.

"Congratulations." Morana grinned.

"Waylon just turned up ahead," Clay said. "His address is in the Stetfield Ridge community, and that's right up there..." He pointed ahead.

"Can you catch up to him before he parks?" Morana asked.

"Maybe." Clay accelerated. "Even if not, the tracker will tell us when he turns off his car's engine."

"I love it."

"Then you'll love that Thane's truck is trackable, too."

"You tagged it?"

Clay nodded. "Transmitters came in a three-pack. While I was back by the garage looking for you, I figured it was the right thing to do."

"Are you sure you hid it well enough? Thane notices every detail of everything."

"He *won't* find it."

They saw that Waylon's car had stopped two blocks from Waylon's house. Clay turned the last corner and pulled to the side of the road. The street was lined with opulent houses separated by manicured hedges bordering spacious lawns.

"He must have driven behind his house. I don't see his car," Clay said, craning his neck to see a sprawling Tudor-style home displayed on his phone.

"You should have heard how vicious he became when Thane trapped him. It took everything I had to not kill him when I had him alone in the sub-lair. Now I regret I didn't squash that bug." She pointed. "He's behind the house."

Clay enlarged the map on the phone screen, showing the car's location. "His car is behind the house. His BMW could be back there, too, and isn't tracked. What if he takes off in it?"

"Give me the third tracker."

Clay pulled the small magnetic device from under his seat and gave it to her.

Morana said, "I need you to put the app on my phone. I need to track Waylon's cars and Thane's truck."

"You got it." Clay held out his hand for the phone.

Before Morana could give it to him, it buzzed. She raised her finger for him to wait. "Hello."

"Mo, it's me."

She covered the phone and whispered, "It's Thane."

Clay motioned for her to keep talking to him.

"Hi, Sweetheart," Morana said.

"Did you catch Waylon?" Thane asked.

"I'm working on it."

"Mo, you m succeed. I found more photographs on his phone."

"No, there couldn't be. I checked it."

"Yes, there were! I'm looking right at them!"

"Okay, calm down!"

"He sent them in an email, and they transmitted."

"What do the photographs show?" Morana asked.

"My garage! My workspace, my tools, and they're clear. I didn't see him taking any photos in the garage before he started chasing me, but maybe I missed it. One of the photos shows my work block in the garage entryway. I wanted none of the blocks to be photographed."

"Who did he email them to?"

"He sent them to himself."

"Then you shouldn't worry."

"Of course, I should worry. He can forward them. And we don't know who has access to his email."

"Thane, I am tracking him right now, and if things go as planned, he won't have time to forward those photos to anyone. You need to trust me.

Everything will be okay. I'll be back soon, and we can put all this behind us."

"I need you to get him—quickly. You told me you could end this."

"I can, and I will."

"Please hurry. Can you call me when you get him?"

"I will."

They hung up.

"That was Thane. He's freaked out," Morana said, handing over the phone.

Clay installed the tracking app.

Morana got out of the car and, before closing the door, said, "Wait here and keep the engine running. My meeting with Mr. Waylon Snells won't take long."

"Wait, are you armed?"

She smirked as though the question was silly, then pulled off a wig and tossed it in the back seat. She slung her bag over her shoulder and walked down the sidewalk to the edge of Waylon's property. She turned, taking cover along a row of hedges separating Waylon's yard from his neighbor's.

Darkness had deepened enough to cloak her as she moved to the rear corner of the house. Waylon's Mercedes was parked sideways in the driveway outside the open garage door. It blocked the BMW parked inside. She felt in her pocket for the BMW key.

A light blinked in an upstairs room on the side of the house. Morana slipped through the shadows, sidestepping toward the open garage door. She looked inside and saw a camera mounted high in the corner, aimed at the garage entry to the house. It seemed to cover most of the garage, not the circuit box on the wall below.

She dropped to her knees and crawled inside, passing the wheels of the BMW. She stood at the circuit box and flipped the switch labeled garage, and the lights went out. She felt her way along the wall to the entry door to the house. Waylon had left it unlocked.

†

Waylon had turned his Mercedes hard enough to skid on the loose gravel at the edge of his driveway. As he sped along the arc to the rear of his house, he reached up to the visor and found the button for the garage door opener, repeatedly jabbing it with his knuckle. When he rounded the corner, the garage door was rising. His tires skidded again, stopping him inches from it. He turned off the engine, leaving the headlights on to illuminate the garage. He ducked under the slow–opening door and rushed into the garage, passing by his BMW. He flipped on the garage lights and disappeared into the house.

He rushed down the hallway to his study and grabbed his landline phone to call the police but stopped when he envisioned law enforcement swooping in to investigate Thane's property. If Thane had kept his magical garage foundation a secret, Waylon intended to get in on it—alone. He needed a better way to deal with Thane and the woman for what they had done to him.

He pressed a speed dial to call his assistant, Angie. Before it rang twice, he checked his watch and realized Angie would have left the office over an hour ago. He called her mobile phone and then realized that her number was stored on his missing mobile phone and he didn't have her mobile number memorized. He slammed the phone down, went to a cabinet, yanked the bottom drawer open, and pawed through some electronics and old phones, examining them one at a time before tossing them into a nearby waste bin. He kicked the drawer closed. "Shit!"

He crossed the room to his computer, leaned over his keyboard, and clicked open his email. Aside from a few scheduling email messages from Angie in his inbox, there were no other significant messages, and his partner had not yet contacted him. He looked up Angie's contact information and was about to dial her mobile number when a message in his inbox caught his attention. It was from himself and had no subject. He opened it. The message contained no text but displayed several photos. He leaned closer to the screen and recognized images of Thane's garage from several angles, showing his tools, work countertop, and two areas of the floor. He frowned and scratched his neck. It would have been impossible for him to have pocket-clicked these photos. Each photo was level and focused. He didn't remember emailing the photos to himself—he wouldn't have forgotten that.

He stepped back and stared at the screen, rubbing his chin. The only person who could have sent these images was that woman—Thane's accomplice. But why?

He pawed through the paperwork on his desk until he found an email from Angie that he had printed out. It had her mobile number in her signature. He grabbed his home phone and called her. "Hey, it's me," he said. "It's a long story… I'm fine and, yes, I know I missed that meeting. Listen, I need you to get me a new mobile phone. I lost mine… No, not tomorrow. I need it now… Bring it to the house, I'm home… Then find a place that's open, Angie… I don't care how. The only thing I know is that I need a goddamn phone!" He hung up and slammed the handset to his desk.

"Useless," he muttered as he walked around his office with his fingers interlocked on his head. He returned to the computer and opened a new tab in his browser. If Angie was pushing back on getting him a phone tonight, he'd find a local phone provider on his own. Before he could enter a search term, he saw a banner at the top of a webpage. A mugshot that had been prominent in the news for a couple of weeks caught his attention. He had seen it probably fifty times and paid little attention to it. This time, the photo seized his full attention. He reached behind him for his chair and slowly sat, keeping his eyes locked on the image of a woman captioned with her name: *MORANA MAHKER.* He opened the story link. The woman in the photo had red hair, cropped short. "It can't be," he said. But something about the jawline, eyes, and expression removed any doubt. And an updated $2.5 million reward sent a rush of excitement through him.

A faint click echoed in the hallway. He tilted his head, listening. He stood and moved to the closet. Without turning on the closet light, he reached in and felt around until he pulled out a golf club.

He heard the sound again, closer.

"I'm armed," he called out, gripping the club with both hands. He held it like a baseball bat, resting it on his shoulder. He crept to the doorway and carefully peered out into the hallway. It was empty. He moved toward the entrance to the garage. As he passed the laundry room, he heard the click louder and stopped.

All the lights in the house went off.

Shit! He wrung the golf club grip as he felt for the wall, then continued moving toward the garage door. His smoke detector chirped every few seconds, warning that it was on battery power.

Behind him, he heard, "Psst."

Before he could react, hands grabbed his neck, and a knee came full force into his groin, doubling him over. A hard shove sent him crashing to the floor. His attacker jumped on him, pressing the side of his face to the floor.

Waylon yelled, "No! Please! What do you want? ...I have money!" he shouted. He struggled until he felt cold steel pressed to the back of his head. Waylon stretched his arms out on the floor in surrender. He gasped, "What do you want?"

While his attacker tied his wrists behind him, a female voice said, "I want to help you get what you deserve."

✝

Eleven minutes after Morana disappeared onto Waylon's property, Clay saw the lights that lined the driveway turn off, followed a few moments later by the lights in all the house windows.

He sat straighter in his seat and checked his phone. He rolled the window down more and listened but heard only the hum of his car's engine. He crossed his fingers, hoping not to hear gunshots.

Four minutes later, his phone buzzed.

"What's going on?" he answered.

"Back your car to the garage door."

"What about cameras?"

"None are powered."

"Shit... did you..."

"We can chitchat later. Get back here!"

"Okay, okay, hang on." Clay turned into the driveway. His headlights cut through the darkness as he rounded the corner to the rear of the house. As he backed his car toward the garage, the door slid open.

Morana's legs came into view, standing in the darkness with a flashlight aimed at what looked like a large bundle beside her. She guided Clay's car closer, then raised her hand for him to stop.

Clay opened the driver's door.

Morana said, "Unlatch the trunk and keep it running."

Clay did so, then joined her in the garage. "What have you done?" he asked.

The bundle moved. Morana put her foot on it and shoved it, rolling it over to reveal Waylon's face. He moaned through a towel Morana had fashioned into a gag and bound it around his head. His body was wrapped in a bedspread, his ankles and wrists bound with zip ties.

"Help me get him into the trunk," Morana said.

Clay lifted Waylon's wrapped upper body, and Morana took hold of his feet. Together, they heaved him into the trunk with a thud that made him groan. Before Morana closed the trunk, Waylon looked at them wide-eyed and yelled something through the towel.

Morana slammed the trunk closed and brushed her hands off.

"Now what?" Clay asked.

Morana handed Clay the key to Waylon's BMW parked behind her. "Meet me at your place. Park at least two blocks away."

"Why my place?"

"Everything I'm suggesting is a means that ends with you becoming wealthy beyond your dreams. Can we chat about this another time?"

"But my place—I don't like it," Clay said.

"You told me in the car that you're all in." She got into the driver's seat of his car and closed the door. She rolled down the window and said, "I wouldn't hang out here if I were you." She drove away.

✝

Thirty minutes later, Morana waited in the assigned parking spot that Clay rarely used in his apartment complex's underground garage. He preferred to park on the street for the shorter path to his front door.

Morana ignored the occasional thumping from the trunk while she waited for Clay to show up.

When he entered the garage and descended the stairs, Morana exited the car and slung her bag over her shoulder. "How far away did you park?"

"Three blocks," Clay said, catching his breath. "I'm still not in love with this idea. My place is too risky, and all my neighbors are nosy. What happened to your paranoia about me turning you in?"

"I'm still paranoid, but you're easier to trust when you're close enough to kill." She reached into the car and unlatched the trunk.

"I wish that was more comforting," Clay said.

"Risk is always relative. Your place is safest for what we need to do. You need to trust me."

The only sound in the garage was the faint hum of a clothes dryer. Clay went to the corner of the garage and looked into the vacant laundry room that also housed the breakers for the building's electricity.

It was a few minutes after 10:00 p.m. Most of the neighbors would be in for the night. He went to the far wall, opened the circuit panel, and flipped the *Courtyard* and *Stairway* breakers. He came out and ran up the stairs to verify the lights were off before returning to Morana. "Let's do it."

"What's the chance one of your nosy neighbors will run down to check the breaker in the next 10 minutes?" Morana asked.

"I can't guarantee it, but not likely. We've had three brief power outages this month, only one attributed to a storm. The residents will think it's more of the same."

Morana opened the trunk. Waylon tried to scream through the gag. She pressed her stun gun into Waylon's side, squeezed the trigger, and slammed the trunk closed. After waiting for Waylon's thrashing to subside, she opened it again and said, "I've got plenty of current. If you make any sound on the way inside, I'll double the juice I just fed you. Understood?"

Waylon nodded emphatically.

Clay went to the garage exit at the top of the stairs, and after making sure no one was walking in the dark courtyard, he ran back, and they pulled Waylon from the trunk.

Morana unwrapped him from the bedspread, then cut the zip tie that bound his ankles. She and Clay guided him up the stairs, through the dark courtyard, and into the apartment.

Inside, Clay locked the door. Morana shoved Waylon to the floor. "Go make room in your closet," she said.

"And turn off all your damned spy cams for your own good."

"For my own good?"

"If you want me here, all surveillance is off, and you need to make me believe that you've done it. Not to mention that your footage will implicate you, too, if it's seized."

Clay rolled his eyes, then got scissors and electrical tape from a kitchen drawer. While Morana watched, he went around the apartment, placing small pieces of tape over all the microlenses Morana had previously discovered and a few more she hadn't seen.

He then went to the bedroom and removed some shoes and a storage box from the closet to make room for their new guest. They pulled Waylon to his feet and guided him to the bedroom, forcing him to the closet floor. Waylon moved his foot to block the closet door when she tried to close it.

"Clay, where's my hand-held encouragement?" Morana asked. "Can you get my bag beside the front door?"

When Clay turned to leave, Waylon shook his head hard. He pulled his feet into the closet.

"Never mind," Morana said, closing the door. She pressed her shoulder to it until the latch clicked.

"It would help me a lot if you could clue me in on your long game here," Clay said as they returned to the front room.

"The plan hasn't changed. We're going to find out how Thane does what he does."

"But what does that have to do with this guy?"

"We have both seen Thane move enormous rocks. I don't know how he does it, but it involves leverage. I'm employing some leverage of my own."

"Listen," Clay said, searching for words. "If this doesn't end well, or exactly like you're planning, can we just let Thane be?"

"You think I would hurt him?"

Clay shrugged. "Not at the moment, but that's what worries me. I never know what makes your reasons materialize, and Thane didn't sign up for any of this."

"Did you see how I'm treating the man who abused him?"

Clay nodded.

"My treatment of Thane is the inverse. Dealing with Waylon isn't about money. It's a gift for Thane. Yes, I want Thane's secret, but you know justice is most important to me, particularly for people like Thane who aren't treated fairly in life. You might not understand what I do, but my scruples are predictable. Thane is safe."

Morana and Clay spent the next hours reviewing Morana's idea of integrating Waylon into their plan to acquire Thane's secret. They brainstormed all the risks introduced by each step. They fell asleep in the living room after working until the early morning to devise their scheme.

Just after 7:00 AM, Clay lay slumped in an easy chair, his legs draped over the arm. The beeping of a truck backing up outside jolted him awake. He rubbed his eyes and checked his watch, cursing the time.

Morana stirred on the sofa.

"I have to get to the office," Clay said, stumbling toward the bathroom.

Morana sat up and returned to Clay's bedroom to check on their guest. When she opened the closet door, Waylon grunted through the gag and tried to roll to his other side. "One night of discomfort. Done. Only a few thousand more to match what you've done to Thane." She watched him for a few moments before slamming the door closed. She went to the kitchen for some breakfast.

Clay emerged from the bathroom wrapped in a bath towel. "I wish I could skip the office today, but the boss man knows I'm back and will expect me to come in. I'll see about getting off early."

"We'll be waiting," she replied.

Clay finished dressing and left for work.

Morana finished eating and heard a commotion from Clay's bedroom as she was putting a bowl in the sink. She grabbed her pistol from her bag and approached the bedroom door. She pushed the bedroom door open with her foot and raised the gun. The closet door was still closed. She crept across the bedroom and pulled it open.

Waylon, lying on his side, looked up at her and tried to say something.

She turned on the closet light.

He squinted in the bright light and repeated something unintelligible.

Morana stepped back, placed her gun on the bed, and then squatted beside him. "We have some work to do," she said. She squeezed his collar with both hands and pulled him up to sit.

Something on the floor where Waylon had been lying caught her eye. A fine dusting of eggshell-colored plastic shavings was below the edge of the wire shoe rack beside his waist, where his wrists had been zip-tied.

Before she could react, Waylon swung, landing a solid blow to her jaw with his fist.

Morana fell back onto the floor.

Waylon launched himself, landing on top of her outside the closet. He grabbed her arms.

He used his full weight to press her wrists to the floor when she thrust her hips upward to dislodge him.

She saw his ankles were still bound, so she bucked and twisted, causing him to fall beside her.

He tried to wrap his leg around her. She landed a solid blow to his groin with her knee. He screamed through the gag, fighting the pain to get his hands around her neck as he struggled to remount her.

She tried to head-butt him, but he held her at arm's length, so she bucked him with her hips again. They rolled over one another several times before colliding into the wall.

Waylon got her pinned again. He let go of her neck long enough to swing his fist, landing another solid blow to her face. Her body went limp.

Chapter 22

WHEN MORANA REGAINED consciousness, only one eye opened wide enough to see, as the other was nearly swollen shut. Her head throbbed, and she clenched her teeth. Clay's bathroom ceiling slowly came into focus. She was on the floor, her head near the tub and her feet toward the door. She didn't know how long she had blacked out, but it had been long enough for Waylon to drag her there and bind her hands behind her back. She shifted her legs and felt a burning pain in her ankles.

Waylon came into view, towering over her, his wingtip loafers pressed against either side of her waist. He leered down at her. "Good afternoon, Morana Mahker. That's been some hell of a game of hide & seek you've been playing. It's over."

Morana turned her head and squeezed her eyes shut.

"You know, I was tempted to leave," Waylon said. He drew Morana's pistol from his back pocket and placed it in the sink. "I could have been long gone by now. But the only thing sweeter than escaping from you will be the satisfaction of claiming the fortune I'll make from your reward. And since I heard your geek friend say he wouldn't be back until this afternoon, I figured we have some time to get to know each other a little better." He leaned down and brushed his finger across her chin.

She pulled away, her temples flared as she gritted her teeth.

"Easy!" Waylon said. "If you don't like my touch, it's gonna be a long morning for you."

Morana lifted her head and looked at her feet. The hacked ends of a cut lamp cord protruded from her ankles like antennae.

"What are you looking at? Ankles too tight?" he asked.

She nodded.

"Good," he said, grinning at her.

Morana thrust her hips, slamming them into his leg. She twisted to her side and thrashed a few times until Waylon dropped to his knees and rolled her onto her back. He mounted her legs to keep her from twisting again.

He grinned at her. "I kinda like seeing your face turn rosy when you strain. I'll enjoy seeing it several times for several reasons this morning."

Morana's writhing had shifted her to a position that relieved the weight of her torso on her wrists. She felt slack under the knot and rubbed the cord between the floor and her back, trying to bring the loose tails closer to her fingers.

"Each time you fight me like that, you'll lose and give me a fun little victory to go with the big one that's coming!"

She tried to head-butt him again, but he dodged it. "Ohhhh, sneaky!" he said. "Maybe I've been too gentle with you." Waylon raised up slightly on his knees to reach for the gun.

When his weight lifted, Morana bent her knees, pressed her feet to the floor, and bucked him harder, raising him off the floor.

"Whoa—easy, easy, easy," he said, waving an arm over his head like he was riding a bronco. He giggled when she stopped. He pushed her shoulders to the floor. When she refused to look at his eyes, he moved his face close to hers, grabbed her chin, and forced her to look at him.

She closed her eyes.

He said, "I know this is all such a surprise, but if you relax, maybe you can enjoy it." he swiped hair from her face, "I wish you'd make more sound while you fight me. I think that would be hot."

Morana's nostrils flared with each breath. Although she had failed to dislodge Waylon, she felt the tail of the cord knot coming loose at her fingertips. She couldn't quite pinch it and continued rubbing it against the floor.

"We better get started," Waylon said. He scooted lower on her legs, keeping them pressed between his knees. "I'm going to untie your ankles. We'll need them as far apart as possible for about seven, maybe eight minutes." He laughed and reached back and pulled her ankle cord loose. "I'm going to stand up. If you fight me, I'll punch you in that pretty little face again," he said. "All they'll need to recognize is your fingerprint for me to get my money."

"Are you sure you want to do this?" Morana said softly, her eyes still closed.

"Oh, she speaks! And I do like your change of tone since our last conversation. Let's see... do I want to do this?" He tapped his chin a few times. "There are three things I like more than anything else." He leaned back and pushed the door closed. "Power, sex, and money. And who's the lucky girl who gets to help me experience all three in one day? This girl!" He squeezed her breast.

Morana winced.

"Of course, there is one way you can skip all the fun I have planned for us this morning."

"I'm listening," she whispered.

"You're going to tell me exactly how Sykes moved that garage foundation like it was weightless."

"I don't know."

"Bullshit," Waylon yelled. "You know goddamn well how he does it! You helped him."

"I had nothing to do with the moving floor while you were trapped. I don't know how he does it."

Waylon wagged his finger at her. "You have to know!"

"If I knew how he does it, why would I have asked you how he did it when you were trapped?"

"Because you were testing me. You and Sykes were trying to determine if I had figured it out."

"You're wrong. But if you untie my hands, maybe we can come to a deal. You'll never get what you want from him without me."

"You can forget about getting untied."

"Then we both lose."

He grabbed her by the neck and yelled, "I know you know. Tell me!" His red face contorted an inch from her face.

"I can't tell you what I don't know." Morana wheezed.

Waylon's jaw tightened, and he let go. He sat back and unbuckled his belt. "Maybe you need some probing to get you to talk." He took the gun from the sink and pointed it at her face. "Now wouldn't be a good time to get squirmy again." He slowly stood up, holding the gun steady. He stepped between her legs. He tugged at his zipper, trying to lower it with one hand.

Morana considered a groin kick as Waylon's stance and her position were perfect, but his finger was on the trigger, and she knew her pistol was loaded.

Waylon got his zipper down, and his pants dropped to his knees. He shook his legs to make them fall to his ankles. "There we go."

"Wouldn't it be better in the bedroom?" Morana said.

Waylon laughed. "Nice try. I heard you and your geek friend discussing all his cameras. I'm not supplying him with any revenge porn—even though I'm sure ours will be hot enough to sell. No, we're gonna play right here."

Morana raised her head.

Waylon pressed the gun between her breasts as he kneeled between her legs. "Get 'em open wider," he barked.

Morana raised her head. She made eye contact with him for the first time and said, "This won't end well for you."

"Since you won't give up the magic you and that little nigger have going on, this is proper compensation for my trouble—I can't think of a better ending."

Morana's eyes bored into him with reptilian iciness before her expression abruptly softened. Her shoulders relaxed, and she let her legs fall apart. With a hint of a smile, she said, "Come and get it."

Chapter 23

CLAY SAT AT his desk in his office, unable to concentrate on any work, knowing that Morana was alone with Waylon at his apartment. Three texts and one voicemail message to her burner phone this morning had gone unanswered. When his boss leaned in to announce that he was heading out for lunch and wouldn't be back for the rest of the day, Clay waited a few minutes, then left early, too.

He checked his phone. Still nothing from Morana. He dialed again, pressed his phone to his ear, and flung his coat over his shoulder as he walked out. In the lobby, the receptionist cleared her throat at him.

Clay looked at her, pointing at his phone.

She mouthed, "Are you coming back?"

He shook his head and pointed toward the parking lot. By the time he arrived at his car, Morana's burner phone had rung for the tenth time. The generic, computerized voicemail greeting answered—again.

"Mo, where are you and what's going on? Pick up or answer my texts or *something*. Call me back. It's important."

He ended the call and re-checked the text messages he had sent earlier to verify they had gone through.

8:14 AM: Everything okay?

9:50 AM: Didn't hear back... Reply to confirm all good.

11:22 AM: Are you there?

A checkmark beside each message confirmed successful delivery. While driving back to his apartment, all the potential reasons for her failure to answer festered in his mind. Maybe she'd lost her phone. Or perhaps she carelessly left Waylon alone at the apartment all day to spend more time with Thane. What if law enforcement had caught up to her? Or maybe Waylon had got the upper hand with her. Every scenario made Clay's fingers sweatier as he wrung the steering wheel. Now, he regretted turning off all the cameras. If Mo hadn't insisted, he would already know what was happening in his apartment. Why couldn't she take two seconds to confirm that things were okay?

The light midday traffic helped him reach his neighborhood quicker than usual. Instead of parking in his usual place on the street, he drove down into the garage. As he climbed up the steps to ground level, he saw the gardener and his neighbor, Carol, talking in the apartment courtyard at the base of the steps to his second-floor walkway. As he closed in on them, he overheard Carol say, "... It's far too much for a nosebleed."

"What's going on?" Clay asked.

"Someone must have been injured," Carol said. "We can't figure out where it's from." She pointed to a line of blood splatter on the bottom four steps, ending with a small pool the size of a tennis ball at the bottom.

A shiver shot up Clay's back.

"It looks minor to me," the gardener said. "We thought it might be you," he said, pointing to Clay. "If you weren't bleeding this morning, it'd have to be from unit 206 or unit 204 since you're the only units that use the stairs on this side of the building."

Clay felt his heart pounding harder. "No, it wasn't me."

"I haven't seen Emily in unit 204 for days," Carol said. "Shall we call the police?"

"No!" Clay snapped, startling Carol and the gardener. "I, uh, agree that it looks minor. A bad nosebleed, a kitchen knife accident, something like that. If this was a more serious injury, you'd have heard it, or they would've knocked on a neighbor's door."

"I suppose," Carol said.

"Could you get these stairs washed down for us right away?" Clay asked the gardener.

"I'll get the hose," the gardener said, leaving.

Carol walked away from the men, muttering, "Apparently, mysterious blood is nothing to worry about anymore. I hope you two are right."

Clay climbed the stairs and saw something that Carol and the gardener had missed. His apartment door wasn't fully latched. It looked closed from a distance, but it was ajar the width of a finger. Clay looked down over the railing to the courtyard. Carol had entered her apartment, and he heard the gardener rustling in the equipment closet below. Clay stepped back from the door and pulled a small pistol from a concealed holster. He set his briefcase down on the walkway and then pushed the door open with his foot, sweeping the gun to clear the room.

"Dear God," he said.

The apartment was ransacked. The sofa had been shifted out of place, and its pillows were strewn all over the floor, one in the kitchen. The coffee table was cracked across the middle, with one of its legs broken entirely off.

"Hello," he yelled.

No answer.

"Mo?"

Again, no answer. Clay kept his pistol ready as he sidestepped toward the bedroom, where he saw its door had been knocked from its hinges and laid diagonally across the hallway. Under it, a smear of blood on the wall from shoulder height ran down to the floor. He looked in the bathroom and found blood smears and spatter on the sink and the floor beside the bathtub. A bloodied handprint on the wall beside the hand towels. "My God," Clay said, taking a deep breath to control the surge of adrenaline.

He ducked under the fallen bedroom door. The bedroom was in worse shape than the rest of the apartment. The bed linen was twisted, some of it spilling onto the floor. His mattress was shifted from the box spring. His closet door was cracked. When he pulled it open, a hinge fell to the floor. The closet was empty.

His bedside table was knocked over, and the landline phone lay on the floor, beeping off the hook.

Clay holstered his gun and texted Morana again.

Where the hell are you?

Someone knocked at his door. He pulled his gun and hurried to the front room. He looked through the peephole and saw Carol. He opened the door a crack.

"What's going on with you?" Carol asked.

"Listen, Carol, it's not a good time," Clay replied.

"What I mean is, I've never seen you forget things." She pulled his briefcase out from behind her and held it up, grinning.

"Those blood droplets you said are not a big deal must have shaken you up to forget your briefcase on the walkway!"

"Oh, thanks." Clay opened the door enough to take the briefcase from her.

"You're welcome." Carol craned her neck, going for a glimpse into the apartment, but Clay closed the door. He went to the kitchen, the only place in his apartment that was relatively untouched. His phone chimed with a text from Morana.

All good.

Clay buried his head in his arm and laughed with relief. He replied:

Don't scare me like that. What the hell happened at the apartment?

It's all under control.

Call me. Need to talk.

Sit tight. Will call later. Don't worry. See you soon.

Clay stared at the message for a long time. It was terse enough to be from Morana, but the *see you soon* didn't sound like her. *See you soon* was too big a commitment for Morana because she never told him when she would see him.

Chapter 24

THANE WOKE SHORTLY after dawn on a set of blankets piled in the garage's corner. After only an hour of sleep the previous night, he yawned as he walked to his work counter to check his phone for voicemail. He hadn't heard the phone ring since yesterday but hoped he had somehow missed Morana's call while dozing. As he neared it, the zero on the phone's base station blinked just as it had since last night.

He went to the center of the garage floor and pivoted, examining the results of the gigantic project that had taken most of the night. The photographs of his shop that he discovered on Waylon's phone yesterday had generated such anxiety that he immediately set out to remove any similarity between his workspace in the garage and the photographs. He wanted every identifiable object from the photos either removed or concealed.

For hours, he transported supplies and tools down to the sub-lair, where he stored them in a hidden chamber. He moved The more oversized items to a space between the rear of the garage and the back fence separating his property from Mrs. Perkins's.

All that remained inside his shop were a couple of sawhorses, two bundles of rolled carpet, and his mother's old upright piano, covered with a dusty tarp. After clearing off everything except his landline phone, he hung sheets to conceal his work cabinets and countertop.

On each ascension from the sub-lair to the garage, he checked the phone for any message from Mo, desperately hoping for news that she'd successfully dealt with Waylon.

He had quarried five new blocks from the west end of the sub-lair and transported them up to the garage, stacking four atop one another to obstruct the inside of the large garage door. After verifying that the knob was locked, he moved the fifth block to the entryway, buttressing the door so it couldn't open.

Only after he was safely barricaded in this reinforced cocoon did he try to get some sleep on the blankets.

The thin outline of the morning sun intensified around the edges of the garage's window coverings. Thane reached down and picked up Gus's bowl on the floor beside the countertop. He momentarily stared at the untouched food before placing the bowl back on the floor. "Gus… Gus?" his voice echoed. He stepped back and looked up to the cabinet tops where he last remembered seeing the cat comfortably curled on a blanket. He didn't remember Gus slipping out through the roll-top or entry doors while moving items from the garage last night. He wondered if the massive changes to the garage's interior had temporarily scared Gus away.

He went to the eight-ton block that buttressed the entry door and moved it away. He tested the knob and was relieved that it was still locked. He opened the door, leaned out, and examined the outside knob. Its talcum powder was untouched. He scanned the yard between the garage and the rear of his house, including the shaded spot under the solar panels where Gus sometimes napped. Gus wasn't there. All was still and quiet, except for some chirping coming from the direction of Mrs. Perkins's bird feeder over the fence.

He stepped out and whistled. If Gus were in the yard after Thane had been absent in the sub-lair, the cat would have bounded to the entrance at the slightest click of the door opening.

He locked himself back in the garage, re-barricading the entry door with the block, and then called Morana again. "Come on, I need you," he said as it rang. He hung up without leaving a message when the call went to voicemail. He hated leaving messages. The idea of giving a permanent recording of his voice to anyone who could share it indefinitely without his knowledge or permission repulsed him. But why wasn't she answering? During their last conversation, she was adamant that he should call her if he needed anything.

He spent the next three hours installing a new turbine vent on the garage roof. He then tested its venting capacity by slowly lifting the Gateway block with the garage roll-up door closed. The turbine vent spun faster than Thane had expected, creating a loud whirring.

Despite knowing that Mrs. Perkins's sound sensitivity was no longer a factor, he returned to work, creating a second slatted vent beside the spinning vent before testing again. The additional opening reduced the sound to a barely audible rush of air. Now, he could travel down to and up from the sub-lair, keeping the garage doors locked without fear of blowing out the windows.

He returned to the center of his shop for another inspection. He wiped the sweat on his sleeve, smearing the fine dusting of coral rock powder that covered his clothes and afro. His fingers were slightly swollen, his arms were tired, and he was finally ready to eat.

Just after noon, he tried calling Morana again, crossing his fingers as the phone rang. When he heard her voicemail greeting, his desperation to reach her finally surpassed his fear of leaving a voicemail. "Hi, it's me. You told me to call you if I needed you. So, I need you. Please call back."

He descended on the lift into the sub-lair. He pushed open a door block outside the lift chamber. He passed through it, then closed himself inside. It was pitch black. He pulled the flashlight from his pocket and sidestepped along a hallway barely the width of his shoulders. After about thirty-five paces, he stepped onto a smaller lift and began ascending.

A hundred feet above him in the main house, air rushed through the fireplace and out the chimney and sucked draperies, pressing them to the windows he always left open a few inches. Less than a minute later, Thane rose through the floor of a bedroom closet in the main house. He opened the closet door and stepped into the second bedroom.

He crept to the door and listened. The house was silent. He stepped into the hallway and cautiously peered around each corner as he made his way to the front of the house. After verifying that the front door was locked, he went to the kitchen and verified that the back door was still locked. He looked out the kitchen window to the backyard, hoping to see Gus, but there was no sign of him. Even from a distance, he could see that the faint dusting of talcum powder was undisturbed along the front edge of the garage.

He wolfed down a couple of sandwiches, then went straight to the master bedroom, where he pulled the soiled and tangled linen from the bed and stuffed it into a laundry basket. He snapped open a plastic garbage bag and dumped in a couple of empty wine bottles, a package of cookies, and a badly torn bag of deep-fried pork rinds, some of which had fallen to the floor.

He hurried from the room and returned moments later carrying a broom and a set of new linen he tossed onto the bed. He swept the crumbs on the floor under the bedside table and wiped down the headboard with a rag and furniture polish. He paused when he noticed a pair of handcuffs dangling behind the headboard from one of its rungs.

After cleaning the bedroom, he went to the bathroom and cleaned the shower and sink until they were spotless. He placed clean bath towels on the shelves, then leaned to check his work from several angles, wiping a few drops of water from the faucet handle.

After putting his cleaning supplies away, he went to the foyer and found a note taped to the inside of the front door. He pulled it off and opened it. His shoulders drooped as he read it. He squeezed the note into his fist and stuffed it into his pocket.

He looked out the peephole. With no one in sight, he took a deep breath and opened the front door. He whistled for Gus. There was no response.

Thane was already averse to spending time in the open, but stepping outside with Waylon on the loose gave him a shiver. He approached the two steps at the edge of the porch and looked around the front yard. None of his neighbors were out. The street had an eerie silence.

On the side of the porch sat 12 trays of flowers, two large bags of potting soil, and a new trowel that had been delivered.

There's no way Morana would approve of what he was about to do after her stern warnings about Waylon's penchant for revenge.

He left the front door ajar, hoping to get inside and lock it before Waylon could catch him. The open door would also allow him to hear the landline phone.

He got to work on his hands and knees, weeding the overgrown flower bed below the living room window. Constantly looking over his shoulder as he worked, ready to run inside.

He spent the next hour planting the flowers while keeping vigilant watch and stewing over Morana's delay in contacting him.

When only two trays remained, Thane crawled to the porch steps and sat, taking a brief break. He looked at the new rows of fresh flowers lined up in a perfect grid pattern on the bed. A lopsided stack of empty flower trays sat by the garbage bags of weeds. Sweat stained Thane's shirt, and patches of dried mud covered the front of his clothing.

He heard the phone ring as he stood up to finish the last flower trays. He dropped the trowel, ran through the open front door, and raced to the kitchen, where he snatched the phone from the holder. "Hello? Hello?"

"Thane, I'm so glad you're there. It's Mo."

"Where have you been?" Thane yelled. "You told me to call you, so I've been trying to call, and you never pick up."

"Sweetheart, calm down. I'm sorry I couldn't answer."

"Did you get Waylon?"

"Well," Morana said, hesitating. "Yes, I did."

"Thank God. Did he have Gus?"

"Gus? No, why would he?"

"Gus is missing."

"Are you sure?"

"Of course, I'm sure. He's been gone since yesterday. He's never gone that long. His food hasn't been touched."

"Maybe he had a successful hunt?" Morana said. "You told me he's a great mouser."

"Except that he doesn't eat the mice after catching them. He brings them to me." Thane walked back to the open front door and looked out. "There are no dead mice in front of the garage or house. There are no talcum paw prints. There's nothing." He closed the door and locked it.

"I have a hunch Gus is out exploring," Morana said.

"Your hunch is wrong. I thought Waylon took him, but you're telling me you caught him."

"There's something I need to tell you, Thane."

"What's wrong?"

"There's more to it than that. I will tell you something, and I don't want you to panic..."

"You're panicking me—just say it."

"I caught Waylon, but he attacked me and got away."

"What?" Thane shouted. "How could you let him get away?"

"I didn't let him get away. I tracked him down and captured him at his house."

"Captured? That's not what we discussed." Thane stomped to the living room, circling the coffee table and squeezing his hair with his free hand.

"Thane, it was out of my control—let me explain. You don't need to worry if you stay in the sub-lair like I told you to. Meanwhile, I have a new plan to get him back."

"A plan? I don't need a new plan. I don't need you to get him. I need you to finish him—*that* was the plan."

"You didn't like it when I raised my voice to you. Please don't raise yours to me."

"Sorry." Thane sat on the sofa and pressed the heel of his hand to his forehead. "The one thing that hasn't changed is my desire to have him out of my life forever. You couldn't have been clearer about how you would help me achieve that. You told me about the whole airplane V1 thing with no turning back. I agreed. Why would we be talking about capturing him?" He got up and returned to the kitchen, peering out the window to the garage.

"Capturing him allows for more options. Let me finish telling you what happened... I had him cornered. We fought and ended up on the ground. I had him pinned. He swung at me, got lucky, and must have landed a solid blow to my head because I blacked out. When I came to, I was tied up in the trunk."

"That's disappointing," Thane said. "You were so confident. You told me you had this under control."

"I *did*, and I do. Listen, Thane, I can throw in the towel now, and you'll be on your own to sort this out with law enforcement and to defend yourself against a legal machine that Waylon is a master at manipulating."

"No, I don't want that."

"Then you need to trust me. The bottom line is that I got away, and everything will work out. You'll see."

Thane sighed. "How did you get away?"

"While riding in the trunk, I found a jagged metal framing near the latch and used it to free my wrists and ankles. When Waylon opened the trunk, I was ready. He must have assumed that I'd still be tied up, which was careless on his part. My legs were free. When he leaned in to pull me out, I kicked him. When I jumped from the trunk, he ran."

"Where did this happen?"

"At Remly City dump. I chased him through a nearby swamp, but he disappeared into some woods at the edge. Thane, this place was so godforsaken. I'm sure he planned to kill me."

"I'll be a bigger prize for him," Thane said. "He'll kill me now, I know it." He went back to the front door and double-checked the deadbolt.

"Actually, I don't think so," Morana said.

"Are you kidding?"

"He made a call while driving. I couldn't hear his voice clearly from the trunk, but understood parts of the conversation. Thane, your trap floor blew his mind. He was more amazed by it than either of us thought he would be. He wants your secret, and he's aware that he can't get it from you if you are dead. I heard him telling someone about it on the phone."

"What exactly did he say about it?" Thane said, peering at his unfinished flower bed through a crack in the living room drapes.

"He told the person that he felt the sensation of dropping on an elevator. He said he was surprised that his feet remained on the floor during such a rapid drop. Then he told them about the darkness and mentioned I was with you, but he didn't know my name."

"Did he mention the photo he took?"

"No."

"Did he describe anything else in my shop or the sub-lair?"

"I only heard part of the call. The conversation was brief. Listen, Thane, I have some new information about Waylon. I planned to wait until I saw you, but this situation may be more urgent than anticipated."

Thane sighed. "You lost him, and he'll kill me. What could be worse?"

"I understand you are upset, but if you had followed my advice in the sub-lair, a perfect plan would have already been executed—so to speak."

Thane quietly replied, "I know. What new information do you have?"

"I asked Clay for help."

"You brought Clay into this?"

"Hear me out. I told him none of the personal information you shared about Waylon. Clay can be useful to us. I've met no one who can sleuth as much information about people as quickly as Clay can. The only thing Clay currently knows about your situation is that Waylon has been after you for some time."

"Did you tell him about the sub-lair?"

"I would *never* do that without your permission."

"Clay talks a lot. If you told him, I'll discover it."

"I understand. Listen, Clay uncovered evidence that the problem of Waylon goes deeper than either of us suspected. Waylon's bullying extends to many more people than you."

"Of course. I would assume that."

"Yes, but this is much more serious. Clay uncovered organized crime ties, specifically an organization called Delboro. You may have seen them on the news."

"I don't watch the news."

"All you need to know is that they are dangerous criminals based here in Florida, linked to credit card fraud, prostitution, and drug trafficking. The bad news is that Waylon has plenty of connections with them. I'm unsure where Waylon ranks in this organization, but if I were to kill him outright, payback for eliminating a key player for these people doesn't appeal to me. It also means that Waylon may not need to come back for you personally with the resources at his disposal."

"My God," Thane said. He walked around the house, turning off all the interior lights.

"What these criminals do is horrific," Morana said. "Clay showed me photos. We can track Waylon's whereabouts if he's in one of his cars."

"What does he drive?"

"He has a black BMW and a red Mercedes, so you need to watch for either of these cars parked on your street."

"I'll try, but I don't pay attention to the cars outside."

"Now is a good time to start, and you understand that there's a possibility that he or someone he works with could show up at your place, right? Because of that, I think it would be safest for you if I stayed with you for now."

"Why?"

"If he's after both of us, he'll revisit your garage."

Thane didn't reply as he went to the bedroom and opened the closet door.

"Did you hear me?" Morana asked.

"And if Waylon trespasses again, how do you plan to handle it?"

"We can use the trap floor again."

"Have you forgotten why I originally released him from the sub-lair? I don't want any crime on my property. I could lose everything."

"And when Waylon gets his hands on you, you will lose your life."

Thane parted the hanging clothes, squeezing between them. "If I use the trap floor, why do I need you?" he asked.

Morana paused. "The other part of this is that… I miss you. I want to be with you. This can work. And this time, I'll take him far away. It'll be a place too distant to have any connection with you."

Thane positioned his feet on the lift. "I have to go."

"Okay, but please call me immediately if you see anything."

"You told me that before, and then you didn't answer."

"Thane, I'm sorry, I just…"

"If you're going to help me, then do it." He hung up, tossed the handset to the bed and closed the closet door. Moments later, Thane dropped through the closet floor as air rushed into the house through the windows and chimney.

Chapter 25

CLAY SPENT THE afternoon restoring his apartment, stacking broken furniture for disposal, and cleaning the bathroom and hallway walls. After he finished cleaning the master bedroom, he tried to call Morana. As usual, she didn't pick up.

He went to the kitchen and pulled a beer and a sandwich from the fridge. He stretched out on the sofa, cracked his beer open, and turned on the TV. After only a few bites of the sandwich, he heard footsteps on the stairway outside. He muted the TV and listened. The creaking of his walkway was distinct, and the footsteps were coming closer. He got up as someone knocked on the door. He slid his hand deep between the sofa cushions and pulled out a pistol he always kept there. He cocked it and held it behind him as he went to the door.

The walkway light outside his unit was out, so all he could see out the peephole was the silhouette of someone's shoulder.

"Who is it?"

"Open up," Morana whispered.

"Goddammit, Mo, you've got to quit unscrewing the walkway light bulb," he said, opening the door.

"Why would you want me to yell my name for your neighbors?" she said, pushing past him to go inside.

"My God—look at you." Clay closed the door and followed her to the kitchen, where the light was better. She had scratches along the side of her face, and one of her eyes was swollen and darkening. He reached to gently turn her chin for a better view, but she pulled away.

"You've got some serious battle scars," he said.

"You should see the other guy," Morana replied. "Sorry about your place."

"Where's Waylon?"

"He's under control."

"What does that mean? Is he in your car?"

"Hold on, and we'll talk." Morana opened the freezer and wrapped a handful of ice in the dishtowel. "There's a new plan."

Clay held up his hands. "Before you go into something new, I need to know what happened to you and where Waylon is."

Morana walked past him and gingerly sat on the sofa. She patted her hand beside her and said, "Sit down. I'll tell you everything."

For the next hour, Morana detailed everything that happened between her and Waylon in the apartment and how the events led her to a new idea for obtaining Thane's secret.

When she explained it, Clay said, "It sounds harsh."

"Any discomfort for Thane should be brief—if things go as planned," Morana said.

"What if it doesn't work?"

"It will work, trust me. More than anything, Thane wants to restore his privacy and return to his life of quiet isolation. This situation has put him on edge, and he'll do almost anything for some stability."

"I don't like it. Your plan seems cruel to Thane."

"It may seem that way on the surface, but sometimes the best result justifies uncomfortable means. Is a surgeon cruel to a patient? Inflicting temporary suffering to improve the patient's life? The way this ends for Thane is that he'll live his dream life with more security and control over his privacy than he could've imagined. My plan is the only thing that will give him that."

"I suppose, but something about it doesn't feel right," Clay insisted.

Morana said, "Suppose we abandon Thane. His privacy and security are lost because Waylon has seen what he does, and we both know he'll leak it. Without us, who will protect Thane's interests? Who will help him when Waylon uses trumped-up charges to extort him?"

"And you think we aren't taking advantage of him?" Clay said.

"No, because our plan benefits him as much as it benefits us. We will not hurt Thane, and I will let no one hurt Thane. If he shares his secret with us, we will help him protect it more effectively than he could alone. The revenue from his secret will allow us to invest in state-of-the-art security, ensuring his ability to continue the research and testing he loves. That's an enormous benefit for the small price of some temporary suffering. Thane will be happy, and despite his lack of interest in money, he'll be rich beyond measure. He has more to gain than either of us."

"I suppose," Clay said.

"Follow my plan and see what it yields. The good news is that we don't have to rush. We have time to make this work. Thane isn't going anywhere, and I can promise that Waylon sure isn't going anywhere."

After taking a deep breath, Clay said, "Fine. I'm in."

✝

Morana drove her Explorer to the town of Shepley, two miles north of Clay's apartment. On the way, she turned on the radio. A local news station reported that prominent attorney Waylon Snells, founder of the famous local personal injury firm, had been missing for three days. Local authorities investigated the matter and asked the public for any leads on his whereabouts.

Before she turned into the driveway of a self-storage facility, she put on sunglasses and a wig and checked herself in the rearview mirror. She rolled down her window and typed in the entry code for the gate.

She drove past aisle after aisle of secure storage units, eventually turning into the one furthest from the office. She positioned the driver's door as close as possible to the padlock before unlocking it. She pulled a flashlight from her bag on the passenger seat. She raised the metal roll-up door halfway and leaned down to look inside.

A muffled voice and a commotion came from the darkness. Morana homed the flashlight in on her precious merchandise on the floor halfway to the rear of the nearly empty storage unit. Waylon lay bound and gagged in the fetal position, trembling.

"Did you miss me?" she asked, resting the flashlight in the center of the floor, aiming it upward to create ambient light. She returned to her Explorer and pulled out a small open box, setting it near the flashlight. She closed the door behind her, triggering another dampened howl from Waylon as he tried to pull his knees up to his chest. She strolled to his sweat-soaked body about six strides from the rear wall where she had left him over a day ago.

Duct tape, wrapped around his neck, held a wire to his throat. The wire draped upward to a pet shock collar hanging from the ceiling and forked to a switch mounted atop a car battery in the floor's corner. Black and red wires ran across the floor from the battery's electrodes, disappearing through the open zipper on Waylon's pants.

In Morana's absence, Waylon had managed to quietly inch his way from the back wall of the storage unit to a place almost halfway to the battery. His temples were raw, one side smeared with crusted blood from attempts to scrape his blindfold off.

Morana went to the shock collar, reached up, and turned it off. "You're quite the silent traveler," she said.

Waylon immediately began humming something through his gag.

"I'm sure you have plenty to say," Morana said, moving to stand beside him. She took hold of the rope that bound his ankles and dragged him across the concrete floor to his original position by the rear wall.

Waylon groaned while she repositioned him.

A few steps away, Gus meowed in a wire cage that contained water, food, and a couple of fluffy play toys. Morana went to the open box by the door and pulled out some fresh cat food and a water bottle. While replenishing Gus's food and water, she asked, "Were Gus's purrs strong enough for a jolt?"

Waylon nodded hard.

Morana shrugged. "Please accept Gus's deepest apologies. I wondered if that might happen after I put the collar on maximum sensitivity. But, in this case, your silence was more important to me than your comfort—I'm sure you understand."

Her attention returned to Gus. A tuft on his newly blunt tail was missing. Gus meowed again. Morana went to him and put her fingers through the wire grid of the cage. She scratched Gus's head as he purred. "Did you monitor him, Gussy? Did you tell him shocking stories all night long? Did you keep an eye on that big bully? Did he say mean things to you like he does to your master?"

She went to Waylon, took hold of his shirt, and pulled him to a sitting position against the wall. She pulled a small water bottle from her coat pocket and removed his gag.

"Please," he gasped. "Listen…"

Morana shoved the water bottle in his mouth, and he guzzled it, spilling down his chin. His last swallow triggered a brief coughing fit. He caught his breath and said, "I have a deal for you."

Morana tossed the empty bottle over her shoulder, sending it toppling across the floor. "You're in no position to bargain."

Waylon watched her momentarily and then said, "Please hear me out—I might be. Obviously, Sykes hasn't given you his secret, has he?"

Morana rose to her feet, straddling his legs. She crossed her arms, glaring down at him.

Waylon continued, "I know a way we can both win. Let me make it easy. I won't pursue any criminal case for the felonies you both racked up by detaining me. You join me in a slam dunk civil suit against Sykes. He won't be able to pay the judgment, and boom, we go after his property—unless he shares his secret with us. If he refuses, he loses everything, and we have equal rights to go in and figure out how he moves that foundation."

Morana didn't answer. She bent down and tightened an ankle binding that had loosened.

Waylon added, "It's foolproof, and we both win—why are you doing this to me?"

"How many times did Thane ask you that on the playground?"

Waylon looked confused. "Is that what this is about? Schoolyard crap? Kids get teased now and then. So, I'll apologize to him if that's what the fuckin' mud bug needs."

. Morana closed her eyes, and her temples flared as her jaw clenched. "An apology is the smallest thing you'll be giving Thane."

"What else do you want? And, please be reasonable. We can help each other here, but you gotta tell me what the hell you want."

"Your radio commercials have inspired me. So, I've decided to help you get what you deserve. You're going on trial."

Waylon rolled his eyes. "You can't be serious. Listen, I don't know what your angle is on this, but if it's money, name your cut and I'll—"

"It won't be a civil case. Your trial will be quick, and you will represent yourself. I'll be the only juror. You'll find that the judge and executioner will look a lot like Thane Sykes." She reached for his gag.

Waylon bucked, saying, "No! Please! You've got the damned shock collar. Please skip the gag. I won't talk!"

She pressed his head to the floor and tried again.

Waylon fought harder, pulling his head away and begging each time Morana tried to secure the gag.

She went to the shock collar. When she reached to turn it on, Waylon went silent, wide-eyed and trembling.

She put her finger to her lips, warning Waylon to keep quiet, and then she flipped the switch on. She exaggerated the motion of tiptoeing back to him.

He pressed his lips together, wheezing through his nose.

Morana put her knee into his gut to keep him from trying to spin away. She put her lips close to his ear and whispered, "You will comply with me, or I will skip the collar and feed current to your nuts until I smell smoke."

Waylon nodded.

Morana secured the gag, pulling one part between his teeth and placing the other over his mouth before tying both tightly behind his head.

Again, she whispered, "Did Thane ever beg you for mercy?"

Waylon hesitated, then shook his head

"Liar." Morana stood, stepped back from him, and clapped once.

The green lightning bolt icon on the shock collar flashed, and Waylon convulsed, slamming his knees into the wall, which triggered a second jolt through his zipper.

Morana went to the shock collar and turned it off.

Waylon's body went limp, his eyes locked onto her.

"You abused Thane for years." She retrieved the flashlight from the middle of the floor and aimed it at him. "The good news for both of you is that you won't need forgiveness because we will make things even. Meanwhile, I expect plenty of helicopters to pass overhead tonight." Before Waylon could protest through the gag, Morana flipped the shock collar switch back on and walked to the storage unit's door.

She tucked the flashlight into her jacket and "Forgive me, in advance, for this." She raised the door, generating a metallic grinding that reverberated inside the unit. The light flashed on the shock collar, sending Waylon into a writhing fit, during which he fought to keep his voice quiet. She stepped outside and said, "Brace yourself... Once more." She pulled the door down, slamming it to the ground.

Thane spent most of the next day holed away in the sub-lair, quarrying new blocks, cleaning, and creating new tools. He waited until the afternoon to ride up to the garage. The latest information Morana had given him about Waylon put him in no rush to go to the surface, but he needed to check for voicemail messages.

He stepped onto the lift and began his ascent. Despite the massive blocks he had placed to obstruct the garage doors, the thought of Waylon miraculously breaching his garage still gave him a shiver. As he approached the shaft opening to the garage floor, he slowed the lift as his head rose above the level of the garage floor. He stopped the lift and looked around the garage. Everything was as he had left it. He finished raising the lift to the surface and stepped off.

He held his breath as he walked to his phone at his workspace. The display showed the blinking zero he had grown to hate recently.

He looked at the floor beside the cabinet. Gus's bowl of food remained untouched. He cussed and kicked it, sending the dry morsels of cat food against the wall before they scattered on the floor. The metal bowl clanged and toppled end over end until it rolled on its rim in a wide arc before falling.

After regaining his composure, he went to a tall cabinet on the opposite wall and retrieved a broom.

The phone rang. His stomach knotted. After getting no voicemail messages for an entire day, why had the phone suddenly rung at this moment? What if someone lurked outside, waiting for confirmation that he was inside?

He examined the windows. They were the only way someone could know he was in the garage unless they heard the toppling cat dish. The windows were all still covered.

Seeing his multi-ton door obstructions still in place reminded him he was safe. But this comfort wasn't enough as he went to the phone. The caller ID was blocked. Although he desperately wanted to hear from Morana, he weighed his reasons for and against answering it. Maybe Morana had a new phone. If he missed a call from her, particularly one with good news, the regret would be too costly. If he let the call go to voicemail, she might not leave a message. He grimaced and picked up the handset as though it might explode.

"Hello…"

"Good, you're there."

"Hi, Uncle Jesse." Thane's shoulders sagged.

"Listen, I'm letting you know I'll be stopping by the house later today."

"Why?"

"I owe you a reason? Don't forget, the house you live in is my property. Is that a problem?"

"No."

"Damned right. I dropped by earlier today. The garage was locked up, and you left a bunch of gardening crap on the sidewalk in front of the house. What's up with that?"

"I'm sorry, something urgent came up. I couldn't finish the flowers."

"Well, you need to get them planted and get that sidewalk swept up. Do you understand?"

"Yes, Uncle Jesse."

"Is that pile of shit your mom left still stored in the garage?"

Thane looked behind him and saw the upright piano against the corner wall, covered with cloth tarps. "Yes, Uncle Jesse."

"Good, there should be a piano there. I might have a buyer for it. I told him it's a Yamaha. He said if it's a studio piano in good condition, he'll pay up to $2,500."

"Why sell it?" Thane asked.

"Do you play the piano?"

"No, but mom used to play—"

"It's taking up space and, just like you, it doesn't pay rent."

Thane was quiet.

"And I need to have a closer look at the property to make sure things are in order."

"I can tell you everything is fine here. I cut the lawn two days ago, I trimmed the tree that was touching the fence. I polished the gas meter, and I will start watering the back lawn just like you asked. You don't need to visit today."

"Doesn't matter. I'm still stopping by. If the property's good, then everything will be fine."

"What time are you coming?"

"On my way now. Probably ten minutes."

"But wait..." Thane looked around the garage. "It's not a good time for me."

"Not a good time for *you*? You hosting a party?" Uncle Jesse laughed.

"Can you make it a different time? A different day?"

"Look, Thane, if you could tolerate conversing with real people, you might hold down an actual job. Then you could pay me some rent; your opinion would mean something. I'm checking the property, and that's final. And I need to see that piano, so get that damned garage door unlocked—which reminds me, I never got the spare key. You were supposed to get me a new key to the garage after you changed the lock without my permission."

"Sorry. I haven't had time to make a copy."

"See, Thane? That was such a small thing I told you to do, and you still didn't get it done. What's the matter with you?"

"I'm sorry, Uncle Jesse. I'll get a spare key made for you right away."

"No, you won't. Remind me when I'm there to take your key. I'll make myself a copy."

Thane walked to the front of the shop and opened the garage entry door the few inches his block would allow. "Is there any way you could wait a half hour?" he asked, looking out to the driveway.

"What the hell for? What's going on with you? You hiding a hooker there?" Uncle Jesse belted out a bigger laugh.

Thane considered moving his truck toward the front of the driveway to block Uncle Jesse from driving to the back. "Never mind. Show up. I'll be ready."

✝

When Uncle Jesse's Cadillac turned into the driveway, Thane watched through the living room window after having traveled to the house by way of his secret lift in the closet.

Uncle Jesse parked within inches of Thane's truck bumper, which now blocked it at the pergola.

Thane went to the porch and climbed down the steps to meet him.

"What's your truck doing there? You never park in front."

"Sorry." Thane shrugged.

"I thought I told you to move all this trash from the flowers you were supposed to have finished yesterday."

Thane scanned the street. An unfamiliar car was parked a short distance away. It was a red Mercedes. Its windows were tinted, and Thane couldn't see if anyone was inside, but this was Morana's description of Waylon's car. Although Uncle Jesse would likely be little help in an assault, having his uncle there encouraged Thane to step from the porch and approach the empty flower cartons. He tripped, staring at the car.

Uncle Jesse went to the center of the front yard and took pictures of the house with his phone.

Thane got on his knees and planted the remaining flowers, looking over his shoulder every few moments at the Mercedes.

Uncle Jesse crossed the yard a few times, inspecting the sides of the house, and said, "It's about time we give the house a facelift. I think we'll start with a new paint job."

"I painted it only two years ago," Thane said. "I think it looks fine."

"Overruled. Weather's been tough on it. It's getting painted."

"The last time painting the house took two weeks."

"I know. You're lucky I'm not in a hurry, but I want it done. I'll get the paint dropped off to you, just like the flowers."

Thane shoved the last flower into the final trowel hole and tossed the empty tray on top of the others.

Uncle Jesse walked to the porch, saying, "Now, I need to go see about that piano."

Thane thought he heard a car start on the street, and his head snapped toward the Mercedes. He kept his eyes locked onto it while rushing to scoop up the empty flower trays and trowel. As his uncle entered the house, Thane ran after him, stumbling with the stacked trays up onto the porch. He rushed through the front door before it closed behind his uncle.

"What are you doing?" Uncle Jesse said, watching Thane navigating the hallway corners with the trays. He pointed down at Thane's feet.

"You're tracking a bunch of dirt in here, boy! Why the hell would you try to carry a bunch of filthy trays through a clean house?"

Because I don't want to be murdered in my driveway, Thane thought. "Because this way is shorter," he said.

"Look!" Uncle Jesse pointed with his toe. "You're making a filthy mess."

"I'll clean it up, I promise," Thane said.

"Damned right, you will," Uncle Jesse said. He strolled toward the kitchen with his hands in his pockets, looking around the place. He drew his finger across a cabinet handle and blew dust from his finger. He wrinkled his nose and said, "I expect that to be fixed, too."

"Yes, I will."

Uncle Jesse went to the window and looked out toward the garage. "Is that the piano?"

"Yes."

Uncle Jesse grinned as he crossed the kitchen and pushed out the back door.

Thane caught the closing door with his foot and eased outside with the trays. He set them on the ground beside the back door.

Uncle Jesse went to the piano and said, "Why is it outside the garage?"

"I thought you wanted to see it."

"Yes, but you could have left it inside." He pulled the tarp off and caressed its top. The pristine black finish and keys glistened. "Did you polish it?"

"No, why?"

"It's shinier than I thought it would be," Uncle Jesse said, grinning. "Maybe I can squeeze out over two-and-a-half grand for it." Uncle Jesse played a few notes, then looked over his shoulder at Thane. "Sounds like at least three grand to me!" He laughed.

Thane watched, twisting his hands in his pockets.

Uncle Jesse pulled out a cigarette and lit it. He walked around the piano, nodded approvingly, then stooped to look at its base. He gave it a half-hearted shove. Then he leaned into it, pushing it harder and failing to budge it. His cigarette flopped between his lips as he said, "This sucker has no wheels. How did you get it out here?"

"I managed," Thane replied.

Uncle Jesse frowned. "You're telling me you moved this by yourself?"

Thane said, "I asked someone to help me."

Uncle Jesse looked skeptical. He took a toke on the cigarette, squinted, and said, "You actually approached a neighbor?"

"No, a man was walking by out front. I asked him if he could help me. It was quick. He was strong."

Uncle Jesse smirked at Thane's explanation. He moved away from the piano and pointed at the small solar array in the yard. "I can tell you the electric bill for the house has been smaller than I've ever seen it lately. Are those panels the reason?"

"No, the bills have been small because I rarely use the house."

"Isn't solar power supposed to get me some sort of refund?"

"These aren't connected to the house. I use the electricity generated by this small array to power my experiments in the garage."

"Why do you need an array for that when the garage is wired for power?"

"I wanted to learn how the solar panels worked. The solar panels themselves were an experiment."

"You realize that they're ugly as hell, don't you? And where you've got them sticking up out of the middle of the yard is weird."

Thane looked away.

Uncle Jesse stepped closer to him and raised his finger. "They haven't made me a dime, so you either need to get rid of them or hide them better."

"Yes, Uncle Jesse."

Thane heard a car slow down in front of the house and felt panic rushing in.

Uncle Jesse flicked his cigarette to the ground and snuffed it with his toe. "I don't know when my piano buyer is available to look at this thing, so let me help you get it back inside the garage."

Thane winced. "No, it's okay. I can move it later."

"Don't be silly! You gonna wait for another passerby?" Uncle Jesse's laugh triggered a brief coughing fit.

"Please leave it to me. I'll make sure the piano gets back inside and is covered."

Uncle Jesse looked from Thane to the garage and back. "What the hell you got going on in there that you've covered all the windows?" He walked toward the large garage door and tried to lift it. It was locked, so he headed for the entry door.

"Nothing!" Thane said. He moved to block his uncle.

"Get out of my way," Uncle Jesse said. He pushed Thane's shoulder and sidestepped him, mumbling, "This is ridiculous." He jiggled the doorknob. "Give me the key."

"But—"

"Give me the goddamn key." He held his hand out.

Thane pulled his key ring from his pocket and flicked through the keys until he found the garage key. Uncle Jesse snatched it from him and unlocked the knob. When he pushed it open, the door opened a few inches and banged against the upright 8-ton block Thane had placed behind it.

"What the hell is blocking this?" Uncle Jesse said.

"I'm working on a… sculpture," Thane said, extending his hand for the keys.

Uncle Jesse handed them over, then tried, and failed, to force the door open with his shoulder. The opening was wide enough for him to see into the garage with one eye at a time. He pressed his face to it, peering in. "Why in God's name would you block the door with some damned sculpture? How are you gonna get in?"

"I'll use the big door," Thane pointed.

Uncle Jesse moved his face to use his other eye and continued inspecting the garage's nearly empty interior. Thane's workbench was concealed by the sheets. All the equipment, area rugs, and Thane's decorative doors that Uncle Jesse remembered hanging all over the walls were gone. All that remained were Thane's mother's leftover belongings, stacked near the back corner. There was a small open space between the items where the piano had been pulled out.

"What did you do with all your crap—your tools and stuff?" Uncle Jesse said.

"I got rid of items I didn't need," Thane said.

"More like you gutted the place." Uncle Jesse spotted the four rectangular blocks stacked high beside the big roll-top door. He turned to Thane with a curious look. "What's in front of the other door?"

Thane fidgeted as he said, "I'm trying to build a barricade."

"I can see that, but what in the hell for?"

Thane cleared his throat, then said, "Just… protection."

Uncle Jesse laughed, turning back to him. "Not exactly practical if you took everything out of the garage, right?"

Thane didn't respond.

Uncle Jesse stared at him momentarily, then said, "What do you have in here that someone would want? I mean, you're acting like you're trying to protect a fuckin' jewelry store in there!"

Thane shrugged.

Uncle Jesse patted his hand on the entry door and said, "And there's no way you brought that piano through this tiny door. And there's no room for it to go around those other blocks, so how are you moving all these things?"

Thane said, "I have some pulleys and… grease and things like that."

Uncle Jesse's phone rang. He pulled it from his coat pocket. He put the phone to his ear and said, "Hold on…" then he moved closer to Thane and wagged his finger at him. "I don't know what you're up to. I don't know where you've stashed all the stuff in this garage, but whatever you are doing, it damn well better not be illegal, and it better not damage the property. Got it?"

Thane nodded.

Uncle Jesse resumed his phone conversation and strolled along the driveway.

Thane followed him to the front of the house.

Before getting into his car, Uncle Jesse turned to Thane, covered his phone with his hand, and said, "Garage key." He held out his hand.

Thane reluctantly removed the key from his key ring and handed it over. As Uncle Jesse backed away, he said, "Expect the paint to be delivered tomorrow. I want the house done ASAP." He pointed over Thane's shoulder and added, "And, come to think of it, the garage could use a fresh coat, too."

After watching his uncle drive away, Thane returned to the garage and moved the piano back inside before descending to the sub-lair. He entered a chamber stocked with the items he had removed from his garage.

Off to one side, his decorative doors were propped against the wall. He searched through them until he found a solid door slightly larger than the current garage entry door. He pulled it from the stack and carried it out with a few other tools he brought up and into the garage. He used a planer to trim the door's edges, and after some sanding, he fit the new door into the door frame with the same precision he achieved with his rock blocks. He transported the old door down into the sub-lair for storage.

On the way, he considered how furious Uncle Jesse would be when he returned with a useless key. Thane no longer cared. The attitudes and intentions of people on the surface couldn't touch him in the sub-lair.

He went into his bedroom and reclined on his mattress. After a few minutes, he fell asleep, well-protected in Earth's fist.

✝

Thane woke up the following day and rode up to the garage. Still no sign of Gus. After checking his phone for messages, he went to the window and peeked through the crack in the edge. The driveway and backyard were clear. He returned to the sub-lair and took his secret tunnel to the bedroom lift, where he ascended to the closet in the house. He cautiously stepped out and listened before checking that everything else in the house remained undisturbed and the doors were still locked.

He prepared some toast and cereal for breakfast and watched out the kitchen window while he ate. He soon saw something that made him stop chewing. Although the distance and angle made it difficult to see the place in front of the garage entry door, he could barely make out a faint smear in the talcum powder. He dropped his bowl in the sink, splashing milk, and leaned closer to the window, straining for a better view. The longer he stared at it, the faster his heart raced.

He ran to the front of the house and parted the living room curtains wide enough to see out to the front yard. It was empty. He ran to the front door and looked through the peephole, feeling his own panicked breath on his face. The porch was empty, too. He ran to the bedroom and looked out the window to the backyard again. That, too, remained vacant. His urge to run out the back door and check the talcum powder was dwarfed by the terror of being ambushed if Waylon or one of his associates that Morana described was still there.

He went into the closet, descended to the sub-lair, and hurried to the garage lift, riding it back up into the garage. He unlocked the entry door and then repositioned the 8-ton block that obstructed it so that he could fit his head and one arm outside. He gripped the doorknob and quietly opened it. He kneeled and examined the area outside the door where he had seen the smear from the kitchen. A shiver shot through him. Along the entire length of the garage's front, his talcum powder revealed footprints and a dark smear where someone had pivoted several times at the entry door. His eyes welled up, and he clenched his jaw. He wondered if his uncle had returned to pick up the piano, but the shoe size was too large. And the tread in the talcum powder was knotty, like that from a boot, not the smooth print from the worn loafers his uncle always wore.

He squatted for a closer look and then scanned the backyard again, checking both sides of the house. He opened the door enough to squeeze his torso out. He looked outside the garage windows and saw smudge marks at the edge of two.

He examined the outside doorknob and felt a rush of terror, as the powder had been almost completely smeared off, and a tuft of hair stuck to the side of the knob. He pinched it between his fingers and examined it. It was the same color as Gus's fur.

He backed into the garage, slammed the door shut, and locked the knob.

Within two minutes, Thane had added a second eight-ton block next to the first—an obstruction a bulldozer couldn't breach.

He went to the phone to check for messages. None. He picked up the handset and had trouble holding his finger steady enough to dial Morana. One ring… Two rings… Three rings… Four rings…

"Hello."

"Thank God," Thane blurted.

"Sweetheart, what's wrong?"

"Where have you been? Why don't you ever call me? I've been trying to reach you. You haven't done everything you said you would do, and now I'm in trouble. I just—"

"Thane, stop!" Morana said. "You need to calm down. Why are you hysterical?"

"He's been here!" Thane replied, hyperventilating. "Waylon was here and left some of Gus's fur on the doorknob. He has my cat."

"Why would he do that? Are you certain it's fur that didn't transfer from your hand after you pet Gus?"

"Gus doesn't shed. This hair is half an inch long, and looks cropped. It's Waylon. He's taunting me. This is what he does."

"Thane, I need you to breathe. Was this today?"

"Yes. You were supposed to have cared for him, but you haven't."

"I know you're frustrated, but there's a logical explanation. I will explain everything, but how do you know it was Waylon?"

Thane swallowed, catching his breath. "I found shoe prints in the talcum and fingerprints on the knob. There are streaks on the outside windows where Waylon put his hands against them, probably trying to spy on me."

"Did he try to break in?"

"Probably. I've fixed it so that he can't."

"Are you worried that he might still be there?"

"If he is, he's hiding because I don't see him."

"I want you to stay there. Do not leave the garage."

"Of course, I'm not leaving. I thought you were tracking him. Why should I call you and tell you he's been here? You should know where he is. You said you would handle this!"

"I know, but there's been a slight problem… I've lost the tracking signal on his car."

"Small? You're kidding me. When were you planning to tell me this?"

"I knew you were safe in the garage. I didn't want you to panic, and I'm telling you now. Clay will fix this problem. I'm on my way to your place."

"Why are you coming here?"

"To protect you."

"I'm safely barricaded. It's far more important that you get Waylon."

"I realize that, but Waylon is after both of us now. He'll assume I'll return to your place. If I can't track him, it makes the most sense for us to be together at a place we know he'll visit."

"Then why didn't you come back sooner?"

"You told me you didn't want Waylon dispensed with on your property, right?"

"I don't care about that anymore. Now, I don't care where it happens. It just needs to happen. And if you can't do it, I need to get a restraining order so he can be arrested. I know you don't want the police involved, but I have no choice."

"Don't do that, Thane. If a restraining order gets Waylon arrested, he'll be released quickly, and you will have angered him more. Meanwhile, he will have told them everything he's seen in your garage. You'll have no guarantee of justice. The system could backfire on you, and your life will never be private again. Investigator's notes about your shop will become part of the public record."

"Stop it!" Thane shouted.

"Okay, so if you let me visit you, you won't need the police."

"I should never have let him go when we had him. Now, he also has Gus. I accept the blame for doing that, but you said you could resolve this problem."

"If you are no longer concerned about something happening on your property, why not use the trap floor again?"

"He won't fall for that again."

"That's why I want to be there with you. Our best chance to resolve this problem to your satisfaction is by handling it together. Let me help you."

"Fine," Thane said, sighing.

"And, Thane, there's another thing… I know you don't like guns, but—"

"I don't care."

"Pardon?"

"Bring as many guns as you want to. This has to end."

"I'm on my way."

"Make sure no one sees you coming onto my property."

"Of course. I'll park at a safe distance."

Thane said, "Okay, but be sure to call me before you come to the garage. I need to open the door for you."

Morana said, "I don't want to risk attracting any attention. I'll just let myself in if you leave the door unlocked."

"No! I need to open the door for you. It's crucial that you don't try to let yourself in."

"Why not?"

"Why can't you just comply with my request?" Thane shouted.

Morana briefly pulled the phone from her ear. "I'm sorry. I'll call."

"When can you be here?"

"Give me twenty minutes."

"Hurry."

"I will."

Thane hung up and looked down at Gus's full bowl of food. He went to the door and cracked it open as much as the blocks would allow. He put his face to it and whistled, hoping the tuft of fur he found on the knob had a benign explanation. He wanted his hunch to be wrong and to see Gus finally come bounding inside. But in the backyard's stillness, there was no sign of the cat anywhere. Thane closed and locked the door.

He spent the next few minutes positioning and measuring a notched block he had brought up from the sub-lair hours ago. This block matched the width and length of the one beside the entry door, but this one was notched evenly along the edges and was thinner. It weighed only 2 tons, which was plenty for its intended purpose. Thane triple-checked its measurements before leveling it over the trap floor and hoisting it to the ceiling.

As he walked back toward his work countertop, the phone rang. Thane hurried to it. The caller ID displayed *UNKNOWN*.

Morana had said she would need 20 minutes to arrive, so the call shouldn't be from her, but missing an important call from her was too risky.

"Hello…"

"Is this Thane?"

"Who's calling?" Thane asked. His stomach clenched even before he heard the reply.

"Thane, this is Waylon. Don't hang up."

Waylon's voice sent prickles up Thane's back.

"What do you want?"

"You may not believe it, but this call is friendly."

"You're right, I don't believe it."

"Thank you for making a deal with me. You had me in a tough spot, and it was admirable of you to let me go, given how I've treated you over the years."

"Part of that deal was to never hear from you again, so it looks like you've already broken it."

"If you will hear me out, you won't mind that I called."

"Say what you have to say."

"I want to make amends with you. After you released me, I started thinking about the many horrible things I did to you when we were children. I'm not proud of them. And I also realize that my behavior toward you after we connected at the job fair only continued that abusive pattern. I want to tell you I'm sorry and ask you to forgive me."

Thane stared down, frozen.

"Are you there?" Waylon asked.

"Yes. I'm just... surprised."

"I expected that, and I wish there was a way I could show you that my apology is sincere."

"You can show it by returning my cat."

Waylon paused. "What are you talking about?"

"You know what I'm talking about—I found the fur on the doorknob. I saw your footprints. Your apology sets me up for another prank—a horrible one."

"Thane, I'm sorry you feel that way. It's too bad that your cat is missing. I wish I could help you with that."

"I think you can."

"Sounds like there's no chance I can change your mind, so we can end this call. But before we hang up, I wanted to tell you that you terrified the shit out of me with the dropping floor."

"I was only trying to defend myself."

"I know. Still, that was amazing... What was that?"

"Is there anything else?"

"Oh, come on, Thane. Listen, I've already apologized for all I've done to you. If you can find it in your heart to forgive me, there is no doubt I could be incredibly useful to you."

"How?"

"Protection."

"The only person I need protection from is you."

"Listen, Sykes, there's probably nothing I can do to change what you think of me anymore, so let's set our relationship aside and look at this from a practical standpoint. You've got something spectacular going on in your garage. I don't think anyone has ever seen anything like it—I sure as hell haven't. If word got out that you can do what I saw you do, you would need legal protection from people who want to steal it from you and people who want to exploit you."

Thane briefly pulled the phone from his ear and rolled his eyes. "People like you?"

"It's not exploitation if all involved parties are compensated fairly."

"First, I'm not interested. Second, you are the last person I would call if I needed a lawyer."

"Fine, I deserved that. Hear me out. I know that a partnership with me sounds crazy, but if you look at your options practically, I've made a tremendous amount of money by protecting the interests of my clients. As my radio slogan says, I help them get what they deserve and could do the same for you. Could you think of the amazing story we'd have? Two kids who grew up together in an abusive relationship make amends as adults in a partnership overseeing a technology that could be worth billions."

"I don't care about money. I don't want to work with you."

"That's too bad, Thane. No hard feelings, though. Good luck finding Gus."

"How did you know my cat's name?"

Waylon coughed.

"Answer me!"

"I heard that woman—your so-called girlfriend—say the cat's name while I was there."

"I don't remember that."

"Listen, Thane, you're under a great deal of stress. Take some time to reconsider my generous offer if you need to, but I can't tell you how long I'll leave it on the table. I can tell you that it would be a lot easier for me to keep your magic floor a secret if I had a vested interest in it."

"You think a threat will change my mind?"

"Not a threat, an offer—and one with huge stakes. Accept it, and not only will you benefit more than you could have dreamed, but I'll also protect you and might even help you find Gus. It's that important."

"I have to go."

"Sure thing, Thane. I have every confidence that you'll do the right thing."

Chapter 26

MORANA SLIPPED TO the side of Thane's house unnoticed. Instead of walking to the garage along the driveway, she sidestepped between Thane's and his neighbor's houses on the opposite side. She squatted when she reached the back and looked out to the garage. She dialed Thane's number and heard the faint ringing in the shop.

"Hello."

"It's Mo. I'm here."

"Where?"

"I'm beside the house at the back. I can see the garage. The front and backyards are clear."

"Okay, come to the door now."

Morana emerged and crossed the backyard, sidestepping the solar panels on her way to the garage door. As she neared the door, Thane opened it.

Thane motioned for her to hurry inside, then locked the door behind her.

She wore a black leather jacket over a turquoise lace-up top, jeans, and black boots and had her bag—heavier than usual—slung over her shoulder. Her hair was tattered. Several scratches lined the side of her face from her ear to her chin. Her left eye was slightly swollen.

He looked her up and down and said, "Your injuries are worse than you described."

Morana leaned to rub her knee. "I'm fine. I'm a quick healer. Any sign of Gus?"

"No," he said, his expression tightening as his missing cat's anxiety rushed back. Thane also wore his own physical signs of wear. Smudged dirt and rock powder clung to sweat patches on his shirt, and his afro was misshapen and dusty.

Morana hugged him gently and brushed off his shoulder with her hand. "Wow, you've been busy." She looked around at the nearly empty garage. Under their feet was a new blue throw rug that covered the entryway and partially overlapped the trap floor. On the opposite side of the garage, a new, larger area rug also covered the seams of the Gateway block. Several long sheets were tacked to a rafter beam and hung like a curtain to conceal Thane's work countertop.

Thane said, "A lot has changed here since your last visit." He patted his hair.

"I can see that. Why have you gutted the place?"

"In the photograph I discovered on Waylon's phone, all the objects in this garage are clearly identifiable, so I have changed or removed everything."

"I can't blame you, but that probably wasn't necessary," Morana said, staring at the makeshift curtain. She masked her urgency as she strolled to where she had placed her micro camera concealed in a pen. The pen should have captured some good footage if he hadn't hung the sheets before starting work. She took hold of the curtain's edge and pulled the corner back. Thane's work countertop was bare. "Where did you put everything? Your tools, your supplies... And even your pens!" She pointed to where the critical pen holder had been.

"I told you—nothing remains that was shown in the photograph."

"So, you just threw it all away?" Morana said.

"Some of it. Other items I set aside."

"But where did you put those items?"

"Why are you so concerned about my things?"

"I'm sorry—I'm just surprised because I know how meticulous you are and how important your tools are to your projects."

"What I've done won't hinder my projects."

Morana's attention shifted to four large new blocks inside the large roll-up door.

Thane noticed where she looked and said, "Eight tons each." He went to them, pulled off a towel draped over the top, and mopped his face. "These will keep a truck out—probably a bulldozer."

"Thane, don't you think that is a little overkill?"

"Actually, I second-guessed the idea until Waylon called."

"He did? When?"

"About an hour after you and I talked." Thane folded the towel and placed it on the floor beside the blocks.

"Tell me what he said!" Morana waved her hand, urging him to hurry.

"He thanked me for the deal that set him free. He said he doesn't have Gus and wants to help me protect my work."

"Like you would ever partner with him," Morana laughed.

Thane waited for her to finish and said, "I have given Waylon what he wants."

Morana took a slow, deep breath through her nose, controlling her reaction. "Are you serious? What, exactly, do you plan to give him?"

Thane slid his hands into his pockets and said, "He wants the secret of moving the blocks along with my agreement that he can help me with the patent."

Morana felt her heart pounding. She tried to mask her visceral reaction by saying, "Thane, I'm shocked. I can't believe you would go along."

Thane shrugged and said, "When I refused, he threatened to go public with what he observed in my garage. I don't underestimate what he's willing to do to get what he wants. Waylon followed this pattern when we were young. He'd lure me with kindness or some generous offer—which was always a snare designed to position me as the brunt of a practical joke. He would skip the joke and retaliate if I didn't respond to his offer the way he wanted me to. He *always* had some other way to get to me. In this case, his retaliation involves Gus—I'm sure of it. Complying with his demand is the only way I can save Gus."

"But he told you he doesn't have Gus."

"He's a liar."

Morana cleared her throat and said, "So, how will you get him this information about how you move the blocks?"

"I've already given it to him."

"Really?" Morana said, slipping her sweating hands into her back pockets.

"That's right."

She cocked her head. "I don't understand. How could you have given it to him?"

"Email."

Morana laughed nervously as she looked around the shop. "You have a hidden computer somewhere in here?"

"No, I used his own phone. I sent it to the same address he sent the photos to."

Morana covered her mouth. "Thane, that is a huge mistake! Someone else could see it."

"When I first discovered the photos on Waylon's phone, you told me not to worry about them. In fact, you said it was doubtful that anyone other than Waylon would ever see them. Why is this different?"

"Unlikely differs from impossible. The risk of someone potentially seeing the photos of your shop differs from someone learning your secret."

Thane smiled at her. "Why do you seem so panicked?"

"No, I'm frustrated. This is the second time you've made a decision that only benefits Waylon! Where is his phone? Let me see it. Maybe it didn't transmit."

Thane gently kicked the block beside him a few times. "You really want to see what I sent him, not whether it transmitted. Isn't that true?"

"Of course, I'm interested, but what's most important is whether Waylon has seen it yet." She wrung her hands. "I can't believe you would use email to transmit your secret to anyone, especially *him*."

"You don't need to worry. I'm confident about what I've done."

"You also felt confident about setting him free when we had him, remember?"

"I'm willing to own that mistake, and it won't happen again." Thane went to the cabinets on the far wall and opened the bottom drawer. He removed Waylon's phone, unlocked the screen, and set it on the countertop. "Come see."

Morana went to him. She picked up the phone and opened an email with the subject: *Ready to deal.*

The message read:

Dear Waylon,

After careful reconsideration, I hereby agree to partner with you to patent my solid aggregate mineral conveyance system. This document provides a preliminary summary of the coral rock manipulation you observed in my garage.

As a show of good faith, I'll provide the following summary of the physics involved:

The key to reversing the gravitational influence on coral limestone is magnetic vectoring using the refraction generated by the electrically conductive coil attached to a modulatory synductor device. When geographically positioned on one of the earth's diamagnetic vortexes, the gravitational force exerted on the object can be manipulated.

When we meet, I will provide complete details, demonstrations, and diagrams illustrating the precise tools required.

Sincerely,

Thane M. Sykes

Morana's heart pounded harder as she read the words. When she finished, she swallowed and then used brute force to contain the excitement in her voice. "So, is this an accurate summary of how you move the blocks?"

Thane grinned at her momentarily and then said, "Of course not! Do you think there's any chance I would give Waylon a crumb of what he wants?" He laughed.

"Oh… good," Morana said, masking her disappointment.

"This agreement buys time for Gus and will bring Waylon to meet with me. After I know Gus is safe, I'm prepared to deal with Waylon in my way. Thank you for your encouragement. A week ago, I would never have considered using my resources to end my nightmare with Waylon, but you showed me how effective, undiscoverable, and safe it would be. I won't be victimized anymore." Thane's voice carried a dark tone Morana hadn't heard before.

"Thane, let's talk this through," she said.

"No, I've decided. What did you call it? V-1? I'm committed and won't squander another opportunity. The only thing that could change my plan is if you keep your word to take care of Waylon beforehand while keeping Gus safe."

"Thane, this could backfire," Morana said. "You shouldn't take him on alone. He's dangerous. If things go wrong, he could take much more from you than a school lunch. He'll kill you."

"Not if I'm prepared," Thane said, putting his hands on his hips.

"I admire your confidence, but what if your plan doesn't work?" Morana thought momentarily, adding, "I don't think it's a good idea to give him misinformation about your secret. What if he asks for a demonstration?"

"Are you suggesting that I tell him the truth about it?"

"Maybe not completely…"

Thane gave her a quizzical look. "You've gone from telling me to kill him to giving him at least a portion of the real secret? What changed?"

Morana thought for a moment and then said, "It was Gus. Gus changes everything. Before, I didn't care how your decisions made Waylon feel. But now, if he really has Gus, then enraging him will be tragic."

"You'll have to trust that I've minimized my risk," Thane said. "When I have Gus safely home, Waylon better hope that a tiny tuft of fur is all Gus has suffered."

"Do you mind sharing your plan?" Morana asked.

"Follow me." Thane led her toward the entry door. "Wait there," he said, pointing to a place just outside the edge of the entryway and trap floor.

Morana did so, and after planting her feet, she looked up and noticed the additional notched block hoisted near the ceiling, parallel to the floor. Except for one wire connected from the block's corner across the rafters to the black box in another part of the ceiling, she couldn't determine what suspended it in midair. "What is that new block for?" she asked.

"It's a trap floor improvement." He pointed to a bent nail protruding from the wall inside the door. A keyring loaded with many keys hung from it. "This nail hook is actually a weight-sensitive lever." Thane pinched the keyring and gently lifted it. The nail hook moved up. He handed her the keyring.

Morana took it and frowned. "I'm sorry, I don't understand…"

Thane pointed to the new blue throw rug that covered the entryway. "The trap floor is activated and calibrated so that anything heavier than a shoe will trigger it."

"But if the door is blocked, how will the trap floor ever be used?" Morana asked.

"That's the point," Thane said. "I'm not going to obstruct this entry door with a block. The locked doorknob will protect law-abiding people from any danger. Any person who breaks in will deserve what they will experience."

Morana said, "That's a beautiful thing. But do you honestly think that if Waylon were to break in, he would go anywhere near this trap floor again?"

"If that memory keeps him away, great. But this isn't just for Waylon. You said he has connections. This way, I'll be prepared to defend myself against him or anyone he sends to break in."

"Sweetheart, if you trap another person, that's another potential lawsuit."

"Like you told me before, that's only true if that person is ever found."

"Wow," Morana said, stepping back. "You are serious, aren't you?"

"I've never been more serious."

"But what if you trap someone, and they send a text or make a call?"

Thane pointed to the notched block above them and said, "That block automatically drops to seal the trap floor shaft within eight seconds. I've tested this, and although it's enough time to press a speed dial, it isn't enough time to complete a connection. The panic and confusion experienced by the trapped person will make it virtually impossible for them to compose and send a text message in less than eight seconds."

"Unbelievable," Morana said, moving for a better angle.

"And there's something else." Thane walked across the shop toward his work countertop.

"Wait! The keys," Morana said. "You didn't deactivate the trap floor."

"I know. Be sure not to step on it."

Morana backed away from the area rug and dropped the keys into her bag before following Thane across the garage to where he stood beside his cabinets.

He grabbed the corner of a second new area rug covering the Gateway block and flipped it back, revealing its seam. He pointed to the faint outline of a new square at its corner, the depth and width of a phone booth. "Stand there," he said.

Morana positioned her feet on it.

"Do you see the seam?" he asked, tapping the square's edge with his toe.

"Yes."

Thane moved close enough to her so that their stomachs almost touched. He tapped his toe near the corner. "Stomp your heel there."

"Will something fall?" Morana asked, looking up into the ceiling rafters.

"Yes, trust me."

She tapped her heel on it. Nothing happened.

"Harder," Thane said.

She stomped harder. Nothing.

"When your heel comes down, keep more weight on it."

On her third stomp, Morana shrieked when the square they stood on sank into the floor. She reached for the edge and Thane grabbed her hand, stopping her. "Don't touch the shaft wall."

"What happened?" Morana asked as they dropped, descending into the darkness of the shaft.

"Your heel, and knowing where to stomp it, is your sub-lair entry key. Rather than having to raise the Gateway block on every descent to the sub-lair, I cut a smaller lift through it. Now the sub-lair is accessible while the Gateway block remains in place."

"So, you're going to allow me to operate the lift?"

"We'll see how it goes."

Through the opening above them, they heard a smooth whirring of air. "Thane, you forgot to crack the garage doors," Morana said.

"It's okay. I installed a new venting system in the ceiling," Thane said. "Now I can keep the garage doors and windows locked while going below."

Morana took his hand as they sank into the darkest portion of their ride.

Thane pulled a flashlight from his pocket and turned it on. He instructed Morana to press each shaft wall panel they came to as they continued their descent.

When they finally slid down into the sub-lair's lift chamber, they stepped off.

"How do I go back up?" Morana asked.

"With me."

"What if I'm alone?"

"I don't expect you to be. But if that happens, you'll wait here for me."

"Every time?"

"Yes."

"But—why don't you show me how to make the lift go up? Having to escort me each time would be inconvenient for you."

"It's not. I'll take you to the surface whenever you need to go."

"So if I'm down here alone, I'm trapped until you free me?"

"That's one way to look at it."

"Sweetheart, as wonderful as it is, being in the sub-lair with no way for me to get out on my own makes me uncomfortable."

"Then you don't have to come down."

"But I want to. I was hoping that you would—"

"Why don't you respect me?" Thane snapped. "I will take you to the surface when needed. It won't be an inconvenience, and it won't be difficult."

"I'm sorry," Morana said. She squeezed his hand. "Please don't be angry. It's just that I worry about what would happen if something happened to you down here."

"We've talked about this. What could happen to me?"

"Nothing—I hope. But accidents are—"

"I don't have accidents. No one is more careful than me," Thane said, letting go of her hand. "The one-way access you have is best for you." He spread his fingers on the chamber wall. "These rocks are unforgiving. Unless you understand them, being alone in the sub-lair is dangerous."

Morana looked around the chamber, considering Thane's ominous words for a moment, and then, in a subdued voice, said, "I'm fine with being here only with you."

"Good."

The empty lift slid upward into the shaft, followed by its solid rock base that sped up. Morana watched Thane, carefully noting his every move. She studied his hands each time they went into his pockets. She memorized the precise areas of the walls he touched and every place he stepped. Nothing he did seemed to be a trigger for any mechanical action that occurred in the sub-lair.

They left the elevator chamber and walked the corridor to Thane's bedroom chamber. Thane plopped onto the edge of his mattress and folded his hands. The tension on his face hadn't subsided since he opened the shop door for her when she first arrived.

Morana dropped her bag on the floor beside the door and came to him, kneeling before him. She took off her jacket and draped it on the mattress. She rested her hands on his legs and said, "You look so stressed."

"Waylon gone forever would be the ultimate relief."

"Yes, I want you to know I haven't given up. I'm confident that between the two of us, that will happen. Meanwhile, I want to talk to you about something else."

Thane looked at her suspiciously.

"Your stack of blocks on the trap floor is fine, but we should further reduce your vulnerability up on the surface."

Thane leaned back on his elbows. "How?"

"I'm going to suggest something, and I don't want you to be upset at me for it."

"I'm listening."

"I think we should introduce Clay to the sub-lair."

Thane looked at her in disbelief. "Are you crazy? After you admitted you don't trust him?"

"I can explain if you—"

"You go from telling me you have a way to reduce my stress, then you suggest bringing an untrustworthy person into my most private world? That's the opposite of easing my stress." Thane pushed her hands away and got up. He went to the doorway of the aquifer room and leaned against it.

Morana said, "When you are down here, you are totally unaware of what's happening up in the garage or anywhere else on your property."

"That's by design. I want to be fully disconnected while down here.

When I'm on the surface, I crave the privacy of my sub-lair."

"But you cannot know what is happening in your garage until you literally slide into it."

"That's not true," Thane said. "If I want to hear what's happening in the garage, I can install a vent for that purpose."

"And listen to it constantly? You need a notification system. A phone down here or some way to communicate would enhance your security, not detract from it."

Thane stared at her before coming back to sit beside her.

She put her arm around him. "What if you were down here when Waylon made his visit? You could have known about it the moment it happened. If Clay had installed cameras, you'd have irrefutable proof of his visit and trespassing. You could have told me sooner, giving me the advantage of ending this nightmare for you."

"Why do you suddenly trust Clay?"

"I can make it worth his while to keep your work secret. He's a useful asset to you."

Thane sighed, fell back onto the mattress, and rolled to his side.

She laid beside him, stroked his back, and pulled a green flower stem from his hair. "I didn't know you had plants in here."

"It's from the new flowers in front of the house."

"I thought I noticed something different in front. You planted those?"

"Yes."

"What were you doing outside? Thane, that was dangerous!"

"I had no choice."

"But I told you to stay locked away. That was a risky move with Waylon on the loose."

"My uncle told me to plant them."

"That couldn't wait a few days?"

"No. When he wants something, he wants it immediately."

"I'm sorry. I don't understand the connection between flowers and your uncle."

"My uncle calls all the shots. He owns the property."

"I thought it was yours."

"Originally, it belonged to my mother. She died when I was 18 years old. I inherited it but couldn't afford to continue making her mortgage payments. My uncle helped to keep possession and eventually had me sign papers to update the title. What I didn't know was that the papers he told me to sign transferred ownership to him. He told me I could live here on the condition that I maintain every inch of the property to his satisfaction."

"You don't pay him rent?"

"He says I don't make enough to pay him what he would charge. He said upkeep and chores were enough, and at first, that was true. I mowed the lawn weekly, kept the house clean inside, and took care of any necessary maintenance. But he's become more demanding. He wants all the outside windows washed inside and out weekly. I scrub every inch of the house's interior. He had some of his mail delivered here, and he makes me sort and neatly stack it on the table by the front door. I take restaurant delivery food to him at least twice a week and clean up the bedroom each time he visits with one of his... guests."

"So, you get to live here in exchange for being a slave."

"I have to do what he says. If I complain, he threatens to evict me. He doesn't know about the sub-lair, but he knows how desperately I want to stay here, and he has leveraged that to his advantage."

"Have you considered finding work to make enough money to pay him rent?"

Thane thought for a moment. "My uncle prefers the current arrangement. If I tried to change it, he would make the rent higher than I could pay. I think he enjoys the power my situation gives him."

"Do you have any other source of income?"

"I told you I don't have much money. That was the whole reason for helping me with the Everett case."

"What about the car washes at the office?"

"I don't get the car wash money. Sometimes, I get tips, but my uncle collects and pockets the staff's payments for my work. He says those earnings still wouldn't cover rent."

Morana scooted closer to Thane, laid down, and slipped her arms around him. She kissed the back of his neck and said, "My feelings are rarely wrong, and I have a feeling we're going to solve all of your problems. Meanwhile, let's get you relaxed."

Chapter 27

THE NEXT MORNING, Thane woke up with Morana's arm draped over his bare chest.

Morana caressed his neck with the back of her fingers while he stared up at the ceiling. "You are so much more relaxed, but I think you could use some more relaxation."

Thane said, "I have a lot on my—"

"Sh, sh, sh," she touched his lips. "Don't bring back the stress." She gently kissed his ear and then his lips.

Thane got up and picked up a towel from the floor. He went into the aquifer room, kneeled, and washed his face.

When he returned, Morana had put on her jeans and was lacing her boots.

"I need to go up to the surface a few times," Thane said. "I have some projects I want to finish today." He removed a shirt and trousers from a plastic bag in the corner and put them on.

"Do you mind if I stay with you?"

"I expected that you'd go out to look for Waylon. Don't you need to know if Clay has reestablished contact with the tracker?"

"We both know that Waylon will look for us here. It makes more sense for me to be here with you." She stood from the mattress and came to him. "My priority is to keep you safe."

"Some of the work I need to do is private," Thane said.

"I won't disturb you—I promise."

"It would be better if you just came back later. I need privacy because—" The conversation was interrupted by a sharp jolt in the floor, followed by the hiss of rushing air outside the bedroom.

"What is that?" Morana said, backing to the wall. She spread her arms out on it.

Thane ran to the open doorway and leaned out into the corridor. The hiss subsided. He looked at Morana and said, "The trap floor dropped."

"Are you sure?"

"Yes." Thane disappeared into the corridor.

"Thane, wait!" Morana said, running after him.

As they entered the lift chamber, the rock column supporting the lift was already sliding downward within the wall. Morana had observed Thane all the way from the bedroom. She had lost sight of Thane only a few seconds after he ducked out of the bedroom. Now, his hands were at his sides. He hadn't concealed them or pressed any surfaces on the wall on their way, nor did he step or stomp on any area of the lift chamber floor. It was as though the chamber sensed Thane's approach and automatically began lowering the lift for him. They stood, watching the sliding rock.

"How did you activate the lift?" Morana asked.

"I told you—that's not something you need to learn."

When the lift's opening slid into view, he stepped aside and motioned for Morana to board first.

"Why are we going to the surface?" Morana asked. "Wouldn't it be safer to remove whomever from the sub-lair chamber like we did before?"

"I need to secure the garage and verify that the trap floor isn't still open. Let's go." Thane pointed, urging her to the lift.

She backed onto it, watching his hands and his feet.

"You're staring," he said as he joined her.

"Sorry. What if there was more than one person, and they weren't all trapped?" Morana asked.

Thane put his finger to his lips for her to be quiet. He looked up through the darkness at the shaft's opening, a tiny square of light 100 feet above them. He froze for a few moments, cupping his ear.

"The garage is quiet. If multiple people broke in, those who weren't trapped would call for help." He dropped his hand to his side. The lift ascended.

She took his hand and whispered, "Even if it's only one person, assume whoever is trapped is armed. We need to be careful."

"No, the person who broke in should have been more careful. And you don't need to be quiet. Whoever is trapped in it cannot hear us."

"What if it isn't Waylon?"

"I don't care who it is. You watched me lock the garage door knob. Whoever is trapped broke in."

"Thane, slow down. All I'm asking is that you first make sure it's Waylon."

"So what if it isn't? You told me he has connections. I can tell you that whoever is on that trap floor will be sorry."

"How? Thane, please tell me what you're planning."

"The lift block you saw hoisted doesn't overlap the trap floor shaft. It's not a lid. I designed it to slide into the shaft like a syringe plunger."

"You're planning to… crush the person?"

"Like a bug," he replied.

A small laugh escaped Morana.

"You don't believe me?" Thane said.

"It's just that I'm surprised by whatever has come over you since my last visit. When I first suggested that you dispense with Waylon when we had him the first time, you couldn't buy into the idea. When I offered to do it, your face looked like you would throw up. Now, you're willing to single-handedly execute him?"

A band of light reflected from the shaft wall slid down Thane's front. "I've put a lot of thought into this. I don't have it in me to kill someone—directly. I certainly couldn't shoot anyone. But when I hear that some monster somewhere has paid the ultimate price for victimizing someone else, I have to admit that I don't feel bad about it. I'm happy for the monster's victims. Most people would admit they feel the same—if honest."

"Then what stopped you the first time?"

"I was worried I'd feel ashamed for doing it with my hands—while he watched. This is another reason I hoped you would take care of it for me."

"If Waylon is trapped, just take him below and let me finish him. You won't have to worry about any guilt."

"No, I've decided to deal with him myself. The trap floor method allows him to be crushed by accident. I won't see or hear any of it."

"So, he dies. You don't see it happen, and you're fine with that?"

"That buffer makes all the difference."

Morana squeezed his hand and said, "I'm glad you're not into bomb-making."

As they neared the surface, the growing ambient light brought the details of Thane's face into view.

Thane said, "What you told me about standing up for myself makes sense to me now. Waylon will never stop bullying me. He will torment me until the day I die. You helped me realize that the sub-lair is the ultimate way to maintain my secrecy. But if you are wrong, and what I'm about to do leads to an investigation, I can promise you that the sub-lair will never be found."

"I love that you want to stand up for yourself, and I don't blame you for feeling as adamant as you do. But you still must be careful. We should talk this through together. Don't let your emotions make you reckless."

"It was reckless for me to let him go the first time. There's nothing more to discuss. I told you I would correct that mistake." Thane's voice quivered, and he swallowed. "I'm tired of being afraid." He stared upward.

"Are you sure you want to do this?"

"There's no other option. I hate him." Thane squeezed the words through gritted teeth. "Why does it feel like you're suddenly dissuading me?"

"I'm not. When you told me how Waylon treated you for so many years, I wanted to make him pay for it. I advise you to be cautious in case you've trapped someone other than Waylon."

"Who else would it be?"

"What if the police came back? I've never seen you this worked up, and I'm just saying we need to have a plan before you drop... the plunger."

"The only other person who would want to get into the garage is my uncle, and I made sure he doesn't have a key. He doesn't know how to pick a lock, and he wouldn't break in because he's too cheap to replace a doorknob."

Morana hesitated and said, "Thane, this is a perfect example of a situation I've been trying to describe. With Clay's help, you could already know who is on the trap floor," Morana said.

"Stop pushing for cameras!" Thane yelled. "You know how I feel about them."

"I'm sorry! Calm down," Morana said, raising her hands.

The lift came to a stop in the garage. The whir of rushing air that spun the new turbine vents in the ceiling went silent. The garage entry door was ajar. Thane hurried toward it.

"Thane, wait!" Morana ran after him and grabbed his arm.

He pulled his arm free and stopped. While staring at the opening left by the sunken trap floor, he said, "Did you bring your gun?"

She felt under her waistband. "No, I didn't. It's in my bag below. We should go get it before you do anything."

"No. We don't need it."

They went to the edge of the opening. The lid block had dropped precisely as Thane had planned, stopping a few feet below the surface. They heard the faint calls of a man's voice from below it. "Thane, is that you? Buddy, help me!"

Thane looked at Morana.

She closed her eyes and rubbed her temples. "It's Clay."

Chapter 28

THANE KICKED THE entry door and then shook his head as he stared at the trap floor.

Morana said, "Let's get him out."

"I don't think so," Thane said.

"Of course, we have to get him out. It's Clay!"

"Buddy, please!" Clay shouted from below.

"You broke in," Thane shouted back. "You violated my privacy."

"I'm sorry—I'm *so* sorry."

Morana approached Thane and quietly said, "Sweetheart, we need him. I know you don't want cameras. I know you are angry, but he's valuable, and we can't make things worse than they are. Please trust me on this."

"Are you guys still there?" Clay hollered.

"Shut up!" Thane said.

Morana's head jerked, surprised by Thane's sharp reprimand.

Thane walked to the opposite side of the garage and slowly came back, rubbing his chin.

Morana quietly watched, not wanting to trigger him again.

"I need to raise the lid block," Thane said as he went to the door.

"Are you going to make me step outside?" Morana asked.

"Unnecessary this time," Thane said. He flipped a switch on the wall. The garage went completely dark.

"Wait, what are you doing?" Morana asked, straining to see.

Thane didn't answer, but his footsteps echoed as they scuffed several times.

"Thane? Sweetheart?" Morana said.

The faint hum came from above. A few moments later, the lights came on. The lid block had moved up to its original position near the ceiling.

Clay, now visible, looked up from the sunken trap floor. "Jesus Christ, you scared the shit out of me. Get me out of here—please."

Thane kneeled at the shaft's edge and shouted, "What were you doing here?"

Morana moved closer and peered over the edge, standing a safe distance from it.

"I was looking for you and Mo," Clay said.

"You should have called," Thane said.

"I did call! Check your voicemail. I left a message before I got here."

"So, because I don't answer, you think that gives you the right to break in?"

"I told you not to come here," Morana told Clay.

"I was worried that maybe Waylon had gotten to the both of you and hid you here."

"Hid us where?"

Morana whispered, "He means the garage. Sweetheart, he's an idiot, but he meant no harm."

"Quiet!" Thane snapped at her. "Let him answer."

Morana stepped back from him with her hands up.

"What do you mean by hide?" Thane repeated. "Where would Waylon hide us, Clay?" Thane looked over his shoulder at Morana.

"I don't know," Clay said. "Somewhere in the garage. Maybe he wanted to see you move the blocks."

"What do you know about blocks? I've shown you only one block."

Thane turned to Morana and glared at her. "You lied to me."

"No, I didn't!" she said. "Clay saw you lift one block. You showed him, remember? Clay knows nothing else."

Thane's expression didn't soften. He grabbed his hair and said, "Why can't everyone leave me alone?"

"Buddy, calm down," Clay said. "If you get me out of here, I can explain, and it will all make sense, I swear. Mo, I thought we were working on this project together."

"What project?" Thane asked, giving Morana a new quizzical look.

"Now is not the time," Morana shouted down to Clay.

"No, tell me. What project are you working on together?" Thane asked.

"Clay refers to our efforts to help you with the Waylon situation. We call it a project," Morana replied.

"That's right," Clay said. "But she won't tell me anything about what you two have been doing. Please, I'm begging you, get me out of this dungeon. I'm getting claustrophobic."

"He's learned his lesson, and the guy is terrified," Morana said, pointing to Clay.

Thane said, "He's no better than Waylon for breaking in."

"But this is different," Morana said. "Clay doesn't want to hurt you.

He isn't a bully. There's a tremendous difference."

"You'd be surprised," Thane said. He stepped back from the edge of the trap floor and walked to another part of the wall next to the trap floor.

"Be still," Thane said to Clay. He then spread his hands on the wall between two wooden support beams. The faint hum overhead resumed, and air rushed out of the garage as the turbine vent above them spun. A brief, soft scrape echoed from the trap floor shaft before it silently rose.

Morana watched Thane, trying to figure out how he had used his hands to trigger the trap floor to rise. Aside from merely placing his hands on the wall, Thane had visibly manipulated no other object.

He stepped back and shook his head, looking down into the dark shaft. "I hope I don't regret this," he said.

"You won't," Morana said.

Clay's head, shoulders, and then his torso rose into view. Clay took a running jump to the edge of the trap floor, where he climbed out beside Morana. He brushed himself off, looking down at his temporary dungeon. "God, that was awful," he said.

The base of the trap floor slowed to become perfectly level with the garage floor.

Clay said, "Thank you, buddy. You gotta understand that I'm on your side."

"No, I don't. You had no right to come in here without permission," Thane said. "It's disrespectful." Thane turned his back to Clay, and while looking up to examine the wire connected to the notched block, he said, "You're lucky."

"I'm sorry. It will never happen again... Would you be willing to show us how you lowered that?" Clay said, pointing to the trap floor.

Morana cleared her throat. When Clay looked, she widened her eyes.

"What?" Clay said. "I'm not allowed to ask?"

Thane walked onto the trap floor and picked up the area rug. He shook it out, spreading it evenly between the trap floor seams. He looked at Clay and said, "Mo tells me you could enhance security for me here."

"Of course," Clay said, beaming. "Whatever you need regarding surveillance, background information on anyone, and electronics. Are you open to that?"

"Maybe," Thane said, interlocking his fingers behind his back.

"Since you've already seen this shaft, I suppose it wouldn't hurt to show you more about how things work here. Let's take a ride." He pointed to the trap floor rug.

"No—no," Clay said. "I don't know if I could take that again."

Thane stepped into the center of the rug. "If the two of you want to learn, join me." Thane pointed beside his feet.

"Oh, come on, Clay. He's giving us an opportunity," Morana said as she came and stood beside Thane.

Clay slowly stepped back onto the trap floor, outstretching his arms to prepare for the floor to drop again.

"Not too close to the edge. It could be dangerous," Thane said, pointing to where he wanted them to stand.

Morana and Clay moved to the center.

"Excellent. Don't be alarmed—you're going to feel some motion." Thane moved to the edge of the trap floor. He squatted slightly and then leaped from it the instant it dropped.

Morana shrieked and dove for the edge as they went down. Her fingertips caught the rim but couldn't support her weight, and she fell. Clay also lunged to grab the edge, but his fingers fell short. After the trap floor's initial drop of 20 feet, it slowly sank, dropping them into the darkness.

Morana yelled, "Thane! What are you doing?"

"Goddammit, Thane!" Clay said.

Thane looked down at them from above, his toes jutting over the edge. Adrenaline had him breathing hard. He stepped away from the edge, disappearing from their view.

"Thane, sweetheart," Morana called out to him. "I don't know what you're doing, but you've chosen a bad time for a joke. Please bring us back up."

As they sank deeper, the shaft darkened. Clay shouted, "Buddy, C'mon! What's going on? We are only trying to help you, and this isn't funny!"

"Shh," Morana hushed him. The trap floor bumped to a stop. Above, they heard the metallic jostle of a wire as Thane's arm came into view, reaching to check its connection to the notched lid block suspended overhead. Moments later, the lid block slowly descended.

"Oh, God! No!" Morana yelled.

"Jesus Christ," Clay said.

The lid block stopped descending knee high above the trap floor shaft. Thane reached out and gently spread his fingers on the side of the lid block, its corners dipping and rising as he manually positioned it over the shaft opening. He held it at shoulder height and moved it with the ease of adjusting a cardboard box. He looked down at them, and his voice echoed in the shaft as he said, "I'm sorry for this. I need to leave because

I don't want to watch. I promise it will be quick."

"Thane, please!" Morana said, slapping the shaft wall with her palm. "What has happened to you?"

Thane disappeared from view for a few moments as Morana and Clay shouted, pleading for mercy.

Thane came back into view and shined a flashlight down at them. "You want to know what's happened to me? I'll tell you... Two weeks ago, my life was quiet. Nobody bothered me, nobody wanted to talk to me, and nobody wanted anything from me. I had virtually no friends, but I had all the freedom and privacy I've always wanted." He aimed the flashlight squarely at Clay's face. "Then I shared part of my private world with you."

Clay squinted and raised his hand to block the beam. "And, buddy, I swear I haven't told anybody about it! Is that what you're worried about?"

"And then you introduced me to her," Thane said, moving the flashlight beam to light up Morana's face. She didn't try to block the beam, only closed her eyes.

Thane said, "You both told me you wanted to help me—gave me every sign that we were friends."

"We do want to help you," Morana said.

Clay added, "Buddy, we *are* friends. I swear." He held up his hand.

"Then why can't I shake the feeling that your friendship comes at an enormous..."

Clay opened his mouth to speak, but Morana nudged him and whispered, "Shut up." She looked up at Thane. "Sweetheart, listen to me. If you plan to harm us, please understand that it will create a bigger problem than the one you're trying to resolve. I've told you we're willing to help you, and you will owe us nothing for it."

"Actually, I already owe you something."

"I don't understand," Morana said.

"I owe you a debt of gratitude. I'm grateful that you convinced me to finally stand up for myself. I'm grateful you've helped me realize how perfect the sub-lair is for containing and controlling secrets. I had never considered using it for that purpose. Your excitement about it was eye-opening. I'm sorry for this blindside, but I have no choice but to use what you explained—the importance of a firm commitment to a decision. You taught me about V1, remember?"

Morana said, "No, I mean, yes, that's true, but this is different. Being reckless ruins it! We need to talk this over—please!"

"All we've done is talk while Waylon remains free to come after me. You couldn't even handle him with a gun. You didn't call for three days when I needed to talk to you. Waylon could have killed me during that time. My situation with Waylon is out of control, and neither of you can do a thing about it."

"Yes, we can!" Clay shouted. "But we can't help you while we're trapped in here. Now let us out, goddammit!"

Morana shoved Clay and said, "Don't talk to him that way!"

"I never meant to show anyone my work," Thane said. "I regret leaking my ability to you two, but I can't undo that. Unfortunately, the only way to restore my privacy is to plug that leak and handle Waylon myself. I'm sorry."

"Thane, wait!" Morana shouted, clasping her hands in front of her. "Think about this... you were concerned that anything you did to Waylon on your property would come back to haunt you legally. I can tell you that covering up for our disappearances compounds that many times."

Thane walked along the edge of the opening to the opposite side and gently tugged the wire. "I never wanted things to end this way."

"Thane, I'm begging you," Morana said. "I only wanted to help you. I care for you. We've spent so much time together, sharing personal stories. We made love."

"What?" Clay said, frowning at Morana.

"Thank you for trying. This isn't personal," Thane said. "I'm not cruel. I've calculated carefully. This slab is 4.2 tons. Technically, you should feel nothing because, with at least one meter to accelerate, your loss of consciousness will be virtually instantaneous."

"Oh my God, Thane!" Clay said.

"What about Waylon?" Morana said. "He's still out there and won't stop coming after you."

"If you had the desire or ability to end Waylon, you would've done it by now."

"No, that's not true!"

"I will stand up to him by myself. If you're right, and he comes after me, I'll soon have him right where you are."

"I don't think you realize how determined—"

Thane yelled, "Nobody will take away what's mine! Nothing you've done has helped!"

Clay prayed aloud until Morana smacked him in the chest. "Knock it off. Thane, please listen."

Thane didn't answer as he lowered the notched block to ankle height and stopped its sway over the trap floor opening before it dropped into the mouth of the trap floor.

The shaft went dark.

Morana yelled, "I know where Gus is!"

The block stopped. A few moments later, it moved upward until light poured in again. Thane peered over the edge.

"Tell me."

"Okay, listen," Morana took a deep breath. "Thane, sweetheart, I can tell where Gus is and more if you let me out."

Thane dropped to his knees and screamed, "You're lying to me— again! Tell me where my cat is, you bitch! Say it!"

"Thane, it would be better if I showed you. *Please!*"

Thane climbed to his feet, and the lid block descended. From inside the chamber, Morana and Clay saw the thin seam of light around the lid block's edges go dark as the block approached them. The massive tonnage sped up.

"No!" Morana and Clay screamed in unison. The air that rushed through the falling block's notched edges generated a hiss that grew louder as the falling block closed in on them.

"My God, we're done. This is it," Clay said.

Morana screamed, "Thane!"

They lay face down. Clay covered his head, bracing for the gruesome impact.

Morana straightened her arms at her sides, her fists clenched.

As the block came within a few feet of them, it abruptly slowed and then stopped. The shaft went quiet. They breathed again. Morana reached up and felt the block, less than an arms-length above them—too close to sit up.

They waited in silence, catching their breath.

Clay rolled to his side. "Now what?"

"Do we have a choice other than to wait, you idiot?" Morana said, panting.

"I'm an idiot?"

"What kind of bonehead move was that to break into Thane's garage after I told you to wait until I called you?"

"Look, Mo," Clay said. "Thane has gone nuts, and you can see it as clearly as I can. You heard the man—he's soured on us and probably planned to get rid of us long ago. This situation would happen whether or not I broke into his garage."

"You're wrong," Morana said.

Their body heat quickly made their cramped space stuffy, fanning Clay's panic.

"He changed his mind about crushing us. He's going to leave us here to die. We're going to suffocate," he said.

"Shut up," Morana said. "He doesn't want to torture us. You heard him say it would be quick. I guarantee he knows the block hasn't crushed us."

A memory gave Morana a shiver. Thane had not constructed drainage for the trap floor. If he had, then cleaning up the soil of the crushed bodies would be simple. Without the ability to wash and drain the trap floor chamber, killing them would produce an unforgettable literal and metaphorical stain on the sub-lair. Maybe Clay was right. Maybe Thane would kill them through suffocation to avoid the mess.

"I think I'm going to throw up," Clay said.

"Stifle it!" Morana yelled.

After being entombed for about ten minutes, a six-inch slat along the bottom edge of their confined space slid open, and light streamed in. They struggled to adjust themselves for a better view. They breathed freely as fresh air flowed in.

Morana recognized the chamber in the sub-lair where they had held Waylon before Thane let him go.

"What in the hell is this place?" Clay said. Pressing his face to the opening.

"Thane created an underground labyrinth," Morana said.

A door block on the opposite side of the chamber opened. Thane entered and walked straight toward them.

Morana said, "Thane, don't make this mistake. You need to let us out."

"Thank you for not crushing us, buddy," Clay said. "You tell us what we need to do to get out of here, and we'll do it."

Thane raised to his toes and aimed his flashlight into the space, illuminating their faces.

"It was a mistake to involve you two in my life. It has resulted in nothing good. Now, tell me where my cat is, or I'll crush both of you thinner than coins."

"Yes, I will tell you everything I know."

"She will," Clay said. "Give her a chance!"

"You have ten seconds to tell me precisely where Gus is," Thane said, looking at his watch.

"He's probably with Waylon," Morana said.

"Probably? I knew you didn't know," Thane said, spreading his fingers on the wall below the opening.

The lid block descended toward Clay and Morana. When it came to within an inch of them, Clay became hysterical, thrashing and pleading for his life.

They lay as flat as possible on their stomachs, and soon, the tonnage made contact, slowly compressing their shoulder blades.

"Thane, for God's sake!" Morana wheezed. "You will guarantee your worst nightmare if you kill the three of us."

The lid block stopped. Thane frowned. "Three?"

"Raise it!" Morana grunted.

The lid block ascended a few inches. Clay coughed, and Morana gasped, breathing deeply.

"What three?" Thane asked.

"Me, Clay, and Gus," she said. "You know you will never see Gus again unless Waylon is confident he has your secret. You can't trick him. If you let me finish dispensing with Waylon, I can finish the job without you having to risk any legal guilt, and if you are sure Waylon has Gus, I will get Gus back safe and sound. You win, and nothing happens on your property. If I fail, you keep your plan in place and handle Waylon because we are both 100% sure he will return. In either scenario, you win. Letting me out carries the least risk and the best chance of getting you what you want."

Thane looked down and scuffed his foot on the floor. "Now you can hold this against me." He pointed along the opening that restrained them.

"What do you mean?" Morana asked.

"You could go to the police and say I kidnapped you just like Waylon threatened."

Clay laughed, "No, no, we won't!"

Morana found Clay's leg behind her and dug her nails into it.

"Ouch! Dammit!"

Morana said, "Thane, you should know how I feel about police and my privacy by now. What would I gain if you were prosecuted? Nothing... Sweetheart, time is wasting. You should let us out before Waylon hurts Gus, or leaks what he knows about your secret."

"Speaking of that," Clay said, "Thane, listen. You need to know that Waylon published a photograph of your garage on a website."

"Published?" Thane said.

"Yes."

"Where? How do I see it?"

"I'd show you, but my hand is stuck underneath me. Can you raise the block a little more so I can show you my phone?"

Thane widened the slat slightly.

Clay worked to fish his phone from his pocket and then found the photograph. He squeezed his arm past Morana and through the opening.

Thane took the phone. "This is the one! *This* is the photo I told you he sent!" He said, turning the phone for Morana to see. "Wait, how did you bring up this webpage on your phone down here? There is no signal."

"That page is cached on my phone. I opened it before I came here to look for you two."

"This is why he emailed it to himself," Thane said. "I knew he wanted to publish it."

Clay said, "Thane, I can remove that photo from the Internet for you."

"Why didn't you do that already?"

"I saw it only minutes before I rushed to your place. Finding you and Mo was more important."

"This is most important! This can ruin everything! Can you remove this photo from the Internet?"

"That's what I'm trying to tell you. At a minimum, I can cripple the site to prevent anyone from accessing it. But I can't do it if I'm dead, so let me the hell out!"

Thane's eyes welled up. He collapsed to his knees and wept. "I don't know what to do."

"Sweetheart, you need to pick somebody to trust," Morana said. "If you don't trust Clay and me, then you have to trust yourself, and you're on your own. Kill us, and you must protect yourself from Waylon while answering for our disappearances and deal with Waylon publicizing the photo of your garage. Release us, and you have a team with a solid chance for justice the law won't give you. But you need to decide quickly."

Thane stood and walked back toward the door. He turned off the lights.

"Thane? Buddy!" Clay said, his voice panicked again.

They felt their platform moving. Moments later, the lights came back on. The opening alongside them had widened enough for them to roll out and drop into the chamber floor.

On the opposite side, Thane leaned against the wall, watching them.

"Thank you. I promise you won't regret this," Morana said.

Clay rushed Thane, grabbed his collar, and slammed him against the wall. "Don't you ever pull that shit again!"

Morana lunged, tackling Clay to the floor.

While Thane backed to the door, smoothing his shirt, Morana

mounted Clay and squeezed his neck. She put her face to his and said, "If you ever lift a finger to Thane again, I will kill you. Do you understand?" Clay's face turned red, and a vein bulged from his forehead. He managed a slight nod. Morana let go, and he gasped for air. She stood up, glaring down at him, then stepped away. She turned to Thane and said, "I will let no one hurt you again. I promise."

✝

Thane led them from the trap floor chamber along the corridor. Clay examined the perfectly sculpted walls, ceiling, and floor, gawking at the precision and craftsmanship of the underground labyrinth.

When they rounded the corner to enter the lift chamber, the column of rock that supported the lift shaft slid downward in the center of the wall.

"What is that?" Clay asked.

"You'll see in a minute," Morana said. "It's the proper way to enter and exit the sub-lair."

Moments later, the lift slid down into view. Thane pointed at it and said, "Go."

They pressed together on the narrow platform and began their ascent to the surface.

"Unbelievable," Clay said as the opening to the chamber slid away, leaving them in darkness.

Morana tried to take Thane's hand, but he pulled away.

"I promise this will end well for you," she told him.

"You've promised before."

"I can't wait to prove it. Just a little more time."

While they rode silently, Clay chuckled a few times as he marveled at their location and the ride on the lift. When they smoothly emerged into the light of the garage, Morana and Thane stepped away from Clay, who stayed on the lift, staring at his feet and repeating, "Wow" and "Unbelievable."

"Let's go," Morana said. "We have work to do."

Clay walked to the garage entrance, directing his attention to his phone as its signal was restored.

Thane hurried to the work counter to check for phone messages.

"Anything?" Morana asked

"No."

As they followed Clay to the door, Morana said, "I'm going to leave you for a while to work on keeping my end of the bargain… Will you feel safe enough locked in here?"

"You know what will make me feel safe," Thane said, opening the door for her.

"Meanwhile, Clay will wait here with you. He has guns."

Thane looked at Clay, standing just outside. He held his hands up and said, "Not on me. They're in the car."

"What about the website that shows the photo of my shop? You said you could get rid of it."

"I can, but I need to get my laptop from my car."

She rested her hand on Thane's shoulder. "Clay will shut down Waylon's web link to the photo, and I'll try to make sure your trap floor won't be necessary. I promise to call you with any news."

Thane nodded and locked the door after Morana stepped outside.

As Morana and Clay walked along the driveway, Clay whispered, "You're pushing Thane too hard and damn near got us killed. If he snaps again, he's FUBARED, and we get nothing."

"I have a new plan with no need to pressure Thane anymore. Thane will only experience relief from now on, but I need a day or two to set it up."

They passed through the pergola to the street.

"Days? The guy is on edge. We'll be lucky if Thane doesn't have police swarming his place before then."

"That won't happen. I've learned some things about Thane that make our plan foolproof."

"Are you going to clue me in?"

"Yes, but not now. You stick to the tech stuff. Just keep Thane safe and calm and get him to let you install a phone in the sub-lair. Everything will work out."

"God, I hope so. You have a lot of catching up to do. You had sex with Thane?"

"I'll call you as soon as possible," Morana waved over her shoulder as she headed down the block.

Clay took the sidewalk opposite to retrieve his laptop and guns from his car.

Morana entered her Explorer and changed her makeup and wig to a different disguise before shopping for a business suit she needed as part of their plan. She changed into the suit while in the car and drove to Clay's office to see if she could meet Uncle Jesse in person. She understood the gist of Uncle Jesse's modus operandi from Thane's description but wanted to profile him for herself in person. She formulated an impromptu sales pitch while walking to the front door, then asked the receptionist to see him.

Uncle Jesse came out to see who the unexpected guest was. One look at her, and he invited her back into his office with almost slobbery hospitality. The meeting provided Morana with everything she needed to know about him.

Afterward, while driving from the office, she called Clay.

"Everything okay?" Clay answered.

"The cargo is fine and secure," Morana replied. "What's going on there?"

"I've been working on Thane. After two hours of consolation, he finally agreed to a single line, wired to the sub-lair."

"That's great news."

"But he wants the line to access only his voice messages, not to make phone calls from the sub-lair. I told him his voicemail was built into his phone. He doesn't care. He told me to figure it out or forget about it. He doesn't want any phone connection in the sub-lair."

"Then design a custom system if that's what he wants," Morana said. "Do whatever you must to get the sub-lair wired today."

"Not happening today. I've already checked with both local hardware stores, and they don't have enough of the cabling line I need. I looked up another supplier who promised to have it in my hand tomorrow by noon."

"Tomorrow works," Morana said. "I'll talk to Thane. I want the sub-lair wired while he still has a powerful reason to."

"There's another thing. Thane won't let me pull the new line. He insisted on doing it himself, so I told him I would come back tomorrow with the cable, supplies, and instructions. He may be great at moving rocks, but that might not translate to electronics."

"Clay, tell him you need to be with him. It could be a prime opportunity for a clue about how he does what he does."

"Believe me, I know. When I deliver the supplies, I'll try again to convince him to let me handle the wiring."

"You have to get his permission. It's critical," Morana said.

That night at Clay's place, Morana arrived, and they met to compare notes. She revealed a new change to her plan and told Clay about her visit to his office and the brief meeting with Uncle Jesse. When she finished, Clay seemed stunned, repeating, "Brilliant."

"It'll be brilliant when it works," Morana said.

The following morning, Morana and Clay continued planning over breakfast. As Clay handed her more cash, she asked, "What's the status of the cabling?"

"Package tracking says I'll have the cabling supplies for the sub-lair later this morning," Clay said.

"Excellent. Get it done."

Clay phoned Thane. While Morana listened, Clay successfully got permission from Thane to visit and wire the sub-lair as soon as the cabling supplies arrived.

Morana left and drove to the storage facility where Waylon was stored. She exited her Explorer, pulled her duffel bag from the passenger seat, and unlocked the unit.

The sound generated by the door triggered Waylon's expected screams and writhing. Morana tossed her bag inside to the floor and closed the door. She reached up, turned off the shock collar from the ceiling, and again placed her flashlight in the center of the floor to light the space.

"Looks like you traveled less last night. That's good," she said, looking around the unit. She unzipped the duffel bag and changed from her business suit into jeans, a thin blouse, a leather jacket, and boots. After repacking her suit, she zipped the duffel bag and then went to Waylon, her feet scuffing to a stop beside him. She took hold of the wires protruding from his zipper and pulled them taut.

He winced, and his face filled with terror.

She wrapped the wires around her fingers and firmly yanked. Waylon bellowed through the gag with his eyes squeezed shut. The wire ends flew out of his zipper, connected to hair-encrusted duct tape that secured the bare copper ends. He writhed and then knotted himself in the fetal position.

Morana opened the storage unit door and backed the Explorer partially inside. She opened the rear door and pulled Waylon up to his feet. "In you go."

When Waylon resisted, she let go of him and returned with a stun gun to the open driver's door. She held it up, pulled the trigger, and showed him the lightning that crackled between the prongs.

Waylon immediately hopped in his ankle bindings to the open door and sat on the edge.

Morana blindfolded him, then pushed his legs inside before slamming the door closed. After loading Gus's cage safely onto the passenger seat, she locked up the unit, and they drove away. As they sped toward Thane's house, she took a few corners hard enough to slam Waylon into the side of the Explorer's cargo area.

As they drove, her phone buzzed with a text message from Clay.

> *Bingo... Thane's taking me to sub-lair to show him wiring options. Will be away from phone...*

Morana pulled to the side of the road and quickly replied:

> *On my way w/ the cargo. Don't tell Thane. I want to surprise him.*

She waited, but no reply came from Clay. She pulled back into traffic and sped up.

When they arrived at Thane's place, it was midafternoon. She backed into the driveway. As she neared the garage, the honeysuckle hanging from the pergola scraped the doors and windows. She stopped and parked at an angle beside Thane's truck, in a place that brought the rear door of the Explorer to within a couple of steps of the garage.

She got out and went to the entry door. It was unlocked. She opened it cautiously and leaned inside. "Hello?... Thane?... Clay?" There was no answer.

She went to the side of the garage and found a shovel leaning against the wall beside a garden hose. She used it to dig a couple of scoops of dirt from the edge of the lawn, placing the dirt into a plastic bag that she pulled from her jacket pocket. She twisted the bag closed and returned to the driver's door. She pulled out a cargo bag filled with supplies, slung it over her shoulder, and opened the Explorer's rear door.

Waylon lay inside, motionless, still gagged and blindfolded.

Morana pulled a stun gun from the bag and gave him a brief jolt, slamming the door closed. When he finished screaming, she opened it again and said, "I need you to show enthusiasm for my instructions. Do you understand?"

Waylon vigorously nodded.

"I'm removing you from the vehicle. You will stand, and you will hop where and how high I tell you to," Morana said.

Waylon nodded again.

She pulled his legs out, guiding his feet to the ground, and helped him stand. She squeezed the back of his collar with one hand while pressing the stun gun into his back with the other, pushing him through the garage entry door, where they stopped.

Morana called out again. "Thane… Clay?"

No answer. She checked the key hook just inside the door. The keys were gone, and the nail was raised. She felt a chill when she looked down at the neatly spread area rug only a couple of steps away on the trap floor, knowing it was cocked and loaded.

She pushed Waylon, navigating him around the outside edge of the trap floor until they reached the shop's center.

Thane had removed the sheets that obscured his work countertop. A large spool of cable and wire-cutting tools sat beside the phone. Pieces of wire sheathing and copper ends were strewn on the floor below it.

"Not a move," she said to Waylon as she released his arm. She exited the garage and returned with Gus's cage, a towel draped over it to keep him calm. She went to Waylon, set the cage down, and threw back the carpet that concealed the small lift on the corner of the Gateway block. She guided him to the square within the faint seams of the lift.

With her bag slung over her shoulder and Gus's cage in hand, she checked to ensure their feet were within the lift's boundaries.

"You'll feel motion," she said. "Don't move, and you won't have to feel my hand lightning again."

She stomped her heel on the corner of the lift twice. Nothing happened. She stomped again, harder. Waylon tensed as the lift descended, swallowing them into the darkness under the floor.

Morana turned on a flashlight, and each time the lift stopped at a lower level, she pressed the wall panel the way Thane had taught her on previous trips to the sub-lair.

Above them, the opening to the lift shaft shrank to a small square. When they eventually reached the opening of the sub-lair elevator chamber, light streamed in, and Morana stepped out into the chamber. She set Gus's covered cage in the corner of the lift chamber. She came back and pulled Waylon's arm. He resisted at first, then hopped off the lift. She noticed that the lift remained in place after they stepped from it instead of automatically ascending back to the surface like it had each time with Thane. She looked at the chamber's walls, floor, and ceiling, still unable to determine how Thane had triggered it. If he was not down here with Clay, she would be trapped here with Waylon until whatever time Thane returned.

Her concern was short-lived as she heard a voice from another part of the sub-lair.

"Be still," she said to Waylon.

"Mo, is that you?"

She recognized Clay's voice.

"Yes, is Thane with you? I have a couple of gifts for him." A metal tool rattled on the floor around the corner, followed by footsteps.

Thane appeared in the entryway to the lift chamber. When he saw Waylon gagged and bound, he smacked the heel of his hand to his forehead and said, "What have you done?"

"I've kept my promise. I told you I would get him."

"After all you've learned about me, why would you bring him here?"

"Look," she pointed to his blindfold. "He can't see anything. He didn't see how we got here. He doesn't know where he is. He can't speak. You have complete control, and you have another visitor..." She went to the cage and removed the towel that covered it.

"Gus!" Thane ran to the cage and kneeled beside it. He slipped his fingers through the wires.

Gus was startled by the commotion and cowered near the back of the cage before skeptically moving forward to sniff Thane's fingers.

"Do you want to take him out of the cage?" Morana asked.

"No, he's scared. He doesn't like it down here. I'll take him up." Thane stood and glared at Waylon. "I knew he had Gus."

Morana said, "The good news is that Gus is back where he belongs."

"Thank you," Thane said. "Did anyone see you enter the garage?"

"No."

"Good... This is very good." He stepped closer and leaned down to verify that Waylon could not see under the blindfold.

"He can't see you," Morana said.

"Can he hear me?"

"Absolutely," Morana said. She snapped her finger beside his ear. Waylon's head turned slightly.

Thane stepped closer to Waylon and said, "We had a deal. I let you go when I didn't have to. I let you go when you were vulnerable to me. I gave you the gift of freedom that I hoped you would give me. And you pay me back with extortion?"

Waylon shook his head and hummed something through the gag.

"It doesn't matter what you just said. Your words have manipulated and tormented me for the last time. Now, sit."

Waylon didn't move.

Morana pulled her stun gun from her bag and pulled the trigger. Sparks snapped between the prongs, startling Clay and Thane and sending a sharp echo crackling throughout the sub-lair. She jabbed the prongs into Waylon's side but didn't have to pull the trigger. He fell to the ground on his side.

Clay went to pull Waylon up to a sitting position, but Thane intervened, saying, "Leave him."

Morana said, "I need to visit your bedroom, and then I need to set something up in the trap floor chamber."

"Both doors are open—why?"

"Trust me. You and Clay watch Waylon and bring him to me when I'm ready." She left them and walked down the corridor to Thane's open bedroom door.

Clay and Thane stayed back at the lift chamber. Waylon groaned and struggled, failing to raise himself to a sitting position.

Thane looked down at him. "After a lifetime of battles, you finally lost the war. You have bullied me for the last time."

Waylon stopped moving.

Thane went to the waiting lift and stepped onto it.

Clay quietly watched him closely, trying to see what Thane could use to trigger it.

"Now that I have my prey," Thane said, "I'm going to the garage to ensure our privacy." He picked up Gus's cage. "If Mo finishes whatever she's doing before I return, tell her to wait. I won't be long."

"Do you want me to go with you?" Clay asked.

"No. You watch my prey. If he moves, make him sorry." The lift ascended. Thane disappeared. The rock column that supported the upward lift slid as part of the wall accelerated.

At the surface, Thane stepped into the garage and looked around, confirming that the entry door was closed and that no one had breached it. He placed Gus's cage on the floor beside his work counter. He opened the cage door, expecting Gus to race out. Instead, the cat sauntered out and purred, rubbing against Thane's leg. Thane gently scratched his head. "It's all over, Gussie. It's finally all over." Gus leaped onto the counter and then jumped again to the top of the cabinet, where he curled up in his bed.

Thane carefully walked around the trap floor area rug and to the entry door. He opened it and looked outside. Morana's Explorer was still backed at an angle to within arm's length of the door.

He disabled the trap floor key hook, locked the doorknob, and moved the 8-ton block to obstruct the door. He brushed off his hands and stepped back to inspect it and the other stack of blocks in front of the larger roll-up door.

He checked again that Gus was safely in his bed atop the cabinet, then returned to the lift. His heart raced as he descended into the sub-lair, now assured of complete privacy and total control over his nemesis.

When he reached the sub-lair, Clay and Waylon came into view. They sat side by side on the floor, facing him.

"Where is Mo?" Thane asked.

Clay pointed to the corridor. "She said to bring Waylon to her as soon as you return."

They pulled Waylon to his feet and guided him around the corner and then along the corridor to where Morana waited in the trap floor chamber. She came to the door and said, "It's time for your trial."

Waylon refused to move into the chamber. They forced him.

Thane closed the door.

Morana untied Waylon's blindfold, tossing it to the floor. When he saw what was before him, his eyes widened, and he wobbled, hopping a few times in his ankle bindings to catch his balance. He looked around at the way Morana had furnished the room. Several items on the floor were spaced in a wide arc around a chair.

"Please have a seat and make yourself comfortable," Morana said. She held out her hand toward the chair.

When Waylon didn't move, Clay pushed his back. Waylon hopped to the chair and sat, wheezing through his nose.

Thane and Clay stepped away to lean against a wall off to one side.

Morana went to the first item on the floor—a bucket of mud. Some mud had dripped down the outside edge, forming a small puddle around its base. She pulled a couple of small pieces of paper from her pocket, handing one to Thane and the other to Clay.

Thane looked at it and briefly smiled.

Clay looked confused.

Morana went to Waylon and held up her paper for him to see. It was a ticket for a *Private Mud Dunking Show*. The price of the ticket: $1.00. "Sales have been dismal, but the show must go on!" she said, stuffing her ticket into her pocket. She moved to the next item and picked it up. It was a piece of paper with tape on it. The paper read: *Kick Me*. She held it up for Waylon to see. "You might remember this. I'm sorry we have only one of these signs—Thane couldn't remember how often you stuck this to his backside. So, he'll tape this one to your ass and kick until it feels right."

Waylon rolled his eyes.

"That's okay," Morana said, wagging her finger at him. "You'll take it seriously soon enough."

She placed the kick me sign back onto the floor and picked up an empty tuna can, its jagged lid raised after being partially opened. She moved toward Waylon and said, "Amazing… Not a single blemish above your eyebrows. Thane, would you mind?" She motioned to him.

Thane stepped closer and took off his glasses.

Morana gently drew her thumb across the scar above Thane's eyebrow. "The hateful graffiti you left on your victim's face remains and has gone unpunished—so far." She slowly walked around Waylon. "Do you feel any shame for abusing Thane?"

Waylon nodded.

"Then this is a wonderful day for you. We're going to remove your need for Thane's forgiveness. What is about to happen in this room will unburden you. Thane will free you and relieve your conscience by removing your debts to him."

Waylon mumbled three syllables, his expression becoming earnest.

"No, no, no!" Morana said. "You don't need to be sorry. That's the beautiful thing about evening the score. Repaying a debt eliminates the need for pesky apologies and unsatisfying forgiveness." She then moved to the next object, a small glass jar, no taller than the tuna can, and filled with cream. She held it up to the light and turned, reading its label. "Here we have the most interesting item of all. Do you know what this is?"

Waylon slumped to one side, and his face returned to a glare.

"I'm not feeling your enthusiasm. Do I need to ask Clay to bring me my hand–lightning?"

Waylon bucked in the chair, shaking his head.

She twisted the jar's lid, opening it. "Whew!" She said, coming closer to Waylon. She squatted and held it close to his nose. At first, he looked confused, then recognition registered on his face. He shut his eyes tightly. A few seconds later, Clay and Thane smelled the piercing aroma of menthol as it filled the small chamber.

"I'm sorry, sweetheart," Morana said to Thane. "I know this scent brings back a horrible memory." She scooped a glob with her finger and smeared it along Waylon's upper lip above the gag. "I want this scent to be top-of-mind while your debts are removed."

Waylon wrinkled his nose and then sneezed.

Morana turned to Clay and Thane. "How many victims fantasize about making things right yet never get the opportunity?" Morana came to Thane and took his hand. "The memories you shared with me are vivid, and you conveyed all your pain. The pleasure he got from tormenting you has ended. You have a unique opportunity to make yourself whole. Your power and privacy are absolute in this place."

Waylon's eyes widened as he looked back and forth between Thane and Morana.

"He's all yours," Morana said, nodding toward Waylon.

Thane said, "I want to be alone with him."

"Of course. We'll wait outside." She came to him and gently kissed his cheek. In his ear, she whispered, "Don't let him go this time?"

"Deals are over," Thane said, holding an icy stare on Waylon, who began bucking and tugging against his bindings.

Morana and Clay stepped out into the corridor.

As Thane closed the chamber door, Waylon fought his bindings hard enough to fall off the chair. The closing door muted Waylon's muffled pleas.

A hundred feet above the sub-lair, Uncle Jesse strolled around the unfamiliar Ford Explorer that was backed up at an odd angle to the garage entry door. He peered into the back window and saw plastic ties, duct tape, and a blanket.

Three men dressed in white stood a short distance away, watching him. They carried paint buckets, brushes, and rollers with extension poles.

Uncle Jesse glanced at Thane's truck, still blocking the roll-up door, then rubbed his chin, his attention returning to the Explorer.

He squeezed past the rear bumper to get to the garage entry door. The knob was locked, so he pulled a full keyring from his pocket and tested each key in the doorknob until he had tried all of them. He took a step back and kicked the door.

The latch broke, and the door flew open about the width of a fist before it slammed against something solid. *Dammit!* "What in God's name?" he said, pressing the door open as far as it would go. He cupped his brow to see into the garage through the narrow opening. He reached in and felt behind the door. It was something solid and heavy, and it had a gritty surface. He took out his phone, reached in, and took a photo. It showed a rock or concrete block, taller than the entry door, positioned inches from the inside knob. *Son of a bitch.* He kicked the door again.

The painters watched, and one of them smirked.

Uncle Jesse shoved the keys into his pocket and turned to them. "Guys, I can't get inside, but start your prep while I make a call."

The men began unfolding tarps along the side of the garage and positioned their paint buckets and supplies on it.

Uncle Jesse walked along the driveway to the front of the house with his phone pressed to his ear. He paused when he heard his call ringing inside the garage behind him. Thane's answering machine picked up. Uncle Jesse cleared his throat. "Where are you, and what the hell have you got blocking the garage door? The goddamn key you gave me doesn't work. I told you I'd be coming back and how you've put me in a horrible position. I've got a guy on his way to pick up the piano, and you better not wreck this sale. Call me immediately when you get this." He hung up and dialed another number coming to the sidewalk in the house's front. "Listen, Roy, it's Jesse Sykes. We have an appointment for you to come by and get the piano today, but there's been a slight delay. I'll call you as soon as the piano is available, and we will have it all polished and ready for you when you show up. Thanks, bye."

He walked back to the garage. "Get over here and help me a second," he barked at the workers. Two of them hurried to meet him at the door, and together, the three of them tried to force the door open, putting their combined weight into it. The block didn't budge.

Uncle Jesse looked inside the garage again. It was cleaner than it had been on his previous visit. Most of the floor was bare except for several oddly placed area rugs. A few open cabinet doors showed they were empty. Four more blocks, like the one behind the entry door, were stacked in front of the larger roll-up door.

As his eyes adjusted to the darkness, he spotted the tarp-covered piano tucked against the far wall in the garage's corners. It was the only item of any size that remained in the garage. *Where the hell did he put everything?*

Chapter 29

MORANA AND CLAY waited in the hallway outside the trap floor chamber.

"So, we're apparently getting into the assisted-killing business?"

"We've had this discussion, Clay. I oppose any undeserved killing."

"Do you think Thane will go all the way?"

"I hope he'll do whatever makes him feel vindicated," Morana said, pulling her hair into a ponytail and tying it.

"Thane isn't like you," Clay said. "And what he's doing in there isn't like him. I don't know how you set him up for this, but he's not a killer."

"You leave town and come back thinking you're an expert on Thane? You know nothing about what Thane shared with me. If you understood, you would be happy for the therapeutic miracle this opportunity gives him. Waylon is an unapologetic monster who incessantly tormented Thane for most of their lives. Thane is convinced, and I agree, that Waylon will continue to abuse him for as long as he's alive."

"So, you feel entitled to take justice into your own hands—just like back in LA?"

"I stand up for victims, Clay—especially if society or the law fails to protect them."

"If we're caught, we will go to prison forever."

"You can't demand justice and then be concerned about the cost. We are committed, and I won't let anything happen to Thane. We are about to get what we want, and Thane will be rewarded beyond his wildest dreams."

"I hope you're right."

Morana and Clay spent the next hour sitting in the sub-lair corridor, talking while waiting for Thane to emerge from the trap floor chamber. When the block door swung open, they jumped to their feet.

Thane stepped out. He was sweaty, and dust covered his misshapen afro. A thread hung from a popped button on his twisted, untucked shirt. He held out his hands, and they looked swollen. One of them had a scratch across the top. "I'm finished," he said.

Clay and Morana stepped closer. She looked suspiciously at him and said, "You mean, finished, as in…"

"No, I didn't kill him," Thane said, backing into the chamber. He motioned for them to enter.

Inside, the chamber had the musty smell of sweat and the piercing scent of menthol.

Waylon sat, his torn shirt hanging around the base of the chair. His trousers were on loosely, with the belt unbuckled. A trickle of blood drained from above his eyebrow along the left side of his face, where it drained into his gag.

Morana glanced at Clay and whispered, "Wow."

The tuna can lie on the floor in the chamber's corner. Blood stained the open lid.

The jar of menthol cream had been broken on the floor, pieces of its blue glass scattered to the edge of the chamber. A glob of the cream centered among the shards from where the jar had impacted was at the base of Waylon's chair.

Morana walked behind Waylon's chair. The crinkled and torn kick me sign protruded through an opening in the back.

Waylon slowly lifted his head and looked toward Clay and Morana. He made a feeble effort to express as much defiance at them as possible, then he turned to Thane and smiled.

Thane rushed to him, leaning into his face. "It's still funny? Is it a game to you?" he shouted.

Waylon looked directly at Thane's face, the smile unchanged.

"It looks like you might need more time with him," Morana said.

"No," Thane replied. "I hate that he's still here—in the sub-lair, my place of refuge."

"Has he apologized?" Morana asked.

"I left the gag on because his voice makes me want to throw up." Thane paused. "But yes, before I leave, I want to hear an apology. He reached behind Waylon's head and pulled the gag loose."

"Wait," Morana said. "Give me just a moment."

Thane stepped back.

Morana came around and leaned on her knees. She put her mouth close to Waylon's ear and whispered, "If Thane doesn't leave here completely satisfied, I promise to make you sorry."

Waylon closed his eyes and gave a slight nod.

Morana yanked the gag off, jerking Waylon's head. His torso relaxed, and he gasped with relief at breathing through his mouth. She held her finger to his face and said, "Remember." Then she turned to Thane and said, "Here's your apology."

Waylon panted a few times and cleared his throat. "Thane, I want to tell you, sincerely, from the bottom of my heart, that she's wanted for murder, and a huge reward can be yours." He motioned with his head toward Morana.

Morana lunged, grabbed Waylon's neck, and swung her knee into his chest. The blow toppled him and his chair to the floor onto his back. The chair came loose and spun until it collided with the chamber wall.

Waylon coughed and writhed as he launched another futile attempt to free his wrists and ankles.

Clay and Thane stepped back against the wall, stunned.

Morana ran to her bag, retrieved a Tonto knife, and rushed to him, her face red and teeth clenched.

"C'mon, Mo, take it easy," Clay said.

Waylon twisted his head on the floor, straining to see Thane and Clay. He shouted, "You're both stupid to trust her! Cash her in, and you'll be rich…"

Morana dove onto Waylon and stabbed him in the chest four times. She threw the knife aside and mounted him, squeezing his neck until all his twitching stopped. She slowly climbed to her feet as a pool of blood spread underneath his body. "You son-of-a-bitch," she said, looking down at his lifeless body.

She looked over her shoulder at Clay. He had moved to the doorway, one foot outside in the corridor, as though he wanted to run. Thane stood motionless against the wall, staring wide-eyed at Waylon's body.

"Sweetheart, please don't be afraid," Morana said.

Thane's gaze went from Waylon to Morana's knee, stained with blood. He cupped his mouth and ran toward the door.

Instead of moving, Clay raised his hand and said, "Buddy, hold on."

"Move!" Thane yelled.

"Let him go!" Morana said.

Clay stepped aside, and Thane ran from the chamber into the corridor, heaving into his shirt.

"But Waylon outed you," Clay said, pointing to the body.

"Shh," Morana put her finger to her lips as she came to join him in the doorway.

Clay stepped out and looked both ways. "He's gone."

"Do you think Thane believed him?"

"I don't know. I couldn't tell if his nausea had been triggered by emotion or the sight of blood."

"Let's go check on him." They walked along the corridor to Thane's bedroom chamber. The door was open, but he wasn't there. Then they heard him heaving in the aquifer room. They went to the doorway and saw Thane kneeling, hunched over the pool. He peeked up at them and then splashed his face with water.

"Are you okay?" Morana asked.

After a final splash, he kept his hands over his face. His shoulders trembled as he sobbed.

"Maybe we should give him a few minutes," Clay said.

Morana held up her finger to hush Clay and came closer to Thane. "Sweetheart, I'm worried about you. I'll give you some time alone if you need it."

Thane shook his head, still covering his face. He pulled off his shirt and dunked it into the water several times. His eyes glazed over while looking down at the aquifer current. After wringing out his soaked shirt, he looked at Morana's bloodstained hands and the patch of blood that spread from the knee of her jeans. He approached her and said, "Thank you."

"You're welcome. Your mom said it would end one day, and she was right."

The slightest smile creased Thane's lips. He stepped aside to go around Morana, but she stopped him. "I want to make sure you understand something."

Thane draped his shirt over his shoulder, keeping his face down.

She took his hand and said, "You heard Waylon say some things about me there. You know he was desperate and would have said anything to disrupt our relationship."

"Waylon lied to me hundreds of times during my life."

"Exactly," Morana looked at Clay with a relieved laugh.

"But for once, I know Waylon was telling the truth this time." He let go of her hand. "I know who you are."

Morana's mouth dropped open. "I—I…"

"Can you deny anything that Waylon said?"

"Listen, buddy…" Clay said.

"Clay, shut up!" Morana said, keeping her eyes locked on Thane.

Clay raised his hands and backed away.

"Your name is Morana Mahker," Thane said, looking down at the floor, wringing his fingers.

"Please look at me," Morana said.

He raised his head.

"I promise I would never hurt you."

"I know that."

"You do?" Morana couldn't mask her surprise. She tried to form a reply, but Thane's expression was difficult to read.

Thane smiled and said, "The fact that I'm not afraid of you is confusing, isn't it?"

"I'm grateful for it... But may I ask why?"

"I've discovered enough about you to draw my own conclusions," he said, moving to the bedroom. He sat on the mattress.

"You've researched me?"

"It should've been obvious to you that research is one of my strengths."

"What do you know about me—exactly?" Morana asked, following him.

"You should sit," Thane said, pointing to a place on the floor beside Clay.

Morana complied.

New worry spread on Clay's face.

Thane leaned back and said, "Would you like me to begin with your childhood or skip to the life events that honed your penchant for vigilantism?"

Morana poked her tongue into her cheek and said, "Surprise me."

"Funny you would say that because I know you hate surprises."

Morana forced a smile and folded her hands on her lap.

"I know you spent two years in Mesa, Arizona, which led me to an archived local newspaper story about an incident at Bresbin High School where charges for a girl's locker room assault incident were dropped against you."

Morana shifted, continuing to use brute force to maintain her smile.

"I couldn't find any records of your coursework or major emphasis in college, but I know you dropped out to become active with *Rigged Justice*, a rather aggressive wrongful imprisonment advocacy group. You were fired from your position for threatening what you felt was an overzealous prosecutor after *Rigged Justice* failed to overturn a case. I know that prosecutor disappeared and was never found."

Morana glanced back at Clay. He looked stunned.

Thane continued, "I know you moved to Los Angeles and became involved with Core Comforts, which provided shelter to the homeless. You worked there for a year and a half until you discovered that the director and several staff members were fleecing the organization. When they dodged embezzlement charges, a mysterious fire destroyed its headquarters."

Morana scratched her neck and finger-combed her hair a few times as she tried to mask her shock at Thane's summary.

"How am I doing?" Thane asked.

"So far, I'm impressed."

"Shall I continue?"

Morana motioned for him to go on.

"There is a gap of about a year of your adult life when I couldn't find anything on your whereabouts, but I know you eventually met up with a man named Aldred Hurd, also known as 'Pop,' who orchestrated a covert mission to end homelessness in Los Angeles. You quickly rose through his ranks, becoming what some described as one of his favored lieutenants. His company, *Trail Bladers,* provided the perfect cover for covert vigilante activities, which grew to include systematic murder for the cause. Recently, its headquarters was destroyed by a bomb, and shortly after that, Clay introduced us. I didn't recognize you on your second visit because you heavily disguised yourself. You have no Florida address. You have no Florida driver's license. The Ford Explorer you drive isn't registered to you." Thane paused because Morana looked like she wanted to say something.

"How long have you known?" she asked.

"I began my research right after your second visit."

Morana took a deep breath. "Given all you know about me, why would you bring me into the sub-lair—alone with you?"

"Because, like I told you before, I love keys and have your key."

Morana frowned. "What does that mean?"

"I hold a key to my safety with you. I learned you hate injustice as much as you love its victims. Your desire to help me get justice equals your desperation to learn the secret of the physics that built this place. Until you have both, I am safe. This was my key."

Morana pulled her knees up and put her forehead to them, burying her head in her arms. Her hair fell to cover her face.

"Are you okay?" Thane asked.

Without looking up, Morana said, "You've described me better than I could have described myself." She looked up at him. "I'm relieved that you know I won't hurt you."

Thane said, "Your ruthlessness scares me, but when I saw it aimed at Waylon, it exhilarated me, and I found it impossible to object to your help."

Morana gave a small laugh. "But now that I achieved half of what I want, and Waylon is gone, hasn't that diminished your key?"

"No."

Morana looked at him quizzically.

Thane spread his arms. "The sub-lair has become the only place on earth you feel safe. No one can see, touch, or prosecute you here."

"Fair enough. Are you saying you'll let me stay here with you?"

"I haven't decided."

She got up and knee-walked to him. She took his arm and gently pulled him to her, embracing him. "In exchange, I'll do anything you want me to—*anything*."

Thane put his hands on her waist, avoiding a full embrace.

"I'm so glad you don't consider me dangerous," she said.

Thane let go of her, got up, and went to the doorway. "I *do* consider you dangerous." He looked around the bedroom. "But that's okay. Down here, I can be dangerous, too."

All the lights blinked off. The entire sub-lair went black.

Chapter 30

TRAPPED IN PITCH darkness, the only sound Morana and Clay heard came from the faint roiling of the aquifer water in the next room.

"Whoa, what the hell?" Clay said, rising to his feet.

"Thane?" Morana hollered. She moved toward the last place she had seen Thane, her hands out, feeling for him. When she reached the doorway, it was empty.

"Sweetheart, what are you doing?" she yelled.

"Buddy! C'mon!" Clay said.

There was no answer from the corridor.

Clay also moved toward the door. When his hand touched Morana's waist, she slapped it.

Morana felt her way around the doorframe and stepped into the corridor door. In the pitch darkness, she heard faint footsteps that faded away in the distance.

"Thane!" she hollered.

"Buddy, this isn't funny!" Clay yelled. Their voices echoed in the darkness.

"We have to catch him," Morana said, feeling her way along the wall.

"Are you sure he went in this direction?" Clay asked, stumbling to keep up with her.

Morana stopped. "What other direction could he have gone?" She cupped her hands around her mouth and yelled, "Thane, if you can hear me, please come back. You know I won't hurt you. I know you are in charge. *Please!*"

Clay said, "We have to get to the lift."

They scuffed along the short corridor wall, repeatedly begging Thane to turn the lights on and come back.

They made a left at the end to enter what they thought was the lift chamber. Clay felt seams with his fingertips and pressed his hand against each new wall block, putting his weight into it, searching for a block that would open. He accidentally kicked Morana's heel, and they almost fell.

"Dammit, Clay!" Morana shoved him away.

Clay cupped his mouth and hollered, "Thane, I don't know what you're doing, but I swear to God I will get you anything you want. Just turn the lights on and come back."

"You can stop begging," Morana said. "If he hasn't answered by now, he won't until he's ready."

"Maybe he went up to the surface," Clay said.

"There's no way he could have gone up that quickly," Morana said. "The lift needs almost a minute to lower and fully raise, so this shaft would still be moving if he had used it. Stand still." She dragged her fingers around the perimeter of the small chamber and found and felt no movement of the lift. "The lift should be right here," she said, slapping her palm on the wall.

"Then where could he have gone?" Clay asked.

"Absolutely anywhere. Have you finished putting in the phone line?"

"He had me run it into the bedroom chamber, but the phone isn't connected in the garage yet."

"Figures," Morana said, stomping her heel on several parts of the floor.

"What are you doing?" Clay asked.

"Every time Thane comes into this chamber, the lift appears automatically, like a valet that knows when he wants it. I haven't been able to figure out how he does it."

"Are you sure it's not as simple as a remote control?" Clay asked.

"If so, it's not handheld because his hands have been in plain view."

"Maybe it's heat, electric, or biometric—it could be anything." Clay pounded the walls and hopped from one foot to the other around the lift chamber.

They split up, taking separate corridors as they continued calling for Thane and feeling the walls.

As Morana dragged her hand along the wall, her fingertips found the faint seams of many blocks that could be doorways, but none would budge. She took her best guess as to the approximate location of the trap floor chamber entrance. She pushed and prodded all the nearby blocks, but each refused to move.

"Where are you?" Clay said.

"Over here," Morana said.

Clay moved toward her voice until they bumped at the center of the main corridor.

"We're dead," he said.

"Oh, calm down."

"He hid it well."

"What are you talking about?"

"He's snapped again. Have you already forgotten that he damn near crushed us before? Remember all those facts he recited about your past? Key, or no key, I don't see how he didn't completely freak out before now."

Morana said, "He didn't look freaked out when he left."

"Maybe not, but don't you find it interesting that his last words were about how dangerous he was down here, and then, bang, the lights go out, and he vanishes?"

"He already knew my history. Were you listening?"

"That's the thing. Why wouldn't Thane turn you in now that Waylon is gone?"

"Because he doesn't care about money."

Clay replied, "Okay, forget about the money motivation. Waylon and I are the only ones who know about the sub-lair. Maybe he's decided that was three people too many."

"He knows the legal mess our disappearance would create for him. He has far too much to lose. My car is up in his driveway. He'd have to dispose of that, and then he'd have to play dumb to your uncle at work about your disappearance—I don't think he'd be able to pull that off."

"I still don't think this sudden darkness is an innocent game."

"Be patient. Thane will be back." Morana's tone had lost its conviction. "Let's go to the bedroom and wait."

As they felt their way back to the bedroom doorway, Morana stopped.

Clay bumped her again.

She swept her fingers around the wall. "Wasn't the doorway here?"

"Yes, move." Clay swapped places with her and felt along the wall, walking a few steps further until he reached the end of the corridor. "It has to be here."

Morana said, "He closed the door."

"How?" Clay said, coming back to her.

A chill shot through Morana. "Move away from me—quick," she said.

"What is it?" Clay asked, backing away.

"Further, don't stand near me!" She backed as far away from him as she could get.

"Why?"

"Thane can move any block, floor, ceiling, or wall whenever he wants to. If he intentionally locked us out of the bedroom, he could be removing our options."

"You think he'll crush us?" Clay asked.

"I don't know." Morana sidestepped along the corridor to create more distance between her and Clay. She beat the wall with her hand and said, "Thane, I don't know what you are planning, but I would never hurt you. I will never hurt you. You should know that by now! Thane, please answer me!"

"God, we're doomed. I feel lightheaded," Clay said. He spread his hands on the wall behind him and whispered, "Where should we go?"

Morana said, "I still think he's coming back, but if you're right about Thane wanting to finish us, it won't matter where we are."

Chapter 31

THE POWER OUTAGE caught Thane by surprise. It was the first he had experienced since wiring the solar panels to the sub-lair. He left Clay and Morana in the bedroom, hurrying along the wall and ignoring their calls to him. His only focus was resolving the problem, not consolation, as he felt his way to the end corridor. He needed to get to the surface as soon as possible.

The solar panels mounted in the backyard were the only source of electricity to the sub-lair. The only explanation for the sudden blackout was a disconnection of the panels. Thane had to investigate, but if he used the garage lift, an intruder who might have broken in would hear the hiss and see the shaft open as the lift descended to retrieve him. He opted for the bedroom closet lift instead.

He rounded the corner at the end of the corridor and used his fingertips to count wall-block seams before he triggered one that pivoted, opening a doorway.

He entered his secret tunnel to the house and closed the block, muting Morana's and Clay's calls. This was his task to correct alone—especially if anyone was at the surface. Leaving them locked below would ensure that they couldn't interfere with anyone he encountered at the surface. It also ensured they couldn't witness any block moving he might need to do in the garage during the repair. A reminder of his control over the sub-lair would be good for them.

He felt his way along the tunnel through the pitch darkness until he reached the end. He triggered the lift, and the column of rock supporting it descended, accelerating. He cautiously reached out and let his fingers drag against the sliding rock. Soon, the lift platform appeared. He stepped onto it.

During his ascent, Thane reflected on Waylon's demise. Thane's stomach clamped again when he remembered the blood spreading underneath Waylon's body. He cupped his damp shirt around his mouth, dropped to one knee, and heaved.

At the end of his ascent, a crack of light slid down in front of him as the lift slowed to a stop in his bedroom closet. Hanging clothes flopped onto his head, and he ducked to avoid a collision with the rack.

Before he stepped off the lift, he waited, listening. He parted the clothes and looked out into the empty bedroom. He heard faint voices that seemed to come from outside the house. He opened the closet door and went to the bedroom window that faced the backyard. Morana's Explorer was still backed to the garage entry door. Three men dressed in white were draping a long plastic tarp over it. He saw the open cans of paint and sprayers. One man twisted a paint roller onto a pole extension.

Thane immediately saw the reason for losing power in the sub-lair. His array of solar panels had been ripped from their stands and stacked atop one another at the edge of the lawn. The mounting stands were severed a few inches from the ground, and frayed wires protruded. A sledgehammer lay a short distance away. *What the hell is going on?*

Thane quickly changed into some clean clothes and went to the kitchen, where he tossed his soiled shirt into the trash. He opened the back door and went outside. "Who did this?" he said as he went to the stack of disconnected solar panels.

The painters looked at him and then at one another.

"I said, who did this?" Thane yelled.

One man pointed his paintbrush toward the house and said, "The boss. He said to take them down."

Thane jogged along the driveway to the front of the house, shouting, "Uncle Jesse... Uncle Jesse!"

As he passed through the pergola, a chainsaw growled to life up ahead, its motor gunned a few times. When he rounded the corner, he saw a man high in his front yard tree, leaning back onto a safety belt while grinding the chainsaw blades into another branch.

A dump truck backed over the curb, stopping with its rear wheels on the lawn near the tree. Two other men tended a chipper that roared to life a short distance away. They began feeding the fallen branches into it. The chipper chewed and spat a stream of chunky sawdust into the back of the truck. Over the roar of the chipper, the chainsaw motor strained, showering sawdust to the ground as the man in the tree pressed the blade into a larger limb.

Thane gaped at the scene.

Uncle Jesse stood at the curb beside the mailbox, talking with a neighbor from across the street who had come out to investigate the sudden frenzy of front yard work.

Thane marched toward the men, clenching his fists at his sides. As he closed in on the men, the neighbor saw Thane's expression and motioned for Uncle Jesse to look.

"What are you doing?" Thane yelled. "You are destroying the

property!"

Uncle Jesse held up a finger to him and said, "Hold on a minute. You need to calm down."

"No, I won't calm down!" Thane shouted louder, competing with the grinding chainsaw. "Why are you doing this?"

"You seem to have forgotten that this is *my* property." Uncle Jesse thumbed at himself.

The neighbor backed away and said, "I'll catch you later, Jesse."

Uncle Jesse nodded and turned back to Thane. "I told you I want to fix this place up, and I meant it. You weren't paying attention if you don't remember that conversation."

As the wood chipper devoured a new set of branches, Uncle Jesse jabbed his finger toward the house and shouted, "I can't compete with this noise. Let's go inside. We need to talk." Uncle Jesse walked to the porch.

Thane looked over his shoulder as he followed, glaring at the man in the tree as another large limb crashed.

As they entered the house, Thane said, "You said I was going to do the painting."

Uncle Jesse went to the living room. "Yeah, well, things change. I did some thinking, and this job is bigger than you can handle, so I went with professionals to get it done—you know—for the sake of speed and quality."

Uncle Jesse pointed to a sofa. "Sit."

Thane moved to a place beside the sofa and remained standing. He folded his arms.

Uncle Jesse turned an easy chair to face him and sat. He rubbed his hands together a few times and said, "You probably wouldn't know it based on the tiny time you spend washing cars at the office, but the tourism business is down. A lot, and your Aunt Gina and I are feeling the financial pinch. From month to month, we're dealing with two car payments, our own mortgage, the mortgage on this place, student loan debt for your cousins, and a great deal of money I've put out for other necessities. I'm sure it's just a temporary downturn in the business. I thought I would weather it, but I can't..."

"Don't say it," Thane said.

"I'm selling this house."

"No! You can't!" Thane said. His face went flush. "No!"

Uncle Jesse stood and pumped his hands toward Thane, saying, "Cool your jets. Don't get all hysterical. That won't change what will happen here, so do yourself a favor and calm down. This house has grown some nice equity, and the property tax and utilities are a burden—not forgetting that you don't pay a dime for it…"

Thane moved to the back of the sofa and shoved his hands into his pocket to keep them from trembling. "Mom's last wish was for me to have this house, and you know it."

"Yeah? Well, she doesn't own it anymore, does she?"

"You tricked me. I should be the owner. You are violating Mom's will."

Uncle Jesse shrugged. "My lawyer has a different opinion. He reviewed it, and it turns out that I was no longer bound to your mother's whims when my name went on the title. It's mine, free and clear. When your mother died, I did what I needed to do to keep the state and lawyers from getting it. You should thank me for letting you squat in this place for as long as you have. Without me, you would have been homeless. Now, look how ungrateful you are for my sacrifice."

Thane kicked the sofa. "You didn't sacrifice. You got a great deal. Taking over payments was a boon for you."

"I figured you wouldn't be thrilled about this decision, but after thinking everything over, forcing you to get a place of your own could be the best thing that ever happened to you. It would do you good to grow up a little, too."

"Uncle Jesse, please!" Thane begged, clasping his hands together. "I have nowhere to go. My whole life is here. I'll do more chores. I'll deliver dinner to your place every night. I'll drive you to work every morning and pick you up every afternoon. I'll wash the outside windows weekly and mow the lawn twice a week if you want me to." Thane's voice quivered. "What will change your mind?"

"A couple hundred grand might change it. You got that?"

Thane stared at him, blinking back tears.

Uncle Jesse shrugged. "That's what I thought. I've made up my mind. The equity in this place is mine, and I need it."

Thane came closer to him. "I'll pay rent! How much do you need?"

Uncle Jesse laughed. "Pay with what? The paltry cash you earn me from washing cars at the office?"

"How could you do this to your own family? I'm your nephew. Mom was your sister!"

"Don't you try to shame me, boy. Your mother should have been more careful with the will. You should be saying, 'It was great while it lasted.'"

Thane grabbed his hair. "This can't be happening!"

"You better hurry and get used to the idea because I already have an interested buyer, and this sale will set your aunt and me up nicely until the tourism business picks up again."

"I have nowhere to go." Thane wiped his eyes on his arm.

"You're going to have at least a month before escrow closes. You should have plenty of time to find a new place."

"I can't deal with this," Thane said, leaving the living room. He went to the kitchen and looked out the window at the fresh paint on the garage.

Uncle Jesse entered the doorway behind him and said, "As a practical matter, you barely use this house. It's too big for you, anyway. You're always holed up in that tiny garage. All of this square footage is a complete waste. You ought to look into studio apartments. Maybe someone will let you manage a property, and you can get your rent down to nothing like you pay me now."

The chainsaw that had been silent for a few minutes roared to life out front again.

Thane said, "You don't get it—my whole life is here. My projects have to happen here, precisely here!"

"Oh? And why is that?"

"You wouldn't understand."

"That's what I thought," Uncle Jesse said.

Thane pushed past him and went out the back door.

Uncle Jesse followed.

The painters had finished a thick coat of white on the side of the garage.

Thane pointed to the stub of the broken solar panel stand protruding from the dirt. "I bought those solar panels with my money!"

"I've been telling you that those panels were an eyesore. They ruin all the curb appeal of this place. I'm not gonna have this place looking like a junkyard, and I sure as hell won't let your experimental crap become a point of negotiation on the sale." Uncle Jesse rolled his eyes. "It would be different if I were making money from those panels—speaking of making money—what about that piano?" He pointed to the garage. "I've got a buyer waiting to give me cash. If you get in the way of that, you'll give me a good reason to kick you out in less than 30 days."

Uncle Jesse went to the garage door, stopped beside the Explorer, and said, "Whose is this?"

"A visitor."

"Well, your visitor damn near ended up with their car painted half white for not being available to move it. Every time I park in the driveway and block your truck, you're all up in arms, but you let somebody park crooked like this, blocking the entry door? Where is this visitor now?"

Thane didn't answer.

Uncle Jesse sucked his teeth and swatted his hand at Thane. He went to the door and tried to open it, but it was still blocked. "What in God's name have you got behind this door?"

"I had to move some things around inside. It's temporary."

"No shit. And you gave me the wrong key to this door. I'm betting you did it on purpose because you were all pissed off about giving me a key."

Thane didn't answer. He twisted his fists in his pockets while staring at the garage.

"Ah, never mind, it doesn't matter," Uncle Jesse said. "But you better damn well get this door open!" Uncle Jesse shoved it. It banged against the block.

"That door is blocked, too." Uncle Jesse pointed to the large roll-up door behind Thane's truck. "You get all these goddamn obstructions moved out of the way. Do you understand, boy?"

Thane glared at him.

Uncle Jesse came closer, getting in Thane's face. "You spite me, and I'll kick you off the property tomorrow. Got it?"

Thane turned and walked away, heading to the house.

"You get back here, Thane!" Uncle Jesse shouted as he followed. "I need that piano, dammit! I'll get it if I have to break the door and get a tow truck to pull it out."

"Go ahead," Thane said as he entered the house and slammed the door closed. He locked it and went to the bedroom. While Uncle Jesse pounded on the back door and hollered at him, Thane eased between the clothes hanging in the closet and quietly closed the closet door. He dropped out of sight as air pulled the drapes from the open window.

Down in the sub-lair, Clay and Morana couldn't rule out Thane's ability to drop a block from the ceiling in any part of the sub-lair onto them with the same speed that he dropped the trap floor. To protect themselves, they felt their way to a place where they could lay side-by-side on the floor between knee-high rectangular blocks in the lift chamber. Thane had placed the blocks there, presumably in preparation to remove them from the sub-lair. If the ceiling dropped, the blocks would seem to create a survivable air space.

"What if he isn't planning to crush us but leaves us down here to starve?" Clay said.

"He won't. If he wants to end us, it will be with a block."

Clay adjusted his position in the cramped space. "I'm telling you that nothing good will come from him ditching us. When Thane moved to the doorway, I got a weird vibe—like he was forcing himself to stay calm before making a run for it. I mean, he knows you're a killer."

"Have you forgotten that he accurately recited all the darkest bullet points on my resume? He wasn't freaked out about me. He was calm."

"He may have looked calm, but if you think about it, we were blocking him in the aquifer. What if he was saying all the right things to get to the door and make a run for it?"

"Shut up!" Morana yelled. "Our only choice is to wait for him to return."

They waited another 20 minutes before Morana said, "Did you feel that?"

Clay sighed. "The only thing I feel is death approaching."

"No, the air… I felt movement."

"Now you're hallucinating."

Morana sat up.

A flashlight blinked on, illuminating the chamber. Thane stood in the corridor entryway, having changed into clean khakis and a white button shirt.

"Oh my God!" Morana said, jumping to her feet. She rushed to him and threw her arms around him. "Sweetheart, you scared us! What happened?"

"There was a power problem above ground," Thane said. He gently pushed free of her, gripping the flashlight with both hands.

"Buddy, you scared the hell out of us," Clay said. "Where did you go?"

"I was fixing the problem."

"If something like that happens again, please take us with you. I'll admit that was terrifying."

Thane didn't answer. Instead, he poked his tongue into his cheek and swept the flashlight beam around the chamber, inspecting the walls.

"My uncle hired a paint crew." Thane pointed up. "He told them to disconnect the solar panels."

"How do you know that?" Clay said.

"Because I just met with him."

Morana looked over her shoulder at the column in the wall where the lift would have appeared. "How did you get there?" she asked.

"That's no longer important." Thane set the flashlight on the floor, aiming it at the ceiling.

In the dim light, Morana leaned closer to him and said, "You've been crying." She gently caressed his chin with her thumb.

"I have some news," Thane said, his voice wavering. "I'm permanently closing the sub-lair."

"What? You can't!" Morana said.

Clay added, "Buddy, what's going on?"

"My uncle is selling the property." Thane twirled his finger above his head. "I need to take you both to the surface—now."

"Before you make that rash decision, please understand that there's no way Clay and I can allow you to lose everything you've worked for."

"No, we'll stop him from selling," Morana said.

"How will you prevent it? Kill my uncle, too?"

"Of course not, but let's discuss other options."

"There's nothing to discuss. My uncle says he already has an offer." Thane wiped tears from his face. "It's over. Some stranger will soon own the garage above us. I'm sealing the sub-lair so no one will ever know it existed."

Clay started to speak, but Morana raised her hand to stop him. "What if there was a way Clay and I could arrange for you to continue having private access to the garage?"

"What new owner would be willing to do that?"

Morana glanced at Clay, then said, "We're aware that this property is on the market."

"How would you know that?"

"Clay discovered it."

"And you didn't tell me?" Thane glared at Clay.

"We didn't want to panic you. Hear us out," Clay said.

"What if we," Morana pointed to herself and Clay, "purchased the property?"

The words didn't fully sink in for Thane. "*You* are the buyers?" he said, frowning.

"Only if your uncle accepts the offer."

Thane put his hand on the wall to steady himself. "So, *you're* the ones who convinced him to sell?"

"No," Clay said. "Listen, Thane, your uncle will sell this place, whether it's to us or not. I saw a listing for your property on a brochure on his desk at the office. I was worried about you, so I accessed your uncle's email and discovered his dismal financial situation."

"You hacked my uncle's computers?" Thane said.

"Wait, Thane," Morana said. "I know how you feel about privacy, but Clay likely saved you from being evicted without a new place to live. If your uncle gets what he wants, he'll sell the property at a profit and with no concern for whether you become homeless."

"I know," Thane said. "He told me that a few minutes ago."

"I think that's wrong and unfair to you," Morana said. "Clay and I can protect this property for you and ensure you aren't victimized—again."

"I can't believe this," Thane said. He put his back to the wall and slid to the floor.

Clay said, "I'm sorry for violating his privacy, but—"

"No, that's not the problem," Thane said, waving off Clay's apology. "I'm glad you hacked my uncle's email. You're right. He wouldn't have told me. He doesn't tell me anything, so thank you." Thane nibbled his cheek, looking up in thought.

Clay continued, "I discovered your uncle subscribed to real estate alerts on this property two months ago. He's way overextended and defaulting on payments to creditors, including his other mortgage and car. His emails show that fights between him and your aunt about money have decimated their marriage. He's even resorted to using company funds to pay some of his personal debts. To save on the real estate commission, he's trying to sell this house himself. Thane, he's desperate. I guarantee the best offer will be in escrow quicker than you can ride to the surface."

"That may be true, but you should have warned me sooner." Their shadows stretched and warped on the wall as Thane picked up the flashlight and wrung its handle.

"We're sorry, Buddy. But now we think we have a solution to this dilemma."

Thane looked at them and said, "You can afford to buy it?"

Clay said, "I'm not loaded, but I just sold my house in Los Angeles. I'm moving to Florida. Using that plus savings, I could make it happen. This property is a smart investment."

Thane got up from the floor and leaned against the wall. His pained expression softened as the realization that Clay and Morana might rescue him from his dilemma relaxed his face momentarily. But then his anxiety returned as he looked back and forth between Morana and Clay. "Do you think owning the property gives you rights to the sub-lair?"

"No," Morana said. "The sub-lair is useless without you, and we understand that. You would maintain one hundred percent control over entry to and exit from it. Buying the property empowers us to protect it for you. This is your masterpiece. We want to preserve it so you can expand it as much as you like."

"And if I say no?"

"Then it will make more sense for me to purchase a house closer to the office," Clay said.

Thane flicked the flashlight on and off a few times, thinking. "No strings attached?" he asked, raising the flashlight to their faces.

"Why are you so skeptical?" Morana asked. "The bottom line is that your situation isn't as dire as it might seem—depending on your willingness to work with us."

"What do you mean by work with you?" Thane asked.

"Actually, we do have an idea for using the sub-lair," Morana said.

Thane raised his hands and let them flop to his sides. "I knew it."

"Don't judge too quickly," Clay said. "You might like the idea."

Thane picked up the flashlight and went to the corridor toward his bedroom chamber.

Clay and Morana followed, staying close, not wanting to risk being abandoned again.

"Sweetheart, please keep an open mind," Morana said, almost tripping into Thane.

As they neared the bedroom chamber, the door slid up. Thane went inside and sat on his mattress.

Morana sat on the floor opposite him, her back to the wall. She patted her hand beside her for Clay to sit.

Thane folded his arms and kept his head down. "I'm listening."

"First, tell me how you feel about your experience with Waylon here in the sub-lair?" Morana asked.

Thane frowned. "What does that have to do with this?"

"Bear with me. What is it like to be free of Waylon's abuse? Be honest."

Thane folded his hands in his lap, and a small laugh welled up in him. "Relief. I must admit, it feels incredible. Knowing that he will never bully me again makes me feel—light." Thane's smile faded.

"But?" Morana said.

"But I feel some shame."

"Why?"

"Because I didn't forgive him." He looked up at her. "They say it's better to forgive. It's better to take the high road—to turn the other cheek—all that."

"All that is bullshit," Morana said. "If you had forgiven Waylon and set him free *again*, he would've abused you and many others for as long as he lived. You said that yourself."

"Still, I wanted to be the stronger person, so I should have forgiven him."

"No, forgiveness does not show strength. People think that the difficulty of forgiveness means that it requires strength. Forgiveness is difficult because it isn't natural, and at our core, we know it isn't fair. Forgiveness creates an imbalance. A person who refuses to be a victim shows strength. The result of permanently ending Waylon's abuse is your freedom and peace of mind. The result of forgiving him would have been to give him a free pass while you take on the burden of ongoing mental anguish about the abuse he would have perpetrated on you and his other victims."

Thane stared at the back of his hands, considering Morana's argument.

She got up, went to him, and sat facing him. "Have you noticed that people most inclined to forgive are those who have no way of getting revenge?"

"That can't be true," Thane said, looking sideways at her.

"It *is* true. And forgiveness is always driven by selfishness. When people are helpless, forgiveness is a crutch used to feel better about themselves. The moral praise a person gets from boasting that they have forgiven comforts the victim. The display of piety distracts observers from the truth of the victim's weakness. Some forgive only because they fear the legal or physical consequences of settling the score. Religious people forgive only because they are taught to defer the vengeance they crave to judgment day when it will be meted out by a beneficient god who will torture those who have trespassed against them. They conjure satisfying fantasies about watching their loving god settle the score on their behalf. They find comfort in the biblical assurance that they'll one day watch the agony of their enemies as a reward for denying themselves the satisfaction of taking immediate revenge."

"Haven't you ever forgiven anyone?" Thane asked.

Morana thought for a moment. "I prefer to remove the need for forgiveness. Righting a wrong does that. Don't forget Newton's unbreakable third law of motion—every action has an equal and opposite reaction. Forgiveness is not equal and opposite. It benefits only the abuser.

Forgiveness causes the victim to suffer more regret, frustration, and inadequacy. It launches an unending effort to forget the injustice they've suffered. This effort creates stress, taking a huge toll on the victim while their exonerated abuser experiences complete stress relief—given a free pass for their wrongs. Revenge completes a perfect, balanced equation." Morana let her words sink in for Thane.

"But many people claim that forgiveness sets them free."

"Of course, they do. This is how the weak avoid embarrassment. I'd say the same thing if I couldn't even the score. Dressing up forgiveness to look comfortable saves face. Forgiveness is a one-sided gift to the abuser and a self-inflicted punishment for the victim. Standing up for oneself by demanding debt repayment makes a person whole and sets them free. Payback fully satisfies Newton's third law of motion."

Thane covered his face with his hands.

"What's wrong?" Morana asked.

"Your argument disturbs me."

"Why?"

"Because its logic makes sense." He dropped his hands and took a deep breath.

"Let me ask you something... Would you repeat your vindication with Waylon if you had another opportunity?"

"Yes," Thane replied without hesitation.

Clay and Morana exchanged a glance. Clay smiled.

Morana got up and sat beside Thane on the mattress. "I understand this might be personal for you, but can you tell me more about what happened between you and Waylon in the chamber?"

Thane briefly studied the back of his hand and said, "The most satisfying part of the experience was his expression. Especially in the first moments after the chamber door closed and we were alone. The gag distorted his face, but his eyes gave me everything I needed. I saw in them his realization of my absolute power over him. I watched him, letting him feel it for a long while. He tried to talk through the gag—begging for mercy. I leered at him the way he leered at me so many times when tormenting me as a child. I expected that evening the score would be satisfying. But what surprised me was how satisfying it would feel to have access to the same tools he used on me. I picked them up one by one and let him feel my power before using them on him. The sensation felt like a balancing. Something was exchanged between us that isn't easy to explain. I felt an emptiness filling up in me." Thane paused and looked up at the ceiling. "Of course, I couldn't settle the score perfectly. Measured throughout our lives, he still hurt me more than I could have hurt him in the brief encounter, but I think the experience balanced things as much as possible. It might have fixed something broken in me that I couldn't fix myself."

"I was hoping you'd feel that way," Morana said.

"I answered your question," Thane said. "Now tell me your idea."

Morana leaned back on her hands and said, "We want to allow other victims to feel the relief you do."

Thane frowned. "You mean more... killing?"

"Not necessarily," Clay said. "Thousands of people have not received and will never receive justice for emotional and physical abuse. When the justice system fails them, they have no recourse."

Morana said, "We want these victims to experience the same relief you feel. Killing wouldn't be mandatory. Repayment could be proportionate."

Thane looked suspiciously at them. "I don't want to introduce more people to the sub-lair. You should know that by now. That's the opposite of maintaining my privacy."

"The victims would never know they were here."

"How? Will you drug them?"

Clay and Morana laughed.

Morana said, "If you're willing to consider using the sub-lair to help other victims like you, this venture could be more fulfilling than you imagine. I can explain."

"Do I have a choice?"

"Absolutely," Clay said. "You can turn us down right now, and we'll call the whole thing off."

"I need to think about it." Thane got up and walked to the entry of the aquifer chamber and stared into the darkness for a few moments before he went inside.

Morana tilted the flashlight to see what he was doing.

Thane kneeled beside the aquifer, spreading his fingers in the water and staring at the ripples.

When Morana looked at Clay, he mouthed, "What's he doing?"

Morana put her finger to her lips.

Thane stayed in the aquifer room for almost 10 minutes. When he returned to the bedroom, he said, "I'm ready to hear the specifics." He provided some paper and, for the next two hours, listened while Morana and Clay presented a plan by which they could use the sub-lair in ultimate secrecy to render justice for victims like Thane and people the justice system had failed. They sketched out security and safety precautions to ensure absolute secrecy. The plan included a solemn oath between them and veto power for Thane to prevent any activity in the sub-lair that he deemed inappropriate.

At the end of their meeting, Thane scratched his head. "This operation is dangerous. What we'd be doing isn't legal."

"You already know my history," Morana said. "You know, I don't mind going to extremes in achieving justice. If you are worried about illegality, remember jury verdicts are legal even when wrong. Inadequate punishments for egregious crimes are legal. Innocent prisoners are too often legally executed for crimes they didn't commit."

"Okay, I get it," Thane said.

"It's not for everyone, but when you introduced me to the sub-lair, and I learned how badly you were abused, I wondered if you'd be inspired to use your amazing discovery to help others hurt the same way."

"Nice pitch," he said. "How long have you been planning this?"

"For years, I've dreamed of an opportunity like this one. I didn't know what it would look like, but I knew I would recognize it when I saw it. Thane, making victims whole is a dream for me, and after learning how Waylon preyed on you and being lucky enough to witness your emancipation, I have the perfect name for our enterprise: *Prey for Us*. I hoped the name would carry special meaning for you."

Thane grinned. "I like it." He sat quietly, studying his thumbnail, then said, "Both of you need to understand that no matter what, I will not disclose my secret."

"We don't need to know it," Morana said. "You will continue to control physical access to the sub-lair."

"There's one other thing," Thane said. "My name goes on the title to the property."

Morana and Clay looked at one another.

Thane added, "If you want to be as fair with me as you claim, it's time to show it."

"I think we can work something out," Morana said.

"Not something—equal ownership," Thane said.

Morana paused. "I have no problem with that."

"Of course, you don't because it's not your money," Clay said.

"Are you seriously going to be greedy now?" Morana snapped.

Thane said, "If my name isn't on the title, there's no deal. Tell me your decision."

Chapter 32

MORANA, CLAY, AND Thane squeezed together on the lift, ascending from the sub-lair. As they neared the surface, the faint ambient light of the garage slowly brightened the shaft.

A few feet before their heads reached the surface, Thane stopped the lift and put his fingers to his lips. Morana examined Thane to determine how he had triggered the stop, but his hands had been in plain view for the entire ride. The lift slowly ascended again, inching up through the shaft opening. As their heads came up over the floor's surface, they looked around the sparse garage interior. Thane expected Uncle Jesse to have broken the door with a bulldozer by now to get the piano, but the door was intact, open a few inches, and pressed against the block that had obviously done its job. The lift brought their feet to floor level, and they stepped off.

"I like your security system," Clay said, pointing to the blocks obstructing both garage doors.

"It's simple, and it works," Thane said, hurrying to the entry door. He closed it and locked the knob. He quickly walked past and checked each window to ensure it was still sealed with its paper covering. He returned to the entry door, spread his hands on the block, and looked over his shoulder at them.

"Do we need to step outside?" Morana asked.

"No, just don't move for a minute," Thane said. He went to the door and flipped a light switch. The garage went dark. The hair-thin seams of light streamed from the edges of the covered windows were inadequate to see what Thane was doing.

His feet scuffed a few times as he moved the block that buttressed the entry door. Then he passed by Clay and Morana to the opposite side of the garage. Through the floor, they felt several faint vibrations a few seconds apart. Thane's footsteps returned to the entry door, and the lights came on.

The work block had been shifted far enough from the entry door to allow it to open.

"Amazing," Morana said.

"You are a phenomenon," Clay added.

Thane opened the door and looked out. He turned back to them and said, "There's no one in the backyard, but my uncle might be in the house. You should leave quickly."

"Why?" Morana said. "He won't recognize me."

"He has already asked about your Explorer. It'll be easier for me if he doesn't see you. He asks a lot of questions."

Morana and Clay exited, and while Clay got into the passenger seat of the Explorer, Morana went to Thane and kissed his cheek. "I don't want you to worry. Remember, you will always be in control."

Thane nodded.

Morana tossed her bag into the back of the Explorer before climbing into the driver's seat.

Thane watched as they drove from the driveway. He went back inside the garage and locked the garage door. He opened a panel on one wall and flipped a switch to change power to the sub-lair from the disconnected solar panels to the garage's wired power. He then descended to the sub-lair and went to the end of the corridor where his expansion of the sub-lair had stopped. He quarried a new block, 7 feet long by 4 feet high. He transported it into the trap floor chamber, where Waylon's body still sprawled. He sliced off the entire face of the block, creating a six-inch slab he set aside. He then hollowed out the block, making a perfectly sculpted sarcophagus.

He took Waylon's legs and worked to heave the body over the edge and into the rectangular cavity. It failed to fall inside. Instead, it hung partially over the edge, twisted in a grotesque position. Thane struggled to push and drag the body until it fell, thudding inside.

He cleaned the blood from the edges and placed the 700-pound slab over it. To prevent any air or moisture seepage from the corpse, he used a mortar epoxy and fluorocarbon aliphatic resin to permanently seal it.

He removed his tools from the chamber, returning with gloves and cleaning supplies a few minutes later. He moved Waylon's sarcophagus to a place beside the door to prepare for transporting it to the surface. Thane had removed all traces of Waylon's demise in less than thirty minutes. After cleansing every drop of blood from the chamber, he had planned to move the body as far away from the sub-lair as possible.

But as Thane stood in the doorway, looking at the sealed sarcophagus, a strange, unexpected feeling came over him. Waylon was now trapped for eternity, placed within a tomb created by the person he had mercilessly victimized for a lifetime. The symbolism of it offset the angst Thane had anticipated from Waylon's intrusion into the sub-lair. The sarcophagus visually represented a permanent end to Waylon's ability to torment him. Looking at it brought about an unexpected comfort.

Thane slowly walked around what felt more like a monument representing victory over injustice. He knew the Egyptians believed that the souls of entombed Pharaohs lived within the chambers where they were buried. If true, Waylon was trapped here and would be forced to observe—according to Morana—many future victims settle scores with bullies like himself.

Thane repositioned the sarcophagus to the center of the floor. After pausing in the doorway to look back at it, he gathered up his supplies and exited the chamber.

He ascended from the sub-lair to the garage. When he emerged through the open shaft, the lift slowed to a stop. He stepped off and checked the door. Not only was it still intact, but it was closed and latched. He went to the corner of the garage and pulled an old gray blanket from the piano his uncle so desperately wanted, revealing its pristine, polished finish.

He covered the piano again and went to the door. He opened it and looked out into the backyard. The painters were gone, and the chainsaw in front had gone silent. Something drew his attention to the kitchen window. He thought he saw the slightest nudge of the curtain. He stared at it for a few moments, but it remained still.

He went to the back door of the house and opened it. "Uncle Jesse?" There was no answer. All the lights were off, and the house was silent. He went inside and called again. "Uncle Jesse?" He passed through the kitchen with his head cocked, listening. In the hallway, he smelled food. After a few more steps, he found the source in the living room. Crumpled fast food bags and ketchup-smeared food containers littered the coffee table and sofa.

He went down the hallway toward the master bedroom. "Uncle Jesse?" Still, no answer. He leaned into the master bedroom. It was untouched since he had cleaned it that morning. He went to the window and checked out front. The workers' truck was gone, and Uncle Jesse's car was no longer parked in the driveway.

Thane was about to turn from the windows when a voice behind him said, "Where did you go?"

Thane spun to find Uncle Jesse leaning against the doorframe, hands in his pockets.

"You scared me," Thane said.

"Guilty conscience?"

"Not at all. I thought you were gone. I was only startled because you snuck up on me."

"Speaking of sneaking, I want you to tell me how you got to the garage from the house?"

"When?"

"When you left me an hour ago—don't play dumb, boy!"

"I walked. How else would I get there?"

"No, no, no," Uncle Jesse waved off the answer. "We were having a conversation in the backyard when you stormed off into the house. I followed you inside, and you were gone. I searched for you every-damned-where in this house except inside the toilet. Then you come strolling out of the garage an hour later after vanishing. I want you to explain that to me."

"I can't explain why you didn't see me. Maybe I went to the garage when you weren't looking."

"Bullshit! I saw that Ford Explorer pull away from the garage. I went to the garage door less than a minute later, and it was already blocked with that big-ass column again. I need to know what you and your visitors are doing on my property and how you moved that tonnage so quickly."

Thane looked at him, not replying.

"If you're gonna be a stubborn ass, I'll kick you off the property tomorrow."

"Go ahead."

Uncle Jesse squinted at him. "What did you just say?"

"Do what you have to do."

Uncle puffed a laugh through his nose. "What the hell has gotten into you, boy? An hour ago, you were begging and crying for me to change my mind about selling, and then just like that, you're over it?"

"You're selling, and I can do nothing about it. You told me the sooner I got used to the idea, the better, right?" Thane went to the door and shouldered his way into the hallway. "It smells in here."

"I had food brought in for the workers," Uncle Jesse said, following him. "You need to get the living room cleaned up."

"No," Thane said.

"Wait a minute," Uncle Jesse said, shoving Thane's shoulder from behind.

Thane stopped in front of his bedroom door and turned back. "Are you going to pay me?"

Uncle Jesse smiled and poked his tongue into his cheek. "Oh, I see… You're feeling uppity because you think you have nothing to lose."

"Clean up your own mess."

Uncle Jesse crossed his arms, gaping at Thane. "You better listen, or I will make you sorry. Now, take your ass into the living room and clean up that goddamn trash."

Thane ignored him and entered his bedroom. He stopped and covered his mouth. The closet doors had been pulled from their hinges, one lying on the floor. The other hung, barely connected. "What have you done?" he said.

Uncle Jesse entered the doorway. "You must have forgotten that I own every square inch of this property—including the closets."

"You had no right to come into this room—we had an agreement."

"Oh, calm down, boy. It's not like you were hiding anything in there. I don't understand why you had the closet all locked up like you were hoarding gold bars, but there wasn't anything inside worth a shit."

Thane picked up one of the closet doors and made a half-hearted effort to reattach it before throwing the door to the floor. He brushed off his hands and said, "You're lucky that you didn't find what these closet doors protected."

"Oh?" Uncle Jesse came closer and looked inside. He grabbed some clothes that hung there and shoved him aside. He examined the floor and walls. "Maybe you're going insane because, like I said, there's nothing in here." He stepped back, stared at Thane, and then wagged his finger. "I always figured something about you wasn't quite right. Like you weren't well in the head, but my news about selling must have triggered a bizarre mental breakdown or something. Whatever it is, you've got problems."

"Your problems are bigger than mine."

Uncle Jesse smirked. "What the hell do you know about my problems?"

Thane leaned against the wall and crossed his arms. "Your marriage would be over if it wasn't for me."

"How do you figure?"

"I wash your car at the office," Thane said. "I see the receipts stuffed under the driver's floor mat… I wonder if Aunt Gina knows about your gambling problem. Even if she does, she does not know how much money you've lost, and it's only getting worse for you. So you have been forced to sell this place."

Uncle Jesse's mouth dropped open. "What I choose to share with your aunt is none of your goddamn business."

"Of course, it isn't. I also wonder if your corporate bosses know you've cooked the books to cover your debt."

"What?" Uncle Jesse's face went flush.

"How about the women you bring into this house from the 'service' you use?" Thane air-quoted. "Does Aunt Gina know about the hookers, too?"

Uncle Jesse covered his face and exhaled through his fingers. "Alright, listen. What if I were to take care of your first month's rent in a new place? You know—help you get on your feet."

"Suddenly, you want to help me?" Thane rolled his eyes.

"Obviously, I'm in a… difficult position. So, I hope we can put the past behind us considering my generous offer. Your past… and my past."

"So, I'd be saving your marriage and helping you avoid bankruptcy for what you call a generous one month's rent? Doesn't seem proportionate, does it?"

"What if I covered your rent anywhere for a year? Think about it… a year would set you up real nice."

"You couldn't afford to pay my rent somewhere else for a year."

"Dammit, boy, what the hell do you want? What landlord will want you as a tenant when you don't even have a job? If you work with me, we can both come out better for it."

"I don't need your help."

"So, you aren't willing to negotiate here?"

Thane shrugged.

"You expect me to walk away and leave you with the ability to hold all this shit over my head? What do you want? Let's settle it."

"Put my name back on the property title."

Uncle Jesse laughed. "You've got to be out of your goddamned mind."

"You wanted a solution. I gave you one. As I said before, your problems are bigger than mine."

"I see," Uncle Jesse said. He shoved the bedroom door with his foot, and it slammed shut.

"What are you doing?" Thane said, backing away.

Uncle Jesse strolled toward him. "I thought you would be a minor problem when selling the property, but I was wrong. I'm not going to let you into my life, but for such a scrawny piece of shit, you've created a big problem." He backed Thane to the wall.

"Wait! I won't tell Aunt Gina," Thane said, raising his hands.

"Boy, you have the nerve to threaten me, then you expect me to trust you to keep your mouth shut?"

"I won't tell—I swear!"

Uncle Jesse came closer, closing in. "I wish I could believe you, but you've shown your hand, and I can't let you play any of those cards. You're stupid, just like your mother."

Thane eyed the closet, wondering if he could hurdle the broken doors and activate the lift before his uncle could get him. Perhaps Uncle Jesse's shock at seeing the lift move would buy enough time to escape out of his reach. But Uncle Jesse certainly wouldn't sell the property after seeing the lift in action, and he would harass Thane for answers—forever. Knowledge of the sub-lair had been shared with too many people already.

Uncle Jesse grabbed his shirt, squeezing it into his fists. "You always were a coddled little shit. I should have kicked you out the day I took the property."

"You will pay for anything you do to me."

"Another threat?" Uncle Jesse slammed Thane against the wall before throwing him to the floor.

The fall knocked the wind out of Thane, and he coughed, then screamed, "No! Let me go!"

Uncle Jesse leered down at him while Thane swung his fists, landing a few useless blows on Uncle Jesse's stomach and shoulders. Uncle Jesse delivered a blow to Thane's jaw.

Thane twisted and pressed his legs against the wall. He used all his strength to thrust, toppling Uncle Jesse to his side.

Uncle Jesse scrambled back onto Thane, his face contorted with rage as he began punching Thane.

Thane blocked as many blows as he could, but several landed.

"This is the beating your mama should have given you," Uncle Jesse said as he rubbed his knuckles. When Uncle Jesse rose slightly, Thane used his knee to land a solid blow to Uncle Jesse's groin.

Uncle Jesse toppled to his side, moaning.

Thane seized the opportunity, scrambling to his feet. He ran to the door and threw it open. While he raced down the hallway, he heard Uncle Jesse stumbling behind him in the bedroom. Thane sprinted through the kitchen and out the back door. He rushed into the garage, closed the door, and locked the knob.

He heard Uncle Jesse come out of the house yelling, "Damn you, runt!" The footsteps raced toward the garage.

Thane's hands trembled as he quickly moved the 8-ton block to the entry door. The doorknob jiggled.

Uncle Jesse's foot slammed against the door, and he yelled, "Now that you're trespassing, I'm calling the police."

Thane staggered to the center of the garage and collapsed onto the floor, panting.

While Uncle Jesse yelled and cussed outside, Thane kept quiet. As his adrenaline rush subsided, the pain of the beating Uncle Jesse gave him set in. He felt a stabbing burn in his ribs, and his face and upper body ached.

The pounding on the door stopped. After a brief pause, Uncle Jesse said, "Listen, I'm sorry I lost my temper, Thane. Let me in so we can talk this out. We're family, and you're making this situation much uglier than it should be."

Thane ignored him, waiting quietly in the garage until he was sure his uncle was gone. He crawled to the countertop and pulled himself to his feet. He grabbed a towel, wiped the blood from his mouth, then picked up the phone and dialed Morana.

Chapter 33

MORANA ARRIVED AT the garage less than 15 minutes after Thane's urgent call. When Thane opened the door, Morana said, "My God, what happened to you?" She lifted his chin to examine his face.

Thane took her wrist and pulled her inside. He quickly closed the door and locked it. "My uncle cornered me in the house. We had an uncomfortable exchange, and one thing led to another."

"Your uncle did this to you?" Morana asked, suppressing her anger while she smoothed his shirt.

"He tried to intimidate me by threatening to kick me off the property today."

"He can't do that. We will have closed escrow before he can legally evict you. You can stay."

"Still, he became angry and attacked me. I freed myself and ran out the back door. He chased me, and then he threatened to call the police."

Morana sucked her teeth. "That's unfortunate."

Thane quickly added, "He bluffs all the time—he didn't mean it."

"You can't be sure." Morana strolled to the countertop and back, tapping her chin while she thought. "We can't allow him to follow through on his threat."

"So, what are you saying?" Thane asked, wringing his hands.

"I'm saying—" Morana paused when she saw the tension spreading on Thane's face. "I know it might be difficult for you to hear, but your uncle is positioning himself to become an ongoing problem that requires an immediate solution. I assume you won't have a problem if I remove him as a concern."

Thane winced.

Morana said, "His threats to bring police to the property risks our future as much as Waylon's threats risked your life. You're lucky to have escaped from both of them."

"I don't think my uncle would've killed me."

"Again, you can't know that. Your uncle knew he was about to lose everything, including his marriage. Permanently silencing you could have felt like his best option at that moment. Your uncle is an example of the problems *Prey for Us* will resolve. When he attacked you, he showed an unmistakable willingness to continue abusing you—or worse."

Thane stared at his feet.

Morana stepped closer and rested her hands on his shoulders, holding him at arm's-length to see his eyes. "Your uncle tried to hurt you. Things need to be made right. Don't forget an eye for an eye and a tooth for a tooth. Don't forget that Newton's third law of motion requires an equal and opposite reaction. If your uncle calls the police, it will ruin our plan to help victims like you. Think of how they will suffer because we let this opportunity go. Your uncle needs to be dealt with."

Thane looked at her, trying to formulate a response.

"Have I misunderstood?" Morana asked. "Do you have feelings for a man who virtually enslaved you?"

"No, but I do for my Aunt Gina."

"Dispensing with your uncle will be a favor to her. He's a serial cheater. He's got a gambling issue. He illegally tampered with his sister's will to steal property she wanted you to inherit. He's verbally abusive, and you and I know your Aunt Gina won't see a nickel of the profit he gets from this property. When *Prey for Us* gets going, we can care for your aunt financially."

Morana's consolation did nothing to soften Thane's expression. He left her and walked around the inside perimeter of the garage with his fingers interlocked on his head. On his second lap, he abruptly turned and came back to her. His face lit up. "I have an idea."

Morana picked up a towel and wiped a smear of blood from Thane's face. "Please tell me. I'm all ears."

Thane moved his remaining tools and supplies down to the sub-lair that evening. Later that night, he returned to the garage and loaded his truck with the blocks he used to obstruct the garage doors. He made three trips, transporting them to one of his secret disposal locations.

To avoid another confrontation with Uncle Jesse, Thane spent most of the following week safely hidden in the sub-lair after Morana gave him a burner phone. With it, he could reach her without using the landline on occasional trips to the garage. Thane eventually permitted her to visit him more than once, always giving her an arrival time after dark. He unlocked the garage door and allowed Morana to operate the lift—for descent only—to meet him in the sub-lair. On each visit, she brought food, and they continued planning for the *Prey for Us* venture.

Two weeks after Uncle Jesse's assault on Thane, Morana broke protocol by visiting Thane in the midafternoon. Although Thane had always given her visiting times after dark, he had not forbidden her to visit during the day. If he was upset by today's visit, she hoped he would forgive her when she explained its purpose.

She stayed close to the house as she quietly approached the garage.

As she expected, the door was locked. She produced a key Clay had made for her after he successfully picked it the night before.

She entered the garage and saw that Thane had the trap floor activated, as expected. She went to the sub-lair lift and threw back the carpet on the Gateway block. Morana stomped her heel on the corner of the lift. It descended, swallowing her into the shaft as she sank into the floor. Not knowing whether Thane would be ecstatic or furious about this visit made her take a deep breath.

When the lift came to a stop, Morana's heart pounded. She should have reached the sub-lair's lift chamber, but she was still enveloped in pitch darkness except for the tiny square of light produced by the shaft opening in the garage above. She stomped her foot on the lift to make it move, but it wouldn't.

She reached out, feeling toward where the chamber should be, and her fingers touched nothing. She reached in further, waving her hand, feeling for a wall, suddenly realizing she had arrived in the sub-lair. All the lights were off. "Thane? …Sweetheart, are you here?"

There was no answer.

Morana cursed herself for forgetting a flashlight. She cautiously put some weight on one foot outside the lift before stepping entirely off it and into the dark chamber.

"Thane!" she yelled louder.

The lights blinked on.

"Thank God," Morana said. But as she looked around the chamber, she saw something different. The corridor was gone. She was sealed in a solid chamber with no exit. She dragged her fingers around the wall, looking for an opening. Thane had to know she was here. When she had almost completed a full search around the chamber's perimeter, air rushed in as a wall suddenly ascended, revealing Thane standing in a new chamber.

Thane stepped toward Morana, his face troubled. "What are you doing here during the day?"

Morana held out a set of keys to him and said, "Congratulations! You are a property owner."

"Already? You said not until next week."

"Next week came sooner. Escrow closed today."

Thane smiled as he looked at the key in his hand, rubbing it with his thumb. "Yes."

"Clay and I arranged a cash sale after we convinced your uncle to accept our own contingencies, which included an as-is sale, skipping all appraisals and inspections."

"He accepted that?"

"Well, he countered with one request: He was adamant about getting that piano from the garage. We agreed to let him pick it up."

"He's coming back?" Anxiety spread on Thane's face.

Morana said, "It'll be the last time you have to deal with him. Meanwhile, we have more planning to do."

They went to Thane's bedroom chamber and sat on the mattress. They continued discussing the logistics and security measures they would require for the sub-lair for the next half hour.

Morana produced an architectural draft of a sub-lair expansion concept from her bag and spread it between them. She overlaid it with parchment paper and used a pencil to highlight the perimeter of a facility that contained twenty rooms. She tapped a pencil on it. "Can you expand the sub-lair to this?"

Thane scratched his neck. "Yes, but it would take some time. I estimate it would require seven to eight months, but it can be done."

"Are you sure there is enough solid subterranean coral rock to encapsulate the type of facility we're envisioning?" she asked.

Thane briefly left the bedroom and returned with an aerial layout of the house, backyard, and easement beyond it. "The mantle is immense," he said, pointing out the property boundaries. "I've acquired data on a recent subterranean geologic survey, and aside from a few aquifer veins, there's no break in the rock for at least a square mile and well over one hundred and fifty feet deep."

"Excellent," Morana said.

Morana checked her watch and said, "I almost forgot to ask—what have you done with your truck?"

"What do you mean?" Thane asked.

"I didn't see it parked up there." Morana pointed up.

"He towed it! My uncle must have towed it."

"Are you sure?"

"There's no other explanation. He must know I'm still here. He took my truck to spite me."

Morana took his hand. "Don't worry. We will get it back for you."

"But when? I need my truck! No sub-lair expansion happens without it."

Thane got up and left the bedroom. Morana followed him along the corridor, saying, "Sweetheart, you have nothing to worry about."

"I have everything to worry about. There would be no sub-lair without that truck."

The lift was still in place when they entered the chamber. Morana squeezed onto it with him, and it immediately ascended. They quietly rode while Thane shook his head and occasionally sighed.

After they reached the garage, Thane went straight for the garage door. When he opened it to confirm the horrible news, he froze. A brand-new Ford F-350 Super Duty pickup truck was parked beside his small, dilapidated truck.

Clay exited the driver's seat and approached Thane, handing him the keys.

"You're kidding me," Thane said, taking them.

"I hope you don't mind—we added the heavy service suspension package," Clay said, beaming. "This should double what you can transport with your old truck and do so with much more comfort. The mobile window tinting service will be here tomorrow to add privacy to your new ride."

Thane grinned as he slowly walked around the truck, shaking his head. He pointed down the driveway to the pergola and said, "This is so big. I can't believe it fit through the archway."

"Barely, but yes," Clay said.

Morana clasped her hands under her chin. "Get in and have a look around."

Clay opened the driver's door for him, and Thane climbed in. He looked up and around the cab, taking in the amenities. He caressed the plush seats and opened the center console. It was fully stocked with an assortment of tools and snacks. He exited and stepped back from the truck to take the whole thing in. "What about insurance?"

"We've taken care of everything," Morana said. "In fact, take this, too." She handed him a gas card. "All the fuel you need for this truck is prepaid."

"How?" Thane said.

"We are embarking on a business venture together. Your gasoline use is a business expense we've already expected."

"Thank you," Thane said.

"You're welcome." Morana smiled at him.

"Thank you for your partnership," Clay added. "Our work makes a vehicle upgrade for you an easy decision."

Morana turned to Clay. "Now, Thane and I have a surprise for you."

"Oh?" Clay said, suddenly uneasy.

Thane looked at her, confused.

Morana went to Thane, put her arm around him, and pulled him close. "We're pregnant!"

Clay gasped.

Thane's face went pale. "You're kidding…"

"You're right, I am kidding. But wouldn't that be wild?" She laughed.

Thane leaned onto his knees to exhale.

Morana laughed as she rubbed his back. "I'm sorry, Sweetheart."

Clay said, "Not funny, Mo. You could have seriously hurt him!"

A buzz echoed inside the garage. Thane spun toward the door and said, "What was that?"

"It's okay," Clay said. "I wired the house doorbell to hear it while we're in the garage."

"It's probably your uncle," Morana said, looking at her watch. "I'll go get him and bring him back."

Thane backed toward the garage door, looking as though he might run.

"Don't worry," Morana said. "Remember, this won't take long, and then he'll be out of your life." She and Clay split up. Morana walked down the driveway to the front, and Clay went straight to the back of the house.

Thane disappeared into the garage and quickly moved the piano to a location just to the side of the roll-up door. As he came to the entry door, he heard voices approaching outside.

"I'm going to need you to move your truck so my buyer can back his truck in for the piano," Uncle Jesse said.

"That truck isn't mine," Morana said. "I'll ask the owner to move it."

Thane came out of the garage.

"Oh, there he is," Morana said. "Sweetheart, can you move your truck?"

Uncle Jesse stopped and gawked. "What the hell are you still doing here?"

Thane didn't answer. He went to the truck and climbed into the cab.

Uncle Jesse turned to Morana. "What's going on here?"

Thane started the truck and slowly rolled toward the front of the house.

"He's the new owner of the property."

"Is this a joke?" Uncle Jesse said.

"It's no joke."

"But Thane's name was not on the title."

"It was a corporate purchase."

"Then he can't be the owner," Uncle Jesse said, crossing his arms.

"Thane has a controlling interest in the organization. You seem upset."

"No, no, not at all," Uncle Jesse said, clearing his throat. "Just… surprised. I'm wondering how he pulled this off."

"You should be proud of him. Thane is a genius, but I'm sure you knew that."

"Right," Uncle Jesse said, kicking a small stone.

"He's told me about you."

"Hmph," Uncle Jesse said, briefly widening his eyes.

"What exactly did he say?"

"Straighten out!" Thane's voice interrupted them, echoing from around the corner.

They moved so they could see the entire length of the driveway.

Thane walked backward, guiding a different pickup truck as it backed through the pergola until it stopped just outside the garage where Thane's new truck had been parked.

Clay kneeled on the living room floor below the window inside the house, typing on his laptop. A wire ran from it through a crack in the living room's window and outside to a receiver hidden in the flower bed below. He opened the software for the radio transceiver kit and showed a successful signal capture of the FOB for Uncle Jesse's car. He plugged in a blank FOB. Within seconds, it was programmed with the unlock codes. He took his laptop and the FOB out the front door and hurried to the car. Pressing the button unlocked Uncle Jesse's driver's door. Clay connected his laptop to the electronic control unit under the dash. After a few mouse clicks, he had disabled the truck's ignition system. He hurried back into the house. He activated a signal jammer in the living room, blocking all mobile phone signals within a 100-meter radius. He checked his phone to verify the signal was blocked, then tucked the laptop under the living room sofa. With his tasks completed, he went to the kitchen window to watch.

A pickup truck with a *Golly Dolly Movers* sign on the door was backed to the closed garage door. A muscular guy wearing a *Golly Dolly Movers* T-shirt climbed from the driver's seat. The piano buyer got out of the passenger side. He had white hair and wore a dress shirt, pressed slacks, and loafers with no socks.

The garage door slid up. Thane stood inside. He brushed off his hands and pointed to the piano he'd moved from the back wall to the edge of the doorway, then joined Morana outside.

After glaring at Thane, Uncle Jesse turned to the other men and said, "Load her up."

The moving guy connected a metal ramp to the bed of the pickup truck. He and the buyer took hold of the piano and rotated it to align it with the ramp. The moving guy gave a three-count, and they lifted one side of the piano, dragging it to rest on the ramp. After another three-count, they heaved, trying to push the piano up the ramp. During the effort, their faces reddened, and their neck veins bulged. Halfway up the ramp, they rested. The moving guy said, "She's heavy—real heavy."

"That's how Steinway makes them," the buyer panted. "This model has a cast iron harp, and all the fittings are brass," the buyer said, freeing one hand to point to the pedals. "She's about 600 lbs. C'mon, we can do this."

"I'm not so sure," the moving guy said. "We might need to come back with a hydraulic lift."

"Any chance we could get some help?" the buyer said sarcastically, pointing to Uncle Jesse.

"Help them, boy," Uncle Jesse snapped at Thane. "You moved it across the garage floor all alone. The least you could do is lift a finger to help them now."

Thane looked at Morana.

She gave him a slight nod.

Thane went to the men and positioned himself at the end of the piano with them.

The moving guy called out another three-count, and they all heaved.

Morana smiled while Thane contorted his face to exaggerate his effort.

They slid the piano the rest of the way up the ramp and into the truck bed.

The moving guy slammed the tailgate closed and threw a blanket over the piano. He began unraveling some ratchet straps to secure it.

Thane returned to Morana's side.

The buyer produced a wad of cash from his pocket. He licked his thumb as he approached Uncle Jesse, whose grin broadened as the buyer counted out hundred-dollar bills into his hand. "…Sixty-two, sixty-three, sixty-four hundred dollars."

Thane's mouth dropped open.

"It was a pleasure doing business with you," Uncle Jesse said, re-counting the money.

"No, I should thank you. It's in wonderful shape." The buyer and the mover got into the truck and drove away.

"Half of that money should be mine," Thane said. "Mom left the piano to me, and you know it."

Morana squeezed his hand.

Uncle Jesse briefly waved the money in front of Thane's face. "If you had any business sense, you would have already sold the piano." He folded and forced the fat wad of cash into his front pocket. He pulled a wallet from his back pocket and pulled out a five-dollar bill. He flung it toward Thane, and it fell to the ground. "That's for moving the piano to the door. Labor's the only thing you're good for." He looked at Morana and said, "I don't know what you see in him, but be prepared to support him—forever."

"Excuse me," Morana said. "Thane is your family. How can you treat him this way?"

"Look, our real estate deal is done, lady. Now is a good time for you to mind your own business."

Thane squeezed Morana's hand.

Uncle Jesse turned and shook his head as he walked up the driveway to the front of the house.

Thane whispered, "Did you make the call?" Thane asked.

"Of course, Sweetheart. Everything's in place."

"But he's leaving!" Thane said. He walked up the driveway, but Morana stopped him.

"He isn't going anywhere. Trust me, your plan is in full effect. I wish I had thought of it."

They went to the house's back door and into the kitchen, where Clay waited. "Come see the show," he said, leading them to the living room window.

Out front, Uncle Jesse had just exited the driver's door of his car after discovering that it would not start up. He went to the front of the car and raised the hood.

"I don't know what he's looking for," Thane said. "He doesn't know anything about cars."

After leaning over the engine to look at nothing specific, Uncle Jesse slammed the hood closed and kicked the car's fender.

"What's taking so long?" Thane said.

"Be patient, sweetheart," Morana said, rubbing his back.

They watched Uncle Jesse pull out his phone.

"This'll be interesting," Clay said.

Uncle Jesse tapped the screen and then put it to his ear. He looked at the phone and walked to the driveway entrance. As he approached the house, he didn't notice a dark gray sedan pull to the curb behind his car. He remained focused on his phone while climbing the porch to the entryway. He rang the bell and pounded on the door.

Morana turned to Thane. "Why don't you take care of this?"

Thane went to the door and opened it.

"My car won't start," Uncle Jesse said. "I need to use your landline."

"Use your mobile phone," Thane said.

"Boy, don't you think I would've done that if I could? I'm getting no signal." He frowned at his phone. "That's odd—the signal is always strong here."

"So you want to use our landline?"

"That's what I said, boy." Uncle Jesse tried to push his way inside.

Thane sidestepped and blocked him. "That'll be $3,200."

"Hilarious," Uncle Jesse said.

Behind him, two beefy men in suits got out of the sedan. One of them opened the car's back door before they strolled toward the porch.

Uncle Jesse didn't notice them because he was too busy glaring at Thane. "Boy, if you think I can't bring you as much trouble as you make for me, you are dead wrong," he said, still not noticing the approaching men. "I need to use your landline, and then I'll be on my way."

"Thane gave you his price," Morana said.

"Fuck you people." Uncle Jesse turned to leave but was startled by the two men standing directly behind him. They stood side by side, blocking Uncle Jesse's exit from the porch.

One man cracked his knuckles, leering at him. "What's up, Jesse?" he said.

"What do you want?" Uncle Jesse said, taking a step back from them.

"C'mon, you know that's a silly question." The men chuckled and looked at one another. "You should remember us. We've helped you many times. You've used us to collect money you owe to the boss, but we need to collect from you this time."

The other guy said, "And the boss made it clear that if you pay his money late, there would be a late fee."

"I'll pay it," Uncle Jesse said, panic spreading on his face.

"And you were also informed that if we had to make a special trip to collect the boss's money and his late fee, there would be an additional inconvenience fee."

Uncle Jesse swallowed hard and raised his hands. "Listen, we can work this out."

The guys laughed. One said, "Oh, we know. That's the beauty of it. And from what we hear, you can handle a couple of extra fees now, so our timing is good."

They stepped closer.

"Listen, guys," Uncle Jesse said, his voice wobbling. "I can pay everything, including all the fees, tomorrow."

"Unfortunately, tomorrow is a day too late. The boss figured you'd say something like that, so he wants you to spend a little time with us until your promises come true."

Uncle Jesse lunged, trying to dart between them, but the men sidestepped, closing the gap. One slammed him against the wall. When Uncle Jesse struggled to break free, the other man delivered a gut punch that doubled him over.

Uncle Jesse gasped and coughed. He caught his breath and said, "Thane, don't just stand there! Do something, boy! Help!"

Thane replied, "If you had any business sense, you would have already paid these guys." He slammed the door and locked it.

Morana, Clay, and Thane moved to the living room window, where they watched the men drag Uncle Jesse across the front yard to the open rear door of the sedan. When he put up a final desperate fight, resisting their efforts to get him into the car, one man delivered another blow to his stomach, shoved him into the back seat, and slammed the door closed.

"Will they kill him?" Thane asked.

"No, not these guys," Clay said.

Morana added, "But we can't make any promises about tomorrow's visitors. He'll need that escrow money."

End of Book 1

Reviews

Thank you for reading **Prey for Us.** Word-of-mouth is crucial for any author to succeed. If you enjoyed this book, please consider leaving a review at Amazon, even if it's only a line or two. It would make all the difference and would be very much appreciated: **Prey for Us Reviews.**

Free Bonus Material

After writing each book, I put in some extra work to create bonus materials to connect directly with my readers. For *Prey for Us*, I've created a virtual tour of the sub-lair as I envisioned it. This POV video footage will take you on a journey where you'll descend from the garage to the sub-lair and move about the corridors and rooms of Thane's creation. (He doesn't know I'm showing you, so keep this under your hat.) If your imagined concept of the sub-lair is perfect and you don't want it affected, move on to the book 2 preview below. But if you'd like to see how the sub-lair looked in my mind while writing the story, tell me where to send your link to the tour. Visit: **https://gneil.co/sublairtour**

What's Next?

Morana, Clay, and Thane have big plans and a great deal of work ahead to prepare for their new venture. The total isolation offered by the sub-lair has provided an unprecedented opportunity for seclusion and protection as they embark on a mission of vigilante justice with stunning effectiveness.

In subsequent books in the *Prey for Us* series, you'll see the rapid expansion of the sub-lair, development of the intricate *Prey for Us* security measures, acquisition of new prey, and a stunning influx of cash beyond even Morana's expectations. With so much going for them, what could go wrong? You'd be surprised.

Enjoy a preview of another book, *HR,* that's been optioned for film and television:

Human Resources - Preview

One

IF SOMETHING SEEMS too good to be true, enjoy the hell out of it before it ends. That was Nelson Dupar's philosophy.

His perfect life began when the hospital elevator closed him in alone with her. She stood six feet tall and dressed to wither other women. A mile of toned leg stretched between candy-apple high-heels and a black leather miniskirt. She flipped her dark hair, sending a wisp of perfume—or something—to his nose. Whatever it was, Nelson smiled. Standing so close to her was a treat. She made the 28-year-old self-confessed slob wish he owned an iron.

Nelson's daily wardrobe was unimportant while buried in a tiny cubicle at the CPA firm. Today, he wore his standard attire: scuffed gray deck shoes, wrinkled slacks, and an untucked button shirt that failed to conceal his gut.

The woman moved forward to crowd the door and closed her eyes. Nelson leaned slightly to enjoy a deeper whiff of her while he sucked in to tuck his shirt. He then enjoyed an unrushed visual tour of this magnificent being's backside, taking in her smooth curves and generous display of skin and hair that shined where it bent at her shoulder.

She sighed and wrung her hands.

"You okay, ma'am?" Nelson asked.

She shook her head, not looking back. "I'm always nervous in elevators," she replied.

Nelson reached to pat her shoulder but reconsidered. "We'll be fine," he said. "And if anything happens, there's a hospital real close."

She laughed a breath through her nose and bowed her head as if praying. When the elevator bumped and lifted, she teetered and pressed her hand against the wall to steady herself.

Nelson watched, intrigued. *I wonder if she might faint,* he thought. The slim chance of a CPR opportunity excited him despite having no training for it. He reasoned that the honorable thing to do if she collapsed would be to give her a little mouth-to-mouth. He'd seen it a thousand times on TV. Just ease her to her back and tilt her head. Her moist lips would part ever so slightly. He'd gently place his mouth over hers. And, not forgetting the chest compressions, he'd need to unbutton...

The elevator door opened, popping Nelson's fantasy.

"Thank God," the woman said as they stepped out.

"See? We're elevator survivors!" Nelson said.

She laughed and turned to him. "Yes, we are!"

The brightness of the hallway added detail to her features. Her hair, almost black, contrasted with piercing blue eyes over a perfect smile. Nelson wished she had fainted.

"You take care, ma'am," he said, reluctantly turning to leave.

"Wait! What's your name?" she replied, fanning her face.

From the side of his mouth, Nelson whispered, "Clark Kent." She laughed again—a bit longer than he expected.

"Nice to meet you, Clark. I'm Morana."

"Actually, my name is Nelson, and it's even nicer to meet you. Come here often, Morana?"

"Only as a last resort."

"Some 'resort' this is, right?"

She laughed harder. Either Nelson was on a roll, or this woman was just incredibly giddy after conquering the elevator.

They walked toward the hospital exit. Morana sidestepped moving gurneys and oncoming foot traffic, hurrying to stay near him. When Nelson noticed they had taken on the appearance of a couple, his chin lifted, and his stride took on some swagger. As they passed through the crowded lobby, Morana drew intrigued smiles and lustful examination from people. Nelson knew she was out of his league, but for this fleeting moment, he relished being the nerd who baffled the jocks by seducing the hottest cheerleader.

Outside at the patient loading zone, their linked journey ended. Nelson pointed to the far side of the parking lot. "My car's way over in the last row. You take care."

Morana smiled. "Thank you for calming me with your comedy." She extended her hand.

As they shook, Nelson said, "Hey, I'm here all week—be sure to tip the veal and try your waiter!"

Morana bent over in a belly laugh that turned nearby heads.

Flattering, but the line wasn't that funny, Nelson thought. Never had his cheesy jokes impressed any of the women he wanted. He scratched his neck, waiting for her to finish laughing.

She caught her breath and said, "You are absolutely adorable."

"Thanks. You know, I get that all the time," Nelson said, finger-framing his face.

She laughed again and touched his arm, saying, "Oh my God—I want to take you home with me."

Nelson felt blood rush to his head as he realized that her flirtation might have traction. *How is this possible?* He knew that when Morana stepped from the dark elevator, her first glance had swept up the details of his grooming and pegged his socio-economic rung, yet her enthusiasm toward him hadn't dimmed.

"Hold on," she said, digging in her purse. She handed him a business card. "Call me."

Centered on the card was one word: *Morana,* printed above a barely visible gray phone number. No company, no title, and no address.

"Secretive much, Morana?" he asked.

"I can explain some other time. Please call me 'Mo' and call me soon."

"Sure thing," Nelson said. He watched her walk away—graceful, confident, gorgeous. *Not a chance in hell,* he thought.

He was wrong.

• • •

Nelson waited outside a hangar at Nadi Airport in Fiji two months later. He rested against the leather headrest in the chartered helicopter and fanned the front of his shirt for relief from the humidity. The twelve-hour flight from San Francisco had him foggy despite the many naps he had enjoyed fully reclined in first class.

On the floor beside him, dangling her feet outside the helicopter door, sat Mo, or *Cover Girl*, a nickname Nelson's envious buddies back at the office had given Morana after seeing her pick him up from work a few times. She wore a denim mini-skirt and a men's dress shirt with the sleeves rolled up—a neglected gift she had purchased for Nelson weeks ago.

It seemed not even jetlag could damper Mo's excitement about this impromptu trip until the helicopter's charter company rang her cell phone to say the pilot would be late. She reached back, gently twisted Nelson's wrist to check the time, and then frowned.

"What's your rush?" Nelson asked.

"We have lunch waiting," she said. She poked out her bottom lip and blew the hair from her face. "And I wanted so badly to have you at the resort already."

After seven weeks of dating, Nelson had given up trying to

understand Morana's infatuation with him. Whenever they ventured out in public, men, and women hit on her. Some of her suitors appeared wealthy, and many were incredibly attractive. She withheld her phone number and dodged all advances with polished finesse. But for some reason, she couldn't get enough of Nelson. When he asked what she saw in him, she would only stroke his chin and say, "You make me crave you."

Nelson didn't know where her money came from—she wouldn't say. But he knew he could never have afforded the lifestyle Mo gave him. She showered him with expensive gifts of artwork, furniture, and concerts. Any material indulgence he mentioned to her in passing seemed to materialize for him within days, sometimes hours. She always paid when they went out, and when they returned to his place, she insisted on massaging him every night before the sex—lots of sex—sex that she joked was all the repayment she needed.

A month ago, he came home to find a new, white Porsche Carrera parked in his apartment's carport, the dealer spec sheet still taped inside the window. After he circled the car twice, grinning, he said, "Mo, there's no way I can accept this—it's far too expensive."

"You are so worth it! Don't hurt my feelings!" she replied, feigning a pout. She tossed him the keys, and when he caught them, she squealed and jumped up and down, clapping. Obliging her by accepting her lavish gifts made her so happy. It was the least he could do. He had it good, real good, too good.

Finally, they saw their pilot jogging toward them from the hangar office. He climbed into the helicopter with a clipboard tucked under his arm and wearing a bright tropical shirt.

"Hi, I'm Captain Kurt. Welcome to my *Skyship Enterprise*," he said. Nelson laughed. Morana rolled her eyes. "I'm sorry for the delay, folks. I can make up the time," Captain Kurt promised. He eased into the cockpit and donned a headset. The helicopter's turbines whined.

Outside, a man in a grease-smeared outfit shut the helicopter's door, muting the whipping rotors. He and Captain Kurt exchanged salutes.

Mo pulled the cockpit's partition closed for privacy in the passenger cabin. She nudged Nelson with her bare foot and said, "I have a new game for later." He grinned and rubbed his hands together. Mo's games for him always included happy endings and two winners.

She pulled a plastic grocery bag from her purse and removed a black leather-studded dog collar attached to a long leash. Nelson wrinkled his nose to raise his thick glasses for a better view. A slow smile of recognition spread across his face. He wagged his finger at her, saying, "I didn't think you were serious!"

They felt the helicopter cabin tilt. They were airborne.

Mo winked at him and said, "Bow-wow-wow." She opened the collar and whistled. "Here boy!"

Nelson laughed and leaned to her. She wrapped the collar around his neck and secured the chrome latch. The lengthy leash bunched on the floor. Nelson picked up the end, swatted his thigh, and said, "I'm such a naughty pup. Teach me to obey—*arff-arff.*"

They laughed. Mo said, "I wish I had my camera."

Nelson pointed to the collar. "Sure you can hold out 'til later?"

Mo nodded. "Your hotness is burning me up, but yes, later."

They looked out the window as the helicopter ascended, nosing its way over the ocean, headed to a surprise paradise for some relaxation, tropical sex, and stress reduction—at least that's how Mo had billed it.

After a few minutes, the view locked onto a two-toned blue portrait of the sky over the sea, so they turned their attention back to one another. Captain Kurt cracked the partition momentarily to say, "Folks, weather's perfect. We'll be about an hour. Get comfortable."

Nelson's inner ear pinched with the pressure change. He pushed his duffle bag under his seat. Morana lowered an armrest and adjusted her vents for some face-on air conditioning. She carried no luggage, only a purse, having promised Nelson that she'd be naked for most of their trip.

Nelson looked around the supple helicopter cabin and then to Morana. He smiled at his life's unfair bounty. He was accustomed to merely counting the money of people who lived like this.

Morana peeled back the wrapper of a homemade energy bar and broke off a bite-sized piece. Nelson held up his bent wrists and doggie-begged. She giggled and popped it into his mouth. Before he could chew it, she pecked him on the lips.

He palmed her knee, rubbed a few circles, and slid his fingers up her inner thigh toward her skirt's opening. She crossed her legs.

"What?" he said as if she had robbed him of an inexorable right. He cocked his head like a curious puppy and whined, "But later feels *so* far away!"

She laughed and said, "Let's wait until we get there."

Nelson frowned. "So you'll bang me in a cramped 747 lavatory with a line outside the door, but a spacious private helicopter cabin is too risky?"

"I'll make it worth your wait," Mo said. Nelson's frown deepened. It was unlike her to deny him anything—especially sex. "Is the possibility of getting caught what gets you off?" he said. "Let's open the partition. The pilot *might* look back." He slid his fingers up her leg again. She gently pushed his hand away, grabbed the edge of her skirt, and wiggled to pull it lower.

"What happened to you?" he said, leaning in for a kiss.

She turned away. "Nothing happened. Trust me, I'm saving my energy for you... Give me your back." She twirled her finger for him to swivel and then pulled a gel tube from her purse. She slipped her hands under his shirt and rubbed the gel onto his shoulders. She put her mouth close to his ear so he could hear her over the smooth hiss of the engines and whispered, "What's most important right now is to get you as relaxed as possible. I promise I'll give you more excitement than you can handle later."

Mo's massage and the gel's tingly warmth weighted Nelson's eyelids, and after a few minutes, his head fell forward. She massaged deeper. He nodded off. She raised the armrests and laid him down on the entire length of three seats. She moved to the facing seats, inserted earbuds, and watched the sparkling ocean slide beneath them.

Fifty minutes later, Nelson awoke when Captain Kurt opened the partition to announce, "We have a ten-minute ETA, folks." Nelson sat up and checked the window. Still only sky and sea. Morana sat with her purse strap over her shoulder and arms crossed as if ready to step out the door at any moment.

"You look worried," Nelson said as he yawned. "According to Captain Kurt, it's our last chance." He slipped off his seat to his knees, reached down, and tried to spread her legs. She kissed him and gently pushed him back into his seat.

"What's wrong? Ever since we got on this helicopter, I'm smeared with shit to you."

"We're almost there. If you can wait until we get to our room, I'll be the naughty stray that dug up your petunias, and I'll wear the leash this time," Mo said.

"Deal," Nelson said. He fumbled with his collar, turning it, tugging at it, but it would not open. "Would you unlatch this?" he finally asked.

Morana made a feeble attempt and then said, "It's broken. We'll get a paper clip at the lodge. It looks good on you. And that you can't get it off gets me hot."

"You tease," Nelson said. "I want it off. I want to see if it fits you." He continued pinching and pulling on the latch. When it wouldn't budge, Nelson wound and tucked the leash into his shirt to hide it. He couldn't understand Mo's need to delay a quickie. She was always game. Damned mood swings. PMS—it must be.

Outside the window, a slit of land on the horizon stretched and became greener as they neared. Like all the small islands within 500 miles, it was blanketed in lush foliage from beach to beach. The helicopter sank into a narrow clearing amongst trees whose branches leaned away and trembled under the whipping rotors. When the struts touched down, Morana moved to rest her hand on the door handle.

"I guess you're eager to get out," Nelson said. "Can't wait to get to the room, right?" he asked.

Morana smirked. "Baby, I want you so bad I could burst," she said.

A man's dark face appeared in the window. He cupped his hand against the glass to peer in, and Morana signed thumbs up. Captain Kurt opened the cockpit partition and said, "Welcome to Mapetoa Island, folks. Have a good time." Morana shook his hand, transferring a folded hundred. Then she pulled the handle, and the door swung open. A motorized step slid out.

A thin white man in a safari outfit—complete with a brimmed hat, shorts, and black boots—stood outside. Six men, islanders dressed in hats and white uniforms, stood in a half circle at the door. One of them leaned on the handles of an empty wheelchair. The safari man offered his hand to Morana as she stepped down.

"Welcome, Sweetheart," he said.

Nelson wasn't crazy about this man calling Mo "Sweetheart" but chalked it up to island protocol that required extraordinary hospitality for high-value guests.

He felt firm hands take his arms to help him from the helicopter, but he shrugged them off and said, "I'm fine." So the man grabbed Nelson's duffle from under the helicopter seat. Some of Nelson's leash slid out from under his shirt. He tucked it into his belt.

"Mister, would you like a ride to the lodge?" the wheelchair man asked.

"No," Nelson said. He looked at Mo, who had walked with the safari man toward the edge of the clearing. The others followed so Nelson did too. They came to a narrow dirt path barely wide enough for the wheelchair pushed behind Nelson.

"Mo, Mo!" he yelled, trying to catch up.

He felt a hand on his shoulder. "Please relax, mister. Why not have a ride?" the wheelchair man said.

"I don't want a ride. What am I? Crippled?" He pushed the man's hand off.

Morana turned back and said, "Sweetie, would you just relax?"

"You're practically jogging," Nelson said. "Would you just slow your roll so I can catch up?"

"Sorry. I'm hungry," Mo replied. Safari man chuckled.

They walked single file uphill on a trail through lush gardens lined with palm and balsa trees, some connected by hammocks. Soon, a grand log cabin lodge enclosed by a wide porch and log railings came into view high on a bluff. Huge picture windows faced a break in the foliage to a panoramic ocean view under the cloudless sky. Waves crashed, and sea birds shrieked on the beach below. Nelson heard the distant sound of their helicopter revving up.

He also noticed a glass-enclosed watchtower atop the lodge. A man stood inside holding a rifle with its butt rested on his hip, barrel angled upward.

"What's with the prison guard tower?" Nelson asked.

Mo nudged safari man and said, "This island has been a target for pirates, so the resort goes overboard with guest security. It was one reason I liked them."

Nelson said, "I wish that made me feel more secure." Safari man whispered into a wire connected to an earpiece. The tower gunman dropped out of sight.

They climbed the steps to the lodge entrance. Above the front door hung an ornate carved sign that read, El Sabor de La Vida. Two other uniformed staff washed windows and swept the porch.

Inside, the lodge was laid out with the care and attention to detail of a 5-star resort. A rock fireplace tapered to a thirty-foot chimney dividing two indoor balconies that overlooked the Great Room. An adjacent dining area featured a twenty-foot table made from a solid balsa trunk, polished to a mirror shine. Sofas, a set of massage tables and reading nooks, were interspersed with painted vases filled with tropical flowers cut from the gardens they had passed. A curved wooden staircase led to the upstairs guest rooms. The aroma of seasoned grilled onions and peppers wafted throughout the space. Nelson's stomach growled.

The delicious smell and fancy accommodations would usually have wowed him, but he'd prefer to take the tour later. Mo had him horny with the thought of a quickie. She should have pulled him straight to their room for some overdue sexual "heeling," but she chatted up Mr. Safari. As they moved to the center of the Great Room, Morana laughed, hugged one worker around the neck, and then kissed him. Jealousy flooded Nelson.

"Did you bring kinky-collars for the help, too?" Nelson said, stepping up to her. His voice had a strained, pre-tantrum tautness.

Safari man stepped between them. "Hold on, pal."

Nelson shoved him hard. "I'm not your pal, asshole. I'm talking to my woman, and I need a private word with her, or we're back on that helicopter." Morana bit her lip to avoid laughing. The staff slowly encircled them. Some shook their heads as they chuckled and watched.

"There is no more helicopter," Mo said.

"What?"

"We aren't leaving."

"The hell we aren't," Nelson said. He pulled her arm, and before safari man could stop her, Morana planted a foot behind Nelson's ankles, grabbed his throat, and slammed him to the floor on his back. His glasses flew off. His mouth froze open to catch his breath as Morana mounted him, her knee in his chest. She raised her elbow behind her to drive the heel of her hand into his face.

"No!" safari man hollered, "Morana! No damage! No damage—please!" He lunged and pulled her off. Before Nelson could make a move, four workers jumped him. They pressed his arms and legs to the floor.

"Get off me!" Nelson yelled. "I'll sue you and own this island!"

The men raised him to his feet and forced him into the wheelchair. A cloth gag pulled firmly over his mouth absorbed his screams. They tied his ankles, wrists, and arms to the chair using lengths of soft cloth in a tight candy stripe pattern. He felt the leash sliding out the top of his shirt as a smiling worker pulled it hand over hand and wrapped it around a bollard mounted to a shoulder-high banister. After the brief struggle, Nelson sat strapped to the wheelchair, his collar moored to the banister like a docked boat.

He bucked once, but the collar dug in and choked off a yell. A worker smoothed the top of Nelson's shirt, brushing the wrinkles from his shoulders and chest. He then pulled a spray bottle from his back pocket and misted Nelson's face with water before dabbing it dry with a fluffy white cloth. Another worker combed and smoothed Nelson's hair, checking his work from different angles.

Safari man and Morana strolled away from the scuffle. They sat on the far side of the Great Room by the front window. Morana's voice pierced the ongoing commotion. "Yes, we have a serious problem, Clay, if I don't see the money."

Safari man held up his hands to her. "Mo, calm down. Try again. I just got the wire confirmation a few minutes ago."

Morana tapped on her phone and waited, watching the screen. After a few moments, she said, "It transferred. Finally. That's more like it."

"See? What did I tell you?" the safari man said, beaming.

He and Morana made their way back to the workers surrounding Nelson. Morana continued to the staircase, saying, "I'm going to my room to freshen up. Begin the rub and include two ounces of shuttle fuel. We have less than thirty minutes."

Two workers yelled, "Yes, ma'am!" and then ran, disappearing into a hallway.

Nelson's heart pounded. What was she talking about? He wiggled under his restraints. His mind raced through the sequence of his two-month relationship with Morana. She claimed to have never visited this resort, yet her familiarity with safari man and the cryptic instructions the staff seemed to understand gave Nelson every reason to panic.

A man dressed in white brought Nelson's glasses to him, and after polishing them with a white towel, he placed the glasses back onto Nelson's face. Another man appeared from a hallway with a silver tray holding scissors and four small bowls. He put on latex gloves and nodded to the men surrounding Nelson's wheelchair. One cut the top of Nelson's shirt to expose his shoulders. The man with the tray dipped his fingers into the bowls one at a time and massaged Nelson's lower neck and shoulders until they glistened. The massage was gentle, and the citrus aroma was familiar to Nelson because Morana had used such scented ointments on him many times. The liquid from one bowl produced heat that penetrated his skin. It was uncomfortable but not excruciating, so Nelson bit into his gag and took it—desperately trying to understand what was happening.

Nelson examined the tether that anchored his neck to the bannister. Without the use of his hands, it didn't have to be strong to deter a run for the door. Even if he made it outside, eluding these people on this small island was absurd and escape impossible.

A worker approached him with a bottle of beer. He placed his finger to his lips, instructing Nelson to be quiet, and then said, "Mister, drink this beer." He loosened Nelson's gag, and it fell to his neck.

Nelson's upper body relaxed with the sudden ease of breathing through his mouth. "Please tell me what is going on," he said, panting.

Immediately, the gag returned, pulled tighter. The man with the beer shook his head and leaned close to Nelson's face. "When we remove the gag, you will drink all the beer without talking, or I will have Miss Morana feed it to you, and she will make you eat the bottle, too." He pointed up the stairs.

Nelson nodded. The gag fell to his neck again.

He parted his lips and took in healthy swallows of beer. The worker cupped his hand under Nelson's chin for spillage, and his smile grew with each gulp Nelson took. "Eeeexcellent, mister," he said as he put the empty beer bottle into a bag slung over his shoulder.

Nelson had looked forward to massages and beer as part of this getaway, but not like this. The forced massage, beer, and careful restoration of his glasses had become forced doting that fueled his terror. He hoped he was the center of a joke that had gone too far.

They re-gagged him and left. He heard voices from the other side of the bannister. One of them was safari man—Clay—giving some sort of instructions. A jarring electronic melody sounded, and Clay answered his phone. "Fantastic. We're ready," he said.

As one worker left the lodge to go outside, the faint beating of a helicopter seeped through the open door. The sound grew, and soon, the windows rattled lightly as another helicopter landed in the distant clearing.

Morana hurried down the stairs, having changed into a safari outfit that matched Clay's, and her hair was pulled back into a ponytail. Nelson tried to call out to her, but his scream only heated the gag. She rushed outside and out of sight.

The gloved man returned and resumed massaging his shoulders. After a few minutes, two men and two women who looked like tourists entered the lodge with Clay and Morana. They led the guests to Nelson and surrounded him. The older gentleman with a camera around his neck turned to Clay and said, "I must admit, this is new for me. I can hardly wait. If price is any indication, this will be spectacular."

"You'll consider it a bargain, I promise you this," Clay answered.

"Oh my, absolutely exquisite," said the older, silver-haired woman. She let go of the man's hand and pointed to Nelson. "May I?" she asked.

"By all means!" Clay said, hands in his pockets. He rocked from his heels to his toes, wearing a broad, cartoonish smile.

"Wait—hold on," Morana said. She stepped forward, rolling something between her fingers. She raised her hand toward Nelson's head. He winced. Morana twisted a compressed foam earplug deep into each of his ears. The foam expanded, and within moments, Nelson heard only his heartbeat thumping.

The silent mouths of his small audience moved. The older woman donned gloves. She approached him and touched his shoulder, gently squeezing it. Her mouth dropped open, and she turned to the others in amazement. When she turned back, Nelson read the word "fabulous."

Clay directed the guests' attention to the edge of the Great Room, where a man entered from a hall door. He wore a stethoscope draped around his neck and a white lab coat with the name Dr. Lawrence Pradin embroidered on it. With a somber, flat expression, he acknowledged the guests, approached Nelson and placed the stethoscope on Nelson's chest. He aimed an infrared thermometer at Nelson's temple and read the results aloud. After he poked and prodded Nelson's upper body a few times, he spoke a few words to the guests. Nelson watched the silent clapping. Morana pointed over the banister to a distant part of the lodge, directing everyone to leave.

When the guests had departed, Clay nodded to Morana. From the banister beside Nelson, she opened a shallow drawer the size of a spaghetti box. From it, she pulled out a ten-inch boning knife with the curve and point of an eagle talon. Crisscrossed hairline lacerations along its cutting edge told a story of frequent over-sharpening. Nelson screamed, but the gag dulled it to a hum. He shook his head hard enough to dislodge one earplug, and his glasses again flew off.

Morana dropped the knife to her side, her knuckles whitening around the handle. She watched Nelson—to see his chest heave like it had so many times after his asinine, animal-role-playing sex games she pretended to enjoy in his shitty apartment.

Nelson squeezed his eyes closed and bit into the gag. *How could she do this?* His too-good-to-be-true had become too-horrific-to-be-possible. He expected searing pain in his chest or across his throat but felt a gentle touch on his legs. He opened his eyes. The knife rested on his lap. Its blade reflected a silent spinning ceiling fan above.

Morana pointed, and a worker rotated Nelson's wheelchair while another untied his tether from the banister. They wheeled him out of the Great Room. The temporary reprieve brought Nelson a flash of relief, but now having to carry his own presumed instrument of execution brought a psychological cruelty akin to Roman crucifixion. Nelson strained to understand. If they were going to kill him, they could have easily done so already. They followed a carefully ordered agenda—that much was clear.

They wheeled him across the lodge, where he passed the visitors, who now sat on sofas in a lounge area. Morana joined them. The joyous, celebratory sounds of Mozart's *Symphony No. 40* filled the air. Laughter erupted from the group as Clay held his phone up for each guest to view a photo on its screen. After viewing the photo, the older woman closed her eyes and rocked back and forth to the music with a slight smile. They were festive.

Nelson's two handlers wheeled him down a dark hallway, stopping beside a door with three deadbolts. They flanked his chair and then slipped their fingers under the cloths that bound his arms and legs, checking for tightness. One worker picked up the knife while the other unlocked the door and pushed it open.

Light streamed into the hallway from the room, and the bouncy melody of Mozart's symphony swelled. Nelson saw his fate in unmistakable clarity. His eyes widened in utter horror. He screamed his muffled scream and bucked, swinging his torso in every direction.

The workers did not try to hinder him. They only steadied the wheelchair by stepping between the rear spokes. The one with the knife leaned against the door frame, whistling along with the music. The other pulled a phone from his pocket and scrolled it for new messages.

- Sample End -

More on *Human Resources*, including the audiobook at:
gneil.co/humanresources

Acknowledgments

I want to thank the following people:

Mom and Dad – You know what you did.

My wonderful wife for her patience, mastery of language and frequent use of that loving, slow-blinking facial expression that gently told me which of my subplot ideas were clearly stupid.

Cyndie Chen for sharing your wonderful eye for logic and uncanny sensitivity to word patterns. Your advice is golden.

Dean Gamburd for the firearms counsel. Any inaccurate references to firearms or their use in this story will have been solely the fault of the author for not checking with Dean first.

Julie "Schmuggums" Harreld for your enthusiasm, sound medical advice and suggestions, and constant support.

Michelle Martin-Stroup for sharing your unusual and extraordinary literary talent with me. I'm amazed by your skill and thankful for you.

Shanna Gray for your insight and keen ability to find unique typos.

Wileen Maldonado for an amazing, thorough proofread and clemency for unnamed characters in this story.